THIS IS ALL I ASK

"In this character-driven medieval romance that transcends category, Kurland spins a sometimes magical, sometimes uproariously funny, sometimes harsh and brutal tale of two people deeply wounded in body and soul who learn to love and trust each other . . . Savor every word; this one's a keeper."
                    —*Publishers Weekly* (starred review)

"Both powerful and sensitive, this is a wonderfully rich and rewarding book."
                                      —Susan Wiggs

" . . . A medieval of stunning intensity. Sprinkled with adventure, fantasy, and heart, *This Is All I Ask* reaches outside the boundaries of romance to embrace every thoughtful reader, every person of feeling." —Christina Dodd, bestselling author
                                      of *A Knight to Remember*

"Sizzling passion, a few surprises, and breathtaking romance . . . If you don't read but one book this summer, make this the one. You can be assured of a spectacular experience that you will want to savor time and time again." —*Rendezvous*

"An exceptional read."   —*Atlanta Journal-Constitution*

Another Chance to Dream

LYNN KURLAND

BERKLEY BOOKS, NEW YORK

THE BERKLEY PUBLISHING GROUP
Published by the Penguin Group
Penguin Group (USA) Inc.
375 Hudson Street, New York, New York 10014, USA
Penguin Group (Canada), 10 Alcorn Avenue, Toronto, Ontario M4V 3B2, Canada
(a division of Pearson Penguin Canada Inc.)
Penguin Books Ltd., 80 Strand, London WC2R 0RL, England
Penguin Group Ireland, 25 St. Stephen's Green, Dublin 2, Ireland (a division of Penguin Books Ltd.)
Penguin Group (Australia), 250 Camberwell Road, Camberwell, Victoria 3124, Australia
(a division of Pearson Australia Group Pty. Ltd.)
Penguin Books India Pvt. Ltd., 11 Community Centre, Panchsheel Park, New Delhi—110 017, India
Penguin Group (NZ), Cnr. Airborne and Rosedale Roads, Albany, Auckland 1310, New Zealand
(a division of Pearson New Zealand Ltd.)
Penguin Books (South Africa) (Pty.) Ltd., 24 Sturdee Avenue, Rosebank, Johannesburg 2196,
South Africa

Penguin Books Ltd., Registered Offices: 80 Strand, London WC2R 0RL, England

This is a work of fiction. Names, characters, places, and incidents either are the product of the author's imagination or are used fictitiously, and any resemblance to actual persons, living or dead, business establishments, events, or locales is entirely coincidental.

ANOTHER CHANCE TO DREAM

A Berkley Book / published by arrangement with the author

PRINTING HISTORY
Berkley edition / December 1998

ISBN: 0-425-20866-4

BERKLEY®
Berkley Books are published by The Berkley Publishing Group,
a division of Penguin Group (USA) Inc.,
375 Hudson Street, New York, New York 10014.
BERKLEY is a registered trademark of Penguin Group (USA) Inc.
The "B" design is a trademark belonging to Penguin Group (USA) Inc.

PRINTED IN THE UNITED STATES OF AMERICA

15   14   13   12   11   10   9   8   7

To Lynn Rowley, dearest of friends, whose opinion of my work given via a gas station pay phone truly changed the course of my life

ACKNOWLEDGMENTS

No author is an island, as it were, and that was never truer than with the writing of this book. The author most gratefully acknowledges aid from the following exceptional individuals:

Elane Osborn, for such fabulous title inspiration;

Dr. Kirk Lorimer, who never fails to enthusiastically ponder the gruesome possibilities of medieval wounds and their complications;

Gail Fortune, editor extraordinaire, for consistently giving the author the freedom to follow her heart;

and Matthew, who gave up vacations and other precious free time to be the author's hands while those hands were tending to the needs of a little one.

Winter

THE YEAR OF OUR LORD 1200

1

Ayre, England

She was going to die.

It was a pity, though, to die so soon, seeing that so much of her life remained before her and that 'twas only now she'd had her first taste of true freedom. But there was no denying the direness of her current plight. Who would have thought it took such skill to ride a horse? Perhaps she should have spent more time in the stables learning of horses and less time loitering in her mother's solar working heroic designs on fine linen. That she could scarce tell one end of a horse from the other should have told her that she knew too little about them to handle one with any skill.

Too late now for regrets. All she could do at present was cling to the saddle with one hand and the horse's mane with the other and watch as both the surrounding countryside and the more noteworthy events of her life rushed past her with dizzying speed. Her sins, too, seemed determined to present themselves to her with all haste—likely before the horse either ran her into a tree or managed to scrape her from his back and leave her in a broken heap on the wild grass.

Stealing. Aye, there was that grievous folly for which she would unfortunately have no time to make a penance. At the time, though, thievery had seemed her only choice. She'd needed a sword to aid her in her new choice of vocation and 'twas a certainty no one would have given her one had she asked for it. It had taken her a pair of days to study the inhabitants of her fiancé's keep intently enough to decide on a likely victim. Fortunately the hall was in enough disrepair and the knights drunken enough for the most part that filching a sword had been an easy task. She half suspected her prey had laid it beside him in the marshy rushes on the great hall floor and then thought he had lost it in the filth. Obviously the like had happened to others, for the lout had only cursed heartily, received condolences from his fellows, and then gotten on with his business.

As far as repenting went, perhaps she also should have done so for the bodily damage she'd done to a pair of knights and a serving wench as she'd struggled to get herself and her newly acquired sword to the stables without being marked as who she truly was. One wouldn't have thought merely walking about with a blade strapped to one's hip would have been so hazardous to others nearby.

Lying. She squirmed in discomfort, but what else could she have done? 'Twas perfectly reasonable to have won booty while dicing—never mind that she'd never thrown a die in her life. And if she were going to win some beast while gambling, why not Alain of Ayre's finest stallion? The stableboy had swallowed her tale readily enough and seemingly been impressed with her wagering skills.

Besides, lying and stealing were perfectly acceptable traits in a mercenary. Indeed, she suspected such talents were more than desirable; they were necessary. Perhaps they would make up for her lack of ability with a sword.

And, of course, with a horse. Her teeth snapped together as she bumped along furiously on the back of her racing steed. A pity the reins were naught but a fond memory as they dangled well out of her reach. They likely would have aided her in controlling the beast.

Her third sin fought mightily for her attention, but she ignored it. Yet the harder the horse's hooves pounded against the earth, the more the very sound of the word seemed to echo in her head: *covetousness*. She coveted a man and that surely was something to repent of. Never mind that his very reputation should have sent any sensible maid fleeing for cover. 'Twas said he wanted nothing to do with wedded bliss, though she believed otherwise. But it had been a handful of years since she'd seen him last, so 'twas possible things had changed. She had cause to wonder. He should have returned from France long ago.

But the man hadn't, so she was left with speculation about not only the state of his feelings for her, but the truth of the tales circulating about him. She had decided to take matters into her own hands and seek him out. And if the rumors were true that he no longer wanted a wife, perhaps he wouldn't be opposed to having another sword to guard his back. And if it took her even as long as a pair of months to hone her skills so she could offer them to him, then so be it. She would have Sir Rhys de Piaget, whether he willed it or not.

His battle prowess was a desirable thing. His foul temper could be ignored. His singlemindedness could eventually be turned from swordplay to her. Convincing him to wed her might entail tidying her person up a bit and unlearning the warrior's skills she currently sought to acquire, but she felt certain she would manage it. No matter the perils of pursuing him, no matter the rigors of living as a mercenary while her swordplay improved, it would be worth the effort if he were the prize.

It certainly was preferable to the hellish future she'd left leagues behind her at Ayre.

She stiffened in fear as a low fence of rocks appeared suddenly before her. Her mount, however, seemed to find it much to his liking if the equine glee with which he sailed over it was any indication. Gwen was reunited with the saddle, accompanied by a mighty clacking of her teeth. She realized immediately that dwelling on her destination was a dangerous activity, given that all her attentions should have been focused on her mount.

She raced through the countryside, feeling as if an eternity had passed since she'd managed to get herself into the saddle outside Ayre's gates. Perhaps speed was a boon. By the time Alain realized she had fled, she would be well on her way to Dover. Surely it would be a simple thing to sell her betrothal ring and find passage to the continent. If not, more lying and stealing would likely be called for. 'Twas a good thing she'd had her first taste of both while still on familiar ground. She suspected she could do either now without so much as a twitch.

She caught sight of something dark out of the corner of her eye. She hazarded a second glance only to find that a man was riding toward her. She would have stiffened in horror, but she feared to move, so she contented herself with a small squeak which was immediately lost in the rushing of wind around her. Merciful saints above, had Alain noticed her absence this quickly and sent someone to fetch her? Or was it instead another mercenary, bent on stealing her blade and her horse?

Ah, so the first test of her mettle would come sooner than she had thought. Perhaps 'twas just as well. Like her vices, her skill with the sword could be first tried while she was still on English soil.

If she could have stopped her horse long enough to draw her sword, that is.

"Away with you, oaf!" she shouted as the man drew alongside her. Then she realized it was more the tone her mother might have taken with a recalcitrant servant. She immediately attempted something more mercenary-like.

"Leave me be, you . . . you . . ." She racked her poor brains for something appropriately vulgar, but soon found herself distracted by the amazing display of horsemanship going on alongside her.

Without so much as a pucker of concentration marring his brow, the young man leaned over, reached out a gloved hand, and swept up her reins. A sharply spoken word and a healthy tug brought her horse to a gradual, graceful, and quite dignified stop. Gwen was so grateful for the cessation of motion, she couldn't find her tongue to speak. That, and she was too busy running it over her teeth to make certain all of them still resided in their proper places.

Satisfied they had survived the journey thus far, she bared them at the man and held out her hand for her reins. Then she pulled back her hand. Dirty as she might be, she looked passing tidy compared to the man facing her. Touching him was not something she was sure she wanted to do.

He'd been traveling, and for a great amount of time, if the condition of his worn cloak told the tale true. He would have been better off to have shaved his cheeks more often, for his beard was ragged and scruffy. Shaving also might have helped scrape away a bit of the dirt that adorned his features. Indeed, the whole of him could have used a good scouring.

She considered. A mercenary, and obviously a good one by the disreputable look of him. A pity she hadn't the time to sit and have speech with him. He might have offered her advice on how to comport herself.

She sighed regretfully and turned her mind back to the task at hand, namely recapturing her reins so she might be on her way again.

"Release my mount, you fiend," she commanded in her huskiest tone.

"*Your* mount?" the man drawled. "Why is it such an idea stretches the very limits of my imagination?"

"Perhaps you use yours less than I do mine," she said, sending him what she hoped was an intimidating glare.

"Horse thieves are hanged, you know."

"Won him dicing," Gwen returned, finding that this time she hadn't even flinched while spouting that bit of untruth. Indeed, she was beginning to think perhaps learning the skill of dicing would be a good addition to her repertoire. Who knew what sorts of things she might acquire thusly?

"From whom, lad?"

"Alain of Ayre, not that 'tis any of your business. Now, give me those bloody reins!"

The man only shook his head with a smile. "Alain is many things, but so poor a gambler he is not. No boy would have bested him so thoroughly as to have relieved him of this piece of horseflesh."

"Then you know little of me," she said, eyeing her reins and wishing her horse would in his shifting but shift a bit closer so she might make a more successful capture, "for I am most skilled not only with dice, but also with the sword. And," she added, "I am a bloody good horseman!"

She leaned over and snatched the reins from his hand.

And with the next breath, she found that her horse was no longer beneath her.

As she lay with her face in the dirt, she wondered if she might have executed her move with a bit more grace. She was too winded at first to notice that she no longer held on to her horse's reins, or that her horse was no longer close enough to step on her and crush the life from her. She could hear the man shouting at her, but it took her several moments before the ringing in her ears cleared enough for her to understand what he was saying.

"—trampled, you fool! Saints above, since when do the lads in England know so little about horseflesh? Bloody hell, but you're just as much trouble as I suspected you'd be. Damn that chivalry; I should make ignoring it more of a habit. As if I had time to aid some fool youth who'll find himself hanged inside a fortnight just the same!"

The tirade went on as Gwen managed to heave herself to her feet. She looked about her for her mount.

"There!" the man said, gesturing impatiently back the way she had come. The bay was nothing but a speck in the distance. "He's gone home to Ayre, likely to look for someone who has the skill to ride him!"

Gwen considered her situation. Horseless and bruised, she stood little chance of walking all the way to France. She eyed the young man before her, then looked at his very well-behaved mount. There appeared to be only one course of action. She twitched aside her cloak, put her hand on her sword hilt, and planted her feet a manly distance apart.

"You cost me my horse," she said. "I believe I'll have yours in trade."

That, at least, was enough to stop the man's tirade. He blinked at her in astonishment.

"Surely you jest," he said, seemingly overcome by the very thought.

Gwen took courage at his expression. Obviously she presented a more intimidating look than she'd dared hope. Perhaps it had to do with the unruly swing to her shorn locks. She hadn't been half satisfied with the work her eating dagger had done on her tresses, but plainly the raggedness lent her a dangerous air. The soot she had liberally smudged on her face no doubt added to her sinister appearance. Perhaps she would need to do less lying and stealing than she'd feared, if her aspect would daunt those about her. That she should intimidate someone even dirtier than she gave her a fresh surge of courage.

She motioned him down with a wave of her hand. "I'm in earnest. Dismount, if you will, lest you force me to draw my sword."

A corner of the man's mouth began to twitch under his scruffy beard. Fear, Gwen noted with satisfaction. Aye, this was much easier than she'd thought it would be.

"Let me see if I understand you aright," the man said, leaning on the pommel of his saddle. "You wish me to dismount and hand over the reins of my horse. To you."

"Aye."

"To you, who could not control that pitiful beast from Ayre's stables."

Gwen gritted her teeth. "He is a very fine horse. Powerfully spirited. Besides," she added when the man looked less than convinced, "even the most seasoned of mercenaries has the occasional run of ill luck."

The man snorted, then began to cough, his eyes watering madly. Gwen toyed with the idea of felling him while he struggled to regain control, then reluctantly let go of the thought. It wouldn't be sporting to do in a man who was obviously having such trouble breathing.

"By the saints," the man said, gasping.

Gwen folded her arms across her chest and frowned. "You've no need to fear. I'll do you no harm if you'll but dismount *now* and let me be on my way. I've many leagues to travel before the sun sets."

He wiped the tears from his eyes with the back of his glove, smudging a bit of the dirt in the process, snorted yet another time, then seemed to master his fear. "Is the whole of Ayre coming after you, or just Alain?"

"Likely the whole garrison," she said impatiently, "so as you might imagine, I've little time to waste. Now, do you obey me or must I draw my sword?"

The man swung down with another muffled exclamation of fear. At least Gwen thought it was fear. He was still wiping his eyes and his shoulders were shaking. There could be no other explanation for his actions.

He took off his soiled cloak and tossed it over his saddle, then stepped a few paces away from his mount. Gwen took a moment to indulge in envy that he possessed a mount who remained where he'd been left, then turned her mind to other matters—namely the man standing before her wearing a sword that seemingly didn't get in his way when he moved. Then there was that ruby the size of a child's fist in the hilt of his sword. Who was he? How had he come by such a sword and a mount that any knight would have groveled to own?

A pity she wouldn't have answers to those questions. Already she had wasted more time on him than she had to spare. She planted her feet more firmly in the dirt and dragged herself back to the task at hand.

"I can see you wish not to cooperate," she said. "You leave me with no choice but to do you bodily harm."

He lifted one shoulder in a negligent shrug. " 'Tis a chance I'll have to take. I have yet need of my horse."

"As you will then. It pains me to do this," she said, gritting her teeth as she struggled to remove her stolen sword from its sheath, "but you are obviously a stubborn''—she huffed as she twisted herself to one side for better control—''soul with perhaps a less developed desire for long life than another.'' She jerked the sword free triumphantly, then almost went sprawling from the movement. She let the sword rest where it seemed to want to— point down in the dirt—and hunched over it as if she'd meant to be doing the like. ''One last chance to spare yourself.''

''You are too kind.''

''Aye, 'tis a trait I'm seeking to rid myself of,'' she agreed, grasping the sword and pulling it upright. ''It only hampers me in my mercenary endeavors.''

''I can see how it might.''

Gwen felt a small twinge of unease at the fact that the man had not yet drawn his sword. It seemed passing unfair that she should cut him down where he stood, but surely she had offered him ample opportunity to save himself, hadn't she?

She lifted her blade and brandished it. Saints, but she should have been hefting other things besides sewing needles these past few months. The blade wasn't that heavy, but to untried arms it was very awkward. With a grunt she got the blade upright and pointing in the man's direction. She gave him her most menacing glance and waved her blade meaningfully at him.

He shook his head. ''I should have remained abed this morn.''

''Too late for regrets now,'' Gwen said, swinging her sword carefully. It moved more easily than she'd hoped, but it certainly was reluctant to give her any ideas on where she should cut first.

''Go to, would you?'' he asked politely. ''I am in haste, with much to see accomplished before the sun sets.''

''I *am* going to,'' Gwen said, through gritted teeth. ''This sword is heavier than those I am accustomed to.''

''Perhaps if you waved it with more enthusiasm, you might manage to nick me here or there.''

''I know that,'' she said, beginning to wonder if he thought her less skilled than he should. She took a swipe at him. It almost sent her sprawling, but she managed to regain her feet before the blade overbalanced her into the dirt. She shoved the remains of her hair out of her eyes and frowned at him. "Are you ready to cry peace yet?"

"Not quite yet."

"Then fight me," she said. She lifted her weapon against him again. "You haven't even drawn your swo—"

Sword, she meant to say. Somehow, though, the word was lost in her astonishment at the feeling of her blade leaving her hand. She stared in fascination as it flipped end over end up into the air and then came back down, flashing in the sunlight. The man caught it neatly with his left hand. He resheathed his own sword—the one she hadn't even seen him draw—then assessed hers with a practiced glance.

"Damascus steel," he noted with admiration. "You've a good eye, at least." He impaled her sword into the dirt next to him. "From whom did you filch it?"

"I won it d—"

"—dicing," he finished with a sigh. "Lying is a sin, you know. As is stealing."

"Desirable traits in any ruthless mercenary," she corrected him. "Now, as you have made off with my sword in such a dishonorable manner, you leave me with no choice but to take my knife to you."

He clapped his hand to his head with a groan. Taking that as a very good sign, Gwen fumbled in her boot for her dagger. She drew it forth with a flourish, hoping it had come out as if she'd planned the whole exercise to come down to this.

The man didn't move, so she took her courage in hand and stabbed the air in front of her with as much fierceness as she could muster.

Stabbing the man before her was, however, quite another matter.

The man shook his head sadly and clucked his tongue.

Perhaps if she merely impaled him in his sword arm it would wound him enough that he would be unable to wield his blade, but it wouldn't finish him off. It occurred to her that she would likely be finishing off a great number of men in her future as a hired sword, but that would perhaps come later when she had more stomach for the deed. For her first conquest, a mere stabbing would have to do.

She lifted her knife and commanded her body to fling itself forward.

Her arm, and her feet for that matter, wouldn't cooperate.

"Too bloody much time at a tapestry frame," she muttered under her breath. She took herself in hand and tried again. She forced the blade to descend and felt a faint satisfaction when she saw it heading directly for the man's upper arm.

And then quite suddenly she found her wrist captured in a firm grip and her knife removed from her hand. And then the man paused. He looked at her and frowned.

"Have we met?"

Saints above, this was all she needed, to be recognized and carried back to Ayre.

"Nay. Never," she said, gritting her teeth and trying to pull her hand from his. " 'Tis my fierce mercenary mien that has confused you. I've no doubt you've seen like expressions on many fighting men's faces."

"Nay," he said, staring at her intently.

He looked at her shorn hair, tucked her knife in his belt, then clamped a hand on her shoulder to hold her in place. Before Gwen could protest, he reached out and started to clean her face with the hem of his tunic sleeve. Apparently that didn't satisfy him, for he licked the fingers of one hand and rubbed industriously on her cheeks.

"What do you—" she spluttered.

He whirled her around so the sun shone down on her face. She blinked against the brightness of it. He reached out suddenly and tucked her hair behind her ears. Then he went still and his jaw hung slack.

"Gwen?" he gasped.

Aye, she almost said, then it occurred to her that no one

loitering so far from her own keep should have known who she was. She frowned up at him.

"And you would be . . . ?"

He smiled dryly. "Ah, how soon they forget, these fickle maids. Though I will admit," he said, reaching out to tug on her ear, "that though you don't look much cleaner than the first time we met, you smell much more pleasant."

And in that moment she knew.

"Merciful saints above," she breathed. " 'Tis you."

"Aye, *chérie*, 'tis I."

Gwen frowned. She hadn't intended to be covered with muck the next time she saw the man before her.

She opened her mouth to begin to ask the scores of questions she had to put to him, then she caught sight behind him of a company of horsemen in the distance. Alain of Ayre's white stallion was easily recognizable in the lead. Gwen closed her mouth around her queries.

"Alain comes," she said simply.

"Damn," he said, looking over his shoulder. He looked back at her. "You've been at Ayre?"

She nodded.

He frowned deeply. "We've much to discuss, I can see. But later," he added, with another look over his shoulder. "Perhaps he won't recognize me in my current state."

"We couldn't be so fortunate." She looked up at him appraisingly. "Obviously we'll have to invent a ruse for why we're together."

The man's eyes widened, then he began to back away. "Nay, not that."

"We must."

"We *mustn't*. I'm not recovered from the last time—"

"What other choice do we have?"

He shook his head firmly. "We have several—"

Gwen knew there was nothing else to be done. With a regretful smile, Gwen drew back her arm and then let fly her fist . . .

Straight into Sir Rhys de Piaget's nose.

2

England, 1190

Rhys rode in the rear of his foster father's company and gaped at the castle that rose up before him. He had seen a great deal of England and France given his tender age of ten-and-four, and considered himself mature and fairly jaded, but all he'd seen as he traveled over Segrave's land had left him almost speechless. He wondered if Segrave looked magnificent simply because of what he'd left behind him at Ayre. Bertram of Ayre was not poor by Rhys's standards, but his modest wealth and small keep paled to insignificance when compared to what Rhys had seen that day.

Segrave's walls were sturdy and in good repair. The land surrounding the outer walls was cleared of all trees and other growth that could have provided shelter to an enemy. And, amazingly enough, the folk here seemed to be using the moat for defense. At Ayre the water was simply a place to fling refuse, leaving the keep's inhabitants suffering as much as any foe who might find himself tripping into the moat. Though as far as defenses went, Ayre might have the advantage when it came to filthy water keeping an army at bay.

The drawbridge came down smoothly and settled gently into a fitting that was seemingly fashioned just for the receiving of it—nothing like the crude bridge that welcomed a body to Ayre's unkempt courtyard. Rhys spared a moment to admire such fine construction, then reined in his mount and looked back over the way he had come. As interesting as the keep might have been, it surely didn't compare to the fields he had just crossed.

By the saints, the land was beautiful.

It had been all he could do to keep himself in the saddle that morn. What he had wanted was to be wandering through those fields, bending to feel the warm earth slide between his fingers, smelling the grasses and flowers. He had wanted to walk over every inch of it, feel it beneath his feet, and lose himself in the dream that such a place might be his.

"Rhys?"

Rhys turned to look at the man who had spoken to him. He jerked to attention out of habit. "Aye?" he asked.

Montgomery of Wyeth, the captain of Bertram's guard, smiled. "Little lad, you're staring the wrong way. The beauty of Segrave finds itself inside the walls, not out."

Rhys shook his head. "Your eyes fail you, Captain. Nothing can compare to what I've already seen."

"Ah, the wisdom of youth," Montgomery said, not unkindly. "Have I not told you enough tales of the maid of Segrave to pique your curiosity?"

"What is a maid but a means to land?" he asked. "Besides, she is very young."

"She has nine summers," Montgomery said with a knowing smile, "and she shows every promise of inheriting her mother's considerable beauty. Come, young one, look on her and see if I don't have it aright."

"As you will," Rhys said reluctantly, and he wanted to add, *What good will such a thing do me?* Gwennelyn of Segrave was so far above him in station he stood little chance of ever being in the same hall with her, much less being allowed to gape at her. Besides, she was a child. He had no interest in children.

Her land, however, was a different tale entirely.

But there was also no sense in lusting after what he could never have, so he followed Montgomery across the drawbridge and into the bailey. Lads came to take their horses. Rhys dismounted and started toward the stable, but then halted when he heard his foster father call to him. He turned to find Bertram approaching.

"Let them, son," Bertram said. "You've no need to see to such things now."

Rhys inclined his head respectfully. "Thank you, my lord, but I prefer to tend my own mount."

Bertram looked at him for a moment in silence, then shook his head with a smile. "As you will, Rhys. Come join us in the hall when you've finished. I'll introduce you to William of Segrave, as he asked specifically to meet you. I suppose he wishes to see for himself how a lad knighted so young carries himself."

Rhys nodded and made his way to the stables. He was accustomed to, if not fairly uncomfortable with, the notice his knighting had garnered him. By the saints, it wasn't as if he'd asked to be knighted at the battle of Marchenoir, especially having just reached his fourteenth summer. But who had he been to say nay to Phillip of France? Especially considering his family's relations with the French monarch. Though he had chosen a different path from his father and grandfather, he was still a de Piaget and Phillip considered him his.

By the time Rhys had tended his horse, he'd ceased thinking of political intrigues and Segrave's soil, and turned his mind to the filling of his belly. Perhaps William would exchange an introduction for a hearty meal. Rumor had it that Joanna of Segrave laid a fine table indeed.

He hadn't taken two paces from the stables when he heard a horrible noise coming from the pigsty. He looked about him, but no one seemed to find it out of the ordinary. Men carried on with their tasks, though some of them were smiling. Rhys shrugged and started across the bailey to the hall, but found himself stopping but a pace or two later.

Those were not sounds that normally came from a piggery.

He found that his curiosity was a more powerful force for once than his desire for a full belly. He turned about and made for what sounded like a beastie from the forests venting its anger. He rounded the corner of the stables and came to a dead halt. There was indeed a body making those horrendous noises, but it wasn't something foul from the forest.

It was a girl.

She sat in the muck and wailed for all she was worth. Rhys suspected that she might have tried to make an escape, for there were smears upon the gate in the shape of hands, and there were indentations in the muck where evidently she had stomped about in frustration. Not being a practiced judge in these matters, Rhys couldn't tell how old she was, though he supposed her to be of a fair age. She was not a girl full grown, though certainly old enough to have escaped the sty on her own. Perhaps there was more to it than what he could see. Rhys approached carefully.

The girl looked up at him and, blessedly, stopped wailing.

Rhys leaned upon the gate and stared back at her. "Trapped?" he asked.

She only blinked, then nodded, her chin beginning to quiver.

"Someone lock you in?"

She nodded again. "Geoffrey of Fenwyck."

Rhys knew of Fenwyck, but nothing of his son. Obviously a lad of little chivalry, but a fair amount of imagination judging by the cleverness of the knots binding the gate closed. Little wonder the girl hadn't been able to let herself out. Why she hadn't climbed the fence he didn't know, but that was a girl for you. The reason she found herself therein, however, was another matter entirely. Rhys leaned on the fence and looked at her speculatively.

"Why'd he do it?"

The girl scowled. "In return for my locking him in the tower chamber I suppose."

Rhys felt one of his eyebrows go up of its own accord. "That took some doing. Is he so foolish then?"

"Nay, 'tis that I have a very practiced imagination. My mother tells me so often." She seemed to take her declaration as simple fact, for there was no look of boasting hiding under all that mud on her face. "I saw him filch a bottle of my sire's finest claret. When he threatened to toss me in the dungeon if I told, I took the empty bottle, put it in the chamber, and sent a messenger to tell him that yet another bottle awaited him there."

Rhys stroked his chin thoughtfully. This was not a normal young girl he faced here. He wondered how many white hairs she had given her sire already.

"I assume you're here," Rhys mused, "because he knew you arranged that. Did you turn the key in the lock yourself?"

"Aye," she said, and there was pride in her face this time. "He deserved it, the wretch. He told me but yestereve that my ears stick out from my head most unattractively and that no wimple ever stitched would hide them."

Rhys put his hand to his mouth and chewed on his finger to keep from laughing. The child wore no wimple at present, and he couldn't help but agree with Fenwyck's description of her ears. But 'twas passing unchivalrous to say so. And he suspected he would do well not to irritate her. She spoke with the tongue of a woman full grown, and Rhys suspected her schemes were just as ripened. Best to remain in her good graces.

He undid the gate and looked at the captive.

"You'll have to hurry, lest the piglets escape as well."

Said piglets were rooting enthusiastically at her skirts. At least the sow was nowhere to be seen. Credit young Fenwyck with some sense about that.

The girl, however, only sat and looked at him.

"Well, come on," he said, gesturing to her. "You're free now."

She started to rise, then her feet slipped out from under

her and she fell back into the muck with a very wet splatting sound. Her chin began to quiver. When tears started to leak from her eyes and forge a trail of cleanness down her cheeks, Rhys knew he had to do something. It was tempting to hasten the other way, but the noise in his head made by his sword kept him where he was. That and the weight of all the lectures he'd heard from his foster father over the years. A chivalrous knight would remain and rescue the maid from her plight. Rhys sighed. He wasn't overly fond of the thought of layering his boots with muck, but there was obviously nothing else he could do if he intended to live up to the standards Bertram of Ayre had set for him.

He stepped into the pigsty. With another sigh he reached down and pulled the girl up and into his arms. He forced himself not to complain when she threw her arms around him and buried her face in his neck. And as he stepped from the pen, he came to a conclusion.

Chivalry was a messy business indeed.

He set the girl down outside the piggery, then shut the gate. Then he turned to her and used the sleeve of his tunic to wipe away some of the mud that was smeared over her face. She looked up at him with pale, tear-filled eyes.

"My gratitude," she sniffed.

" 'Twas my pleasure," he said, trying to ignore her smell, which had now become his smell.

She looked down at her gown. " 'Tis ruined," she said sadly.

"Perhaps if you let it dry."

" 'Twas my finest stitchery," she said, showing him the hem of her sleeve. "See?"

He meant to obey, but made the mistake of looking at her and truly seeing her. And for the first time in the extensive experience fourteen years had given him, Rhys felt himself grow a tiny bit weak in the knees.

The girl had the most beautiful eyes he had ever seen.

"See?" she repeated.

It was with effort that he dragged his eyes down to her sleeve. He looked at the mud-encrusted fabric and nodded gravely, as if he actually could see the stitches worked there.

"Terrible tragedy," he managed. "Truly."

"I should be avenged. The knave should pay for his dishonorable assault upon me."

Well, obviously this one had been listening to too many *chansons*, but Rhys refrained from saying so. 'Twas a simple matter to remain silent, actually. The girl had rendered him speechless.

"I'll need a champion," she said, looking up at him appraisingly.

"Um . . ."

She looked down at his sword. He could feel the metal heat under her gaze. It came close to burning a stripe down his leg even through the sheath.

"You're young to be wearing a sword," she said.

"Well, I—"

Then her eyes widened. "By the saints," she breathed, "you're Rhys de Piaget. My father told me of you. You were knighted but a pair of months ago for saving Lord Ayre's life. Why, you're a knight of *legendary* prowess!"

She wiped unconsciously at her face, leaving a large swath of mud running down her cheek. Then she seemed to remember her ears, for she reached up to rearrange her hair about them. More dung was left behind.

"My mother's minstrels already tell tales of your skill." She looked at him worshipfully. "You could be my champion."

Rhys blinked. *This* was Gwennelyn of Segrave? Lays had been written describing in intimate detail the beauty of her mother's face and her goodness of heart. Bards, players of instruments, and artisans all came to kneel at the feet of the former lady-in-waiting to Queen Eleanor and offer up to her their finest work. Rhys had not been so distracted by his swordplay that he hadn't listened now and then to the rumors of the woman's beauty, or the rumors of how the promise of that beauty rested heavily on Joanna's daughter.

Was everyone blind, or was he himself so distracted by

the overwhelming stench of pig manure that clung to the
both of them that he couldn't see what others had been
raving about?

As he contemplated that, he found himself torn between
looking at the muck now in Gwen's hair and squirming
under the weight of her assessing gaze.

"Aye," she said with a smile, "I couldn't ask for a
more chivalrous knight to restore my honor to me. Already
I can imagine how the battle will go."

So could he and it would finish with him trotting off to
her father's gibbet. But before he could tell her that Geoffrey of Fenwyck was a baron's son and mere knights did
not go about challenging baron's sons, she had taken him
by the arm and started back to the hall.

"Challenge him after we sup," she advised. "I'll have
a wash so that I might look my best while I watch you
dispatch him. You will dispatch him, won't you?"

One thing he would accord her; she had the most stunning pair of aqua eyes he'd ever seen. How could a man,
even a young man such as himself, say nay when finding
himself lost in them?

He tried to shake himself back to some semblance of
reason. He reminded himself that she had no more than
nine or ten summers and that it could not matter what she
thought of him. He would never have a one such as she,
so disappointing her should mean nothing to him. Yet
when she turned the full force of her shining eyes on him,
he found words rushing out of his mouth he surely hadn't
intended.

"Aye, I'll challenge him," he blurted out.

And then he knew that the only course of action left to
him would be to draw his sword and fall upon it. As if he
could actually dare such cheek. By the saints, he should
have clamped his lips shut!

"You will?" she asked with a dazzling smile.

"Ah . . . I'll demand an apology," Rhys amended
quickly. Perhaps he could shame the fool into giving Gwen
one.

"Will you use your sword?" she asked breathlessly.

"If necessary," Rhys said, feeling the urge to drop to his knees and pray for deliverance from his own wagging tongue. "But first I'll give him a chance to comport himself well without violence."

"If you think it best," she said, sounding somewhat disappointed. "Though I would surely like to see him poked a time or two for his crimes."

Evidently her disappointment was not so great that she was ready to release him from his errand. She took hold of his hand and dragged him back toward the keep. Rhys searched for a means of escape, but saw none until he happened to glance upon Sir Montgomery. Montgomery stopped the sharpening of his sword to look at them.

"Escorting our lady to the hall, Sir Rhys?" he called.

"He is my champion, Sir Montgomery," Gwen returned promptly. "He's going to avenge my bruised honor. Plans to use his sword if he has to."

Rhys threw Lord Bertram's captain a beseeching glance, but Montgomery only smiled.

"Well done, lad," Montgomery said approvingly. "Trot out that chivalry as often as possible. Keeps your spurs bright, as Lord Ayre always says."

Rhys wondered what Lord Ayre would say when he found out his foster son had been talked into taking to task the son of one of the most powerful barons in the north of England. Likely something along the lines of, "Best of luck to you, you chattering fool," as he headed back to Ayre, leaving Rhys to be carried off to Fenwyck and left to rot in the dungeon. Considering Fenwyck was a good two weeks' travel north from Ayre, Bertram could rest easy knowing he'd never have to hear Rhys's dying screams.

"I'll deserve it," he muttered. "Never should have picked up a sword."

"You said something?" Gwen asked.

Rhys shook his head. "Nothing of import."

"Then let us be about our business," she said enthusiastically.

Rhys sighed and let her pull him toward the great hall.

He should have contented himself with the keeping of a field or two instead of lusting after knight's spurs. It would have been safer. It also might have been safer had he paid more attention to filling his belly than to rescuing a fair maid in the mud—only to find himself Gwennelyn of Segrave's champion.

But in his heart of hearts, he found that being chosen as such was quite possibly the sweetest pleasure he had yet had in his fourteen years. Foolish or not, he felt his step, and his heart, lighten. Gwen turned on the threshold to look at him and he gave her his best smile. He suspected that even his mother had never had such a smile from him.

Gwen smiled in return, and the sight of it smote him straight to the soul.

Aye, he found himself feeling that there was much indeed he would do for the girl before him.

"A favor," she said, patting herself.

"Another one?" he asked with a gulp. By the saints, serving this girl could take up a great amount of his time.

"Nay, I meant a favor for you to wear upon your arm. 'Tis how it is done, you know," she informed him.

"Of course," he said, wondering if he should have spent more time paying heed to Bertram's minstrel.

Gwen continued to pat until she pulled forth from some unidentifiable portion of her mud-encrusted gown a thick ribbon. Rhys could only speculate upon the color. He thought it might have been green. It likely still was, under all that dirt.

She tied it around his arm with great ceremony, then smiled up at him again. "Now you are truly mine. Coming?" she asked, taking him again by the hand.

How could he say her nay? He loosened his sword in its sheath and cast one last prayer heavenward before he ducked into the great hall behind his lady.

3

Gwen lay next to her mother in the large, comfortable bed and found, for a change, that the events of the day were far more interesting than the happenings she usually made up in her head to put herself to sleep.

"Gwen, please stop squirming."

"Oh, but, Mama, was he not wonderful today?"

Her mother sighed, but Gwen recognized the sigh. It was her I-wish-this-girl-child-would-fall-asleep-but-even-so-that-won't-stop-me-from-listening sigh. It was a sound Gwen was very familiar with. She'd overheard her mother say that she had only herself to blame, that it was her fault that Gwen's head was so peopled with characters from *chansons* and bardly epics, so she as well as anyone should pay the price. But it had been said gently and followed by a loving laugh from her father, so Gwen knew her parents weren't displeased with her.

But now she had a very live, very brave champion to think on, and that was better than anyone from her imaginings.

"He didn't even have to use his sword," Gwen said, relishing the moment yet again. "Just his reputation and the drawing of his blade was enough to set that Fenwyck demon to trembling.''

"Aye, love."

"Would he have bloodied Geoffrey, do you think, Mama?"

"Likely so, if he'd had to."

"Was he so serious then, think you, about avenging my bruised honor, Mama?"

Her mother laughed and hugged her close. "I think he was very serious, my girl. But do you not think you earned a bit of Sir Geoffrey's ire? You did lock him in the tower."

"He told me my ears were overlarge."

"Only after you pointed out to him that he has a gap in his teeth."

"He's vain, Mama, and I couldn't bear him swaggering about. Besides, he tweaked one of my plaits when your back was turned. Sir Rhys would never have done such a thing."

"Likely not."

"Is he not wonderful, Mama?"

"Aye, my Gwen, he is. But do you not recall that you are betrothed to Alain of Ayre? As fine a lad as Sir Rhys may be, he will not be your husband. Perhaps you would do well not to think on him overmuch."

What Gwen didn't want to give thought to was Alain, so she agreed quickly with her mother, turned away, and pretended to go to sleep.

In truth, she dreamed with her eyes open of a gallant lad who had taken his life in his hands to challenge a man at least six years older than he. Gwen could still see the steadiness of Rhys's hands as he rested them upon his sword hilt, telling all who watched that he had the courage of a score of Geoffreys of Fenwyck. She had no trouble recalling the fineness of his dark hair as it fell to his shoulders, or the noble tilt to his chin and the regal shape of his nose.

And he had such marvelous ears.

She sighed in pleasure before she could stop herself,

then coughed, lest her mother think she was dreaming instead of sleeping.

If only he could offer for her instead of that foul-tempered, lackwitted Alain of Ayre. Then would the truth of her life be as glorious as what she imagined up in her head.

Was there a way? Rhys was but a knight, true, but would not his glorious deeds count for something? Could her father not be persuaded that Rhys was far more desirable as a son-in-law than Alain? She was discerning enough to know that land and alliances would decide whom she wed—indeed, such things had already decided the matter. But could that not be set aside this once? Her father denied her nothing. Perhaps he would continue the practice with this. She would ask him first thing.

She yawned and closed her eyes, and then she dreamed in truth.

Of a splendidly chivalrous young man with serious gray eyes and a bright, sharp sword.

Rhys had watched the rest of the keep seek their beds, yet he found himself standing guard near his lord. He wasn't in truth a member of Lord Ayre's guard, but he volunteered for the duty willingly. Bertram had given him much; it seemed the least he could do in return. Being near his lord tonight was especially soothing, given the busy afternoon he'd had. He'd come away the victor, but it hadn't been without price—namely his peace of mind.

No sooner had Gwen washed her face and brushed the mud from her hair than she had reappeared, waiting for him to do something. Rhys had entertained one last hope that perhaps her mother might have talked her into reason, but he had found said mother sitting beside his championed lady, watching just as expectantly. His promise to avenge resting heavily on his shoulders, he had taken his cheek in hand and approached Geoffrey of Fenwyck with as much seriousness as he could muster.

Fenwyck's son had laughed at him at first. It had taken

a great deal of courage to stand there and not flinch, but Rhys had done it. Then he'd drawn his sword and rested it point down in the rushes before him. It was but a borrowed sword, as Bertram had only recently ordered another to be fashioned for him, but a sword was a sword when it came to the finer matters of chivalric duty. Evidently Geoffrey had seen that the point was sharp enough and that Rhys's determination was firmly fixed, for he had stopped laughing and started blustering about. His bluster had soon turned to uncomfortable silence when Rhys had invited the older lad to have a go in the lists. Uncomfortable for Geoffrey, that was. By that time Rhys had begun to feel that his reputation for fierceness on the battlefield might indeed serve him well.

It had certainly earned him a look of worship from Gwen after the deed had been done.

By the saints, but it was enough to make him believe there was something to Bertram's lectures on chivalry after all.

William rose, startling Rhys from his reverie. He waited until Lord Bertram had risen as well before he fell in behind them. He stopped outside Segrave's solar and stood with his back to the partially open door. And much as he tried not to, he couldn't avoid hearing the conversation going on inside.

"You missed the excitement this afternoon, my friend," William said. "While you were napping, your foster son was going about correcting injustices."

Bertram laughed uneasily. "He didn't challenge your entire guard, did he?"

"It wasn't my guard he was taking on, 'twas that rascal who locked my Gwen in the piggery."

"Young Fenwyck?"

"Who else? The boy's a menace."

Bertram whistled softly. "A full score of years he has, yet he's still causing the maids to weep. It doesn't surprise me that Rhys took him on."

"Indeed he did. He swaggered up to Fenwyck's get just as boldly as you please and told Geoffrey he'd throw *him* into the piggery if he didn't apologize to Gwen. He added that he would escort him there by way of the lists if necessary."

"Ah, that's my lad," Bertram said, his voice full of pride. "I take it young Fenwyck did as he was bid?"

"Ungraciously, but aye. Young Rhys's reputation is the stuff of legends already."

Rhys stood straighter. He couldn't help himself. That William of Segrave should compliment him was something indeed. He fingered the ribbon he wore on his arm. His first favor, and from a lord's daughter no less. He had lived up not only to her expectations, but her father's as well. 'Twas something to be proud of.

"He'll be a fine man," Bertram said quietly.

"Aye," William agreed. "A pity he'll have no land. He would make a good husband and lord."

There was silence for a goodly while. Then Bertram spoke.

"He would make a fine husband just the same. Especially to a girl whose antics would terrify the bravest of men."

"Bertram," William said with a half laugh, "you insult my sweet Gwen. She's merely adventurous."

"You told me yourself that just a se'nnight ago you found her preparing to scale the outer wall to assure herself that your defenses against such a thing were what they should be. The girl thinks far too much for her own good!"

William's chuckle was enough to make Rhys begin to sweat. If he found that bit of mischief amusing, what other things was Gwen about that he indulged? Saints, the girl would kill herself before she reached a score of years.

And he found, unsurprisingly, that the thought was deeply distressing to him, the saints pity him for an impractical fool. As if anyone would care that he felt the sudden compulsion to make sure she didn't dash her dainty toes against a sharp rock.

"William, she deserves someone who will appreciate that."

"One would think, my friend, that you would rather me give Gwen to him than your son."

"Rhys has many things Alain lacks."

"And he lacks what Alain has, which will be a barony in time. I cannot wed my daughter to a simple knight, Bertram."

Bertram sighed heavily. "I know, William. I know."

And that, it seemed, was that.

Rhys swallowed with difficulty, surprised by how much such simple words pained him. It wasn't as if he hadn't had the same words hurled at him all his life, and by those with certainly purposefully crueler tongues than Segrave's. He should have been used to the sting by now, but he wasn't. For a moment he had actually believed that he might be looked on as more than just a knight.

He should have known better than to allow himself to hope that he might have a baron's daughter, or any other woman of such exalted station. He'd heard the truth of the matter and straight from William's lips.

Rhys sensed eyes upon him and looked up to find Sir Montgomery watching him. He stiffened.

"How long have you been there?" he demanded.

"Long enough," Montgomery said quietly.

"Must you always lurk in dark corners?" Rhys snarled.

Montgomery only clapped a hand on Rhys's shoulder and urged him down the passageway.

"I'll remain," he said, and the tone of his voice warned Rhys that he would accept no argument. "Go sleep. You'll want to be in the lists early."

Rhys would have gone to the lists then if he could have, to relieve the feelings of shame that coursed through him. Of course he'd known he could never have someone like Gwennelyn of Segrave. Hadn't he told himself as much as he rode through the gates that morning? He wouldn't have her and he wouldn't have her land. Instead they would be given to Alain of Ayre, a young man whose thoughts ran no deeper than to which falcon to choose for his day's hunt. Gwen's soil would turn into a wasteland under his care. For all Rhys knew, Gwen herself would turn into the same with Alain as her mate. And there wasn't a damned thing he could do to amend either.

A pity that he wanted to.

By the saints, desire was a bloody awful thing.

He set off down the passageway, and as he did so, the ribbon she had given him fluttered with the movement of his striding. He fumbled at it, then found that he couldn't release the knot. By the saints, who had taught the girl to tie things so securely? He worked at it with frantic intensity. He pulled, then yanked, cursing the favor and its giver. Finally it came loose and he cast it to the ground, the stinging in his eyes blinding him to where it had fallen. He walked away, leaving it behind him in the passageway.

He cursed the day he'd ever gazed into those aqua eyes and prayed the day would never come when he had to look in them again.

It was very much past the wee hours of the morn when Rhys crept back up the steps. The torch had burned low and the passageway was empty. Rhys inched his way along the wall, stopping at the place he thought he'd been before.

The ribbon was no longer there.

He leaned back against the wall and swore softly. Then he gathered his wits about him. It had been a foolish idea, just as foolish as all the hopes he had entertained that day. He made his way back down the great hall to return to his sleeping place. On the morrow he would rise before dawn and train. He felt confident in the lists, secure in his abilities and proud of his performance. He was safe there. It was a far safer place to be than anywhere near Gwennelyn of Segrave.

Aye, deciding to keep as much distance from her as possible might be the most rational decision he'd made all day.

It would likely serve him just as well in the future.

4

England, 1196

Gwen peered into her mother's polished silver goblet, trying to see if the wimple sat properly on her head. Upon closer inspection, she discovered a pair of smudges on the white fabric near her ears.

"By all the bloody saints," she exclaimed, "who dirtied this?"

"Gwen," her mother chided, "such unattractive words to come from your mouth."

"My finest wimple is ruined."

"Perhaps if you wore them more often," Joanna said, "you might become more acquainted with their state of cleanliness, or lack thereof."

"I am endeavoring, Mother," Gwen said with as much patience as she could muster, "to make a good impression."

"On Lord Bertram?"

"Who else?" Gwen lied. Her future father-in-law could have seen her covered in leavings from the cesspit and she wouldn't have cared. Nay, there was only one whose good opinion she craved.

And the bloody lout hadn't looked at her once since he'd arrived.

She couldn't understand it. He had departed the keep with Lord Bertram the day after he'd challenged Geoffrey of Fenwyck those six years ago, which was unexpected, but she had assumed he'd done it not to cause Fenwyck's son further embarrassment. That was far more than Geoffrey deserved, the wretch.

She had been at the gates to watch Rhys ride away. She'd exchanged no words with him, but certainly a good long look. His eyes had been clear and bright and his jaw set strongly as if he sallied forth to do more heroic deeds to delight her. She'd recognized the look that hid all emotion. All fine champions did so, lest prying eyes discover the innermost feelings of their hearts. It was a ruse they put into play, and Gwen had been greatly cheered to know Rhys was doing the like. It could only mean he had given his heart into her keeping. She had nodded to him gravely, then escaped to her mother's solar to imprint upon her memory her last sight of the man she was certain she loved.

It had troubled her occasionally to find Lord Bertram arriving without Rhys in the ensuing years. It had troubled her even more to see Alain arrive with his father from time to time, but she had comforted herself with the knowledge that one day Rhys would come for her and claim her as his own. That made enduring Alain's poor manners and feeble-minded conversation less difficult than it would have been otherwise.

And then today had dawned. She'd been loitering on the battlements, observing her father's archers and wondering how difficult it would be to filch a bow from one of them to learn their skills, when what she had seen but Ayre's banner coming toward them. She'd groaned at the sight of it, but remained on her perch that she might see if she were to be burdened with her betrothed's presence or not.

And then she'd seen who rode in Lord Bertram's company.

She'd almost fallen off the walkway in surprise.

Her mother had kept her busy in the solar for the whole of the day. Gwen had sewn tunic sleeves shut, hemmed sheets too short, and stitched a three-footed falcon onto her father's finest surcoat. Her mother had finally put her to playing the lute to entertain Segrave's ladies, but even that had proved too taxing a duty. Gwen couldn't for the life of her remember her notes.

He was below.

She could hardly breathe for the excitement that coursed through her.

Then she'd finally been allowed to go to the great hall and partake of a meal. It had been a very long meal, and Rhys had sat at the table below her father's for a very long time.

Ignoring her.

If she'd dared, she would have walked up to him and demanded an explanation. Concealing his feelings was one thing, yet even that demanded the occasional stolen glance filled with love. What had she had from the champion of her heart?

Not a bloody nod. Nary a wink. Not even a twitch of an eyebrow when she'd accidentally knocked a pitcher of wine over into Lord Bertram's lap.

Events were not progressing as she had planned.

Which was why she found herself on this, the second morning of Sir Rhys's stay in her keep, digging through her trunk for a suitable wimple to cover her ears. Perhaps he had thought better of wanting to champion her because he had spent too much time dwelling on the state of filthiness she'd found herself in the last time they'd met. Not so this time. She fully intended to show him that she could keep her clothes clean, her demeanor demure, and her ears covered. He couldn't fail to be impressed by that.

Only now her plans were dashed by the discovery of dirt on her finest wimple. How was she to make a good impression with a filthy headcovering? She was in mid-contemplation of a selection of curses when she felt her mother's hands on her head.

"Here, my love," Joanna said gently, removing the soiled cloth, "you'll wear one of mine."

"Nay," Gwen protested, "you know I'll only ruin it."

"For such a tidy girl, you do manage to wear a great deal of dirt," Joanna agreed placidly.

Gwen didn't bother to argue. She did find herself smudged quite often, but it came from the places she went and the things she investigated. She needed fodder for her own tales and 'twas a certainty she wouldn't find it in her mother's solar. Women's gossip, no matter how entertaining, was not interesting enough for the elaborate lays she wrote out in her head. But her father's armory was. Never mind that she had never hefted a sword in her life. She needed no hefting for creation.

She stood still as her mother fussed with tying the wimple under her chin and tucking her hair under the cloth. And she found it very difficult to meet her mother's eyes, lest she see the plots and schemes lurking therein.

"Gwen."

Gwen looked at her mother reluctantly. "Aye?"

"Your course is set before you, my girl."

"Would that I could alter it," Gwen muttered.

"I had no choice in the wedding of your father," Joanna reminded her, "and see you how well that has turned out?"

Ah, but her sire was a far different man than the volatile, selfish Alain of Ayre. That his temper was matched only by his stupidity made him a very disagreeable prospect indeed.

But with any luck, he would be searching for a new bride very soon. Sir Rhys would see to that. Gwen had faith in him.

Now, if she could just convince him to agree with her.

"I must go down," Gwen said, feeling the need to escape from her mother's assessing glance. "It will show Lord Bertram that I will be a good chatelaine if I am there to tend to our guests."

Her mother sighed. "Be careful, Gwen."

Gwen fled before she had to hear any more. She had the feeling what her mother didn't know, she'd guessed. Had she been so obvious then, over the past six years? She'd lived for every scrap of news about Sir Rhys and made any bearer of such tidings repeat over and over again what they'd heard. She'd reminded her parents that she was composing heroic lays as a tribute to Queen Eleanor's fondness of them, and it only served her to hear of the gallant Sir Rhys's remarkable adventures. He had gone on many errands for Lord Bertram and somehow always managed to extricate himself in the most glorious of ways from impossible situations, using his sword and his wits with equal skill.

Gwen stopped at the bottom of the steps and hung back in the shadows where she could observe the occupants of the great hall, yet remain unseen herself. It was yet early in the day and the men had returned from their morning business to break their fast. Gwen had given much thought to the timing of her entrance. Sir Rhys would have to acknowledge her as he left the hall after finishing his meal. And if he did not do so then, she had other plans to plant herself in his path and leave him with no choice but to look at her. What she would say to him then, she didn't know. She prayed something would come to her. For now, it was enough to have him look on her and see her.

Even by the light of torches on the walls, she had no trouble finding him. There were many who sat at her father's lower tables, but none who set the very air about them to trembling merely by being there.

He sat with his back to the fire, his helm on the table next to his arm, and a dark cloak pushed back over his shoulders. The torchlight shone on his dark hair and glanced off his perfectly chiseled features. His clothing was simple and unadorned, though as Bertram's favored foster son he likely could have bedecked himself as lavishly as did Alain and his brother Rollan. Gwen decided then that he had no need. Not even the simpleness of his garb could hide the nobility of his bearing and the beauty of his face.

And to think he was a mere knight with nothing to his name but his sword and horse.

By the saints, 'twas no wonder Alain hated him so. He was everything Alain wasn't.

He ate quickly, speaking gravely to those about him only when he was spoken to. Gwen watched him finish long before those around him had satisfied themselves, rise and beg leave of Lord Bertram to depart the hall, and make his way out the door. He was gone before Gwen had realized that her initial plan to put herself in his path before he left the hall had failed miserably. She would have to exert better control over herself. Gaping at the man while he escaped the web she set for him would get her nothing but fodder for her dreams at night. She fully intended to have more. Her parents might have intended her for Alain of Ayre, but she had a different idea.

Even if it entailed wedding only a knight.

But that wouldn't happen until she had speech with him, and that surely wouldn't occur until she had found a way to attract his notice. She certainly wasn't going to roll about in the pigsty again to have it. She was a woman now. Though she'd been but a child the last time she'd encountered him, she'd known then he was what she wanted. Now that she was grown, surely he would take her desire for him to be her champion more seriously.

She walked from the hall as quickly as she dared, hoping her father would think she had ignored his calls to come sit and eat due to a sudden loss of hearing on her part. She breathed a sigh of relief when she found that no one was following her from the great hall. She might succeed after all.

Sir Rhys had gone to the stables. She knew this because it was his habit to check on his mount after the morning meal to assure himself it was being treated well. And after his visit to the stables, he would return again to the lists, where he trained for several hours a day. Surely he wouldn't mind interrupting his habits this once.

She ran toward the entrance to the stables, fearing she might have missed him already. She had almost reached the opening when her toes made contact abruptly with a sharp stone. She greeted the pain with a most unladylike expression and hopped about on one foot, clutching her offended toe with her fist.

She hopped, of course, directly into Rhys de Piaget's substantial chest.

He caught her by the arms. She looked up, her pain forgotten. Indeed, she had to remind herself that breathing, not standing there gaping at him like a halfwit, was the best way to make a favorable impression.

She lowered her foot as casually as she could. She made no move to straighten her garments, for that might have induced him to release her and that she couldn't have.

"Hurt?" he asked.

Ah, but he did have such a rich voice. Surely the stuff of any maid's dreams.

He frowned. "Are you unwell?"

It was all she could do not to fling herself into his arms and blurt out her love for him right on the spot. Instead, she shook her head and prayed she looked even the slightest bit dignified while doing so.

"Well, then," he said, releasing her abruptly and taking a step backward. "Good morrow to you, lady."

He was halfway across the bailey before she managed to gather up enough wits to realize he had once again escaped her clutches.

"Sir Rhys, wait!"

He didn't stop. Gwen couldn't credit him with rudeness, so she assumed perhaps too many victims screaming for mercy had ruined his hearing. She hiked up her skirts and dashed off after him.

"Sir Rhys, wait," she repeated breathlessly when she caught up with him. His ground-eating stride did not slow, which forced her to keep running alongside him. "Won't you stop and have speech—"

"Have things to do," he said curtly, increasing his pace.

"But," she said, breaking into a full run.

"No women in the lists," he threw over his shoulder as he fair sprinted to his destination.

Gwen realized how foolish she must look, so she stopped and frowned. No women in the lists? So *he* thought. He obviously was unacquainted with her determination. She would have the chance to win his heart before his visit was up or perish in the attempt. Surely he couldn't resist her. She was wearing her mother's finest wimple, for pity's sake. Had he no idea what kind of sacrifice that was?

She thought about following him to the lists, then realized that perhaps she might need to rethink her strategy.

But he would succumb in the end. She would give him no other choice.

Rhys leaned on his sword and forced himself to take deep, even breaths. It wasn't that honing his skills against the majority of Segrave's garrison wasn't enough to cause him to pant; indeed, any man might have been forgiven a bit of gasping after the morning's exercise Rhys had just taken.

But not every man had Gwennelyn of Segrave loitering along the walls, watching his every move.

He could feel her gaze on him, just as surely as it had been for the past three days. Relentless, that's what she was, relentless and determined. He'd never felt so scrutinized in his entire life, and to be sure he'd had his share of souls watching him to mark any misstep. But he'd never forced himself not to pant for any of them.

The saints preserve him, he was losing his mind.

He'd done his best to ignore her. He'd even gone so far as to be rude to her on more than one occasion. Once he'd realized she knew his habits, he'd changed them, thinking that she couldn't possibly outwit him. Obviously there was a very clever girl under all that beauty, for she'd discovered him straightway and thereafter taken to shadowing him. She would have made a bloody good spy.

He had no idea what she wanted of him. Likely to talk him into another rescue. He scowled. He'd learned his lesson the last time. It hardly mattered what he did for her, for he would never have her. What was the point in pleasing her?

A pity the thought of pleasing her was the one that had haunted him for six years.

Out of the corner of his eye, he checked to see if she still held her position. Still in place, aye, but seemingly overwhelmed by the taxing nature of her chase. In spite of himself, Rhys began to smile. He walked over to the wall quietly and stopped a few paces away from her. He fussed with his gear, lest he be observed, and surreptitiously drank in the sight of the young woman snoring so peacefully where she sat with her back against the wall.

Six years had done nothing but enhance the promise of beauty he'd seen in her. No wonder Bertram wanted her for his son. She would bring a loveliness to his table no jewel-encrusted goblet could hope to equal, and she would likely do all Alain's thinking for him. It was a wise choice to have made as far as Ayre's future was concerned. Rhys would have done the same thing in his lord's place, only he never would have given such a one as she to his son; he would have taken her for himself.

He sighed, and it felt as if it had come from the marrow of his bones. It had been a mistake to come to Segrave. He'd told himself he would come because Lord Bertram had asked him to come. He'd been asked before, of course, but he'd never dared think he was equal to the task of gazing upon Gwen and remaining unmoved.

Fool, he thought with another sigh. All it had taken was one look at her and his carefully constructed defense against her had crumbled.

He resheathed his sword and cursed softly. He should have gone to France in the spring. He'd planned to. Lord Bertram had been willing to free him from all current obligations in order for him to do so. Rhys had envisioned a few years' tourneying yielding enough gold to purchase some fine bit of soil somewhere. He'd sketched out in his mind the sort of keep he might build and tallied the number of knights he would have about him calling him lord.

He had, of course, studiously avoided peopling his keep

with any kind of family, especially a wife, *especially* after his first musings had cast Gwennelyn of Segrave in that role.

France had, in the end, seemed a rather unattractive destination that spring. His duty to Lord Bertram, given of his own free will, was almost over. He'd offered seven years of knightly service and had it accepted willingly. Six had been fulfilled and Bertram hadn't seemed reluctant to collect the seventh at a later time. Still, Rhys had been unable to move himself from Ayre.

And, as he stared at the young woman before him, he wondered if this might have been what he had waited for. Against all reason, he suspected one last glimpse of her had been what had kept him off the continent. Bertram traveled to Segrave often enough. It had certainly been no difficulty to come along.

Now the difficulty would be leaving.

And if he had even a grain of sense in his head, he would have packed up his gear and fled for France that very day.

His feet, however, had a different idea. They seemed to have no intention of responding to his command that they carry him far away from certain heartache.

"Oh, you're finished!"

The sound of her voice startled him so badly, he stumbled backward. Gwen leaped to her feet. The look of delight she gave him slammed into him like a dozen fists and left him gasping more surely than his morning's exercise.

Run, you fool!

His common sense had that aright. He made Gwen a low bow and turned to flee from the field.

"Sir Rhys, wait!"

If he had to hear that phrase one more time from her, he knew he would scream, so he did the only sensible thing he'd done since he'd first clapped eyes on her. He fled to the guardtower and closed himself in the garderobe.

After all, how long could she possibly wait for him to come out?

5

Gwen's feet hurt. Standing outside the guardtower for most of the day had been mightily taxing on them. At least she had the chance to rest them for a bit. She currently did so as she sat at her father's table and scowled at Rhys's profile. Who would have thought the man could be so stubborn? He had escaped every snare she'd set for him, resisted every attempt at polite conversation, and resorted to flight when all other avenues had been closed to him. But the most irritating thing of all had been the length of time he'd remained in the garderobe that morn. Who would have thought a man's business could take him so long? If she'd had a sword, she would have prodded him into an empty corner with it and kept him there with it at his throat until she'd had speech with him.

She nursed the wine in her cup and gave that thought more consideration. She had no sword at her disposal, but she was clever enough for a young woman of her tender years. Perhaps a message, delivered by someone he trusted, would lure him to a private meeting.

After the meal she penned a quick missive, approached Sir Montgomery, and smiled a most innocent smile at him. And bless the man if he didn't do as she intended, which was smile back at her just as foolishly as did anyone her mother chanced to grace with her attentions. Though people told her she resembled her mother, Gwen couldn't see it somehow. Blessedly Montgomery seemed to think so as well, so she without hesitation used what wiles she had.

"A favor, good sir?" she asked him.

"Anything," he said, blinking at her as if he had stared too long at the sun.

She handed him the tiny scrap of parchment. "Might you deliver this to Sir Rhys? Discreetly, of course."

"Of course," he said, though she could see in his eyes that he was wondering about the wisdom of it.

"A few harmless words," she said with a dismissive wave. "Nothing of import." She smiled again for good measure.

He took a step backward as if he'd been struck, nodded, and turned to walk obediently, if not a bit unsteadily, to where Sir Rhys sat at the table.

Gwen escaped the hall and ran for the roof before Rhys could suspect that she might be behind the meeting. She went out onto the battlements and secreted herself in a darkened corner. No sense in having the whole of her father's guard watching her as she was about her business. She had every intention of convincing the gallant Sir Rhys to snatch her away before she was forced to wed with Alain of Ayre, but that was best done in secret.

'Twas but a moment or two later that the door next to her creaked. Rhys slipped from it carefully, as if he expected to be attacked. Even the very sight of him, dark and full of stealth, was enough to set Gwen's heart to racing. Aye, this was surely the man for her, and what a man! Her father could not help but be pleased with his prowess. Gwen tucked that thought away for future use. Perhaps she could suggest to her sire that Rhys would be a far better protector than Alain. Surely he would be swayed by that.

Rhys closed the door behind him softly. Gwen took her courage in hand and reached out to touch his arm.

And before she could even open her mouth to greet him, she found herself slammed back against the wall with a knife at her throat. She would have squeaked, but she didn't have the breath for it.

As suddenly as it had appeared, the knife disappeared into a sheath somewhere up Rhys's sleeve. Rhys hung his head and let out a shaky breath.

" 'Tis only me," she managed.

He lifted his head and glared at her. "I could have slain . . ." he began, then he shut his mouth and started to pull away.

"Nay," she said, grasping him by the tunic sleeve more firmly, "don't leave."

He paused.

"Please," she added.

The moonlight shone down on him, casting his face into shadows. There was no smile that she could see, but she had no trouble hearing a sigh of resignation. It was a sound her father made regularly.

"What is it?" he asked.

Gwen feared he would disappear if she released him, so she kept hold of his arm. It was the same arm she had tied her favor around seven years earlier. She wondered if he still had it.

"What is it you want?" he asked again, more roughly this time. "I've things to do."

"Well," she said, wishing this were turning out a bit more like she had dreamed it would, "I thought we could talk."

"I've no time for talking." But he didn't move.

He wasn't declaring undying love, but he wasn't running off either. Gwen rifled through what pitiful wits still remained her for something clever to say to keep him there a bit longer until she could discover for herself if he had tender feelings for her. Then she would present her plan to him.

" 'Tis a lovely night, is it not?" she asked.

He growled something unintelligible.

"The moon is quite large," she added.

"Did you lure me here," he said through gritted teeth, "to discuss the contents of the heavens or something more interesting? I pray you, lady, come to a decision quickly for I have little time to waste upon foolishness."

Gwen took a deep breath. Had she been made of lesser stuff, she might have been cowed by his grumbles. Or, worse yet, she might have taken them to mean he cared nothing for her. She wasn't about to believe that. He'd agreed to be her champion once before. She felt certain that, given the chance, he would do so again. And if he wanted her to speak frankly, then frankly she would speak.

"I asked you here to discuss my hand in marriage," she said as calmly as she could.

"Your marriage to whom?" he asked curtly. "Alain of Ayre?"

"Nay," she said plainly. "To you."

He blinked. Then he blinked a bit more. And then his jaw went slack.

"You cannot be serious," he managed.

"Oh, but I am."

He shook his head. "You're daft."

"I believe I'm quite in possession of all my wits. Hence the craftiness of my ruse to get you here."

He seemed to give it some thought, then a look of coldness came over his face. "Is Ayre so unappealing," he asked flatly, "that you would lower yourself to wed with a mere knight?"

"Alain is unappealing," she agreed, "but that is not why I chose you."

"How arrogant you are, lady, to think the choice is yours."

It was her turn to stare at him, speechless. That he might not want her had never occurred to her. She had imagined him rescuing her from her current plight so often that she had come to believe that he cared for her as greatly as she cared for him.

She shut her mouth as casually as she could, then gathered her courage about her. She released his arm, though it was done most reluctantly. Then she tried a smile. It wasn't her best effort, but she persevered.

"Could you not," she ventured, "be persuaded to be mine?"

He seemed suddenly to have difficulty swallowing. Supper had been delicious as always, so she couldn't credit the fare for his trouble. Perhaps 'twas that he was suddenly confronted with something he'd tried to deny. She'd seen the condition in other men, and it usually meant they were overcome by some strong emotion. Could it be affection for her? Perhaps he wasn't as unmoved as he seemed.

"Hmmm," he said, looking as if he were giving her proposition serious thought, "I would need to think on it."

"You were my champion once," she said, hoping to spark a bit more enthusiasm from him. "You could perhaps be that again."

"Your champion?" he echoed. "Of course it would be only that. What else could it be?" He started to turn away.

This was not going at all as she had expected.

"Champion, husband, 'tis all the same to me," she said in exasperation. "The point is, 'tis you I love and 'tis you I would wed."

He froze. Then he turned to look back at her. " 'Tis me you love," he echoed, blinking at her.

"Aye, and now 'tis your task to accomplish my rescue and carry me off to a priest."

"But . . ."

"I know you can do it. I'm quite familiar with your exploits."

"But," he spluttered, "I cannot wed you."

"Of course you can. You said you might somehow be persuaded to want me."

He waved a hand impatiently. "That isn't what hinders me."

"Then you *do* want me." She smiled. She'd known it. Only a man who wanted a woman badly could have ignored her as thoroughly as Rhys had.

"Of course I want you," he said in an angry whisper. "I've wanted you from the moment I bloody clapped eyes on you."

He sounded none too pleased about it.

She smiled happily. "How lovely—"

"But I can hardly have you," he interrupted. "Or have you forgotten that your father would never give you to me?"

"He would if he could. He said as much to my mother not six months ago."

Rhys pursed his lips. "Words prompted, no doubt, by a visit from your betrothed."

"Alain slipped rather heavily in his cups and vomited upon my father's finest mattress."

"I see."

" 'Twas a most unpleasant se'nnight." She shrugged. "My mind, however, was made up long before that. And even though my father's hands are tied, mine are not."

"And you think your sire wouldn't tie your hands and lock you in your mother's solar until the wedding if he knew what you have proposed this night?"

Gwen would have liked to think not, for her father was enormously patient with her antics, but she wondered if Rhys might have it aright. She settled upon another course of action.

"We won't tell him," she said.

He fell silent. Gwen looked up at him and felt hope begin to spring to life in her breast. He was giving it thought, she could see that. He'd said that he wanted her from the moment he'd clapped eyes on her, never mind how irritated he'd sounded over it. 'Twas obviously a powerful love indeed, for she remembered vividly her liberation from the pigsty and how she must have smelled.

He was what she wanted, she was certain of it. Memories of the gallantry and kindness of a fourteen-year-old lad were forever emblazoned upon her memory.

He looked down. Gwen watched as he slowly reached out and took her by the hand. He rubbed his thumb over the back of her hand slowly, as if he sought to memorize how it was shaped.

"You'll see to it, won't you?" she asked.

He said no word, but continued to look at her hand. Gwen would have prodded him further, but she was too distracted. His fingers were callused and warm against her skin. How odd. His touch was far different than she'd imagined it might be. She'd held her father's hand often enough; he had calluses from wielding a sword and his hands were warm.

Rhys, however, was not her father and the touch of his hand on hers was entirely different. Shivers went up her arm and scattered themselves over the rest of her poor form.

She watched, mute, as he lifted her hand and brought it to his lips. The touch of *them* upon her skin sent a rush of something through her she'd never felt before. Not even almost falling down the barbican steps after having snuck up on her father's garrison captain to see if he performed his duties sufficiently well had sent such tingles of fear through her.

Only, somehow, she thought what she was feeling wasn't fear.

"Aye," he said, taking her hand and resting it against his faintly scratchy cheek, "I will."

Gwen blinked at him. "You will?"

"I'll see to it."

"See to it?" She was so overcome by his nearness, by the sheer height and power of the man that she could scarce remember her name, much less what they'd been discussing. He smiled and the sight of that almost sent her pitching backward off the wall. By the saints, he was beautiful.

"I'll see to the rescuing of you from Alain's nefarious marriage designs upon you," he reminded her.

"Oh," she said, nodding. "That."

"Aye," he said, with another smile, "that."

His smile faded. He closed his eyes and sighed. Then he opened his eyes and looked down at her. The longing in his gaze was like nothing she'd ever seen before on any man's face, not even those men who came to look at her mother knowing they would never have her. That a man, much less Rhys de Piaget, should look at her thusly was a marvelous thing indeed. She studied his look intently that she might call it to mind during the next few months while he was conceiving a way to have her as his.

And then before she could ask him to turn a bit more to the left that the moon might light his features the better, he had taken her face in his hands, bent his dark head to hers, and kissed her very sweetly upon the lips.

Gwen was certain the stones had moved beneath her feet.

"Oh," she managed as he lifted his head and looked down at her.

He looked as dazed as she felt.

"Aye," he said hoarsely. He shook his head, as if to clear it. "We should return below, lest someone see us."

But he didn't move.

Neither did she.

All she could do was stand there with his rough hands upon her cheeks, the remembered warmth of his mouth lingering upon hers, and his beloved form standing but a hair's breadth from her, and wonder if any maid in the annals of time had ever had such a man willing to champion her.

Or to kiss her, for that matter.

Before she could ask him if he wouldn't be so kind as to do the like again, he had taken her by the hand and pulled her along behind him down from the roof.

"We must return," he said over his shoulder.

"But—"

"Short of snatching you away in the night, I don't know how I'll manage this," he muttered as they descended the steps.

"But—"

"Bribery, perhaps," he mumbled. "Very expensive, but you're well worth the price, I should think."

"Well, thank—"

"Aye," he said as they reached the bottom of the steps. "I will take up my journey to France and there frequent a tourney or two."

Gwen jumped in before he could interrupt her again. "And then you'll return? Well before I'm to wed with that fool?"

He turned around to face her. "Well before, with bags of gold in hand."

"Then—" *Perhaps another kiss,* she started to say as she leaned up on her toes and aimed for his mouth with hers, but a bellow from down the hall interrupted her.

"Gwen!"

The sound of her father's voice echoed down the passageway. Gwen gasped and pulled her hand from Rhys's. A look of intense alarm fixed itself upon his features.

"Do something," he whispered fiercely, "lest he cast me into the dungeon and then there will be no hope for us at all!"

Another ruse. She sighed. She was destined to be called upon to think them up.

"Why, Sir Knight," she exclaimed, putting her hands on her hips and affecting a look of outrage, "how dare you!" She threw him a look that she hoped said *'Tis the best I could think of,* and pulled back her fist. "Father, I'll dispatch him myself," she called down the passageway, then with an unspoken plea for forgiveness, firmly and with deadly accuracy, let fly her fist.

Very ungently into Rhys's nose.

6

For the second time in all the years he had known Gwennelyn of Segrave, Rhys clutched his nose and cursed. He'd thought that four years ago would be the first and last time he would have to endure such a smacking from her.

"Damn you, Gwen," he exclaimed, "why must you always do that?"

"For the same reason I did it the last time," she said. "That we might not be discovered!"

Rhys felt his nose gingerly and wondered if it was worth it. He couldn't argue that it hadn't been the last time. William of Segrave had stood at the end of the passageway and watched with ill-concealed amusement as the blood dripped down Rhys's face. He'd only nodded to Rhys as Rhys had escaped past him to the safety of the garrison hall. Rhys had fled the next morning after having begged leave of Bertram. His request hadn't been refused and he'd been fortunate enough not to encounter Gwen's sire again.

He hadn't exchanged any words with Gwen, either. She'd only watched him ride out with a look of perfect trust and confidence. It had been enough to send him straight to France with only a brief stop at Ayre to collect his few belongings.

And now, against all odds, he stood staring down at the
woman he'd spent the past four years working to buy. It
hardly surprised him that he didn't have the peace or privacy to greet her properly. Then again, he was close to
having enough coin at his disposal to offer for her, so what
should he care what her betrothed thought?

"I wonder if it really matters what you reveal," he said,
dabbing at his face with his sleeve, "for in a few more
months I'll have plenty of gold—"

"A few more months?" Gwen echoed, whirling on him.
She jabbed with her finger toward where Rhys could see
Alain's white stallion approaching rapidly. "I'm to wed
him within the se'nnight!"

Rhys stopped dabbing and gaped at her. "You aren't.
You can't. You weren't to wed him—"

"Until I was a full score and one, aye, I know! But who
is to stop him? My sire is dead two years now, and my
guardian cannot wait to rid himself of me."

Rhys had known of her sire's passing but hadn't dared
return to comfort her. Besides, the news of it had taken
half a year to reach him. He'd grieved for her and hoped
she would know as much.

But Lord Ayre was still alive, and Rhys knew his foster
father wouldn't allow her wedding to happen before the
agreed-upon time. Gwen had been convinced incorrectly
by her guardian as to the date of her nuptials.

Nuptials which, of course, wouldn't take place with
Alain of Ayre.

"Bertram will see to it," he assured her. "He sent for
me less than a month ago, which is why I am here and
not in France still filling my coffers." He smiled at her.
"Fear not, Gwen. He will not allow this to happen yet."

Rhys wasn't sure why, but she seemed not at all reas-
sured by that. She looked over her shoulder, then turned
back to him. "This may be the last time we have speech
freely together."

"Surely not—"

"You've no idea what has transpired."

Rhys looked at Alain's rapidly approaching figure and

cursed the inconvenience. "I'll see to it all," he said confidently. "We'll just tell this fool here to be off—" He stopped at her warning look. "Very well, we'll keep up the ruse a bit longer. Shall I clutch my nose again to please you?"

She opened her mouth to speak, then shut it. Rhys would have been more satisfied with some kind of declaration of affection, but obviously 'twas not to be. Whatever catastrophe had occurred, he felt certain Alain was responsible for it. It could be solved, if they could just avoid displaying before the entire garrison of Ayre their true feelings. Rhys fingered his nose gingerly. It might not be so difficult after all if the alternative was another fist in his nose.

He suddenly had no more time to contemplate the significance of the last few moments of his life, for he was standing surrounded by Alain's men. He watched Alain expertly cut Gwen off from Rhys's own horse. Rhys had never doubted Alain's skill with horseflesh. It was his skill with handling the souls about him that Rhys had never felt sure of. Alain sat there, his chest heaving, and stared down at Gwen for several moments, likely trying to choose the appropriate word to voice his obvious displeasure.

"Bitch," he said finally. Then he bit his lip, looking faintly appalled at what he'd just said.

"Fool," Gwen shot back.

Alain only stared at her, his mouth working a bit. Rhys surmised that Alain's mind was not keeping pace, for no sound came out. Perhaps an impasse between thought and utterance had been reached already.

Alain seemed to gather his wits about him. Then he looked at Gwen in faint disbelief. "You ran from the keep," he managed finally.

"Aye, I did," she said.

He scratched the side of his head with the leather crop he held. "Why?"

"To escape you, you halfwit!"

"Halfwit," he echoed, gaping at her. "*Halfwit?*"

Rhys wondered just what response Alain might find to

that insult in the recesses of his overworked brain when to his complete astonishment, Alain leaned over and backhanded Gwen full across the face.

Rhys caught her only because the force of the blow sent her sprawling into his arms. He looked down into her soot-smudged face and felt a white-hot rage well up in him. His sword was halfway from its sheath before he even realized what he was about.

And then a slighter hand came down upon his suddenly. He looked down into Gwen's eyes and saw the pleading there. It was the hardest thing he had ever done, that releasing of his blade. And he suspected, in the back of his mind, that 'twas only the beginning of the things he would have to do to keep his desire for the woman in his arms a secret.

By the saints, this was a difficult path they'd chosen.

Alain glared at him. "I don't know who you are, but you've a manner about you I don't like. Release the wench, for I've yet more blows to deliver."

Rhys was the first to admit his appearance left something to be desired, but surely Alain had seen him often enough in the past to recognize him. Obviously Alain's wits had not increased during Rhys's absence.

"Your sire, my lord," Rhys said, "does not approve of the beating of women."

"And what would you know of my sire, you . . . you . . ." Alain spluttered furiously. He seemed to be searching again for a term foul enough to express his displeasure, when his gaze fell to Rhys's sword and his mouth dropped open.

Rhys knew then that Alain had finally realized whom he was looking at. Lord Bertram had given Rhys not only his sword, but a fat ruby to put into its hilt. Alain had never forgiven his father for it, for he surely hadn't received the like. Bertram's reasoning was that since Alain would eventually inherit everything else, he had no need of gems adorning his blade. Alain, though, being Alain and not precisely overendowed with logic, had raged over the injustice of it for years. He hadn't, however, raged thoroughly enough to invite Rhys to step into the lists to soothe his bruised feelings.

Rhys wondered, in the back of his mind, if he just might end up paying for his foster father's generosity all the same.

Alain spat at Rhys's feet. "My sire is dead, de Piaget, which means he's not here to disapprove—"

Rhys felt the ground grow unsteady beneath him.

"Dead?" he echoed. "He lived but a month past."

"It came upon him suddenly," Gwen said quietly. "He had but traveled to Segrave most recently—"

"And I was until recently being paid attention to!" Alain interrupted angrily. "By the saints, I hate being ignored!"

Rhys could hardly believe Alain's father was dead and he was now staring at the current lord of Ayre. If he'd known the truth of that, he never would have left France so ill-prepared.

"Now, brother," a voice said from behind Alain. "Surely you should save your irritation for a more private display."

Rhys pulled Gwen behind him while Alain's notice was off her and onto someone else.

Alain looked at the man who had spoken. "She called me lackwit," he complained.

"Actually, she called you halfwit," Rollan said gently, "but who remembers such trivialities?"

Rhys could hear Gwen muttering under her breath behind him, and he wished mightily that she would cease with it. Never mind that Alain was a fool. His younger brother, Rollan, was as crafty as the devil himself, and just as ruthless. Even if Gwen's insults eventually slipped Alain's mind, Rollan would choose the worst time possible to refresh his brother's memory.

"She should be punished," Alain grumbled. He glared at Rhys. "And you should step out of the way so I can be about it."

"Her guardian surely would not approve of such treatment," Rhys said, hoping to spark some small sense of reason in the man.

"Who are you to tell me what to do?" Alain demanded.

"Aye," Rollan agreed. "Who indeed, Sir Rhys? I daresay you forget your place. You have no title, no rank, no lands."

No lands. Well, that was always the heart of the matter, and Rhys felt the sting of it almost as keenly as he had the first time the insult had been hurled at him.

"I am a knight," he said curtly, his bruised pride demanding some kind of assuagement, "and therefore sworn to protect those weaker than myself."

"Indeed," Gwen said, with an approving poke in his back.

"I should have thought these years of battle, mock battle though it was, would have taught you the truth of the matter," Alain said. "The strong rule the weak. Isn't that so, brother?" He looked at Rollan for a nod of approval. "And so I will rule you," he continued. "And I'll rule that headstrong wench once I beat some obedience into her. I think I'll begin now."

When I'm dead, Rhys thought to himself. He would have said as much, but he hadn't earned his reputation by ignoring the odds of success in any given battle. It was him and Gwen against Alain, Rollan, and a score of Alain's guardsmen, several of whom had reason not to care for him overmuch. Better to talk his way out of this one.

"You might want to leave her with her strength of will intact," Rhys offered. While Alain digested that, Rhys spit his next words out with as much haste as possible. " 'Tis something she may well pass on to your sons."

"Ha," Gwen said from behind him. "As if I would ever bear a son of his!"

Alain urged his horse forward, and Rhys backed up a pace to avoid being trampled.

"She's bound to wed me," Alain said. "Her father promised."

Gwen snorted. "He was in his cups at the time—"

Rhys looked over his shoulder and spared Gwen a

frown. She left the rest of her words unsaid, but scowled at him. Rhys turned back to Alain, ready to move should he need to, but the newly made lord of Ayre only caressed his whip and chewed on his thoughts. Not a substantial meal likely, but seemingly an enjoyable one.

"Perhaps there are more effective ways to drive her cheek from her," Rollan offered smoothly.

Alain looked at his brother. "Are there?"

"On your wedding night, perhaps," Rollan said.

Alain looked faintly perplexed, then shrugged. Obviously uncovering the hidden meaning in Rollan's words was too much for him. Alain looked down at Rhys.

"I see by your nose that she's marked you. I take it you were trying to stop her from fleeing?"

"Of course," Rhys managed. "What else?"

Alain grunted. "Then I suppose you'll serve me well."

"Serve you?" Rhys echoed. "Why would I serve you?"

"You owed my sire one more year."

"Aye, your sire. Not you."

Alain scowled. "Before he died, my sire commanded that you give that year to me. As part of my inheritance."

It wasn't the first time Rhys had heard of the scheme, but he'd always managed to avoid agreeing to it. He found, as he stared up at Ayre's new lord, that he could say nothing in return. How often had Bertram tried to convince Rhys to tend Alain? *"Just a year or two, son,"* Bertram would say. *"Stay by him for a year or two after he weds. Perhaps you can be a steadying influence."* *With the way he feels toward me?* Rhys would always argue. *I'll be serving out my year in the dungeon.* Bertram had always promised Rhys it would be worth his time, but Rhys had never been able to imagine anything that would have made such a sacrifice bearable.

In return for Segrave perhaps.

Or Gwen.

Damn you, Bertram, he swore silently. *Why did you do this to me?*

"I'm still itching to beat her," Alain announced. "Everyone stand out of my way so I might do so."

And with that, Rhys had his answer. Bertram had obviously wanted Rhys close by to protect Gwen. Rhys snorted to himself. What was he to do, sleep between the pair?

Nay, it would never come to that. Gwen would never wed with Alain.

Rhys would see to that personally.

"Perhaps you should wait until you reach home," Rollan suggested. "Beat her in the privacy of your solar with a goblet of wine at the ready. You'll be more comfortable there."

Alain considered, then nodded. "Someone give me a rope," he barked, dismounting. He shoved Rhys out of his way and reached for Gwen. "Perhaps the walk back to Ayre will teach you not to run away again," he said as he jerked a coil away from one of his men.

Rhys clenched his hands at his sides as Alain bound Gwen's hands together. He mounted and turned his horse toward Ayre, holding on to the rope's end. "Mount up, de Piaget. I have important things to see to. A hunt, perhaps, though 'tis certain she's ruined the morning already for that kind of sport."

Rhys hardly had time to fix Gwen's stolen sword to his saddle before Alain had led her a goodly distance away. He grasped his horse's reins and hastened after the company. He fell into step next to Gwen, leading his mount. They walked together for a time in silence before she spoke.

"I was coming to find you," she said quietly.

He sighed. "I wish you had waited at Segrave."

"I was already at Ayre and I couldn't bear the thought of staying there another night. Besides, I thought you might have wanted someone to guard your back."

He almost smiled at that. "Indeed."

She scowled at him. "Think you I could not have done it?"

"Ah . . ."

"Today was my first day as a mercenary. I assure you I would have improved with practice."

The thought of Gwennelyn of Segrave guarding his back was enough to make him break out in a sweat. Saints, but 'twould be enough to get him killed.

"Besides," she said quietly, "I'd heard rumors that you were uninterested in taking a wife." She looked at him from under her eyelashes. "I thought I might appeal more as a mercenary."

"Oh, by the saints," he groaned, wondering what other untruths she'd heard bandied about the garrison hall. He generally kept enough to himself that the only tales people had to tell of him were ones they made up themselves. He turned to ask her just what she'd overheard, but found himself looking at air.

Alain had jerked the rope so hard, he'd tugged Gwen completely off her feet. He was currently dragging her, ignoring her struggles to regain her footing. Rhys dropped his reins and ran forward to pick her up. Alain wheeled around and lashed out at Rhys with his crop. Rhys ducked, pushed Gwen to her feet, and backed up a pace.

"This is most unseemly, my lord," he said sharply.

The riding crop came at him again so quickly, he barely had time to react. He caught it before it struck his face.

"You forget your place," Alain snarled.

"I haven't yet agreed to serve you," Rhys returned before he could think better of his words.

"Such cheek," Rollan said with a shake of his head. "Truly a disturbing trait in him."

Alain looked at his brother. "It is, isn't it?"

Rollan nodded. "I don't know that I wouldn't worry about his lack of humility, given his station."

"True enough," Alain said.

"Perhaps a taste of your displeasure," Rollan suggested.

Alain fingered his crop, then nodded suddenly. "Ten lashes for his disobedience. Guards, come hold him."

Rhys was surprised enough to just stand still and gape at his lord's son.

"I will not be flogged," he managed.

"You will if I command it."

"I will *not* submit willingly," Rhys said, wondering how many of Alain's men he could do in before he was overcome just the same. A full score surrounded him. He could take perhaps half of them if he could mount quickly enough.

"Then I'll whip *her* instead for your cheek," Alain said, jerking on Gwen's rope.

"Nay," Rhys said, aghast. "You cannot mean to—" He didn't bother to finish. It was all too clear that Alain would do whatever he pleased, the consequences be damned.

"Submit, then," Alain said, dismounting. "Kneel at my feet and submit."

'Twill keep her from his wrath, Rhys told his knees, but they weren't listening. It took all his willpower not to draw his sword and use it liberally on the fool standing in front of him.

"Perhaps he needs aid," Rollan suggested.

"Likely so. Guards!" Alain called. "Take him and bend him over something solid."

Rhys considered. If he didn't have to kneel on his own, perhaps he could submit. Besides, ten lashes were a small price to pay for keeping Gwen on her feet and out of Alain's whip arc. Damned annoying chivalry. He was far better off when he ignored its clamorings.

He looked at Alain's guardsmen and recognized most of them. Those were the ones he had met previously in the lists while training. There wasn't a bloody one of them he hadn't left crying peace more than once. They were the ones who were slow to dismount and even slower to draw their swords.

The others bounded down enthusiastically and surrounded Rhys. Rollan, of course, was still safely sitting atop his horse a healthy distance away. Rhys looked at Alain's brother and hoped the man could see the promise of retribution in his eyes. Rollan only lifted one eyebrow and smiled. He didn't, however, come any closer.

Rhys looked at the other handful of Alain's guards who

had encircled him. Either they had heard nothing of his skill or had heard it and didn't believe it. Rhys told himself it would do him no good to wipe those smiles off their faces, but the temptation to draw his sword and do just that was almost overpowering.

This will save Gwen from Alain's whip.

That was the only thing that kept his sword in its sheath. He didn't think, however, that he would be condemned overmuch for using his fists a time or two. He bloodied several noses and felt the satisfying crunch of teeth coming loose, but in the end there were simply too many hands for him to avoid. They stripped off his upper garments and bent him over a stump.

"You vicious whoreson!" Gwen exclaimed. "He did but try to protect me from your foul temper!"

"My foul temper?" Alain echoed. "You're the one with the shrewish tongue!"

"At least I don't flog innocent men for my flaw!"

"He's hardly innocent," Rollan said, "and far too cheeky for his place. I'd say that deserved twenty lashes not ten, wouldn't you, brother?"

Rhys fixed his gaze upon Rollan and gave himself over to the contemplation of revenge. That unfortunately didn't last long, for it took all his concentration to keep his own mouth closed.

There were two things Rhys could say for Alain of Ayre: he was very strong and he wielded his crop with great skill. Rhys would have bitten off his own tongue before he cried out, but he did his fair share of grunting. Alain paused in his work, came around, and lifted Rhys's head up by his hair.

"Have you found obedience yet, Sir Rhys?"

Rhys took stock of his strength and measured his fury. Aye, there was a bit more there yet to sustain him. He immediately thought of half a dozen vulgar things he could suggest Alain do to himself, but he had no breath for the voicing of them. So he contented himself with spitting at Alain's feet.

"Another ten!" Alain thundered, stomping off.

After those were accomplished, Rhys decided he'd perhaps had enough of the building of his character for the morning. He could see that Alain was almost beside himself with rage. Rhys suspected if he pushed the man any further, he would be seeing a great deal of Ayre's oubliette. That hardly served his purposes.

It galled him to do it, but he gave Alain the answers he wanted and was deposited none-too-gently back on his feet. He thanked those who helped him back into his clothes, memorizing their faces for future reference, and then imprinted upon his memory every pull, twitch, and drop of blood that his back had produced.

Alain would pay for them all.

And then Rollan would pay as well.

Rhys walked stiffly over to his horse and swung up into the saddle, biting his lip to maintain his silence. And then he found the presence of mind to look for Gwen.

She was watching him with tears streaming down her face.

Rhys looked away before he himself wept. This was not how he had intended their reunion to go. What he wanted to do was snatch her up in his arms and flee with her. All he could do at the moment, however, was concentrate on keeping himself in the saddle. He was hardly in any condition for successful rescuing.

He would repay Alain for that as well.

He would return to Ayre with her. He would see his back tended and take a day or two to shore up his strength. And then perhaps it would come to him just how he intended to see the future come about. If they fled, they would leave behind her mother, which Gwen would not do, and her lands, which he would not do.

He closed his eyes and wondered if his desires were too greedy to merit a heartfelt prayer for deliverance.

He looked at her again as she stumbled along behind Alain's horse, and watched the woman who had kept him on his feet for the past four years. Saints, but she was beautiful. And so full of fire she fair left him gasping for air. To think he'd had her ragged, dirt-smudged self within his grasp and he'd been too stupid to recognize her while they'd had the time.

He should have asked for another ten lashes as repayment.

7

Gwen felt her face flame as she trudged along up the way to the castle. Her mother would have been appalled, her sire incensed at her current plight. She herself was simply mortified. She'd gone off in such a rush of glory. This was not exactly how she would have chosen to return. Given that she'd never intended to return at all, the insult was doubly painful.

"You could release me now," she said distinctly, jerking suddenly on her rope to gain Alain's attention.

He only glared over his shoulder at her. Gwen thought briefly about fighting, then abandoned the notion. Alain would just drag her along as he had before. Considering the wretched condition of Ayre's bailey, she preferred to have her face remain as far away from the ground as her legs could manage.

She did her best to cross the drawbridge without breathing any of the stench wafting up from the moat. It was no wonder Alain employed so few upon his walls. The reek of the water alone was enough to cause his enemies to swoon.

Unfortunately, the smell in the inner bailey was no better. She could hardly believe her father had actually wanted her to pass the rest of her life in this hovel. Surely no political alliance was worth this.

She sighed. She knew she had no cause for complaint. Her sire had made the best match for her he could and trusted her to use her wits to improve her surroundings. Which she would have done, of course, if she'd ever found herself misfortunate enough to be at Ayre for any length of time. As it was, she didn't plan on being there long enough to gather up the rubbish and refuse and carry it well away from the walls. What freedom her attempts at being a mercenary hadn't earned her, Rhys's appearance in England certainly would.

Though she had to admit that she felt the tiniest bit anxious about how he would manage to free her from the wedding Alain had planned for less than a se'nnight hence.

She breathed through her mouth as she trudged over the hard-packed dirt. Alain dismounted before the great hall. He was no taller than she, which afforded her a fine view of his angry eyes as he released her hands from their bonds. Gwen prayed her disdain didn't show. Alain was a bit on the plump side, nigh on to losing the greater part of his hair, and had teeth that would likely rot from his head before spring. And he was bowlegged. She suspected that came from his spending most of his time on horseback, either hunting or using the perch as a means to intimidate those who might have been taller than he.

All in all, not her first choice for a husband.

That soul, whom she could see out of the corner of her eye, was stiffly dismounting his horse. His feet hit the ground with an unsteady thump. He leaned his head briefly against his horse's withers before he suddenly straightened. She suspected that he wished no one to know of his pain.

He looked over his shoulder, and she found herself staring into pale gray eyes. He said no word, nor did his expression reveal anything of what he felt. But in his eyes she could see it.

We will be free of this place.

Then, as if he knew she'd understood him, he nodded.

He turned and slowly led his horse toward the stable.

Gwen winced at the stiffness of his gait. Perhaps she had made a mistake by stopping him from drawing his sword. Then again, had he done so Alain likely would have had his guard cut him down where he stood. This was a painful alternative to death, but likely a better one, though she wished she hadn't been privy to it. She had made herself watch Alain take his whip to Rhys's back, partly so she might meet his eyes should he look up and need strength, and partly to imprint on her mind another example of Alain's cruelty. It had taken every smidgen of willpower, though, to remain where she was and not fling herself at Alain and maim him with her hands alone.

"I see you found the gel."

"No thanks to you. You were to watch over her and see she comported herself well!"

Gwen looked up. Alain was currently expressing his displeasure to her guardian, who stood on the steps leading up to the great hall. She indulged briefly in the wish that she could have hied herself off after Rhys to the stables. Listening to Hugh of Leyburn and her betrothed argue over who was responsible for her flight was something she would have been pleased to avoid.

"I am but a simple man," Hugh said, reaching into the pouch at his belt for something else to put into his mouth. He slurped up a fig or two, then chewed diligently. "I am unused to such disobedience. I surely threatened her properly."

"How?" Alain sneered. "By vowing to take away her sewing needle?"

Her guardian shrugged. "It worked for my gels."

Gwen wondered if Hugh's daughters had also been threatened with losing their place at the supper table. Hugh was not a slender man and neither were his girls, or so rumor had it. The only reason Gwen could divine as to why her father had chosen him to watch over her and her dowry was because Hugh was more interested in Segrave's larder than he was either in Gwen or her mother. Tallying up the rents with one hand while stuffing his maw with the other left no hands free to investigate either of Segrave's ladies. Gwen was most grateful. She suspected her mother was even more so.

"Might I go now?" Gwen asked, moving past Alain before he could say her yea or nay.

"To my mother's solar," Alain commanded. "Fitzgeralds! Finish your duties, then put yourselves at the wench's doorway and see she doesn't go anywhere else."

Gwen gaped at the two blond giants who stepped from the great hall and came down the steps as one. Admittedly she hadn't been at Ayre but a pair of days, and she had pleaded pains in her head at every opportunity that she might miss the filth of the great hall, but she should have noticed the two before her.

Twins, they were; identical pillars of ruthlessness, and surely possessed by foul demons as well. Who knew what was left of the twisted soul who had been split to make its home in two bodies? Why hadn't someone drowned them both while they could?

She bolted past them with a squeak. She slipped and slid across the rushes in the great hall but didn't slow her pace. Once she reached the stairwell, she scraped the bottom of her filched boots on the lowest step, then climbed the steps as quickly as she dared. She gained the solar, then paused at the door to look back down the passageway and make certain the demons weren't following her.

All clear, but she had no idea how long that would last. How many duties did they have? She entered the solar and closed the door behind her. She didn't envy Rhys the besting of those two, for best them he would need to if they were to leave Ayre.

Perhaps she should take her courage in hand and find him before the devils sent to guard her could take up their posts outside her door. It would certainly save his strength. She suspected he had little enough of it at present to spare.

She thought on the possibilities for a goodly length of time. She had just decided that perhaps a brief journey to have speech with Rhys would have been a good thing when the door opened. Too late. She turned, steeling herself for the worst.

"Oh," she said with a scowl as the other soul entered, " 'tis only you."

A lad of no more than fourteen summers made her low bow and then straightened, grinning. "You overwhelm me with your delight at my arrival."

"I was expecting someone else," she grumbled. "How did you manage to slip past my guards?"

"None there yet, though it wouldn't have mattered. I would have told them Alain had sent me."

That made sense enough, she supposed. John was Alain's youngest brother and as much unlike Alain as she was. At least he didn't look to have come out of the morning's events any worse for the wear. He'd been the one to find clothes for her. He had also given her much advice on how to walk like a lad. Perhaps she had been too quick a student. If she'd looked more like a girl, Rhys perhaps might have recognized her more quickly and they both could have avoided their encounters with Alain's temper.

"Sir Rhys is here," John announced. "I saw him in the great hall."

He was as enamored of the man as she was, she noted with another scowl. John had fostered with her father, then remained at Segrave at her mother's request, leaving Gwen amply acquainted with John's worship of the gallant Sir Rhys. John had the most amazing talent for ferreting out the most insignificant details about the man. Where he came by all his information was still something of a mystery, but she suspected he acquired most of it by eavesdropping either in the stables or the garrison hall. She hadn't allowed herself to believe that John had exaggerated either Rhys's fierceness or his skill. She was as ready to believe any and all tales of the man as Alain's brother was.

Except, of course, for those rumors that he wanted no wife.

"You'll not believe what has happened to me," John said, fair frothing at the mouth. "Ask me what happened but moments before. Make haste and ask me."

"Did you see Sir Rhys?"

John made a sound of impatience. "I told you I had. This is more glorious even than that. Ask me what could be more glorious than that."

Gwen sighed. "What could be—"

"Well, as you know," John interrupted, "your mother bid me remain by your side that I might report to her your antics—"

"John!" As if she wanted to be reminded that her mother had saddled her with a keeper!

"And once I realized you were to wed Alain so soon and knew I would be continuing on here at Ayre," he continued animatedly, "I found myself at a loss as to what to do with myself. There was the thought of immediately earning my spurs, of course. 'Tisn't unheard of at such a tender age. Sir Rhys himself had earned his at ten-and-four, and by King Phillip's own hand you remember, though was against the wishes of my father, who was his master at the time, but who was he to argue with the king of France—"

"Who indeed?" she muttered as John drew another great breath for more speaking. She knew all of that, of course, but it never hurt to hear it all again. It helped remind her that Rhys was infinitely capable of extricating himself, and her as well, from any impossible situation.

Or so she hoped.

"So, I supposed that it was possible to be knighted so young, but to be sure I haven't Sir Rhys's skill as yet, though 'tisn't because I haven't worked very hard to acquire it, as you know from having watched me in the lists where I spend most of my time—"

"The event, John. The glorious and noteworthy event that just transpired!" Saints, but there were times the lad could babble on more expertly than the giddiest of serving girls.

John took a deep breath and with great ceremony announced his news. "I am to serve him."

"Whom?"

"Sir Rhys," he said, his joy fair exploding from him. "Can you believe my marvelous fortune?"

"And Alain said as much? In those words?" John had certainly wasted no time in realizing his desire. Would that she could do the same.

"He said, 'I don't care what you do, John. Serve the devil for all I care, just stay out from underfoot.' I took that as permission."

"And the chivalrous Sir Rhys? What did he have to say about this?"

For the first time since he'd burst in upon her, John looked the faintest bit unsure. "He seemed rather absorbed with downing a goodly quantity of ale, so I thought it wise to approach him with the glad tidings after supper."

"A sensible choice."

"I thought so, too."

Gwen paced the short distance to her window, then turned and leaned back against it.

"Why is he here?" she asked. She knew the answer from Rhys's own lips, of course, but there was no harm in hearing what tales John had heard.

"Sir Rhys? Why, my father sent for him. Likely to bid Sir Rhys farewell before he passed."

"Perhaps your sire thought Rhys was finished with his business in France."

"Oh, nay," John disagreed. "I daresay Sir Rhys planned on another full year of tourneying, at least. He needs the gold, you see, to buy his land."

His wife, Gwen corrected silently. She cleared her throat. "You told me several months ago that he had gone to France to make a name for himself."

"Aye, and to earn gold to buy the land he wants. He has no title and to be sure his sire's antics have done nothing to aid him in acquiring one by name alone."

"Hmmm." She nodded, as if she understood what John was talking about. This was a tale she knew nothing about. She'd heard rumors about Rhys's sire coming to a bad end, but she had no idea what he'd done to arrive there.

"Why then," she asked carefully, "doesn't he spend his gold on a title for himself and then seek out a rich heiress to wed?" She realized with something of a start that while she was almost certain Rhys would have her or die in the attempt, she had no idea how he planned to accomplish the deed. *'Tis all in the details, my love,* her mother always said. Gwen was beginning to understand what she'd meant by it.

"He's given some thought to doing that," John informed her, as if he'd been privy to Sir Rhys's most intimate deliberations with himself. "Of course he'll have a wife in time, but that isn't what concerns him the most and it surely isn't what concerns him now. He needs land. Unless," he said with a frown, "unless she came with a large dowry. Then he might be persuaded to burden himself with a bride. And I suppose only the richest would suffice."

Gwen thought of her dowry and of the enormous estates it entailed. Aye, Rhys would not suffer by having her. But would he manage it?

As she stood in her small chamber, she began to wonder just what her worth to him might be if she came with just herself.

Nothing?

She shook her head sharply. He'd just bent himself under the rod for her sake. He'd promised her several years ago that he would find a way to have her. Surely he hadn't lied about something so serious.

"I'm certain," she said, prying a bit further, "that if he met the right woman, he would wed her despite her poverty."

John looked at her as if she'd just sprouted horns. "Of course he wouldn't," he said promptly. "What good would she be to him then?"

There was no point in trying to explain to John the finer points of chivalry. He should have spent more time eavesdropping at her mother's solar door.

She turned him around by the shoulders and pointed him

toward the door. "*Adieu*, little lad. Go nip at your new master's heels."

"He wouldn't wed a woman with nothing, Gwen. He has to have land. He speaks of nothing else—"

She pushed John out the door and shut it behind him. He couldn't be right. After all, what else would Rhys say? That he only wanted to wed for love?

He'd said as much to her. The size of her dowry was something she had no control over. She wouldn't begrudge him the wanting of it. He had no land of his own. Why not have hers?

They would have to have speech together, and the sooner the better. Perhaps she would do well to have a small wash and become presentable. Her hair was a detriment in its shorn state, especially given how much of her ears it revealed, but she could unearth a wimple from the bottom of her traveling trunk. Surely there would be a clean one lurking there.

Then again, perhaps the tidying of herself could wait yet awhile. The events of the day had caught up with her, and she felt a sudden weariness descend. She sat down on a stool near the window and closed her eyes, giving herself over to contemplation of her gallant champion. It was better to first shore up her courage by imagining how it would be when she and Rhys actually managed to flee from Ayre. She propped her elbow on the edge of the window, rested her chin on her closed fists, and concentrated her considerable powers of imagination on the memory of his kiss.

And to think it could quite possibly happen within hours.

Perhaps her destiny had taken a turn for the better that day.

8

Rhys finished his ale and helped himself to another cup. It was quenching his thirst but hardly dulling the pain in his back. Not even his thoughts, absorbing as they were, were enough to distract him completely from the discomfort. But at least giving them his attention was more interesting than concentrating on the throbbing.

He could hardly believe Bertram of Ayre was dead. Had it been a natural death? He could believe many things of Alain, but murder was not one of them. His lust for the title was not so great. But there was always Rollan to consider. With Rollan, anything was possible.

Rhys frowned. Perhaps he should have left France sooner. Once Bertram's messenger had found him at the tourney, Rhys had collected his ransoms, gathered up the rest of his gold, and deposited it with his mother for safekeeping. That had taken him a se'nnight, then he'd wasted another se'nnight traveling to the shore. After that he'd sacrificed a fortnight to pass through London and leave a bottle of costly claret with the king's steward. He hadn't even paused for a bit of bathing along the way, not that such a thing was fashionable in England. He scratched his cheek in annoyance. Shaving would be the very first thing he would do once his back was seen to.

He sighed. A pity he hadn't known Bertram's true condition, else he would have made more haste. He vowed to discover the truth behind Bertram's demise in time. For now, all he could do was assume Bertram had known he was failing quickly and had called Rhys to his side to inform him how he would exact Rhys's final year of service.

Rhys scowled and took another mighty pull from his cup. By the saints, the very last thing he wanted to do was stand at Alain of Ayre's elbow and steady him before he made a fool of himself. And it was something he *wouldn't* be doing if he had his way. Bertram might look down upon him from heaven and forgive him the lapse. Far better that Gwen should be out of Alain's sights than Rhys fulfill a vow of service to one who was dead and perhaps wouldn't know the difference. In this instance his honor could be damned for all the heed he would pay it.

He put his shoulders back and flinched at the movement. The time for seeking out Ayre's healer had come. He rose carefully and turned, then found his way blocked by two expansive chests with beefy arms folded over them. Rhys looked up, no small feat given his own formidable height, and met the gazes of two men who were even taller than he.

Despite their advanced age of at least five-and-thirty winters, the identical features were as smooth as marble, and just that unyielding. Long blond hair flowed over impossibly broad shoulders and great paws of hands were tucked under arms, hands that easily could have snapped a back in two without any effort.

The Fitzgerald brothers returned his stare with those great, unblinking eyes of theirs and not a flicker of emotion on their faces. Rhys folded his own arms over his chest and stared back at them. It would take a warrior of the most courageous mettle, the surest hand, and the stoutest heart to face these two and come away the victor. Rhys quickly took stock of his weapons and the damage already done to his poor form that day. He cursed silently. Besting these two would only come at great cost, but it might very well turn out to be something he couldn't avoid—

"Told you he wouldn't write."

Rhys blinked. One of the statues had spoken.

"Young ones never do," the other grumbled.

"That is the thanks we get for all our tender care of him," the first added, a small pucker of irritation beginning to form between his eyebrows. "Looking after him when he was a wee lad."

"Tending his cuts and bruises."

"Making sure he ate as he should."

"Spinning yarns of Viking splendor for him every night so he would have glorious dreams of war and bloodshed."

The first's expression had turned very unpleasant. "I vow, Connor, 'tis enough to make a man rethink his desire for seed to carry his sword after he's gone."

"Aye, Jared, you have it aright. Children. Bah."

Rhys smiled weakly. "I was busy," he offered.

"Too busy for a handful of words on a scrap of parchment?" Connor demanded.

"Or scrap of skin," Jared suggested. "I would have been well satisfied with that."

"I was much consumed with traveling about earning the gold I need," Rhys said.

The twins were seemingly unimpressed. Connor's scowl was formidable. By the thoughtful look on Jared's face, Rhys suspected he was still contemplating the possibilities of skin as a missive instrument.

"I was never bested with the sword," Rhys continued. "And I held over a hundred souls for ransom—"

"And the lance?" Connor barked.

Rhys gritted his teeth. "Bested once."

"Once?" Connor fair shouted. "Saints above, boy, did I teach you nothing?"

"It was once, Connor—"

"Once?" Connor repeated, in much the same tone. "Once is one time too many! Kill, or slink off in shame. Vanquish, or don a hairshirt for a full year. Humiliate, or forgo the pleasures of the flesh for *two* years—''

Rhys wanted to put his hands over his ears and disappear under a handy table. "I know, I know," he groaned. "Saints, but I've heard the list for what feels like every day of my life! I've too much to see to today for the listening to it yet again."

"See?" Connor grumbled to his brother. "These young ones are always in haste. Never time to sit and speak of their travels to those less fortunate."

"Aye," Jared agreed sadly. "Or to quaff a companionable cup or two with the aged and infirm—"

"Oh, by all the bloody saints!" Rhys exclaimed. "I traveled, I humiliated, I vanquished. Satisfied?"

Connor's expression darkened considerably. "Should I cuff his ears, brother?"

"Turn him over your knee and leave welts on his arse," Jared advised. "Such cheek and disrespect from a little lad deserves no less."

"I'm a score-and-four, if you'll remember," Rhys growled. "And if you'll also remember, you haven't executed either of those threats on my poor form for the last twelve years. Since I was ten and two," he added as he watched Jared begin to count surreptitiously on his fingers. "Not since the day I bested you both, one with each hand."

"Aye, and the proudest day of my life it was," Jared said, reaching up to dab away a bit of moisture from the corner of his eye. "Me with your right and Connor with your left."

"Aye," Connor said, beaming with paternal pride, "and using all my own stratagem on me. That little feint to the left—"

"The forward thrust—"

"The graceful backhand sweep aiming for the knees—"

"The dodge and disembowel parry—"

"The delicate slice across the throat—"

Rhys knew just how long the list was, so he endeavored to refocus his former nursemaids' attentions on the present moment.

"If you'll excuse me, I've a need for Master Socrates."

"In the cellar," Jared said. "Lost his place near the weaver's shed. You can imagine why."

Rhys could. It only made sense that Alain would go through the keep and do his best to make everyone as miserable as possible.

Connor looked at Rhys critically. "You're wobbling."

"An encounter with Ayre's strips of leather."

"Ah," Connor said wisely. "Couldn't guard your tongue, eh?"

"He slapped the lady Gwennelyn."

The twins blinked at him.

"I encountered her this morning," Rhys explained. "I thought she was a he, and that he had stolen a horse. She tried to fight me for my mount."

Jared seemed to be trying to decide whether he approved or not. Connor continued to blink, as if such a thing were simply beyond his comprehension. Or perhaps it was the mere mention of a horse to send him into a stupor of such proportions.

"Who bloodied your nose?" Connor asked, at length.

Rhys gritted his teeth again. "She did."

Two jaws fell open in unison.

"I was taken by surprise," Rhys said defensively.

Two sets of teeth clicked together as jaws were retrieved.

"Well," said Connor.

"Well, indeed," agreed Jared.

Rhys squirmed at the bit of untruth he'd just told. Never mind that he had known what she had intended. That she had actually carried out the threat was surprising enough. Then again, this was Gwennelyn of Segrave. He should have known better.

"I hadn't expected to see her there," Rhys added. "I didn't recognize her."

"You had plenty of opportunity to go to Segrave to look at her," Connor said. "Lord Bertram went often enough."

"You didn't go, either," Rhys pointed out. He'd been

to Segrave twice, twice more than he likely should have gone.

The twins paled as one. Then they began to shake their heads.

"Couldn't go."

"Best not to leave the keep."

"Lord Bertram needed us to stay."

"Important tasks for us to see to here."

Rhys knew the reason why they hadn't left the keep and why they kept as much distance between themselves and anything that moved faster than their own two feet, but he chose not to say anything. There were things a body could torment the Fitzgeralds about, and then there were things one didn't dare. Rhys knew very well where to draw the line.

"A pity I recognized her too late," Rhys said with a sigh. "The day might have ended differently otherwise."

Jared sighed as well. "Poor child. I fear we gave her quite a fright when she first saw us."

"How could we help it?" Connor asked. "You give me a fright, and I've looked on you all my life!"

Rhys shook his head, wishing he could stave off the inevitable discussion of who they resembled more: their axe-wielding mother or their dual-broadsword-wielding sire. It was impossible and he knew he wouldn't be noticed even if he tried to interrupt the argument, so he sidestepped them and limped through the hall to the kitchens. Gwen was in good hands. If Alain had sent the Fitzgeralds to watch over her, he had no intention of troubling her again that eve. If there were any bodies who could make the new lord of Ayre nervous, it was these two. They had been Bertram's favorite guardsmen for precisely the effect they had on others.

Rhys gingerly made his way down the stairs to the cellar, pausing often to catch his breath. Alain's crop had taken more out of him than he cared to admit. Perhaps he had been too hasty in submitting to Alain's display of displeasure.

He came to a halt under a torch and leaned his head

against the stone. Never had it crossed his mind that Alain would disobey his sire's wishes, though he now wondered why he'd been so stupid. Of course Alain would wed with Gwen as quickly as possible. Her dowry was enormous.

"Who are you mooning over now, or should I guess?"

Rhys peered back upward into the gloom. Montgomery of Wyeth came down the steps, holding a cup of what Rhys assumed to be ale.

Rhys looked at him in surprise. "You're still here?"

"Apparently so."

"I would have thought Alain would have buried you with his sire."

Montgomery raised his cup in salute. "It wasn't for a lack of trying, believe me."

"Fortunately for you, you're harder to do away with than that."

Montgomery only smiled. "Indeed I am. Now, what of you? It took you long enough to come back. Bertram had been anxious to see you."

Likely to give me the details of his command that I serve Alain, Rhys thought with a scowl. "Trust me, I was busy."

"I'll wager you weren't," Montgomery said with a snort. "Just dawdling, as usual."

"I hurried, but I've no time to tell you of it. I'm off to see Master Socrates for something useful. Care to come?"

Montgomery shuddered. "Don't like to watch him make his potions. I like the taste of them even less well."

"You've a weak stomach, my friend. They're always very effective."

"Aye, they work simply because your poor form heals itself to avoid having to down any more of his brews."

Rhys laughed and the movement made him catch his breath.

"Saints, Rhys, what befell you?"

"An encounter with our new lord and his riding crop," Rhys said, pausing to let the pain subside.

"The lash *and* a fist in your face? You must have let your tongue run mightily free at his expense."

Rhys pursed his lips. "He only saw to my back. I earned the other mark from someone else."

"Brawling again, good Sir Rhys? I'm disappointed in you."

"It was Gwen," Rhys muttered, feeling as disgruntled as he had the last time she'd clouted him on the nose and he'd been forced to explain to Montgomery just where he'd gotten the mark.

"Again?" Montgomery asked with a laugh. "By the saints, lad, you'd think you would have been expecting it this time."

"She took me by surprise—"

"I can see that."

"—and bloodied my nose while I was gaping at her, amazed to find the heiress of Segrave traipsing about the countryside pretending to be a mercenary," Rhys finished darkly.

Montgomery shook his head with a fond smile. "The girl has an imagination, I'll give you that."

"And a ready fist," Rhys agreed.

Montgomery stared at him thoughtfully. Rhys wanted to squirm, but he was too old for squirming.

"What?" he asked defensively.

"I was just wondering what it is you keep doing to the girl that causes her to abuse your poor nose thusly."

" 'Tis no affair of yours."

"And I was wondering how your tourneying went on the continent and what it was you intended to do with all that gold you no doubt earned."

"Again," Rhys growled, " 'tis no affair of yours."

Montgomery scratched the side of his face thoughtfully. "Was it a very large amount of gold you earned? Enough for, say, a bribe?"

Rhys scowled at him.

"And is it possible that he whom you intend to bribe is disposed to accepting your bribe?"

"You think too much."

"Have you thought that perhaps your gold would serve you better in other ways?"

Rhys had no answer for that. His only goal for the past four years had been to earn enough to buy Gwennelyn of Segrave. What other use for his gold could he have?

"Your sword might buy you a better heiress than you think, especially if you could convince King John your allegiance ran more toward the English crown than the French."

As if John would give Gwen to him merely because of his skill with a sword! Rhys almost laughed out loud. "He is uninterested in a blade which has seen the clasp of a French king. Gold, however, could come from the devil himself and John wouldn't care. Besides, he knows I want land here. And surely he knows it was hardly my fault Phillip knighted me."

Not that Rhys could have argued with the French king anyway. His father and grandfather had ties to the crown of France that Rhys certainly hadn't been in a position to break. Even though he had chosen a different path than the other two men of his family, he was still a de Piaget.

"England is my home," Rhys continued. "What greater display of loyalty could John ask of me than that?"

"I daresay he still has fond memories of his brother wearing the English crown and keeping his feet mostly on French soil."

Rhys sighed as he dragged his hand through his hair. "I have few ties to France, Montgomery. My mother is there, true, but she has her own vocation and no interest in political intrigues. My grandsire is old and well past posing any threat to any king." A small lie, but a necessary one. "The land I want is here. I've never kept that a secret."

"Ah, but you have kept secret just what little plot of ground it is you covet so fiercely." Montgomery leaned forward conspiratorially. "Just a hint, Rhys. I vow I won't tell a soul."

"Until you slip into your cups later this evening," Rhys said dryly. "Then the entire keep will know."

"Your doubt cuts me to the very quick. For all you know I might be able to aid you in your quest."

Rhys pursed his lips. "The only thing that might help me in this quest is another few chests of gold."

Unfortunately, he didn't have time to earn any more. What he had already would have to do.

"Go see Socrates," Montgomery said, retreating back toward the stairs. "I'll find you later and pry more of the truth out of you."

Rhys pushed away from the wall and continued down the passageway. Gwen's guardian was a greedy man. Perhaps he could be convinced to hold off the wedding for another pair of months until Rhys could return to London and convince John fully that he intended to remain on English soil, loyal to the English crown. Rhys smiled grimly. Perhaps he would even be able to convince the king that he wasn't interested in following in his father's footsteps.

Or perhaps he would merely snatch Gwen away during the night and flee.

It was tempting, but that would leave them no choice but to go to France. England was her home. England was where he wanted to dwell. He would just do as he intended from the beginning and settle for bribery. And he would see to it first thing in the morning before Alain could do anything else to foul up Rhys's plans.

"Let the gold be enough," he muttered under his breath as he made his way to the healer's chamber.

It would have to be.

He had no other choice.

9

The child sat on a stool near the cooking fire and watched the contents of the kettle boil frantically.

"Nay, not that," a wizened old man muttered to himself, stooping over to peer into the recesses of his collection of pots. He shoved aside what he didn't want and reached in with bony fingers to pull out a leather pouch of some moldering substance. He opened the pouch, sniffed carefully, then smiled in triumph. "Knew I had a bit more left," he said, turning back to the pot. "Keep stirring, child."

"Aye, Grandfather," the child replied, giving the bubbling brew a hearty stir. She watched as the old man dropped a pinch of something into the thick potion. It disappeared under her awkward strokes into a rather unappetizing mass of greenish paste.

"Mmm, something smells wonderful," a voice said from the doorway.

The child looked up without surprise. She'd known the knight would come home today. She'd seen it, though she hadn't said as much to anyone else. Her grandfather would have thought her fanciful, but she knew better. It was a gift she had, this seeing.

"Ah, Sir Rhys," her grandfather said, drawing the young man into the tiny chamber, "you've returned safely! And not a moment too soon, I'd say. Terrible things afoot in the keep, terrible indeed! Knew you'd come put an end to them as quick as you could."

"Master Socrates, your faith in me is, as usual, greater than I deserve."

"Not at all, lad. Here, come and sit. I've something especially tasty on the fire."

"I could smell that from fifty paces, despite the foul odors from the kitchen. How is it you find yourself in this hellhole instead of near the weaver's shed where I left you?" He paused and smiled down at her. "Good to see you as well, *ma petite*."

The child found her hair ruffled gently as the tall knight moved past her to sit himself down with a wince on the stool near the fire. She didn't understand the little words he always called her, but she liked how they sounded against her ear and she knew by his tone that they were good words. Her heart warmed within her as she continued to stir diligently, stopping only long enough for her grandfather to ladle out a cup full of his current combination. It smelled not at all tasty, but the knight sipped, then complimented her grandsire lavishly on not only the strength and texture but the unique flavorings of his brew. When her grandfather turned his back to putter amongst his things, his face aflame with the pleasure of the compliment, the knight winked at her and put a finger to his lips. She nodded, her heart full of love and appreciation. There was not another soul in the keep who tried to save her grandsire's pride.

"I wonder, Master Socrates," the knight said politely, "if you might have something for the soothing of cuts and bruises? I seem to have run afoul of a few stripes this morn."

The knight's back was soon bared to view, and the child watched as her grandfather ran his gnarled fingers over the lash marks. He clucked his tongue in grave disapproval, then turned away to prepare his poultice.

The child stood against the wall and watched the knight. He was digging in the pouch attached to his belt for something, and she wondered if he might be searching for something to rid his mouth of the less than pleasant taste that no doubt lingered there. She loved her grandfather, true, but she would be the first to admit he was not a very skilled cook.

The knight beckoned to her. "I've something for you, *chérie*. They called your name when I saw them."

The child approached, stunned that he should think of so small and insignificant a personage as herself while on his travels. She held out her hand and blinked at the sight of the pieces of colored sea and sky he laid there.

"I happened upon a glassmaker putting in a chapel window," the knight explained. "He assured me these colors were pleasing together, but I've no eye for such things. I thought you might make use of them somehow."

The child ventured only a peep at the three smooth pieces of glass, green, azure, and yellow, but already she saw more in them than she ever had in the still water of her grandfather's wooden cup. She closed her small fist about them and looked at the knight. She could scarce see him for her tears, and she could find no words to express her gratitude.

The knight only laughed softly. "Ah, if only others were so well pleased by so little." Then he turned his face away and sighed. "If only I were so satisfied with so little."

The child watched as the knight bowed his head. She wondered if it might be the wounds he bore that grieved him so, then thought better of it. Though she knew little of men and their sorrows, she suspected this gallant soul was carrying a heavy burden indeed.

She waited until her grandfather had applied his healing salve and turned back to his brew before she approached. Her mother had warned her to use her gifts sparingly, for men would not understand them, but also to use them generously when called upon. If ever there were a time to be unselfish with what little good she could do, now was the time.

The child stepped up to the knight carefully and touched his back with her small hand. Though she could not ease his heart, perhaps she could ease his body.

The knight stiffened in surprise, then looked over his shoulder at her, his eyes wide.

"In return for your gift," she said, lowering her eyes and pulling away.

She saw the knight stretch. She chanced a look in time to see him appear mightily surprised at his pains being taken from him. Then he lifted his hand and ran it over her head gently. "Little one, 'tis I who should thank you, I think." He looked at her grandfather's back, then shook his head as he arose as if he just wasn't sure what had eased him—her touch or her grandfather's brew.

Her grandfather turned and looked at the knight expectantly. "Are you soothed, Sir Rhys?"

"Aye," the knight said with a faintly bemused smile. "'Tis nothing short of a miracle."

"Ah, good," her grandfather said, looking very pleased. "A new recipe, but obviously a good one!"

The knight stretched again as he redonned his tunic, then looked at the child with another glance of wonder. He shook his head with a small smile, bid her grandfather farewell, and then left the chamber.

The child waited until her grandfather had turned back to his pots before she opened her hand and stared down at the glass pieces there. They were so much clearer than the water in her grandfather's cup.

And she told no one of what she saw.

10

Rollan of Ayre was smiling as he sat at the lord's table in the great hall and nursed a cup of ale. It had been a particularly interesting day, what with all the excitement over Gwen's escape and recapture, and that savory flogging of Rhys de Piaget. Rollan had wondered, as he'd wandered about the keep, just what could happen to possibly improve on the day's events.

To his surprise and delight, the day had indeed improved. After returning to the keep, he'd descended to the cellars to visit his favorite ale spigot. He'd just settled down for a fine afternoon of imbibing when he'd heard Rhys and Montgomery begin to speak together. He'd slipped back into the shadows immediately. Uncomfortable, aye, but the rewards had been well worth the trouble. He'd ignored the rats and spiders crawling about him and listened raptly to the discussion going on just in front of him.

Rollan had eavesdropped until he thought he couldn't bear any more. The pair had parted ways with Montgomery ascending the steps and Rhys continuing on to Ayre's pitiful excuse for a healer. Then, feeling as full and satisfied as if he'd just spent hours at the king's table, Rollan made his way back up to the great hall where he could watch the goings-on and give thought to what he'd learned. He'd relished the idea of spending a full evening pondering just what the ever truthful Sir Rhys was about. With Alain still raging in his solar over Gwen's short-lived flight as violently as a pricked boar, Rollan had had ample time to turn over in his mind the possibilities. Never in his most vivid imaginings would he have suspected such a devious notion as bribery of his father's beloved foster son.

Rollan was momentarily tempted to do a bit more lurking to see where Rhys went and to whom he spoke, but he stopped himself. He would speculate a few more hours and decide for himself what sort of scheme de Piaget would try to put into motion. Discovering the details any sooner would be an insult to his own imagination and plotting ability.

Nay, he would give de Piaget ample time to ruin himself, then do the honorable thing and step forward and expose the subterfuge before it went any further.

After all, a knight was bound to tell the truth, wasn't he?

Rollan nodded to himself thoughtfully. It was the least he could do for the cause of chivalry.

11

Gwen stared out the modest window that had earned her chamber the lofty title of solar. It wasn't much of a view, what with the courtyard of Ayre right below her. She'd been studying the piles of filth gathered here and there for an hour since the sun had risen, and devoted much thought to the merits of a sewing needle as a weapon. She'd used them before with good success. It was all she had at her disposal given that Rhys still possessed her filched sword.

Unfortunately she suspected that a small needle, even a sharp one, would be of little use against the Viking demons who guarded her. She'd had two meals brought to her since her imprisonment, and both times her guardsmen had been standing like unmoving trees in front of her door. They looked far too substantial for a good poking to do them any harm.

It was not an encouraging sign.

A frantic pounding on her door almost sent her pitching forward into the window enclosure. She turned and hastened to the door, flinging it open.

"Alain wants you," John panted. "Immediately."

Gwen would have given John an earful of her displeasure over being ordered about, but the look on his face stopped her. "He's furious, obviously. Over what?"

John's eyes were very wide. "I've no idea, but it has something to do with Sir Rhys. He's been commanded to come as well."

The Fitzgerald brothers parted in Red Sea–like fashion, and Gwen slipped out of her chamber behind John before her shadows could decide she shouldn't be allowed any freedom. She heard them fall into step behind her. She suppressed a shudder.

The journey to Alain's private solar was far too short. Gwen entered the chamber and looked about her. Alain, Rollan, and her guardian all sat in chairs as if they'd been royalty and she the lowly servant come to receive instruction. She was sorely tempted to comment on the ridiculousness of the situation, for to be sure if she were a man and owned her property by herself she could buy and sell the three before her several times over, but she knew it would not serve her. The less attention she drew to herself, the better off she would be. Perhaps if Alain thought she was malleable, he would ease his scrutiny of her and she would stand a better chance of escaping his clutches.

And then there was Rhys. He had obviously had a bath. A dangerous activity, but then again here was a man used to risking his life with his sword. Gwen looked up at his face and wished suddenly that someone had provided a chair for her as well. Even a small stool would have served. This was a sight that required something sturdy beneath one's backside.

How four years could have made him more enticing she surely didn't know, but it had. He was beautiful and forbidding and so darkly handsome that she could hardly look at him. She wondered if the men he fought were as overcome by the unyielding strength of his features as she was, or were they merely chilled by the coldness of his pale eyes? She very much suspected the women he met could only stare at him and wonder where their minds had gone. She understood completely.

And then she realized two things: she was gaping at

him, and he was returning her look—only he wasn't seeing her.

She dragged her attention back to Alain and his companions.

"You sent for me?" she said, hoping she sounded calmer than she felt. She'd given it thought on her way there and could divine no reason why she and Rhys should find themselves having an audience with Alain at the same time.

Unless he knew of their feelings for each other.

Alain, as usual, merely stared at her as if he rehearsed in his mind all the things he found so objectionable about her person. He frowned and chewed on the inside of his cheek.

"Is it possible then, my lord," Rollan asked hesitantly, "that she knows nothing of this scheme we've discovered this morn?"

Hugh of Leyburn snorted and then smacked his lips. " 'Tis a scheme I could easily credit her with dreaming up. Her sire let her run too freely in her youth, I say. I never would have allowed such daydreaming in my household."

Gwen sent a heartfelt prayer of gratitude flying heavenward that her sire hadn't been this corpulent lump of lard. She pitied his daughters.

"I'll rid her of the habit," Alain grumbled. "I've no mind for a headstrong bride."

"But she'll breed well for you," Hugh said, reaching for another fig and slipping it between moist lips. "Got good hips, does this one."

"And what would you know of it?" Gwen demanded.

Hugh's face turned a very unattractive shade of red. Alain's eyes had narrowed, and he looked to be considering something foul. Rollan's eyes had lowered, and she thought he might be judging her hips to see if Hugh's observation had any merit.

Saints, but she could hardly believe she found herself in the same chamber with three such poor specimens of manhood.

She stole another glance at Rhys, just to remind herself what a man could be. Perhaps it was the contrast between him and the other men in the chamber to make her realize just how magnificent he was. Perhaps it was the way he carried himself, as if he had acres of soil under his feet and a powerful title to shield himself and his loved ones behind. Perhaps it was the simplicity of his garb that presented such a pleasing diversion from the baubles, feathers, and gaudy trappings that bedecked the buffoons before her.

Or perhaps it was that fat ruby in his sword that screamed he was not a man to be toyed with, else his victims would be finding themselves covered with a like color.

She sighed. A pity Rhys couldn't just do Alain and the other two in. That would have saved her the trouble of this current foolishness which the three before her seemed determined to drag out as long as possible. Alain was fingering his ever-present riding crop. Hugh, of course, was shoving figs into his furiously working mouth as fast as he seemingly could. Rollan was looking far too contemplative for her peace of mind. It could only mean trouble where she was concerned. At least he wasn't salivating at the very sight of her. She'd cured him of that during his last visit to her keep with his father.

He'd caught her alone in a passageway and proceeded to acquaint her with his kissing. His groin had been impervious to her knees and his skin resistant to her pinches. His belly, however, had seemed a fine place to stick her sharpest needle a time or two. At least her steel had worked well enough for her then. She'd left him howling and quickly retreated to her mother's solar to there spend the duration of Lord Ayre's visit.

She looked at Rollan and rubbed her belly pointedly. He seemed to take the hint well enough and turned his attentions elsewhere.

"Hugh," Alain said, "tell me again what happened this morn, just so this pair hears it clearly."

"Of course," Hugh said. He licked his fingers thoroughly, then wiped them on his tunic front. He pointed a now clean finger at Rhys. "He came to me first thing this morning, before I'd had a chance to break my fast, mind you, and tried to—"

He belched a time or two, then started to choke. Gwen sighed. Not another brush with death. The man ate so much and so swiftly, he spent at least once a day fighting for air. She looked at her love and lifted one eyebrow in question. He wouldn't meet her eyes. She would have been much relieved by a small look in her direction, but perhaps 'twas better this way. After all, she would soon be his and she would have all the looks she wanted. She turned back to the predicament before her.

Both Rollan and Alain were pounding on Hugh's back. Gwen normally would have suggested they cease and leave Hugh to his fate, but she was too curious about what Rhys had done to say anything. Finally Hugh spat forth a great lump of something she had no desire to investigate more closely and sucked in great gasps of air. He wheezed for a moment or two, then pointed again at Rhys.

"—bribe me," he finished with another gasp.

"Bribe you," echoed Rollan, putting his hand over his heart as if it stood ready to fail him at the very thought. "Almost too dastardly a plan to contemplate."

Hugh nodded enthusiastically. Alain looked momentarily perplexed, and Gwen wondered if he were having trouble with Rollan's assessment of Rhys's scheme.

So Rhys had tried to bribe Hugh. For her hand in marriage. Bold indeed.

"He wanted Segrave," Hugh continued. "Said he'd been working for the land for years."

Gwen nodded. A clever ruse. Of course he would have said the like.

Alain snorted. "I can understand that, seeing as how he has no land of his own."

"Just for the land?" Rollan asked. "Nothing else?"

"What else would he want?" Alain returned. "Her? He probably would have tried to bribe Hugh into keeping her if he'd thought she would come with the soil."

Gwen looked at Rhys. She knew she shouldn't. She

knew that any look other than bored disinterest would be marked and remembered by Rollan and tucked away for use at the worst possible time, but she couldn't help herself. She began to wonder what the truth was.

"Just the land?" she asked.

He looked at her and his eyes were chilly. Or bleak. She couldn't decide which until he spoke.

"Just the land," he said flatly. "What else?"

What else indeed. She searched his expression for any sign, however small, that perhaps he lied, or that he told less than the truth to cover his true feelings for her.

She saw nothing of the kind.

She could hardly believe what she saw, but there was no sign from Rhys that she should deny it.

She turned back to her tormentors and schooled her expression into one of complete disinterest. Let them speak of her disparagingly. Let them pick and prod at Rhys and hope to force from him some sort of confession. She cared nothing for either.

He didn't want her.

She could hardly believe it, but Rhys's eyes were so cold. Obviously, he'd had a change of heart. Or perhaps he had lied to her all along.

She wasn't sure which thought hurt her more.

Rhys stood in Alain's solar and had but one thought rage through him with the force of an angry gale: Hugh had betrayed him.

He should have known as much. He'd approached Gwen's guardian but two hours before with more naïveté than he'd obviously ever possessed in his entire life. For being as skilled a warrior as he was, he'd been blindingly stupid.

He knew little of the man, but watching him at supper the night before had revealed a soul whose interest lay primarily in his gullet. How was he to know that behind all that belching and burping lay a man devious enough to place a substantial amount of gold in his purse with one hand, continue to throw food into his mouth with the other, and yet still have enough presence of mind to plot another man's ruin? If Rhys had thought he could have gotten his fingers about Hugh's throat to strangle him, he would have. Unfortunately, Gwen's guardian was every bit as corpulent as he was untrustworthy.

By the saints, he had been a fool.

What gold he'd brought with him to England was lost. His chance to have Segrave was lost as well. He could hardly bear to think on what else he had lost in the bargain, but it was hard to avoid as she was standing not three paces from him, her back as straight as a blade. He'd hurt her, he knew, but there had been naught to be done about it. 'Twas bad enough that Alain suspected Rhys wanted Segrave. If Alain suspected Rhys truly wanted Gwen, Rhys knew he would find himself in Ayre's dungeon in truth.

And then *all* hope would be lost.

"Her land alone?" Rollan mused, breaking Rhys's concentration. "I'm surprised, Rhys. One would think your lofty chivalry would have dictated you desire the woman as well."

Saints, but wouldn't the man let the matter drop? Rhys clenched his fists. Strangling Rollan of Ayre would be too swift and easy a death for the man. Rhys wished he had the time and the leisure to think of a more painful way to end his life, but there was no time to spare. Alain was thinking again and that never boded well. Rollan generally did all the contemplating for the pair, but that didn't improve matters, either. Rhys had no doubts Rollan was somehow at the bottom of this catastrophe, but he could afford to spare no thought to how that might have come about. What he had to concentrate on now was how to distract the fools before him until he could think of a way to free both himself and Gwen. Obviously, he would have to go to the king.

"I want land," Rhys said, dragging himself back to the present. The three men were still staring at him waiting for him to say something.

"It must be very hard to have never had any of your own," Rollan said sympathetically.

"And you do?"

A swift flash of loathing swept across Rollan's face, but it was gone as quickly as it had come.

"I am full well content to do nothing but serve my brother," Rollan said humbly. "And should he see fit at some time to gift me with a poor bit of soil, I would only count it graciousness on his part."

Gwen snorted.

Alain ignored her. Rhys felt a shiver of apprehension course through him at that. That the lord of Ayre should overlook such cheek could only mean Alain's attention was fixed upon him.

"Alain," Rollan said quietly, "perhaps you should speak to Sir Rhys about that matter that concerns him so closely."

Alain scowled at his brother. "Don't want to."

"Now, brother, a desire for land is not such a poor thing."

Rhys had no idea where Rollan intended to go with that, but he knew it couldn't be a good place.

"Our sire would have wanted him to have what is due him," Rollan continued.

"Why should he have anything more than what he's already received?" Alain demanded. "Father gave him enough. Besides, 'tis my land now."

Rollan shook his head and gave his brother a patient smile. "How can it be yours, Alain, when our good sire had other plans for it?"

"It wasn't his to give, either!"

"Ah, but it will be once you wed with Segrave's lady." He put his hand on Alain's shoulder. "You must do the right thing in this matter, my lord. 'Tis only fair that Sir Rhys have everything that should be his. Regardless of the cost to you."

Rhys wished desperately for a chair beneath him, for he was beginning to wonder if he would manage to stand through whatever madness these brothers intended to spring upon him.

"Very well then," Alain said, sounding extremely reluctant. He looked at Rhys. "You're to have Wyckham."

Rhys blinked. And then he blinked again. Yet for all that, Alain still sat in the same place and Rollan still stood behind Alain's chair with his hand on his brother's shoulder. Hugh still shoved figs into his mouth at an alarming rate.

"Wyckham?"

"My sire wished for you to have it," Alain said. "And so you shall. When I see fit."

"Alain," Rollan began soothingly, "do not torture poor Sir Rhys thusly. Making him wait yet more time for what he desires so mightily . . . why 'tis nothing short of cruel."

Rhys wouldn't have been any more surprised if Alain had offered him Gwen.

"Wyckham?" he repeated, stunned. "But how . . ."

" 'Tis mine upon my marriage to her," Alain said, with a negligent gesture toward Gwen. "My sire commanded me to give it to you afterward."

"When Rhys had reached his score-and-sixth year," Rollan corrected, "for then he felt the lad would be ready for the challenge."

Lad? Rhys ignored the urge to glare at Rollan. He had more important things to keep from reacting to—such as the fact that a piece of land might possibly be within his grasp and all he had to do to win it was stand there and keep his mouth shut.

"So you will serve me until that time," Alain continued.

"That is two years, not one," Rhys replied, somewhat amazed he'd found his wits to say even that. "I was bound to your sire for but one year."

"And *I* say you will serve me two," Alain said angrily, "in whatever capacity I choose."

Cleaning the privies, no doubt, Rhys thought to himself.

" 'Twas bloody foolish of him, if you ask me," Alain groused. "Don't want to do this at all."

"But 'tis the honorable thing to do," Rollan said gently.

"And no one can argue that you do not always strive to be honorable. Besides, 'tis but a small token of esteem from our father for his beloved foster son."

It wasn't a small token. It wasn't Segrave, but it was land enough. But in return for two years of service to Alain? Rhys found he simply could not voice any sentiment, either of shock or disbelief. Not even the thought of having to serve Alain for an extra year was enough to clear the haze of surprise away.

He could, though, see clearly enough that honoring his father's wishes galled Alain to his depths. Rollan, however, was the mystery. Rhys had never once had anything but venom from Ayre's second son. There had to be something he'd missed. He glanced at Rollan and saw the slight smile. And he knew then there was a great deal more to the proposition than there seemed.

"Where is the deed?" Rhys asked.

Alain glared at him. "I say 'twill be yours. That should be enough."

"It isn't," Rhys said. He listened to the words come out of his mouth and was astonished at his own audacity. Never mind that he would be beholden to Alain of Ayre for another pair of years. It meant land would be his, and he should have been willing to do anything, believe anything to have it.

Then again, this was Alain of Ayre he was bargaining with.

Rhys watched as Alain came up out of his chair, his face a mask of fury. If Rollan hadn't caught his brother by the shoulders and jerked him back, Rhys was certain Alain would have tried to cut him down where he stood.

"'Tis a perfectly reasonable request," Rollan said calmly. "Not very politely stated by our gallant Sir Rhys, but reasonable enough." He kept a hand on Alain's shoulder. "The deed will be drawn up after the wedding."

"Two copies," Rhys said. "One to be held here, the other to be held in London."

Rollan laughed softly. "By the blessed saints, you would think Sir Rhys had been acquiring land the whole of his life. I suppose when one doesn't have the burdens of nobility resting upon him, one has ample time to think on these things.''

''Greedy bastard,'' Alain muttered. He looked at Rhys narrowly. ''You'd best serve me well, else I'll rip up the deed.''

All the more reason to have another copy in the hands of the king, Rhys thought to himself. Yet even as the distrust of Alain washed over him, he was also overwhelmed by the truth of what he'd just learned.

Bertram had left him land. He could hardly take it in.

''Are you finished with me?''

Rhys blinked at the sound of that voice, then realized just what he'd forgotten.

Gwen.

''Come now, Rhys,'' Rollan said ignoring her. ''Can you not assure my brother that you will serve him well? I vow were it me standing in your place, I would be throwing myself at his feet and kissing his boots.''

Which is exactly what I will be doing for the next pair of years, Rhys thought sourly.

''I will serve you well,'' Rhys heard himself say, and he wondered where the words had come from.

''Ah,'' Rollan said with a sigh of contentment, ''chivalry in the flesh. He possesses it in abundance, wouldn't you say, Gwen?''

''Oh, aye,'' she said quietly. ''There is a veritable glut of it in this chamber this day.''

Rhys cleared his throat. ''If there is nothing else, my lord? I am certain there are duties I should be about as quickly as possible.''

''Duties,'' Alain repeated. ''I must give thought to what those might be.''

''Perhaps something else as a reward for his morning's work,'' Rollan suggested. ''I daresay it should be something that only the honorable Sir Rhys could fulfill.''

''Aye,'' Alain said, scratching his head, then looking at his brother. ''Perhaps I should think on it later.''

''A wise decision, my lord,'' Rollan said, inclining his

head submissively. "And I will be at your disposal to hear anything you might suggest, of course."

The saints preserve me, Rhys thought to himself. Then he shook his head. What duties Alain might decide upon did not matter. Rhys would not be there to fulfill them.

Or would he?

If he could just remove himself from the chamber, he was certain he could think more clearly. Land was within his grasp. And Gwen was within Alain's grasp. And in order for him to have his land, he would have to watch Alain take Gwen to his bed. And if Gwen wed with Alain, her life would be nothing but a misery—if she survived life at the man's hands. Rhys knew that if her sire had known of Alain's true character, he never would have allowed the union.

And if Segrave had never allowed the union, Rhys never would have had Wyckham.

It was a situation more fiendish than the devil himself could have imagined up.

"Now to the wedding," Rollan prompted. "Surely it should be accomplished with all haste? Perhaps on the morrow?"

Alain scowled. "I had a hunt planned for the morrow."

"Ah," Rollan said, sounding immensely regretful, "and I know how you love a good hunt."

"Best tame her as soon as you can," Hugh offered between slurps and gulps. "Can't start too soon with a wench, or so I've always said."

Rhys felt the words sink into him like blades. *Tomorrow. The wedding on the morrow.* It was too soon. He needed more time. He had to speak to the king, to promise the man gold, fealty, his own sweet neck if that was what was required. Tomorrow was too soon.

"Tomorrow, then," Alain said, waving his hand at them. "You both may go. We'll have the ceremony at noon. I might yet get in an hour of falconing beforehand. And remember, de Piaget, obedience in exchange for your land."

"Of course, my lord," Rhys responded, and he said as

much because he was too numb to do anything else. Numb and terrified.

He was on the verge of losing the two things he'd spent the last four years paying to have with the price of his own sweat and tears.

Gwen passed out of the chamber before him without looking at him. Rhys was silent until the Fitzgeralds had come out behind him into the passageway and closed the solar door.

"Gwen," Rhys began.

She turned and looked at him and her expression was bleak. "I seem to have misunderstood you."

He shook his head sharply. "You've misunderstood nothing. I've always wanted land, of course—"

"And I possessed an abundance of it," she interrupted. "Thank you, sir knight, but I understood that very well."

"It isn't as it appeared—"

"And to think I thought you were different than the rest of them," she said.

"I—"

Am, he meant to finish, but she had already turned and walked away. The Fitzgerald brothers trailed after her in her wake. Rhys started to go after her when the door behind him opened and Alain appeared, looking at him with irritation.

"Loitering?" Alain demanded. "Lazy already?"

Rhys made the new lord of Ayre a very low bow, ignoring the protests of his damaged back, then turned and walked away before his visage betrayed him. Or his tongue. He already knew what that would win him, and the last thing he could afford was to find himself with a lock between him and Gwen.

Bertram had given him land, and all he had to do to have it was give up the love of his soul.

By the saints, but he'd never expected any of this.

12

A knock sounded on the door.

Gwen ignored it. She was far too busy contemplating the shattering of her dreams to disturb such morose musings by answering what could only be yet another disaster for the day. As if the thought of becoming Alain's bride on the morrow wasn't disaster enough.

The knock came again, more firmly.

"Leave me be, I'm brooding!"

The knock came again and Gwen cursed. Well, at least it couldn't be Alain; he wouldn't bother to accord her the courtesy of a knock. Perhaps it was John with a sharp blade on which she could impale herself. Feeling that such a thing would be a vast improvement on the day's events, she crossed over to the door and opened it.

The Fitzgeralds stood there, looking down at her from their great height.

Gwen, feeling emboldened by her impending doom, stared right back at them without so much as a flinch. A pity she hadn't felt this hopeless when she'd first escaped Ayre. She might have passed more easily for a mercenary. The horror of these two was nothing compared to the terror she would face on the morrow at Alain's hands. Somehow she doubted very much he would woo her to his bed with sweet songs and wine, as did the heroes of her mother's favorites *chansons*.

"Aye?" she said finally, when it became apparent that the twins were bent on doing nothing but staring down at her with those fierce expressions. "One of you knocked?"

The one on the right cleared his throat. "I did."

"Fool," muttered the other.

"She should know of this," whispered the first.

"Babble on then," grumbled the second. "I've no mind to listen to the tale." And with that, the second stuck his fingers in his ears and stared up at the ceiling.

Gwen looked at the first who had spoken and wondered how anyone told them apart, themselves included. The only possible way was that this one on the right seemed to scowl just a bit less than the other.

"He wants you," he said.

Gwen waited. Then she found herself scowling up at the twins. Saints, but it was contagious this foul humor of theirs. "How was that?"

"Him," the first said, inclining his head back down the passageway. "Young Rhys."

"He sent for me?"

"Nay. But the words he spoke today were not the words of his heart."

Gwen wanted desperately to believe that, but she'd heard the words come out of his mouth with her own ears. They were very hard to deny. Despite his expressions of affection yestermorn, it had been four years since she'd seen him. Much could have changed.

The other demon started to tap his foot impatiently.

"Enough, Connor," the first said, elbowing him in the ribs. " 'Tis rightly your tale to tell and you won't see to the telling of it, so it falls to me to do it."

The second, apparently Connor by name, unplugged his ears. "I've no mind to relate this to such innocent ears, Jared."

"She deserves to know."

"He won't like it that you've said aught."

"She won't repeat it. Will she?"

Gwen found herself pinned to the spot by bright blue eyes that seemed to demand a response in the affirmative. She wasn't, however, above reserving the right to remember the tale for use in future extortion. But she shook her head, as if the thought of repeating such tidings was simply beyond her.

"Well then," the one named Jared said, looking a bit more comfortable, "this is how it all came about. 'Twas a night several years ago that we were roaming the hall—"

"Looking for makers of mischief," Connor interjected.

"Overenthusiastic revelers—"

"Oppressors of the weak and helpless—"

"Filchers of savories from the kitchens—"

Gwen sighed heavily. "I think I understand what you were about that night."

Connor frowned fiercely at her, but she was too weary in mind and spirit to give him any reaction of fear he might have wanted. She looked at Jared expectantly.

"Well?"

"Well," Jared said, "as we were going about our business, we happened upon the chamber where Rhys was making his bed for the night."

Gwen wondered if this could possibly be something she would want to hear. Jared seemed to think it necessary, for he plunged on ahead.

"Connor, being the inquisitive soul he is, put his ear to the wood to see how young Rhys's labors were progressing."

Gwen snorted before she could stop herself.

"My thoughts exactly," Connor grumbled. "Must the child hear this?"

"Aye, she must," Jared said with another elbow in his brother's ribs. He turned his attentions back to Gwen. "Finding the moans the wench was making little to his liking, Connor opened the door with the purpose of observing Rhys to divine just what it was he was doing so poorly as to wring such inadequate sounds from his companion.''

"Well," Gwen said, hardly able to believe her ears. "This is news."

Connor pursed his lips and resumed his contemplation of the ceiling.

"Aye, well to be sure what Connor saw inside was news indeed."

Jared paused in his tale and waited expectantly, as if he desired some sort of response from her. All Gwen could do was return his stare. He frowned at her a bit, as if by so doing he could wring from her the reaction he wanted. Finally he frowned again in exasperation and spoke.

"Well," he asked, "will you not know what was occurring inside?"

Gwen shrugged helplessly, feeling completely at a loss. Did she need to know this? Then again, how could the tidings possibly make her any more wretched than she was at present?

"Um," she began, "well, I don't know—"

"Nothing," he interrupted.

Gwen blinked. "Nothing?"

"Well," Jared said with a thoughtful look, "it wasn't as if nothing at all was happening."

She waited. And when he said nothing more, she prompted him with an "I beg your pardon?"

"Aye, that was what Rhys said at the time, too, as he turned from his game of dice to look at Connor."

"Then he was . . ."

"Dicing," Connor said, shaking his head in disbelief. "And a fine-looking wench she was, too. I could hardly believe my eyes."

"Then he wasn't . . . they weren't . . ." Gwen hardly knew how to voice her question.

"Wasn't," Jared confirmed. "Didn't. Not then."

"Not ever," Connor added in a disgruntled tone. "If you can believe that."

She couldn't. "That isn't the tale I've heard." Rumors of Rhys's prowess in many areas had reached her ears thanks to John's finely honed eavesdropping skills. Men bedded women, and some men bedded as many women as possible. Rhys, by all accounts, fell into that last lot.

"I should hope you hadn't heard differently," Connor said. "Think on the embarrassment for the lad!"

" 'Tis highly chivalrous, if you ask me," Jared countered. He looked at Gwen. "He invited the wench to leave, then relented under our questioning—"

"Which was most fierce," Connor said. "Had to rough the little lad up a bit to pry the truth from him."

"In the end," Jared continued, "he told us his true motive."

"Unwillingly enough, though," Connor said. "And to be sure I can understand why he was loth to give voice to such a ridiculous notion."

"It isn't a ridiculous notion," Jared argued. " 'Tis most romantic."

" 'Tis foolish."

" 'Tis not!"

"Please," Gwen interrupted, wishing she had the courage to knock their heads together and stop them from arguing. "Tell me what his motives were!"

Jared looked at her and smiled proudly. "He was saving himself."

"Saving himself?"

"Aye," Jared nodded. "Nary a taste of those pleasures has the lad had in all his years."

"Not that he's a gelded stallion," Connor hastened to add. "He's a man sure enough. Ruthless."

"Fierce," Jared added.

"Merciless."

"And quite the swordsman, if I do say so myself," Jared finished. "Taught him all he knows," he boasted.

"*I* taught him all he knows," Connor said, turning to glare at his brother. "That two-fisted thrust through the ribs and out the back—"

"*My* axe in the thigh with the right hand and dagger across the belly with the left—"

"*My* ferocious swipe with one blade and a delicate slice the other way with the second—"

Gwen had the feeling this kind of argument could go on for more time than she had to spare. Besides, the descriptions were starting to make her more than a little queasy. Perhaps a mercenary's life was not for her.

"Let me understand this," she said, interrupting them. "He has never made any of the conquests he's credited with."

They looked at her as one and nodded.

"Why?"

"Why?" Jared echoed. "Why, for you, my lady."

"Me?" She shook her head. "He doesn't want me. He wants my land."

"Bah," Connor said, " 'tis a bad habit he learned from Jared, that lying."

"From me?" Jared gasped. " 'Twas from you he learned to deny the feelings of his heart! I taught him to express himself in the most tender of ways. If he'd spent less time listening to you and more time to me, he would have told this girl years ago of his feelings for her!"

"But he did tell me," Gwen said.

Both Jared and Connor turned to look at her, their mouths hanging open.

"He did?" they asked, as one.

She nodded. "It took me a bit to wring them from him, of course."

Jared's ears perked up. "Did you stick him?"

Connor snorted. "She wouldn't stick him. She's a passing sweet girl." He turned his fierce gaze on her. "What'd you do, then? Loosen his tongue with sweetmeats cooked right proper? Well-cured eel smothered in savory sauce? Roasted pheasant with all manner of little nuts and pleasant things surrounding it on a fine platter?"

Obviously Connor had heard of the delicacies produced by her mother's kitchens.

"Nay," she said, "I used my womanly ways to convince Sir Montgomery to deliver a message for me—"

"That Montgomery always was soft," Connor said in disgust.

"And I cornered Rhys on the roof and told him I wished him for my champion."

"And he agreed," Jared stated, as if there could have been no other outcome.

"Of course he agreed," Connor groused. He frowned at her. "He's had tender feelings for you since he was a lad, sadly enough. Ruins him for serious swordplay, I've always said. He spends at least a handful of moments each day mooning over you, and has done for years. That time was better spent honing that little dodge to the groin, or perhaps the blade carving artistically along the jaw-bone—"

Gwen could hardly bear another listing, so she turned to Jared, who seemed much less inclined to catalog his warriorly moves than his brother.

"Why then do you suppose he said what he did?" she asked.

"What else was he to do?" Jared said with a shrug. "It wasn't as if he could admit the innards of his heart to Lord Ayre. Wouldn't think he thinks on it overmuch himself, though. And that isn't because of any lack on my part, of course."

"Of course," she murmured.

She felt suddenly as if her world had righted itself again. Rhys loved her. He had for years, just as she had him. He couldn't have said as much to Alain or Rollan, and he certainly wouldn't have said the like to her guardian. After all, hadn't he tried to bribe Hugh that morning? Bribery for land was one thing; bribery for a woman was another. It wasn't something Hugh would have understood, so Rhys approached him with something he *could* understand. A pity Rhys hadn't used a few wagons of foodstuffs instead of gold. It might have had a better effect.

But what were they to do now? She stood to marry Alain in the morning. She looked up at the twins.

"Escape," she said distinctly. " 'Tis our only hope."

They only blinked at her.

"He lied to distract Alain and Rollan," she said, "so that we might escape." Her heart lightened so greatly and so quickly, she thought she just might be able to fly from the keep. "I'll find him, then we'll flee," she announced. She smiled up at the brothers and then parted them with ease. "My gratitude, twins. You've been a great deal of help to me."

She ran down the passageway and thumped down the circular stairs to the edge of the great hall. Alain would likely be engrossed in his plans for his hunt on the morrow. Rollan's whereabouts were always a mystery, but with any luck she could avoid his notice as well. All she needed to do was find Rhys, tell him she understood his plan, and decide how they would accomplish their flight.

And then she came to an abrupt halt.

Every exit from the great hall was under heavy guard.

She looked to the high table only to find Rollan sitting there with a goblet at his elbow. He smiled pleasantly and raised his cup in salute to her.

And it was at that precise moment that she knew there was no hope of escape.

She could not flee to the kitchen. She certainly couldn't slip out the hall door. There was no other way from the keep besides leaping off the parapet into the moat, but she suspected she wouldn't survive the trip down, and it wasn't as if she could keep herself afloat in the water.

She was doomed.

Her breath came in gasps and she began to see faint specks of light all over the room. She stumbled back into the stairwell and leaned against the wall. There was no leaving Ayre. Not even had she been able to find Rhys and convince him she was for him would she have been able to sneak away from the keep. It was tempting to give in to the fancy that perhaps during the changing of Alain's guard she might slip past them . . . but nay. If Alain had taken this kind of trouble now, he would surely take just as much trouble to ensure the changing of the watch went just as smoothly.

She mounted the steps and walked slowly back to where the Fitzgerald brothers waited. She looked up at them and smiled sadly.

"No escape."

They seemingly had no reply for that, so she entered her chamber and shut the door behind her. What else was she to do? She had no wings to fly off over the walls to freedom. She suspected that not even Rhys could single-handedly take on the entire garrison of Ayre, no matter his reputation. At present she would be of little help to him. There would be no evading her fate: she would marry Alain of Ayre whether she willed it or no.

And after he wedded her, he would most certainly bed her, and she very much suspected that would not be a pleasant experience. She had given him one taste too many of her insolence. Aye, she would pay for her cheek.

And that was enough to make her think that perhaps she *should* throw herself into the moat.

She walked to the window and looked down. Saints, even the barbican was swarming with guardsmen. If she hadn't been so panicked, she might have been flattered at the precautions Alain seemed to be taking to keep her safely within the keep.

Now it only forced her to realize that there was indeed no escaping her fate.

She would sacrifice herself on the morrow to a man who cared nothing at all for her when but a handful of paces away would stand a man who loved her enough to have denied himself his entire life that she might be the one he first took to his bed in truth. A pity she could not somehow find a way to switch bridegrooms at the altar. Or to switch herself. Perhaps there was more advantage to being a twin than she'd suspected at first, though she certainly wouldn't have wished her fate on anyone else.

The knock on the door startled her so badly she almost fainted. She put her hand over her heart to soothe its pounding and turned to the portal.

"Aye?"

The door opened. John stood there, looking as dejected as she felt.

"He doesn't want me now," he said with a long, drawn-out sigh. "Says he has too much to brood about tonight."

"Sir Rhys?"

"Who else?"

Gwen refrained from informing John that while Rhys might not want him, he most certainly wanted her. Her straits were too narrow for such disparaging comments.

"And Alain had no task for you?"

"Too busy planning his hunt on the morrow."

"I'm happy to see he isn't overly consumed with thoughts of his wedding."

John looked at her and she thought she might have detected the hint of tears in his eyes. "I wish you could wed with Rhys, Gwen. Even if he wants you just for your land. I think he might become fond of you eventually."

"With any luck," she agreed, "he just might."

John sighed again and fingered the hem of his tunic. "I even put on clean clothes to present myself to him. And the new helm your mother gifted me. Just so he might see I was ready for battle at any moment." He looked at her. "He was unimpressed."

"Poor lad," she said, unable not to smile. It was difficult to have one's idol take no notice of such efforts.

And then, of a sudden, a flash of brilliance overcame her. She pulled John into her chamber, feeling more grateful than usual that Alain had chosen to put her in a solitary cell, and shut the door behind him.

"I had wished for a twin," she said, shoving aside the nagging thought that this was a very poor idea indeed, "but I think you'll do just as well."

"Uh," he grunted as she released him, "what are you—"

"Strip."

"I beg your pardon!" he said, aghast.

Oh, the finer sensibilities of a lad of ten-and-four. Gwen put her shoulders back and prepared to put forth her arguments for the scheme, which she was sure John would hardly agree with, for 'twould be his neck as well as hers in the noose if they were to be caught. Perhaps she would do well to clout him over the head before she left the chamber. At least that way he wouldn't be completely responsible for her flight.

"What do you want my clothes for?" he asked. "Are you thinking of escaping again?"

"With Sir Rhys," she admitted.

"Not without me," John said stubbornly. "You'll not leave me behind this time."

This was going to be a problem. Maybe she'd have to do damage to him before she relieved him of his clothes. Either that or tell him a falsehood and make off with his garments.

"Gwen . . ." he warned.

Lying and stealing, she thought with resignation, were indeed vices determined to become part of her character.

Not many minutes and the promise of a hefty bribe to John later, Gwen opened the door to her chamber and parted the Fitzgerald brothers in what she hoped was a John-like fashion. She spared no time in trivial speech with them, but immediately set off down the passageway. John had been soothed with the knowledge that he could indeed escape Ayre on his own more easily than she, as no one would likely mark him as he left the gates. Thusly appeased, he had informed her where Rhys was keeping himself and given her directions on how to reach the guardroom in the north tower.

Gwen made her way down the passageway with a confident air. She would reach Rhys, convince him she knew the truth of his heart, then they would set off together for France.

Unfortunately, her journey took her through the great hall once more. She couldn't deny the number of men there, nor the completeness of their weaponry.

No matter. She and Rhys would manage it.

But by the time she'd managed to gain the stairs to the north tower, she was beginning to have her doubts. She had no sword. Would Rhys's sword, lethal though it was, and his formidable skill be enough to win them their freedom?

She hazarded another glance into the bailey on her way

up the stairs. Even though the arrowloop was small, she had no trouble marking the number of men crowded into the inner bailey. She paused on a step, finding that more than doubts were assailing her now. They would not manage it, she was almost certain of that. As fierce as Rhys might have been, there was virtually no hope of him subduing all the men in the great hall and still having enough strength left over to see to the men outside.

She leaned against the stone wall. There was no hope. She should have realized it before.

She looked up the stairwell, defeated.

And then a thought occurred to her.

She might not be able to flee, but she wasn't without a choice about one thing. After turning the idea over in her head a time or two, she nodded to herself. Perhaps Rhys would find the idea foolish, but then again, perhaps not.

Alain, if he noticed, would be livid, but that was something she could face on the morrow.

Heartened, she turned and marched purposefully up the stairs.

13

Rhys paced the confines of the small chamber and cursed the walls that surrounded him. And when that gave him no relief, he cursed the circumstances that surrounded him in just as unyielding a fashion. Gwen, or her land. That he was even faced with such a choice was enough to send him straight to the cellars to cozy up to a keg of ale for a fortnight.

Wyckham.

Or the most beautiful, courageous, perfect creature ever to set her dainty foot to English soil.

By the saints, if he'd had but a grain of sense in his head, he would have recognized Gwen the moment he'd seen her, then fled with her then and there to France. Alain would have eventually decided that perhaps some foul fate had befallen her and gone on to wed with some other heiress. Hugh would have savored Gwen's wealth for several more years. Rhys would have bought himself a little piece of ground in France, and he and Gwen would have lived out their lives in perfect bliss. But now where did he find himself?

In a tiny upper guardroom, staring at walls that would imprison him for another two years, and contemplating

what tortures Alain and Rollan might invent for him during
said two years.

But it was not how his future would come about if he
had anything to say about it. To be sure there were guards
aplenty, but couldn't he take them? Perhaps he and the
Fitzgeralds could fight their way through the press, pulling
Gwen along behind them. Even if he were forced to leave
Gwen with his mother while he and the twins earned a bit
more gold, it would be worth the sacrifice. To be sure,
three such hired swords would be enough to set any lord's
tongue to lolling.

Assuming, of course, he could convince Gwen her
sword was better used as an ornament in the abbey. The
saints preserve him if she insisted on guarding his back.

He jerked open the door, ready to storm down the passageway and inform the Fitzgeralds of his plans, only to
run bodily into a lithe form standing before him. He cursed
silently. Saints, but this lad was persistent. Rhys couldn't
deny that he was somewhat flattered by John's blatant worship, and then there was the added pleasure of knowing
that at least one of the Ayre brothers held him in esteem
and by so doing irritated the other two no end, but now
was not the time to begin the training of his new squire.
He had men to slay.

"John," he said, mightily annoyed, "did I or did I not
tell you I've no need of you this eve?"

To his complete astonishment, John put his hand in the
middle of Rhys's chest and shoved him back inside the
chamber. The lad followed him in, then shut the door behind him. Rhys was so shocked, all he could do was just
stand there and gape at the lad's cheek.

"I should leave welts on your arse," he exclaimed.

"Wouldn't if I were you," John responded promptly.
"It would put a mighty damper on the evening's events,
I'm sure."

And with that, John pulled off his helm and before
Rhys's very eyes appeared none other than Gwennelyn of
Segrave dressed, of course, like a lad. Rhys felt his jaw
slip downward.

"By the saints, lady" he managed, "you don't wear gowns all that much, do you?"

"I'm in disguise," she confided.

"Can I assume John is left in your solar in skirts?"

"And none too happy about it, I assure you."

"Well," he said, completely at a loss. "Well," he tried again, wishing that the chamber contained more than just a pair of chairs and a table, for he wished desperately for a bed on which to put himself until his head ceased spinning.

"I couldn't agree more," she said.

Rhys felt for a chair and lowered himself into it, then realized what he had within his grasp. He leaped up and reached for her arm.

"Come," he commanded. "We'll fetch the Fitzgeralds and cut our way from the great hall. The stablemaster will saddle our mounts for us, for he has little love of Alain. You'll ride behind me, aye?"

"But—"

"I know you want your own mount, but 'tis safer this way. I'll teach you what you need to know to have your own once we reach France. I have gold enough to at least see us passage across."

"But—"

He reached for the door, but she put her hand on the wood and shook her head. He shook his head as well, uncomprehending.

"Haste, lady," he informed her, "is of the essence at the moment."

"Have you peeked into the great hall of late and seen the number of men?"

"Perhaps you have had a recent lapse of memory regarding my reputation," he said pointedly. "I can take them."

"I didn't doubt you could as well after I gave it some thought," she agreed, "but then I saw the courtyard filled with the rest of the garrison. I think even you might be outnumbered there."

It occurred to him that she just might be right. And then something else occurred to him.

She had obviously seen through what he'd said in the solar.

"You would come?" he asked.

She leaned back against the door and smiled up at him. "Despite the fact that you want nothing but my land?"

" 'Tis good land," he reminded her.

"The best, I should think."

"Without land I am nothing," he reminded himself.

She smiled. "That's a matter of opinion, but 'tis a manly thought and one I can understand."

He sighed. "I've gold enough to buy us a poor bit of soil in France."

"Rhys de Piaget, keeper of a small vineyard?" she mused. She shook her head. "It seems a waste somehow."

"Then we'll travel the world living off my sword."

"Nay, not just your sword. I could learn—"

"My sword," he interrupted.

"But—"

"Trust me. I am capable of protecting us."

"I could be a very dangerous mercenary," she informed him archly.

"Aye," he agreed, with feeling. Dangerous to him, but he didn't dare say as much. She'd planted her hands on her hips, and there was the beginnings of a glare forming on her face.

And then just as suddenly she shook her head and leaned back against the door. Her arms came around her waist, as if she sought to comfort herself.

"Nay, Rhys, 'tis not possible."

"I could take them all," he said desperately.

She looked at him and shook her head again. "There are too many. Besides, 'tis what Alain expects. Either you would finish on the gibbet or in his dungeon, and neither of those things could I bear."

"We have no choice."

"Aye, but we do. I will wed with Alain. You will give him your two years and have your heart's desire."

"The land be damned," he growled. "You know that isn't what matters the most to me."

"But it does matter."

"Of course it does," he retorted sharply, "but only because I need somewhere to build a keep. How will I protect you without walls? How will I protect our children without men to man those walls? I need a place to take you!"

She didn't answer. She merely moved away from the door, slipped her arms around his waist, and gathered herself close. She laid her cheek against his chest.

"Rhys, we cannot leave. It is not possible."

He put his arms around her and rested his chin on the top of her head. It had to be possible. He would accept nothing less. Much as he wanted Wyckham, he wanted Gwen more.

"At least," Gwen said, pulling back, "there is one thing I will not give Alain."

"There are several things you will not give Alain," he managed. It was the most rational thing he could say as the sensation of having Gwennelyn of Segrave in his arms was as distracting as it had been the last time he'd held her. It had taken him almost four years to recover from that. He put his arms around her, lest she think better of her action and try to pull away. She only leaned against him and nestled closer. "You won't give him your hand in marriage, for instance," he said.

"I cannot escape it."

"I'll see that you do—"

"Nay, Rhys." She pulled back only far enough to look up at him. "The land should be yours. The saints only know you will have earned it by then."

"I'll not have it at the expense of you."

"Go carefully, Sir Rhys, for you lead me to believe that perhaps you might begin to value me for something besides my dowry."

He scowled at her. "You shouldn't believe everything you hear."

She only laughed softly and laid her head back against his chest. Rhys closed his eyes and wished with all his heart that the castle would fall down upon him at that very moment. He would have gone to his grave a perfectly contented man.

"Nay," she continued, "Alain will have my hand and you will have your soil. But he will never have what I intend to give you this night."

Rhys felt a frown begin. He looked up at the ceiling for an answer to her riddle, but saw nothing but cobwebs. No aid from that quarter.

"Well," she said, pulling back to look at him. "Will you have it?"

"Have what?"

"My virginity."

"Your *what?*"

She started to smile. He, however, saw nothing amusing at all about the fact that his ears had already started to fail him. Deaf at a score and five. It was a tragedy.

"You heard me. My virginity. My virtue. Call out the mounted knights and let us breach this maidenhead."

He took a step away from her. Then he took a few more steps backward until he found himself with a sturdy chair beneath his backside. He knew he was gaping at her, but he couldn't stop himself.

"Surely you aren't serious."

"Then you don't want me?" She took off John's cloak and dropped it onto the floor. "I apologize that I have no gown, but it seemed a bit imprudent under the circumstances, and I also apologize for my hair, but you know how that tale came about."

And as she continued to describe and apologize for her failings, all Rhys could think was, *The woman I dreamed about for almost half my life has just come and offered herself to me.* And if she'd had any idea just how appealing hose and a tunic were on her, she wouldn't be speaking at all.

"Ah," he managed, "I couldn't. Unchivalrous, I think."

"Don't you want me?"

He crossed his legs in self-defense. "That isn't the point."

"Do my ears trouble you then?" she asked, pulling her hair over what she deemed to be the offending features.

"Of course not."

She considered. "Perhaps, then, a game of dice might soften you to the idea."

"Dice?" he echoed.

"I understand you're an excellent teacher."

He could only stare at her, uncomprehending. And then the light began to dawn. He'd been exposed, and by the most unlikely of sources.

"Damn those Fitzgeralds," he grumbled.

"A talkative pair, indeed."

He scowled at her. The saints only knew what else they had told her. It was obvious he had no more secrets.

"Think of tonight as a chivalric duty," she coaxed.

He groaned and dropped his face into his hands. He was so bewildered he groaned again for good measure.

And then he felt a soft hand against his hair and heard a knee pop as she knelt before him and took his hands.

"Rhys," she began, and there was no light of jest in her eye, "this is not how I would have it."

Nor I, he wanted to say, but no words would come.

"But 'tis the only choice I can make. I cannot escape my fate. And I will not ask you to give up what you have worked your whole life for."

"But you are asking me to give her up."

She blinked very rapidly. "Cease with that romantic foolishness, lest I lose my resolve."

"Gwen, the land means nothing to me."

"Well, it should, for the price is very dear."

"But it would be you to pay the price for it," he argued. "And that I cannot have."

"You haven't asked me to pay anything," she said. "Our course is laid out before us, Rhys. We are both bound to Ayre, and the time for flight is well past. I can make no choice there. But I can choose to whom I will give my virtue. And if doing so means I must spend the rest of my life with Alain of Ayre, then 'tis a price I will gladly pay.''

"But, Gwen—"

"Please, Rhys," she said, and for the first time he heard fear in her voice.

And that frightened him.

"He will not be gentle," Gwen added. "I have provoked him one time too many. I can only pray that he will use me quickly and be off to other matters."

He swallowed with great difficulty.

"I would truly prefer it if I had some pleasant memory of what it should be like to concentrate on while enduring the other."

"Oh, Gwen," he said miserably.

She smiled, but it was done too brightly to be believed. "So, let us be about our work while the night lasts. The morrow will take care of itself soon enough, I'll warrant."

He drew her up onto his lap and cradled her against him. He thought he might have managed a solid front until he felt her hot tears on his neck. His own eyes burned and his cheeks were soon wet with his own grief.

Saints, but this wasn't how he had planned things.

And so he rocked the woman in his arms, as much to soothe himself as to soothe her, and wished with all his might that he might somehow bend time to his will and place them both back outside Ayre's gates with her manfully struggling to lift her blade to do him in. He would have caught her hand, hauled her into his arms, and kissed the breath from her, then fled with her to France. Their mutual deflowering would have taken place in the most expensive inn he could have found, preceded by a fine meal, rare wine, and as many *chansons d'amour* as a minstrel could have racked his brains for.

It certainly wouldn't have happened in a filthy guardroom on the night before she was set to marry someone else.

She pulled away, took his face in her hands, and kissed both his cheeks softly. Then she smiled at him.

"Come, my gallant knight, and let no other soul come between us tonight."

"But how can I have you," he asked, "and then never have you again? Live in the same keep with you and know you are forever out of my reach?"

"Perhaps Alain will put you to cleaning the cesspits, and we will see little of each other."

He considered. "There is that."

"I will likely be confined to my tapestry frame in the solar." She brushed his hair back out of his eyes. "We will see each other now and again and know in our hearts that we shared what no one can ever steal from us."

"It isn't enough."

"It will have to be. 'Tis all we are allowed."

"If we are allowed even that."

"If it is a sin, then I will bear the burden of it. Surely I will be forgiven this desire for such a small comfort."

He couldn't help but agree, though he suspected the comfort would certainly not ease either of them over the next pair of years.

And that didn't begin to embrace the rest of his sorry life.

To have Gwennelyn of Segrave, and then to lose her?

"Chivalric duty," she reminded him.

"How you can possibly make that out of what we intend to do this night, I do not know."

"I use my imagination more than you do."

He sighed and dragged a hand through his hair. "Very well, then," he said, feeling somewhat at a loss. "We should begin, I suppose."

"Aye."

But where? Saints, it wasn't as if he had any experience in those matters. He fished about in his almost empty purse, sparing Hugh of Leyburn one last hearty curse for its lightness, then pulled forth a pair of dice. He fingered them nervously.

"Perhaps a brief game," he conceded.

"Time is of the essence," she agreed.

"A very brief game, then," he said.

And as he began to teach her all he knew of dicing, he marveled at the absolute improbability of the situation in which he found himself. Wooing the love of his heart by divulging to her the finer points of a game of chance. His most recent encounter with her had come while she was posing as a mercenary, lying and stealing as enthusiastically as if she'd been doing it all her life. That they were now playing not only with dice but also with their lives shouldn't have surprised him.

And he studiously avoided thinking about the very real possibility of someone, Rollan for instance, stumbling in upon them.

"I'd best bolt the door," he said.

He returned from his errand to find Gwen studying the dice intently. Would that she would study him with like concentration.

And then she looked up at him and smiled.

The sight of it almost felled him where he stood.

"One final game?" he croaked.

She nodded happily, and he knelt down next to her. His hands were shaking, and he wondered if she would respect him less if he indulged in something of a swoon before he indulged in her. He later remembered nothing of their game except the sight of her hands, the warmth of her body next to his, and the sound of her laughter in his ears.

He thought he might just perish from it all.

"I won," she said suddenly, smiling smugly at him. "Didn't I?"

"Aye," he managed, dazed by the sight of her.

"And my prize?"

He felt very self-conscious as he held out his hand to her. "Will I do?"

She put her hand in his. He looked down and remembered the last time he'd reached for her hand. It had been on the roof of her father's keep when she had chosen him for her champion. Champion, husband, 'twas all the same to her. Rhys looked at his lady and wondered if it was sweat running down his cheeks. They were very wet.

"I don't think I can—" he croaked.

She put her finger to his lips and shook her head. Then she brushed the damp from his cheeks, leaned forward, and very gently kissed him on the mouth. And this time her sire was not standing at the end of the passageway to stop her.

At least his nose was in no peril.

He thought, however, that his heart would be much worse for the wear.

"This moment is ours, my love," she whispered against his lips.

He wanted to argue, but her mouth distracted him from his thinking. He wanted to flee, but her hands touched him and left him caring nothing for anything outside their chamber. He wanted more than what they would have that one night, but her arms went around his neck, and he found himself pulling her so closely against him that clothes were stifling.

And so they shed their clothes, layer by layer, with nervous hands and embarrassed smiles, until they had made a nest of them in the corner. Rhys lifted Gwen into his arms, then laid her down carefully on their poor bed. He followed, drawing her tightly against him, praying that the night might last far into eternity.

And then there was no more time for thinking, no more room for arguing, and no more will for fleeing.

They were alone, and no other would intrude upon their bliss.

14

Rollan of Ayre stood behind his brother's chair on the morn of his brother's wedding and observed the two standing next to each other in the midst of Alain's solar. They had been slow to answer Alain's summons and both looked exceedingly weary. Even with their drawn and spent expressions, Rollan had to admit that they made a fitting pair. De Piaget, damn him anyway, with his commanding height and muscular build made even Gwen look slight and fragile. Not that Rollan cared how mannishly tall she was. He would have taken her against whatever surface was handy at any time, any number of times, and not regretted it once.

And now she was on the verge of becoming his brother's wife.

It had been enough to sour his stomach that morn.

He suspected the only satisfaction he would have out of the day would be watching de Piaget's reaction to what his new duties would be. Rollan had come up with the idea himself, based on a nagging suspicion he'd had for years. He could hardly wait to see if his instincts ran true. Alain hadn't been happy about cutting short his hunting that morn, but Rollan had managed to convince him that getting Rhys settled was best done that day, preferably before the wedding.

"I've come to a decision on your duties," Alain announced.

"Then why am I here?" Gwen demanded.

"Because, you wasp-tongued wench," Alain growled at her, "you're involved as well."

Rollan could have sworn he heard her mutter something about a cesspit, but he could have been imagining it. He watched Rhys raptly, waiting for the reaction he fully intended to savor for many months to come.

Rhys, however, made no move and spoke no word. His face wore a mask of impassivity even Rollan had to admire.

"She's been left to run wild too long," Alain said, pointing at Gwen. "She'll embarrass me at some important moment. Or so Rollan says, and I believe him."

Alain paused. Rollan realized that only he himself seemed to be enjoying the drama of it. Gwen looked as if she might lose the contents of her stomach. Rhys was as still as stone.

Interesting.

"She needs a guard," Alain ground out, "and you are to be its captain."

Rollan could have wished for a much better delivery, but the crack in Rhys's armor was all he could have hoped for. The man flinched as if he'd been struck. Rollan spared Gwen a quick look to find her as pale as an altarcloth.

So, he had been right. There was something between them.

Could it possibly become any more entertaining than this?

"Everywhere she goes, you'll follow. Everything she does, you'll remember and report on. Everything she says, you'll repeat to me when I demand it. Understood?"

Rhys was, to all appearances, speechless.

Gwen looked as if she would faint.

"Excitement over the wedding?" Rollan asked her, unable to resist the question.

She only looked at him with eyes as bleak as a winter sky. In spite of himself, Rollan felt a twinge of regret for her. It wasn't as if he would have looked forward to marriage to his brother, either. The man was a rutting boar, and a stupid one at that.

But, Rollan consoled himself, it would only make her appreciate him all the more when the time came.

"De Piaget, your duties begin immediately," Alain said. "See her safely to the chapel. Then you'll stand guard outside the bedchamber door tonight as well. Don't want to be disturbed in my labors."

Gwen turned and walked from the chamber. Alain pointed a finger at Rhys.

"And see that she stops that. I hate it when she leaves before I can tell her to go!"

Rhys bowed his head. "My lord, if I may?"

"Aye," Alain said, waving his hand dismissively, "go. Two years, de Piaget."

"As you will, my lord."

Rollan watched him leave and leaned against the back of Alain's chair, full well satisfied with the morning's events. Gwen's hell would begin in a few hours. Rollan rubbed his belly with a frown. She would deserve every second of pain.

And Rhys's hell had already begun.

Truly, it was a fine morning's work.

15

The child crept up to the top of the steps, then hastily hid herself at the end of the passageway. It wasn't as if she needed to be there to observe the events, but compassion drew her. The knight and his lady suffered. If only she could have done something to ease it.

Earlier that day she had watched the lady go to the chapel, pale and drawn. As evening shadows fell, the lady had gone to her marriage bed.

The knight had stood guard outside the bedchamber door, his face pale and drawn.

Even the child had paled at the muffled sounds of discomfort.

And then the two Vikings had appeared and led the knight away.

"I must stay," he had protested.

"You've been there long enough," one of the blond ones had growled.

"Aye, and now you can hear him snoring from here," the other had snarled. "He'll not know you've gone."

"But she will."

" 'Tis better that way, lad."

"There's wine aplenty downstairs," the other stated.

"I don't want any."

"Best to have some, young one."

"Aye, it will ease you."

The knight seemed not to agree, but the child could see that he was in little position to argue. Never mind the fierceness of the men who escorted him down the steps. His heart was broken and his will bent under the load he carried. He had no strength left for arguing.

She wondered if she could have eased his burden, but she suspected even the touch she had inherited from her mother would have been too small and mean a thing to aid him. All she could do was stare into the glass stones in her hand and watch.

And then even her tears blinded her to that.

16

Gwen stood at the door of her solar with her hand on the bolt and fought with herself. She wanted to leave the chamber. She also wanted to repair immediately to her bed and never emerge again from beneath the coverings.

It was the morn after her wedding, and she suspected that she had passed better nights.

She couldn't hide forever. She would have to face the keep, Alain, and his filthy living conditions. She would also have to face Rhys.

She drew in a deep breath and opened the door. The Fitzgerald brothers stood in their accustomed places. They parted without comment. She stepped between them, then looked up at them. Connor, and she could tell it was he by the intense scowliness he seemed to wear like a fine cloak, would not meet her eyes. She turned to look at Jared. He seemed determined not to look at her, either, but she had come to suspect that he was less resolute about his gruffness than his brother. His lips pursed, tried to form a scowl, and failed. He unbent enough to let his gaze dip down to meet hers. She smiled up at him as best she could, but it was a less than happy smile. He unfolded his arms from across his chest and briefly rested his hand on her shoulder. Connor growled at him, and he hastily reassumed his tree-like pose.

So much for sympathy from the Fitzgeralds.

Gwen started down the passageway only to find them grumbling along behind her after only a few paces. In spite of herself, she felt comforted. At least she would have some sort of companionship.

And then she looked up.

There, standing in the dim light coming in through an arrowloop, was the very person she had hoped with all her heart she could avoid. He leaned negligently against the wall, resting one shoulder on the stone, his arms folded over his chest. The ruby in the hilt of his sword was dull and lifeless in the gloom. His face was cast in shadows.

All hail, captain of my guard, Gwen thought to herself without humor. She should have been flattered. Any number of women would have been overjoyed to be looked after by a man of such a reputation.

But not her. She wanted to weep.

He didn't move. Indeed, he seemed to be waiting for her to come to him.

She came to a stop before him. She couldn't smile. She couldn't even speak.

Rhys, apparently, hadn't much more to say than she did. He stared down at her, his expression grim and forbidding. He looked as if his most recently passed night had been more taxing than hers. His eyes were very red and his hair and tunic damp. She might have suspected that he'd drunk himself into a stupor and then stumbled into the moat, but he did not carry that stench with him. Perhaps he had spent the night pacing, then dunked his head into a rainbarrel to refresh himself.

And then she had no time for speculation, for he straightened and pushed himself away from the wall. He folded his arms over his chest again. She had first thought that it was a posture he so often assumed because it intimidated. Now she thought he might be trying to protect his heart without realizing it.

Rhys cleared his throat.

"Did he h—"

He cleared his throat again.

"Did he hurt you?" he whispered hoarsely.

Gwen shook her head, mute.

"Then he lives another day."

She nodded. She believed him. She suspected that if she ever answered any other way, Alain's time to linger in his mortal frame would be very short indeed.

"It was very impersonal," she began, then came to an abrupt halt as Rhys flung back his head as if she'd struck him.

"I don't want to hear of it," he said through gritted teeth.

"Then we won't speak of it," she agreed. Nothing could have suited her better.

Rhys unfolded his arms and started to reach for her, then he jerked his hands down by his sides. He glared at her instead.

"You are mine," he whispered harshly.

"Rhys—"

"You were mine before you were his."

"But now I am—"

"You are still mine, and I will have you or die in the trying."

She shook her head and reached up to put her hand over his mouth. He backed away sharply, shaking his head.

"I *will* have you."

And with that, he spun on his heel and walked swiftly away.

"Fitzgeralds," he barked over his shoulder, "come with me."

Gwen's keepers trailed after him obediently. Connor's hands were already caressing his swordhilts, so Gwen assumed he anticipated some sort of sport in the lists.

She contemplated what her options were for tasks to keep her busy that day. She could have written to her mother to let her know that she should have been grateful that Hugh hadn't allowed her to come to the wedding. He'd claimed there wasn't enough room in the baggage wains, but Gwen suspected he'd wanted one less wedding guest to stand in the way of his ingesting the finest Ayre's larder had to offer. But writing to her mother would only remind her of what she had lost, and that she couldn't bear. Not even the thought of beginning to make Ayre habitable raised any sort of enthusiasm in her.

All that was left was to make her way stealthily to the lists and see what the men were about. It looked to be a gray day outside. She could put on a cloak and remain unmarked. If nothing else, her day as a mercenary had prepared her for that much.

Without any more thought, she returned to her chamber for her cloak, then made her way to the lists. She'd almost reached them when she ran bodily into Sir Montgomery. He made her a low bow.

"My pardon, lady. I should have been watching for you."

She waved aside his apology. "The fault was mine. Think nothing of it."

"Oh, but I must think on it. I am a member of your personal guard now, and my captain would be mightily displeased to know I'd come close to plowing you over."

Gwen blinked. "But you were captain of Lord Bertram's guard. How is it . . . ?"

He smiled. "The fortunes of fate, my lady."

"Rhys possesses much cheek to think to order you about."

"He possesses more skill with the sword than cheek, and believe me when I say he has the latter in great abundance. Had he not bested me so thoroughly when we discussed the matter, I might not have been so willing to do his bidding."

"Well," she began, unsure if she should feel sorry for him or not, "I am glad to have you, if that matters."

His smile was as sunny as ever. "It matters a great deal, lady, and I am happy to serve you. Where go you now? I will see you safely there."

"I thought to hug the walls of the lists and see the goings-on there."

He lifted one eyebrow. "Your husband is there. As well as Captain Rhys, of course."

"Fighting each other?"

His eyes twinkled merrily. "Now, wouldn't that be something to see. Nay, lady, I daresay Lord Alain has little desire to cross blades with any but those in his own personal guard."

She didn't doubt it. None of them would dare best him.

"But Rhys's back is still not fully healed," she said. *And I would know.*

"Ah, but his mood is powerfully foul. That is more than enough to make up for what strength he lacks."

And likely more than enough reason for Alain to keep a safe distance. It was the first wise choice Gwen had seen the man make.

Within moments she had chosen a handy rock to rest herself upon and turned her attentions to what went on before her. Alain was easily marked. He made more noise with his mouth than his sword, and his ridiculous boasts and comments about his own skill filled the air. Gwen wondered how his men stood training with him. Given the somewhat ineffective way he seemed to be puttering about with his sword, she suspected he didn't spend all that much time in the lists.

Not like the man at the other end of the field.

Gwen watched Rhys facing the Fitzgeralds and wondered which one he intended to fight first. The twins each drew a sword. Rhys drew two himself.

It was then she realized he intended to fight them both at the same time.

Montgomery whistled low under his breath and laughed a huff of a laugh. "What cheek that boy has."

"He'll never manage it."

Montgomery looked down at her and smiled. "Have you never seen him do it?"

"I saw him fight at my sire's keep, but that was several years ago."

"He's improved since then. He must be powerfully irritated this morn. He doesn't usually take them both on at once.''

Gwen knew he was angry and she knew exactly why. And she wondered, as she watched Rhys take on those two enormous men, if Alain knew what sort of raging storm was brewing inside his keep. She turned to look for her husband only to find him staring at Rhys. She watched him watch her captain fight and suspected that Alain knew very well what lived beneath his roof. She also suspected he had no desire to admit as much.

Rhys continued to keep the Fitzgeralds at bay. Alain turned back to his own exercise, raising the volume and the arrogance of his boasts.

Rhys had said he would have her. As she watched him work, she decided that if anyone could make good on those words, it was he.

She rose and walked back to the hall before she could think on it any longer. Going out to watch him had been a mistake. Better that she concentrate on something she could control, such as the filth in Alain's keep. She would attack the piles of refuse and see them thrown far beyond the walls where they would trouble her no longer.

A pity she couldn't have done the same thing with the man to whom she now found herself wed.

Rhys came in from his morning's exercise the same way he had for the past two months. Silently. His anger unappeased. He'd worked the Fitzgeralds to the bone, driven Montgomery into the dust, and made his squire John weep with exhaustion.

And yet still the sun rose.

Alain breathed.

Gwen was still wed.

His only comfort was knowing that he was commanded to stay near her at all times. Taking the time to train was probably something he shouldn't have done overmuch, but he felt no guilt over it for Gwen came to the lists frequently to watch him. When she did not come, he left the Fitzgeralds to guard her door.

John and Montgomery did not like those days.

But that was how the days had been passed. He had trained. He had contemplated all the ways he could extricate Gwen from her marriage. He had spoken to her of trying to obtain an annulment.

He had prayed for a miracle.

None had come.

Rhys glanced at the high table to see who was there. Alain reclined in his chair, obviously having enjoyed a fine meal already. Rhys pursed his lips. The current lord of Ayre never spent more time than necessary in the lists when it stood to interfere with his time at the table. Hugh would have been proud.

Rollan sat in his accustomed place next to Alain, as close as possible to his brother. It was likely easier to whisper his venom into Alain's ear thusly.

Gwen sat on Alain's other side, leaning as far out of her chair as she could. Rhys half wondered why she bothered. The one thing he could say for Alain was that the man was determined to ignore his wife. Rhys couldn't have been happier about that. Now if he could just be counted on to ignore her at night as well.

Satisfied that there was no mischief afoot, Rhys retreated to one of the lower tables and sat down to what was left there. He'd had worse. Indeed, there had been times during his first few months in France when he'd gone to earn his gold that he'd had none at all. But he'd definitely had better. Try as she might, Gwen had been unable to improve the kitchens at Ayre. She'd seen the hall and the bailey rid of most of its filth, but she'd been unable to remove Alain's cook from his post, or encourage him to produce better fare. Rhys indulged in a fond memory or two of the meals he'd eaten at Segrave. Well worth the journey. Hopefully he could convince Gwen that a trip home would be good for her. He could use something tasty to eat.

"There's nothing wrong with the fare."

Rhys looked up to see Alain glaring at Gwen. She only blinked at him, obviously surprised at his outburst.

"The fare?" she echoed.

"This is the first time you've managed to stir yourself to come down for a meal in days. You'll not shame me by refusing my food!" he shouted as he shoved back his chair and leaped to his feet.

Rhys didn't think; he leaped. How he managed to cross all that space and clear the high table in so short a time, he couldn't have said. All he knew was Alain's hand was coming toward Gwen's face, and he would be there to stop it.

"Forbearance, my lord," Rhys said, pulling Gwen behind him.

"Insolent cur, stand aside! I'll beat her where all can watch. Perhaps 'twill cure her once and for all of her disobedience."

"I will suffer in her stead," Rhys began, but Gwen poked him sharply in the back.

"Beat me if you will," she said, looking around Rhys's arm and glaring at her husband, "and lose your child in the process."

Rhys turned to look at her. "A babe?"

"A son?" Alain asked, as if the child he'd just learned of could be nothing else.

"Aye, a babe," Gwen said, pushing past Rhys to stand toe-to-toe with her husband. "And you'll drive it right from my body if you take a hand to me."

Alain looked her over critically. "I suppose you could be breeding. You haven't had your courses yet, and we've been wed nigh onto four fortnights."

Rhys looked at Alain and, for the first time ever, saw him smile.

It was, somehow, not a very pretty sight.

"Well," he said, smiling a bit more, "now that's done, I can see to other things. De Piaget, see that she cares for herself well, else you'll answer to me. I'm for Canfield this afternoon. Long overdue for a visit there. I think I'll have a bit of a hunt before I go. Aye, I've missed that."

He walked away, continuing to enlighten those around him as to his immediate plans for the future.

Rhys turned back to Gwen in time to find her nigh onto slipping down to the floor. He caught her by the arms and lowered her into her chair.

"You're feeling poorly?" he asked, bending to peer into her face.

She waved him back. "Not so close."

He straightened, wondering if he should feel as offended as he wanted to.

"Your breath," she said, waving her hand in front of her nose.

Now he *was* truly offended.

"All manner of smells," she continued. "I can scarce bear them."

Well, that left him feeling a bit better.

"I think I can find someone to aid you," he offered. "If you like."

She looked up at him, and he could see something in her eyes. He wasn't sure if it was pain or embarrassment.

"I'm going to bear him a child," she said quietly.

He nodded.

"Now there can be no—"

Annulment, he knew she meant to say, and he coughed loudly to cover it up. He hoped Rollan hadn't seen her mouth move.

"Off to Master Socrates," he said, reaching for her hand and pulling her to her feet. He looked at Rollan and inclined his head. "If you will permit us, my lord?"

He didn't wait for an answer. He pulled Gwen along behind him, felt rather than saw the Fitzgeralds fall into step behind her, and managed to collect Montgomery and John as well as he passed through the kitchens. And all the while he tried not to think about what he'd just learned.

A child.

Aye, there would be no annulment now. Their chance for a miracle had just passed. If he managed to free her, it would be through his own sweat. He wondered if he had enough of it for the deed.

He kept walking because there was nothing else he could do.

17

Gwen followed Rhys through the kitchen, trying to hold her breath as best she could. Damn Alain's cook for being so stubborn. Gwen suspected she likely would have felt better if she'd been able to install someone with a bit more skill and a great deal more tidiness.

"Where are we going?" she managed.

"Master Socrates. Lord Bertram's healer. Out of favor with the current lord, of course, and therefore consigned to the cellars, but a fairly skilled maker of potions just the same."

Anything to settle her stomach. But the closer they drew to their destination, the more certain Gwen was that she wouldn't keep down even the crust of bread she'd managed to ingest that morn, much less any potion.

Her guardsmen wouldn't even come down the passageway with her. She left them loitering by the ale kegs and walked with Rhys into a tiny chamber. She put her hand over her mouth as a precaution. A wizened old man stood over a kettle, stirring intently. A girl-child stood nearby, watching just as intently.

"Master Socrates," Rhys began, "the lady Gwennelyn

is feeling poorly this day. Perhaps you have something to help?''

The old man looked up at her from under bushy eyebrows and frowned. ''Feeling poorly? Perhaps 'twas something she put in her belly. Sour wine? Overrotted eel?''

'' 'Tis the babe,'' the child whispered.

Gwen looked at the girl in surprise. It wasn't as if she'd announced her tidings to anyone as of yet.

''A babe, eh? Then come in, my lady, and I'll fetch you a cup of what's on the fire at present. 'Tis a concoction of my own making with several things that perhaps another might not think of combining.''

Gwen came closer, holding her hand even more tightly over her mouth. Then she abruptly used her fingers to pinch her nose closed.

''What are the black spots?'' she managed.

''Flakes of dried vermin. Adds a bit of unexpected flavor—''

As did, subsequently, the contents of her stomach. Gwen knew she should have felt more remorse than she did, but there was only one pot to retch into, and it was right there before her.

She heaved until she had no more strength, then felt herself turned around and gathered into strong arms.

''Ah, *chérie*,'' Rhys whispered, stroking her back gently, ''don't you know you should never ask a healer what he puts into his potions?''

''I know it now,'' she croaked, clutching the front of his tunic to keep herself upright.

''Perhaps a brew of soothing herbs, Master Socrates,'' Rhys suggested.

''Oh, um, aye,'' the healer said.

Gwen looked over her shoulder to see him peering down into his kettle with a look of intense regret.

''I suppose I could do that,'' he said slowly. ''I have some extra things I could add to it—''

''Perhaps but a simple herb or two,'' Rhys interrupted gently.

Master Socrates looked ready to argue, then he looked at Gwen.

"But one or two?" he asked, fingering his wooden spoon.

Gwen belched miserably before she could help herself.

"Just one," Master Socrates said with a sigh.

Gwen soon found herself deposited on a stool with her back against a chilly wall. She wasn't sure what helped her more, the cold or the sitting. Or perhaps it was knowing that Alain would leave the keep and the oppressiveness of his presence would be lifted.

Then perhaps she could see a bit more of Rhys. It wasn't in the best interest of her poor heart, but she could hardly stop herself from wanting the like.

She looked at him as he squatted down before the little girl and spoke to her with soft words and gentle smiles. Envy seized her. Even the luxury of such effortless speech with the man was something she couldn't enjoy. Never mind that he was near her so much of the day. There wasn't a moment that passed that she didn't guard against a gaze that might linger too long upon him, or a smile that might soften overmuch and alert those around her as to her true feelings.

If only she'd had the chance to perfect her mercenary skills subterfuge would have come much more easily to her and she would have been able to outwit her husband. It wasn't that such a thing required a great deal of effort, but there was always Rollan shadowing his elder brother, pointing out to him what Alain himself missed. Would Alain leave Rollan behind to report on her activities, or would he trust Rhys to do as he was bid and keep his own memories of her behavior? But if not Rollan, then a score of others who would take great pleasure in marking and relating every glance, every smile, every manifestation of her affection for the man not five paces from her.

And the very thought of it was enough to make her want to retch again.

She tucked her clammy hands beneath her arms and leaned back against the stone wall. They'd spoken in

snatches of how her freedom might be won. The only solution they could see was an annulment. Not that such a
thing was possible now.

What was she to do, flee to France with Rhys, taking
Alain's heir with her? Or was she to leave the child behind? It hardly seemed possible that she carried so quickly,
but there was no denying the strange illness that coursed
through her. Perhaps she would feel nothing for the babe
after it was born, but she suspected that wouldn't be the
case. She had been undone by every babe she'd ever held.
Nay, she could not leave her babe behind, and she could
hardly take him with her. She meant nothing to Alain and
she suspected he might be somewhat relieved if she were
to vanish, but his son?

He would comb the earth looking for him.

Nay, there would be no peace there.

She felt large, warm hands come to rest upon her knees
and she opened her eyes. Rhys knelt before her, a small
frown on his face.

"You are still feeling poorly?"

"Aye," she managed.

He reached up and brushed away the tears she hadn't
realized were coursing down her cheeks.

"Ah, Gwen," he whispered, reaching for her, "come
here, my love."

"Nay," she said, with so violent a shake of her head
that the entire chamber went spinning.

He blinked in surprise. "But—"

"Nay, Rhys. You cannot touch me."

"I cannot touch you," he repeated.

"Not even an innocent touch."

"But Alain is leaving today. There will be no one here
to see anything." He looked at her, then frowned again.
"I hardly see the harm in an innocent touch now and then.
It isn't as if I'm proposing a little adultery to pass the
time."

"I didn't think you were. And it isn't for them; it is for
me."

"For you?"

She nodded. "Aye. I cannot bear it."

"You cannot bear it," he repeated.

This wasn't going at all well. She took his hands and gently pushed them away.

"We must forget what happened between us."

"We must—" he spluttered.

"I cannot live in the same keep with you for the next pair of years and have your touch remind me of the night we shared!" she exclaimed, starting to feel rather exasperated that all he could do was repeat what she had said. "We'll survive better if we put it behind us."

That, at least, had seemingly rendered him silent.

"We'll have speech together," she said, feeling as if that might just be the thing to save them both. "You can sing to me, as do the knights in the *chansons d'amor* my mother's minstrels performed." She paused. "You can sing, can't you?"

"Nary a note," he growled.

"Ah," she said, feeling slightly disappointed. "Well, then perhaps you could just relate to me the lays you have no doubt heard on your travels. You have heard lays, haven't you?"

"More of them than I could stomach."

She had the feeling he was less enthusiastic about her plan than she was. But she knew it was the only way, so she forged ahead, ignoring the formidable frown he was now wearing.

" 'Tis how it is done," she informed him. "The knight worships his lady from afar, riding off into battle with her favor on his arm, composing lays to her beauty and goodness, and doing all that he does in her name and for the glory of his love for her."

"All from afar?"

"Aye. Or so I've heard."

"And your favor?"

"I think you've already had it," she said, feeling her cheeks grow warm. "And more than once, if memory serves."

He only glared at her.

" 'Tis the only way," she pressed on, clutching her hands together to keep from reaching for him. "How can it be otherwise?" Then she had a flash of insight. "Perhaps 'twould be easier if we considered ourselves comrades-at-arms."

His mouth fell open.

"John is at your side constantly and rejoices in it. If we were to attempt the same thing, always speaking of swords and such other knightly endeavors, perhaps it would go easier for us."

"Swords and such," he repeated. "Swords and such?" he said again, in a more enthusiastic tone.

At least she thought it was enthusiasm to prompt him to raise his voice in such a manner.

"See? Already you begin to appreciate the wisdom of my plan. We must put aside whatever passed between us and consider ourselves nothing but comrades from now on. It is a most reasonable scheme."

She looked up to see Master Socrates bearing down on her with a steaming mug of something. She accepted it hesitantly, then sniffed. It smelled passing sweet, and there was a conspicuous lack of dark spots floating along the top, so she took her courage in hand and sipped.

"Very pleasant," she said, smiling at the old man.

"Bland if you ask me," he said with a sigh, "but a mama's belly is nothing to trifle with."

Gwen finished the brew, handed the cup back to the healer, and looked again at Rhys, who had not moved, nor had his expression of intense irritation changed.

"Come, my friend," she said brightly, "and let us be away and leave the good man to his work. Perhaps you might help me improve my swordplay this afternoon. I'm feeling remarkably better all of the sudden."

"My friend?" he repeated in a choked voice.

"Aye," she said with a firm nod.

He looked as if he would have truly liked to throttle her. Gwen saw the idea come into his head, then watched as he contemplated the merits of it. He scowled most fiercely at her and rose to his great height.

"If you think," he began in low, gravelly tones, "that what passed between us can be so easily forgotten—"

"I never said forgotten—"

"Dismissed then!" he hissed. "Set aside as a thing of naught."

"I never said naught, either," she managed as he drew a deep breath.

"I will not be your friend!" he roared. "Saints above, woman, what sort of man do you think me to be?"

"An honorable one surely," a voice drawled from the doorway. "And one whose lord is preparing to depart for another keep. Perhaps you should be there to at least bid him farewell?"

Gwen looked around Rhys's long legs to see Montgomery standing near the doorway wearing a most speculative glance. She rose carefully, found that her feet were steady beneath her, then looked up at Rhys.

"We'd best heed him. Alain will no doubt wish to see us appropriately heartbroken at his leave-taking."

"You are bound for your bedchamber where you will rest," Rhys growled. "And I'll brook no argument from you on that score."

It seemed a more appealing alternative than seeing her husband, so she nodded and moved past him. She thanked Master Socrates again, smiled at the child who stood by the cooking fire watching her, and then left the chamber.

She kept walking even though she was fair to dropping on the spot in a fit of weeping. Though she'd put a bright smile on her face and suggested the most sensible plan she could think of, she was more than a little miserable. By all the saints above, how was she to endure another pair of years with this man always at her side but ever out of her reach?

By thinking of him as a comrade, she reminded herself.

"Friend, my arse," Rhys muttered from behind her.

Gwen almost smiled at that. He would agree with her in time, for she knew she was in the right. They would form their own garrison of two. He would teach her swordplay and other warriorly skills. She had little to offer him, but at least she could sing. And she could read. Perhaps she could teach him that in return for a few lessons with the blade. And perhaps with the dice.

Nay, she thought sharply, not with the dice. It would only bring back other memories she simply couldn't bear to think on anymore. But the other she could manage.

Aye, 'twas a most sensible plan.

18

It was the most ridiculous plan he'd ever heard.

Rhys deposited Gwen inside her bedchamber before he was tempted to give in to the overwhelming impulse that raged inside him—that of strangling her. As he'd tromped up the steps behind her, he'd managed to reacquire the rest of her guard. Said guard was now clustered around him as he stood outside Gwen's door. He fixed John with a steely glare.

"Tend her."

John's expression fell. "Must I?"

"Aye, you must."

"But where are you going?"

"To the lists," he growled. "I've a need of sport to cool my temper."

"I could stay behind as well," Montgomery offered with a small smile.

Rhys considered the Fitzgeralds, how long it would take him to dispatch them and what there would remain of his irritation after that was done. He shook his head.

"I'll have need of you later. You'll come with me."

Montgomery shook his head. "I think I would rather stay here."

"Aye, he should stay," John agreed, "and then I could go with you."

"I assure you, John," Rhys growled, "that you would be much safer guarding your sister by marriage."

He motioned for the twins and Montgomery to follow him as he strode back along the passageway and down the steps to the great hall.

Alain and Rollan stood near the fire, dressed for travel. That boded well.

"Godspeed, my lord," Rhys said to Alain as he passed him.

"Remember your duties," Alain said.

"And remind him not to add to them, brother," Rollan replied.

Rhys made Alain a low bow, then walked briskly for the door. The last thing he wanted was to listen to Rollan's gall by way of Alain's mouth.

He made his way quickly to the lists, trailed by the three members of Gwen's guard. He paused, then contemplated who would give him the least trouble and the most pleasure to dispatch first. Montgomery would be a fine choice if he'd wanted nothing but to stretch his muscles, but he would be of no use in cooling the white-hot irritation that flowed so strongly through his veins. Perhaps he would save Montgomery for later, as a sort of sweet to be enjoyed after a full, hearty meal.

He looked at the twins and decided on Jared first. Connor was smiling, never a good sign, and fingering a pair of swords. Rhys would need to do a bit of warming up before he took on those flashing blades.

Not to say Jared was any less the swordsman than his brother was. Indeed Rhys had to admit, as he fended off Jared's sudden attack, that he couldn't have had two better masters when it came to swordplay. They were overly large, uncommonly strong, and wily as two foxes. But it was also not without reason that Rhys had held over a hundred knights for ransom on the continent. It took a bit of effort, but the time soon came that Jared cried peace. Rhys had but a moment to reach out and take Montgomery's sword, then pull it from the sheath before Connor was coming at him, still smiling.

Saints, but it was enough to give a man the chills.

Connor certainly seemed to be enjoying the two-handed sport, for his smile soon turned into a grin. As he caught Rhys with an especially wicked backhand, he actually chortled. The blades flashed in the sunlight, and Rhys found himself hard-pressed to keep the larger man at bay. It wasn't an everyday occurrence to fight with swords in both hands against a man who wielded either with like skill.

"Come now, my little friend," Connor chided, "surely you have more to show me than that."

My little friend. Well, at least Gwen hadn't added the little. But the reminder of just what she had called him brought to the fore a fresh surge of annoyance. He wasn't about to become her comrade-at-arms. That she would no doubt get either herself or him killed with her swordplay was beside the point. He didn't want her as a comrade, he wanted her as a . . .

Montgomery's sword went flying from Rhys's hand. Rhys looked at his empty fingers in surprise, then looked at Connor who had chortled yet again.

This was not good.

Rhys put aside his uncomfortable thoughts of just what he wanted from Gwennelyn of Ayre and concentrated on finding a way of either ridding Connor of his second sword or regaining Montgomery's that Connor seemed determined to keep under his heel.

It was the beginning of a very long, unpleasant morning.

By the time Rhys had finally beaten Connor back, it was past noon. Rhys was dripping with sweat and wished for nothing more than several mugs of cold ale.

"My turn," Montgomery said brightly. "Come, Rhys, and let me see what you have yet in reserve for me."

"Go to the devil," Rhys wheezed.

"Before you have a go at me? Surely not."

Jared clapped Rhys on the shoulder. "I'll fetch you something cold, lad. You deserve it."

"Deserve it?" Connor echoed. "What did he do to deserve ale? I had him the whole time. If he just hadn't avoided my lethal jab above the knees with both blades."

"You'll note," Jared said, "that he used my defense against just such a womanly move. 'Twas my training that won the day for him."

"Your training? Bah, 'tis a wonder he can lift a sword after what you taught him!"

Rhys suppressed the urge to stick his fingers in his ears until the argument was over. Fortunately, Connor seemed as inclined for something cold as his brother did, and he and Jared made straightway for the great hall, still arguing about who had taught whom what. Rhys leaned on his sword and sucked in great gulps of air.

"If it will soothe you, I doubt I could have stood against them," Montgomery offered. He shuddered. "That Connor frightens me."

"Tame as a bunny once you know where to scratch," Rhys panted. "Distract him with a compliment on his swordplay and he's yours."

"Don't think I want him, thanks just the same. Now, tell me what it is that has you in such a temper. It can't be the thought of seeing the last of Alain until he tires of his mistress at Canfield."

"As I'm certain he'll move on from there," Rhys said, "I doubt we'll need endure him again before the babe is born."

"Ah," Montgomery said, looking at him closely, "then 'tis the babe that troubles you?"

"Now why would Alain having an heir trouble me?"

"Ah, Rhys, I am not so great a fool as you think. I know where your heart lies."

Rhys glared at him. "As I always say—you think too much."

"Ah, but when thinking yields such delicious insights, how am I to help myself?"

Rhys would have cut off Montgomery's head to stop him from babbling the more, but he found he was simply too weary to lift his sword at the moment.

"I wonder just what it was you and our sweet Gwen were discussing in the healer's hovel," Montgomery mused. "So many hints, but so few details."

"Eavesdropping is a very unattractive fault, Montgomery."

Montgomery only smiled. "You wound me. I was merely shadowing my captain. Is that not one of my duties?"

"Why do I have the feeling I'll live to regret having asked you to be a part of this foolishness?"

"Come now, Rhys," Montgomery chided. "You chose me for Gwen's guard, which kept me from Alain's clutches, and I am most grateful. I can only assume it was as a reward for past service to you."

"Past service?" Rhys asked. "What past service have you ever done me besides your efforts to corrupt my sweet soul?"

Montgomery waved aside the accusation. "Stretch yourself to remember, Rhys. Who was it who fed you tales of Gwennelyn of Segrave all those years when you wouldn't travel with us to her keep, hmmm? Who was it who laced descriptions of her soil with equally as interesting descriptions of her person as she grew into the beauty she is today?"

Rhys only scowled at him.

"And these are the thanks I receive for such heavy labors? All those hours of being forced to observe her at close range, just so I could bring you tidings of the girl?"

Rhys felt his fingers begin to flex of their own accord.

"Hour upon hour of following after her with my eyes, marking her every movement, seeing how her hair moved as she walked, how the sunlight turned those pale eyes of hers to something the shores of southern France would envy, watching her bloom from a girl into a beautiful, pleasingly proportioned wom—"

Rhys wasn't at all surprised at how well his fingers about Montgomery's throat silenced the man to mere gurgling. He contented himself with but a mere shake or two, for after all, Montgomery had provided him with visions of Gwen he'd been too cowardly to go and obtain for himself. That alone was likely worth sparing the wretch any further punishment.

Montgomery only knocked Rhys's hands away and backed up a pace, grinning like the empty-headed fool he was.

"Saints, lad, but you are smitten."

"As if it served me!"

Montgomery shrugged. "You never know what the future holds—Ah, my lord Ayre," he said, putting on a less open expression, "a pleasant journey to you."

Rhys turned and saw that Alain and Rollan had begun to make their way to the stables. He bowed along with Montgomery and hoped his relief at seeing them gone wasn't as obvious as he feared it was. He had no doubts Alain would have his spies everywhere marking his and Gwen's every move, but that could be borne.

Then he shook his head in wonder at his own conceit. Could Alain possibly care what either of them did? It wasn't as if Alain had any intention of holding to his marriage vows. Canfield was the home of Rachel, Lord Edward of Graundyn's sister. She was unwed and likely to stay that way, for her brother was very loth to give up her lands. She did manage, however, to warm her bed with any number of men, married or not. That Alain believed himself to be the only one loitering there between the sheets merely proved the extent of the man's stupidity. The saints only knew what Rollan would be about for the next while, but Rhys contented himself with knowing he would be about his business in some other keep. At least he and Gwen would have peace from that pair of prying eyes. Though what there would be to see, he surely didn't know.

The truth of it was enough to make him want to sit down and weep. She was Alain's. She was now carrying Alain's babe. The time for an annulment was surely past. The only alternative left them was divorce, and proving that Alain continued to bed his whores would be difficult indeed. Rhys wondered if Alain had even maintained the sanctity of his wedding night before he'd sought out other companionship in the castle.

Rhys couldn't have said, as he remembered so little of the eve thanks to the amount of spirits the Fitzgeralds had poured down him. And should he have by some miracle even marked the events of the night, he would have forgotten them straightway thanks to the awakening he'd had before sunrise the next morn. He'd been snoring in peaceful oblivion one moment, then snorting under the deluge of cold water the next. He had sat bolt upright only to find he was in a makeshift bed in a forgotten corner of the cellar, naked, with no idea how he'd gotten there. The Fitzgeralds had been standing over him, frowning fiercely, both holding empty buckets in their hands.

Such had done nothing to begin a day he'd been sure would be one of the most hellish of his life.

Gwen was wed. And not to him.

"Speak of our angel and suddenly she appears," Montgomery said with a happy sigh. "Just looking at her is enough to break my heart."

Mine as well, Rhys thought with a slow shake of his head. How could anyone possibly expect him to have the keeping of her for the next two years and not want her? Just the sight of her was enough to bring him to his knees.

She was dressed, and by now this came as absolutely no surprise to him, in John's clothes. At least the lad wasn't wearing her skirts. Rhys was just as grateful for that as he was sure John was. She carried her filched sword, and Rhys wondered at whose feet to lay that blame, for he was just certain he'd concealed it well enough with his gear. Someday he would have to take the time to find its rightful owner and pay the poor soul for it. Either that or he would have one made for her strength of arm. She would never learn any swordplay with this blade.

"Is he gone yet?" she asked.

"Aye, lady," Montgomery said with a low bow. "You can be about your sport freely now." He looked at Rhys and raised one eyebrow.

Rhys ignored him. "I thought you were resting."

"I rested," she answered promptly, "and now I am here for my lesson."

He remembered vividly the last lesson he'd given her. He saw by the immediate flush on her face that she remembered it as well.

"In swordplay," she added.

"What else?" he grumbled.

"What else indeed?" Montgomery murmured.

Rhys gave him a healthy shove, then turned back to his would-be apprentice. From all appearances, she seemed ready and eager to learn.

"What will you have me do first?" she asked.

Take off that bloody ring of Alain's and flee to France with me, was on the tip of his tongue, but he refrained from giving voice to the thought. Unfortunately, that was just the beginning of the things he wanted her to do.

He wanted her to look at him again as she'd looked at him the night she came to him. He wanted her to put her arms about him and tell him that she couldn't live without him by her side. He wanted her to fumble hesitantly with his clothes as she had that night, touch his flesh with cold, trembling fingers, and lift her mouth to his for sweet, lingering kisses.

She is not yours.

Rhys scowled at the voice in his head. Surely there was some angel somewhere recording the deeds of his life, and it would be noted that before Alain of Ayre laid a hand upon her, Rhys had taken her as the wife of his heart and the love of his soul. He had bound himself to her just as surely as if he'd stood with her before a priest and spoken the vows aloud.

Now, if only that angel also kept a book of ways to take a woman away from a husband who most certainly did not deserve her. And if they both could but survive the next pair of years, Wyckham would be his, and he would have a place to take her when he managed to free her from Alain.

She is not yours to take.

"Nay, but she will be," he vowed as he looked at her.

"I will be what?" Gwen asked, leaning on her sheathed sword.

Rhys put aside his schemes. There would be ample time to think on them later.

"A damned good swordsman by the time I'm finished with you," he said with a sigh.

"Think you?" she asked with a smile so bright he almost flinched. She lifted the sword with gusto.

Predictably it overbalanced her, and she stumbled backward into John, who, obviously unused to dealing with these sorts of crises, fell straightway upon his arse. Gwen fell upon him just as directly, and the sword hilt smacked her solidly in the face.

She blinked for a moment or two in silence, then began a most unladylike round of howling and cursing.

Rhys clapped his hand to his forehead and groaned. He would surely have no time at present for plotting and scheming. Keeping Gwen unbruised would take all his attention.

Saints, but it was going to be a long afternoon.

And an even longer summer. There was surely nothing they could do about escape until the babe was born, and by his count that wouldn't happen until early spring, at least. Swordplay would have to occupy their time until then, for at least as long as she could lift one safely.

"John," he said, "you'll be the one to help show her how to hold the blade."

"Me?" John squeaked from where he was still sprawled in the dirt.

He looked as terrified by the prospect as Rhys was.

Heaven help them all.

19

Gwen sat under the lone tree in Ayre's garden, enjoying the spring sunshine and the fact that she'd managed to lower herself to a sitting position with almost no help at all. Given the fact that she was ripe to bursting with her babe, it was a feat to be proud of.

She savored the smell of the herbs and flowers that were clustered in neat, orderly patches about her. Her keepers were clustered about her as well, but not nearly as neatly and certainly not in as orderly a fashion. Montgomery was sitting near a patch of yarrow, rubbing his nose and looking about him in irritation as if he could thereby divine what it was that was making his eyes water so fiercely. The Fitzgeralds stood a few paces off with their arms folded over their chests and their customary frowns adorning their faces. They had declined her invitation to sit and enjoy the day. Gwen supposed when a pair of men seemed less likely to bend than oak trees, standing was preferable to trying to find a place between pasque-flower and Saint-John's-wort.

Rhys was sprawled out next to several hills of lavender, twirling a stalk of it between his fingers and staring off unseeing into the distance. Gwen told herself she was happy with the turn of events. Her lessons in swordplay had progressed for a pair of months' time the previous fall, then abruptly ceased when Rhys decided it was no longer safe for her to practice. Safe for whom was still the question. She hadn't cut John that often, and she'd only bloodied his nose a handful of times as he struggled to show her how to hold the blade. She'd wondered at the time why Rhys had chosen his squire for such a task. Perhaps Rhys had pressed John into such service because he thought it would train his squire at the same time.

Or perhaps he had decided that he truly felt nothing more for her than friendship and therefore had no reason to want to be near her.

"Which is what I wanted, of course," she said.

"Huh?" John asked, looking up from the manuscript on his lap. He sat the closest to her, burdened with the task of reading aloud.

"Nothing," Gwen said.

She could feel Rhys's eyes on her, but she didn't dare look at him.

Comrade-at-arms. By Saint George's crossed eyes, what had she been thinking?

"Gwen, this is too hard," John complained.

"How can you be a great lord if you know nothing of reading?" she asked, then she bit her tongue. For all she knew, Rhys couldn't read. Insulting him was the last thing she had intended.

John sighed heavily and started up the tale again from the beginning.

" 'Not so many . . . um . . . years a . . . ago, there lived a lady who . . . who . . . ' "

"Whose," Gwen said.

"Aye, 'whose beauty was re . . . renowned through . . . out all the land.' " He rolled his eyes. "Why would anyone care?"

" 'Tis a most marvelous story of love and devotion," she informed him.

"I'd rather read of war and slaughter," he said, turning up his nose.

"No war today, though I'm certain I should be apologizing most heartily for it. This was my favorite tale from my mother's finest minstrel. She had it copied down, and I learned to read from it."

"Indeed," Rhys said with a cough.

"Oh, aye," she said, nodding. "I daresay I have it memorized by now."

"All that romance has warped her thinking, if you ask me," Montgomery muttered, looking as if he were on the verge of a mighty sneeze. He gingerly tried to move aside a few flowers that were leaning toward him. "What is this weed here?"

"Yarrow," Rhys said absently, firming up a bit of loose soil near the base of the plant nearest him.

"Yarrow?"

"Bloodwort," Rhys said. "Good for staunching wounds. Don't crush it."

Montgomery put his hands in his lap and looked at the cluster of herbs with new respect.

" 'Tis a most romantic tale we are hearing," Gwen said defensively, feeling somewhat slighted by Montgomery's criticism of her favorite story.

Montgomery scowled. "And romance is what is wrong with the world toda . . . ah . . . hachoo!"

"Ignore him," Rhys said, casting Montgomery a dark look. "Press on, John. The lady Gwennelyn has it aright. Learning to read will serve you well in the future."

"But this?" John asked plaintively. " 'Tis drivel! I've heard the tale before. The knight does nothing but worship her from afar."

"Ugh," Montgomery said, looking down with intense dislike at the herbs that had somehow migrated onto the front of his tunic.

" 'Tis very—" Gwen began.

"Feebleminded," John interrupted. "He sighs, he swoons, he beats upon his breast with his fist, and moons over her for pages. Saints, Sir Rhys, look you how many pages of mooning there are!"

" 'Tis highly chivalrous," Gwen said stiffly. "And I find the tale much to my liking."

"All I can say," John grumbled, "is I think the knight's time would be better spent in the lists. At least then he would be seeing to something of value—"

"Oh, by the bloody saints," Rhys growled, "give me that thing."

John blinked at him. "Can you read?"

The look on Rhys's face should have alerted John he was treading in dangerous waters. John, however, as Gwen well knew, was oblivious to such unspoken warnings.

"After all," he said, plunging ahead heedlessly, "your sire was merely a—"

"John."

"Aye, Sir Rhys?"

"Do you wish to continue to be my squire?"

Even John seemed to realize he had perhaps gone too far. He gulped audibly.

"Aye, Sir Rhys."

"Then hand me the manuscript and do it silently."

John handed over the manuscript without another sound, then shifted as far out of Rhys's sights as he could get.

Gwen watched the entire scene with fascination. It was almost more interesting than the tale Rhys held in his hands. Rhys's parents were a mystery, though she knew his grandfather had been a knight of some renown in the French court. It was he who had seen Rhys sent to Bertram of Ayre, though why he had chosen an English lord instead of a French one, she couldn't have said.

Perhaps Rhys's sire was a mere knight. Based on her experience, she had to conclude that being a nobleman did not necessarily guarantee that a man was noble. Perhaps Rhys had been well served by having no nobility flowing through his veins. Gwen could find no fault with his conduct because of it.

" 'Not so many years ago, there lived a lady whose beauty was renowned throughout all the land.' "

Gwen caught her breath. Now, there was a voice that any bard would envy—deep and rich. Gwen found herself immediately under his spell. She gave a passing thought to the fact that Rhys could indeed read very well, spared one last question as to where he might have learned such a thing, then gave herself over to the magic he was weaving with his voice alone.

" 'Many a knight came to gaze upon her beauty, then depart with a solemn vow on a quest to win her, whatever the cost. The lady knew of none of these vows, of course, for her father kept her sheltered, and the lady herself saw not her true love amongst the men who came to her father's hall.' "

Gwen closed her eyes with a sigh of pleasure. How many times had she heard this tale? Too many to count. Only never had she heard it told in such a fashion, even when it had been put to music and sung by her mother's most skilled minstrels.

And as she continued to listen, she felt the babe begin to stir within her. Obviously he was just as charmed as she by what he was hearing.

And then she realized, with a start, that it wasn't just the beauty of the poetry that moved her babe.

She was on her feet before she knew how she had gotten there.

"Gwen!"

She would have replied, but she found quite suddenly that she couldn't. She held out her hands and immediately found a pair of strong forearms there, ready to support her.

"The babe comes," Rhys announced.

The pain passed and she found that she had the strength to scowl up at him. "And what would you know of it? It could be anything. Supper. The saints only know Cook is incapable of preparing anything edible."

He looked down at her solemnly. "Have the stirrings of your babe come more closely together than before?"

"Aye, but—"

Before she could answer, she found herself off her feet and into his arms.

"Rhys, put me down!" she exclaimed. "What will Alain—"

"I would imagine, given how he's passed his afternoons for the fortnight since his return, that he will be occupied for several hours still."

"Rollan—"

"Is a fool I will see to when the time comes. Why do you not save your energy for the birthing of your babe and leave your other troubles to me?"

He certainly wasn't giving her much choice in the matter. Gwen found herself being carried back into the keep before she could clear her mind enough to voice any more protests.

The afternoon passed slowly. Rhys had cleared her solar of her ladies straightaway, which had suited her very well, as most of them had spent ample time in her husband's bed and she cared not for them as a whole. Fewer souls had also meant more room to pace, which she had done for what seemed like hours.

She'd wanted the midwife from the village to come, but Alain had refused. He'd sent instead his surgeon, who had done nothing but lay out the sharp tools of his trade. Gwen had done her best to ignore him. A birthing stool had been brought by one of the serving maids, and Gwen had been tempted to have her stay just for the companionship of another woman, but the surgeon had banned her from the chamber. Gwen would have protested to her husband herself, but evidently he had already been in his cups when he'd learned that his son's arrival was imminent. The tidings had only heralded the opening of another keg of ale.

And still the surgeon sharpened his knives.

And Rhys stood in the corner of the chamber with his arms folded over his chest, glaring at the man. At least Alain had been too drunk to wonder about Rhys's whereabouts. Rhys was no midwife, but he was companionship.

The pains came harder. The surgeon rubbed his hands together as if he itched to be about some business. Rhys glowered all the more. They began to exchange insults. Gwen felt her tongue loosen as well, and she began to use it generously on the other two souls in her chamber.

Somehow, though, that did not help her pass the time any more easily.

The sun had set and candles had been lit. Rhys stood in the middle of the chamber staring down in satisfaction at Alain's senseless surgeon. At least now the evening could progress without anymore threats, blasphemy, or taking of Rhys's name in vain.

At least from the surgeon.

Gwen was still sharpening her tongue on him, but Rhys couldn't blame her. He'd only made the mistake once of telling her that her body was designed to birth babes, which had resulted in another string of aspersions being cast at him. Her having likened labor to his passing a large egg through his . . . well, it had left him crossing his legs in discomfort and racking his brains for something else with which to distract her. Suggesting that perhaps it was due recompense for Eve and the apple—

He still marveled that a woman in labor could move so fast or use her fist so liberally. At least she hadn't had the energy to reach up for his nose. He rubbed it absently, somewhat relieved to find it still unbruised.

With a sigh, he hefted the surgeon and deposited him in a corner, out of the way of Gwen's pacing. Then Rhys leaned back against the wall, half afraid to say anything for fear of saying the wrong thing.

Not that Gwen would have noticed him by now, likely. Where she had gone he didn't know, but her spirit was certainly far away at present. She was pacing the confines of her chamber, pausing frequently to grab hold of whatever sturdy object was handy to lean against until her pains passed. She was making a great deal of noise, and the groans had initially frightened him. He'd made the mistake of interrupting her pacing and paid the price in the blistering of his ears. After that, he'd done his best to stay out of her way and make certain that no one else disturbed her.

Her pacing brought her his way, and he remained perfectly still as she clutched his arms and rested her head on his chest. He didn't dare touch her.

"Gwen?"

His only answer was something of a grunt.

"Shall you have a potion from Master Socrates? It might ease your pains."

She grunted again and pushed away from him to resume her slow, deliberate pacing.

This at least was something he could do. He walked toward the door, wishing his mother had been in attendance at least. Much as he might have wanted to believe that he alone would suffice Gwen in her times of need, he was fast beginning to believe that birthing was women's work. A pity he didn't trust any of Ayre's ladies, else he would have called for them. Perhaps a softer touch would have soothed Gwen.

He opened it to find Rollan leaning against the far wall of the passageway. Rollan's eyes widened as he caught sight of Rhys.

"What are you—"

"Saving her life," Rhys said shortly. He looked about the passageway and espied Master Socrates and his granddaughter. He'd had John fetch them earlier that afternoon, should Gwen need them. "She has need of one of your potions."

"I should be unsurprised to find you here," Rollan said with a snort. "I suppose you would have the skills to do this thing, seeing as how your father's skills lay there. Son of a healer," he sneered. "How you came to earn your spurs is a mystery to m—"

Which just went to show how little Rollan knew of Rhys's family. His father had healing skills, 'twas true, but he'd also earned his spurs. It just hadn't served him to let others know the like.

Rhys retreated inside the chamber with Master Socrates and his granddaughter, then slammed the door shut. The last thing any of them needed that eve was to listen to any more of Rollan's spite.

Rhys turned to Master Socrates. "Can you ease her pain?"

"Aye, Sir Rhys. I have brought with me all things needful."

"And can you birth the babe?"

Master Socrates looked down at his gnarled hands, then met Rhys's eyes. "My wife and daughter were midwives. But I do not know—"

"Better you than me," Rhys said grimly. He intercepted Gwen in the midst of the chamber. He was surely no midwife, but even he could tell there was a change in his lady. "Gwen?"

"My time is upon me," she said with a gasp.

And so, apparently, it was. Rhys found that now the moment had come, he felt as if he shouldn't be near her. Surely she would be better off in the company of women.

He shook himself. There were no women to be had. He would have to suffice.

He stood behind the birthing stool and put his hands on her shoulders. At least she wasn't cursing him anymore. She was, however, coming close to drawing blood on his hands with every wave of labor that came over her. He didn't care. 'Twas surely the least he could do for her.

Not a handful of moments had passed before the chamber door burst open and Alain himself stood there. He looked at Rhys, his mouth working furiously. Rhys only returned the stare, unruffled.

"Y-you!" Alain managed finally.

"Aye, my lord?"

"Who do you think you are?" Alain bellowed.

"I am the one charged with protecting her life," Rhys said calmly. "And so here I am."

Alain frowned, as if he knew there was something amiss with that, but couldn't divine what. He turned his attentions on Master Socrates. "Him!" he said, pointing furiously. "I told you I wanted nothing to do with that filthy old man!"

'Twas obvious Master Socrates had heard this before,

for he took no notice of Ayre, but continued to speak to Gwen in soothing tones.

"The babe comes," Rhys said shortly, "and he can keep both the child and its mother alive."

"Then why are you here?" Rollan said from where he had come up behind his brother. He smiled coldly. "Gazing upon what you can never have?"

"I was protecting my lady from that," Rhys said, jerking his head toward where the surgeon lay in a heap against the wall. "It is my duty."

Alain looked at Rollan for aid. Rollan's returning look was one of grave concern.

"I would worry, my lord," Rollan began, "about Sir Rhys's parentage. You know what a poor reputation his sire had. Never amounted to much, or so I remember."

Alain blinked. "I thought his sire was a healer. Roamed the countryside plying his craft."

Rhys didn't stir himself to comment.

"Or was he a minstrel?" Alain asked, sounding very unsure of his information. "I've heard both tales."

"Does it matter if he was both?" Rollan asked. "The man was burned as a heretic, accused of using witchcraft to heal his victims."

"Ah," Alain said, nodding. He turned to Rhys. "Leave."

Rhys clenched his jaw. "Nay."

Alain's expression darkened. "I'll not have your reputation tainting my son!"

"My sire was unjustly accused."

"Was he?" Alain asked, frowning. He looked at Rollan. "Was he?"

Rollan shrugged. "Who's to say? Perhaps 'tis the truth. And perhaps I spoke out of turn. Considering Sir Rhys's heritage, perhaps this is the place for him."

Alain waited, seemingly for enlightenment.

"Birthing is peasants' work, after all," Rollan said.

"The lady of Ayre is no peasant," Rhys said, wishing he had the right to throw the lot of them off the parapet. "Rollan insults both her and your son."

Alain looked to be working that out in his head. He finally pushed Rollan toward the door.

"You insulted my son," he said sternly. He shot Rhys a final look. "The babe dies and you die, understood?"

Rhys nodded and breathed a sigh of relief when the chamber door closed behind Ayre's lord and his brother.

"Finally," Gwen gasped. "I learn some of the tale. Why—" Another pain shook her and left her breathless. "Why I had to be suffering this before I heard of it I surely do not know."

"Ugly rumors," Rhys said shortly. "My sire was no heretic."

"Healers are ofttimes misunderstood," Master Socrates informed them. "Add a pinch of something unusual to a potion, and one becomes labeled a witch."

"And here I thought . . . your sire . . . was a knight," Gwen said, gasping for air. "Or so . . . I'd heard."

"He was several things," Rhys muttered. "Push, Gwen. Let us have this babe out."

The candle on the hearth had not burned down but another hour before Ayre's son had indeed made his entrance into the world. Rhys watched Gwen weep with relief. He watched Master Socrates pull the babe from beneath Gwen's gown.

Socrates' face drained of all color.

Rhys looked at the babe.

It wasn't breathing.

20

The child stood in the corner of the chamber and watched the babe come into the world. Her grandfather's hands shook as he held the lad. The babe was still.

The knight took the babe in his hands. He rubbed the tiny body, crooning to it in soft tones of command, bidding the child to take his place in the world.

Yet the child did not respond.

And then she watched as the knight leaned over, brushed aside the matter that covered the babe's face, then put his own mouth over the tiny nose and mouth that had not yet moved.

Once.

Twice.

Three times the knight gave the babe his own breath, his own means of life, as if he strove to breathe into the wee one his own will to live.

The tiny chest moved.

And then it moved again.

And then, to the child's relief, the lad set up a weak wail.

The child watched the lady take her firstborn son and cradle him close to her breast. She watched the young woman's tears and felt tears course down her own cheeks at the sight.

Then she looked at the knight kneeling at his lady's feet and saw that he wept as well.

The child looked at his hands and saw that they were full of healing. His heart was full of love for both mother and son, unlike Ayre's lord. The child wished she could have changed things, but that was far beyond her modest arts.

The breath of life. Aye, 'twas what she would have done as well in his place. Her own mother had done it often enough. The knight was powerfully wise to have thought of it.

"Come, granddaughter. Our work is done here."

The child obeyed the whispered command of her grandsire. She cast one last look behind her as she walked to the chamber door, saw the knight lift his lady's hand and kiss it tenderly.

Ah, that she could have changed things!

She suspected the pair behind her likely felt the same.

Gwen lay back against the pillows of the bed, exhausted in body and spirit. Aye, the laboring had been hard, but 'twas almost losing her son that had stretched her to the very limits of her endurance and reason. At least the babe was safe. And she had Rhys to thank for that.

There was a sudden commotion by the doorway. Gwen looked up to see Alain and Rollan entering the chamber, shoving aside Master Socrates and his granddaughter in the process. As tempted as she was to chastise her husband for his ill treatment of the old man, she found she had little energy to do aught but lie where she was and cradle her son close.

"Let me see the babe," Alain said, reaching for him.

Gwen reluctantly allowed Alain to have the boy. Much as she would have liked to deny it, Alain was the father and had every right to at least hold his son.

"Ah," he said, looking at the boy with satisfaction, "a healthy son."

"No thanks to you," Gwen whispered. " 'Twas Rhys who saved the babe."

Alain frowned at that, then looked back at his son. "I did my work well with this one," he said, sounding supremely satisfied. "He resembles me, don't you think?" he asked his brother.

"Oh, aye," Rollan said, bobbing his head obediently. "Very strongly."

Alain contemplated the babe in his arms. "Fragile little beast," he said, hefting him. "What if I lose him?"

"Surely you won't," Rollan said gently.

"But if I did," Alain argued. "Damnation, but I had thought not to need to sire any more on her." He sighed heavily. "I suppose I'll need another, in case something happens to this one."

"Perhaps you should make certain nothing happens to this babe," Rollan suggested. "If he were mine, I would give thought to who might best care for the lad."

"Aye," Alain said, seemingly giving that what he thought to be an appropriate amount of thought. He smiled suddenly at his brother. "I'll take him to Canfield to be raised by someone with experience."

Gwen felt a coldness rush over her. "Nay," she croaked. "You'll not take him from me."

"I'll do what I like—"

"I am his mother," Gwen said, sitting up with great effort, "and I will be the one to care for him."

Alain looked at his brother. "What think you?"

Rollan smiled. "Take him to Canfield. That is a most sensible plan. Indeed, I'll find a wet nurse immediately, and perhaps we could take up our journey this afternoon."

"Nay," Gwen said, reaching for the babe.

"Rachel would care well for the child," Rollan continued.

"Aye, my thought as well," Alain said. "Let us be off then—"

Gwen found herself on her feet, reaching for the dagger

in Rhys's belt almost before she knew what she had intended. She rushed at her husband with blade bared. And if she hadn't been so enraged at his cheek, she might have found the way he and Rollan both squeaked and stumbled backward to be somewhat amusing.

But there was nothing humorous about their plan.

"Give me the child," she commanded.

Alain hesitated.

Gwen brandished the knife, and Alain promptly handed the swaddled babe over to her.

"I'll kill you if you try," she said hoarsely.

"I doubt very much—" Alain spluttered.

"I'll kill you if you try," she repeated, dropping the dagger and clutching her son to her. "And if you think I won't turn over every stone on the isle to find you and end your life, consider it again, my lord. You will not take my son from me."

Alain looked rather startled. Then he seemed to gather what wits he possessed around himself.

"I'll give it more thought," he promised.

"Begone from my chamber," Gwen rasped. "You have your son, but you'll take him from me at the peril of your own life. And if you slay me, I'll haunt you for the rest of your days until you're driven mad."

Alain was, if nothing else, a superstitious soul. Without another word, he turned on his heel and scurried from the chamber. Rollan, however, was slow to follow his brother. He lingered at the doorway. When he opened his mouth to speak, Gwen pointed her finger at him.

"Don't," she warned. "Say nothing at all, if you value your sorry life."

He shut his lips around the saints only knew what kind of foolishness, then inclined his head.

"Hearty congratulations on the birth of your son," he said simply.

Gwen looked at him narrowly. "That is all? Just congratulations?"

Rollan shrugged. "I could not be happier for you. If there is anything I can do . . . ?"

"You can leave," Gwen said shortly. "I need to rest."

Rollan made her a low bow. "As my lady wishes." He straightened and looked at Rhys. "Surely your presence here is no longer required, Sir Rhys."

Gwen watched Rhys pick up the dagger she had filched from his belt, resheath it carefully, then incline his head to Rollan.

"My place is, as always, outside her door as captain of her guard," he said with a grim smile. "After you, my lord."

Gwen gingerly sat back down on the bed, clutching her son close. Rhys waited until Rollan had departed, then went down on one knee in front of her.

"I know of a trustworthy woman or two from the village," he said quietly. "Perhaps you would care to have them attend you rather than your ladies?"

"I daresay I could use the aid," she admitted.

"Then I will see to it. Once I am returned, if you have need of me, I will be immediately without your chamber. All you must needs do is call."

Gwen nodded and bent over her newborn son. She knew she should have been thinking a score of other more uplifting thoughts, but all she could think was how she wished this child had a different father than Alain.

Rhys, for instance.

A short while later a pair of women appeared at her door, waiting hesitantly for permission to enter. Gwen was grateful for them. The very last thing she wanted was to have any of Alain's whores in attendance.

Once she was made comfortable and had made her first fumbling attempts at nursing the babe, Gwen laid him by her side and watched him sleep. It was a miracle the babe lived. If Rhys hadn't been there, he wouldn't have. The thought of that caught her tight around the heart and wrung grief from her she didn't realize she had.

And then as relentlessly as sleep had claimed her babe, it began to claim her. She fought it, knowing there were things she had to consider before much more time passed.

Already ten months of Rhys's service to Alain was fulfilled. What would she do when he left?

It was surely nothing she could bear to think on at present. Perhaps it was best that weariness was so heavy upon her. Rhys would be keeping watch outside her door, and for the moment both she and her son were safe.

It was enough.

Rhys knocked softly upon the door, and one of the women he had fetched opened it hesitantly.

"She sleeps, Sir Knight," the woman whispered.

"And the babe?"

"He sleeps as well."

"You made them both comfortable?"

"Aye, good sir. Will you have us remain?"

"Yet a while, if you will."

The woman nodded and withdrew back into the chamber. Rhys lingered at the doorway, unable to tear himself away.

Gwen slept with her babe cradled in her arms. The sight was such a peaceful one, nay, 'twas a sacred one. Rhys looked at the tiny babe and blessed his father wherever he currently resided—heaven or hell—for having passed on if not his gift for healing, his gift for quick thinking. Rhys had seen life breathed into a body before, but had also watched his father be carried away by furious envoys from the church after having done such a thing. A flimsy excuse to put him to death, of course, but no one had seemed to find it unreasonable. One life had been saved, the other destroyed as a result. At least Rhys hadn't had to watch his sire die.

And at least he'd avoided the same fate. The saints be praised Alain hadn't seen what he'd done to the boy.

Nay, it had been worth the risk. Gwen was delivered safely, and her son breathed on his own now. Rhys could ask for no better end to the day.

Unless, of course, he were to have the right to shoo the

women from the room and lie down next to his lady, wrapping his arms about both mother and child.

It was what he wanted more than anything else. More than land. More than the saving of Gwen's reputation from scandal. More than his own honor, truth be told. He wanted these two as his.

It would take a miracle for that to come to pass.

His vision blurred and he dragged the back of his hand across his eyes. It was then he realized Gwen was watching him. Her own eyes filled with tears, but she made no move to brush them from her cheeks.

It was an intolerable situation.

He made her a low bow and backed from the chamber before he broke down and wept. He closed the door softly, then turned and leaned back against it.

The rest of Gwen's guard was leaning against the opposite wall. They looked at him in silence for several moments, then Montgomery cleared his throat.

"What say you," he said roughly, "to seeking out a full keg in the cellar?"

Rhys shook his head. "Nay."

Montgomery frowned. "A go in the lists?"

Rhys shook his head again. "Nay."

"Well, *I'd* like to go to the lists," Montgomery grumbled. "I'm feeling passing edgy at the moment."

"I'll oblige you," Connor said, fingering the hilt of one of his swords. "With my left, I think."

Montgomery looked at him narrowly. "Think me to be easy sport, do you?"

Connor only shrugged and followed a cursing Montgomery down the passageway. Rhys almost smiled at that. If Montgomery only knew the left was Connor's better hand and he only reserved it for his more challenging sparring partners. Rhys looked at Jared.

"Perhaps you'd best go keep watch. Wouldn't want Connor to truly do him in."

Jared nodded and took John by the neck. "Come, little one. Let us leave your master in peace."

"But," John protested, "he might need me."

"What he needs is quiet," Jared said, pulling him down the passageway. "If you stop digging in your heels, I might even give you a small lesson in swordplay."

John's heels abruptly stopped trying to find holds in the floor. "You taught my master, did you not?"

"Aye, lad. All his most deadly moves."

John was now moving along quite willingly. "Think you you could teach me how to fight with two swords as Sir Rhys does?"

"Why don't we begin with one, young John."

Rhys watched them disappear into the stairwell, then leaned back against the door and closed his eyes. His men were happily engaged in their business. Alain and Rollan had no doubt descended to fill themselves full of drink. Gwen had likely fallen asleep peacefully again with her son.

And there he stood outside her door, acting the proper guardsman, when all he could think about was how badly he wanted to snatch her away.

He shook his head sharply. He couldn't think on it. Alain would never give up his heir, and Gwen would never give up her son. Rhys knew he could never ask it of her. Whether he willed it or no, he would have to take the situation he faced and bear it.

Though how he could, he certainly did not know.

But he would have to. He would have to smile, look content, keep up a façade for Gwen's sake. She would have more than enough to occupy her mind with the raising of her son. Perhaps she had it aright and they could truly think of each other as nothing more than comrades-at-arms. Rhys wasn't sure he would manage it, but he knew he had little choice but to try to pretend it was so. At least for the next few months.

"By the saints," he muttered, "I wish my father had been an actor instead of a knight!"

Fall

THE YEAR OF OUR LORD 1202

21

Two years wasted. Two years of scheming lost. Rollan of Ayre prowled through the passageways in the cellar, seeking for something to soothe his foul humor. He tried a pull at one of the ale kegs. It was sour, almost as sour as his mood.

Saints, but his plans had gone awry. He'd suspected it before the birth of Gwen's son, of course. He remembered well that spring. Spring was such a wonderful time, with all things springing to life. It was his favorite time to hatch plots. He'd spent a pair of months despoiling a pair of noblemen's daughters, then joyfully wreaking some choice havoc at court. He'd looked forward, with his customary gleeful anticipation, to returning home to find Gwen and her captain wallowing in misery.

But, to his dismay, what had he found?

Gwen growing great with child, but still cheerful. Rhys seemingly concerned, understandably, but not frantic.

It had not boded well.

Rollan had been certain the birth of Gwen's babe would be the thing to truly make the pair realize what they wanted yet could never have. He had looked forward to a rich bit of suffering to enjoy. Yet what had occurred?

Gwen had continued to smile.

Rhys had continued to look if not content, almost resigned.

And damn that bloody babe if he hadn't grown into a strong little lad of an age to be walking and looking about as if he already owned Ayre and all in it.

Damnation, but it had been enough to turn Rollan to drink.

He had watched Gwen and Rhys together as often as he could manage since then, but had seen nothing that indicated they were more than lady and loyal knight. No touching. No lingering looks of love. Saints above, not even a stolen kiss to report to Alain. Rollan had been tempted to brew up a fabrication as large as his irritation to spew at Alain the moment his brother came up for air from all his wenching, but it had offended his finer sensibilities, so he had refrained.

And now the son, yet another soul who stood in the way of Rollan's desire. A son, a doting mother, and a protector of both mother and child in the form of Rhys de Piaget. Events had certainly taken a decided turn for the worse since Alain's marriage to Gwen.

Two years had not improved matters any.

Gwen wouldn't flee the keep now, not with her son to consider. Rhys wouldn't leave the keep because he wanted Wyckham and likely Gwen as well. Captain and lady together always and seemingly content with it. The situation Rollan had thought would drive the pair of them straight off the parapet had turned out to be something the two of them couldn't have designed any more pleasingly if they'd been planning it themselves.

And now, most distressingly, Rollan found himself fresh out of ideas for further mayhem.

He stomped back up to the kitchens, latched on to a likely serving wench, and pulled her behind him up the stairs to his bedchamber. Perhaps a fortnight of wenching and drinking would restore his good humor and provide him with a few new ideas for making Rhys and Gwen miserable. It would take a cleverness that only he could muster, however. And he felt certain it would take something that would stretch even his considerable powers of imagination.

He snagged a second wench as he walked down the passageway.

It was going to be that kind of fortnight, he could just tell.

The child stood at her grandfather's elbow and watched as he scratched upon the parchment with his quill dipped in ink. It was easier to see the strange marks now that she had passed almost another pair of years on the earth and was a bit taller, but easier to see did not necessarily mean easier to read. Her grandfather had taught her a few letters, but those few she recognized were so hopelessly intertwined with the others that she couldn't make sense of any of it.

She could, however, make sense of the pots and pouches littering her grandsire's worktable. Indeed, he had always told her that her gift lay more in the making of potions than in the writing down of them. And so she had trained her nose and her eyes and her hands to weave together things that would heal, and she hoped that would be enough skill for the tasks life would send her way.

But still there was a part of her that wished, wistfully, that she, too, could make those graceful sweeping lines on paper.

Her grandfather sat back on his tall stool and smiled in satisfaction. The child peered at the page.

"Very beautiful," she said admiringly.

"Aye," he agreed. "Much like life has been of late, aye, granddaughter?"

He spoke truly. Though they still lived in the damp cellars, a few comforts had come their way, borne of course by souls who swore not to know the identity of the senders.

The child knew, but she chose to say nothing.

Sir Rhys visited frequently, as did the lady of the keep. The child still rarely dared speak to the lady, for her beauty was almost painful to look upon, and the child's own lack shamed her. But the lady was gentle and kind and came often bearing little gifts for her alone. With the added joy of a baby to tickle and laugh with from time to time, life was indeed very sweet.

"This page is much like life," her grandsire began. He made a sweeping gesture, the one he always made when telling her something very important.

Only this time his sleeve caught his pot of ink and sent it splashing over his finely wrought words.

The child cried out in distress and used the sleeve of her dress to try to stem the tide. It was, unfortunately, hopeless. The page was ruined, the letters covered by a wash of dark ink.

Her grandfather sighed and looked at her.

"As with life, little one, sometimes one must begin the page again."

The child thought this a very wise, if not exactly pleasant, observation. So much work and patience, all undone with one chance gesture.

How like life indeed.

22

Gwen transferred her squirming son to her other hip and glared at her collection of keepers.

"How am I to eavesdrop with young Robin in tow?" she demanded.

To a man, well, and John of course, the souls facing her gave no answer. They did, however, wear almost identical looks of panic.

"Oh, by the saints, you are the most useless group of warriors I've ever encountered," she groused. "Afeared of such a small lad. You'd think the child was fierce enough to subdue you all with nothing more than a glance."

There was no change in their expressions, unless it was absolute certainty that such a thing was indeed possible.

Obviously humiliation was not going to work, either. There seemed to be no other choice but to take a drastic measure.

Gwen gave Robin a last cuddle, then turned him about and thrust him at the man nearest her. Jared, the soul so selected by default, held up his hands as if to ward off certain doom. Instead of avoiding his fate, he found himself with his hands full of a squirming lad of nigh onto sixteen months of life. Jared held the boy at arm's length as gingerly as he might have a striking snake. Gwen took one last look at her son who, though likely slightly uncomfortable at his precarious position, seemed to find Jared's features to his liking, for he merely stared at the man with as unblinking a stare as Jared possessed. Then he popped his thumb into his mouth and settled back for a substantial contemplation. Satisfied that both would survive the next few moments, Gwen slipped away and hied herself to her husband's solar.

It was only moments later that she stood with her ear pressed against the wood of the door, struggling to hear even the faintest sounds of conversation going on inside. That all was deathly silent could only mean one of two things: Alain was gloating and Rhys had chosen to remain stoic, or Alain had betrayed her captain and Rhys had slain every soul inside the chamber. The latter wouldn't have surprised her overmuch. Rhys was near the breaking point.

How they had managed to survive this long she surely didn't know. She told him often that it was because her powers of imagination were certainly more well exercised than his—she spent a good deal of time pretending that she was living one of her mother's bard's tales. It was far easier to think of Rhys as an unrequited suitor who worshipped her from afar. Of course that was more difficult than she'd anticipated given that he spent so much time at her side. But he'd been true to his word. He hadn't touched her. He hadn't spoken to her of love. He'd treated her with the same comradely affection that he used with John, Montgomery, and the Fitzgeralds.

Damn him anyway.

Only once had she suggested that perhaps even if he didn't commit the acts in truth, giving her an indication that he might have wished deep inside himself to touch her hand or perhaps kiss her fingers wouldn't be such a poor thing.

The look he'd given her had been enough to make her regret her suggestion most sincerely.

And so she had distracted herself with other things.

She'd practiced swordplay. Rhys had had a sword fashioned for her and somewhere procured a jewel for the hilt which perfectly matched her eyes. The edges of the blade, however, were most distressingly blunted. And damn the man if he hadn't threatened every blacksmith within a ten-mile radius with death if the blade had any killing powers placed upon it. Gwen might have tried to sharpen it herself but the steel was beautiful as it was, and she feared to mar it with her clumsy attempts. Besides that, it was something Rhys had given her, and she treasured it for that reason alone, despite its lack of ability to do damage to any foe.

And she had doted on her son. Alain had never mentioned again his intent to carry the boy off to some other keep and she had eventually given up sleeping with a blade in her hand and her other arm wrapped around Robin. She had no doubts Robin would be sent away the very hour he reached seven years, but until that time she had the full keeping of him. Alain rarely found himself at home, and even when he did, he never troubled her at night. Even Rollan spent little time at Ayre stirring up mischief. Gwen raised her son in peace, practiced her swordplay, and spent the rest of her time at her tapestry frame.

And she told herself she was content with her life, for she knew no other choice was left to her.

Which made her wonder what she was doing standing pressed against Alain's door like a lover, straining to hear the faintest sound of speech inside. More disturbing was what she hoped to hear. That Rhys had indeed obtained his land as Alain had promised?

Which meant he would be leaving Ayre no doubt as quickly as he could.

The door opened with such suddenness that she almost fell face-first into Alain's solar. She jerked herself back upright, hoping no one had noticed her. Rhys came out of the solar so quickly, she liked to believe no one had.

He slammed the door shut behind him. He glared down at her. "We spoke of Wyckham."

"Of course," she said. It wasn't something she was overly glad to hear about, for it spelled the end of his time there. She had the feeling, however, that things had not gone as well as he might have liked. The fact that he looked fair murderous was a good indication.

"He told me, and I'll repeat exactly what I heard, 'Take it from under my troops if you want it.' "

Gwen blinked. "He said *what?*"

"You heard me," Rhys snarled. "He's bloody encamped his men on it! If I want it, I'll have to take it by force!"

"How many men?"

"Too bloody many to do in myself!" he roared. "Damn the man to hell!"

She sensed a logical conversation about Rhys's options would not be appreciated. She also suspected that bidding him to stop shouting lest her husband hear his words would also not be received well. So she folded her hands sedately in front of her and tried to look soothing.

"Well?" Rhys demanded.

"Well what?" she asked, lifting one eyebrow. "I daresay you don't want any of my suggestions."

He pursed his lips. "I might."

She shrugged. "You could turn your back on the land."

"Turn my back on the land?" he mouthed, but no sound came out. His face turned a rather bright shade of red, and he began to make inarticulate sounds of fury.

"Not an option," Gwen noted. "Then you could perhaps make a visit to court and petition the king."

"Petition the king, my arse!" he exclaimed. He shook his head sharply. "I like neither of those."

"You could stay with me," she said.

His lips tightened. "As what? Captain of your guard?"

"You needn't make it sound as if it has been that great a burden."

"It has," he said shortly.

Gwen felt as if he'd slapped her. "I see."

"Do you?" he demanded. "Do you indeed?"

"I see that it has been a place you would have rather not taken," she said stiffly. "I regret the trouble it has caused you."

"Merde," he snarled under his breath.

Gwen found her hand captured in a grip that obviously wasn't going to be broken any time soon.

"Rhys, nay," she attempted.

He ignored her and pulled her along behind him down the passageway, leaving her no choice but to run to keep up with him.

She thought to wonder why no one seemed to glance at them more than once, then she caught sight of the expression on his face and the mystery was solved. Never before had she seen him so angry.

"This isn't my fault," she said.

He ignored her. He strode down the passageway to her solar. He threw open the door and swept her ladies with a look Gwen surmised by their expressions she had been glad not to be the recipient of.

"Out."

One word sent every woman there scurrying for the door. Gwen would have scurried right along with them, but her wrist was still prisoner in his hand. The women rushed past her, then Gwen found herself propelled into the chamber. The door slammed with a resounding bang.

"Do not begin patting yourself for potential weapons," he growled at her.

Gwen realized she had been doing just that, so she clasped her hands behind her back.

"As you wish," she said.

"As I wish," he repeated. "Do you have any idea what it is I wish?"

"To throttle me?" She tried a teasing smile.

"Nay." He did not smile in return.

"Then I vow I have little idea, for one would think by the expression on your face that a throttling appealed to you most."

He gritted his teeth and resorted to merely glaring at her.

Gwen searched frantically for something to say that would cajole him from his foul mood. But what could she say? *Enjoy your land, you've certainly earned it? Find yourself an army and take the soil by force? Leave me behind and never give me another thought?*

It was the last she found that troubled her the most.

She took a deep breath.

"You *could* stay," she said. She'd said it before, but it was a sentiment that bore repeating.

He lifted one eyebrow, but said nothing.

"You make a fine champion," she pressed on. "It has been tolerable, has it not? Reading together, walking in the garden together, having speech together. Could we not go on as before?"

"Nay, we cannot," he bit out.

"But why—"

"Why?" he interrupted. *"Why?"*

He looked as if throttling her had suddenly become a very appealing idea, so she took a pace backward.

He advanced, his expression thunderous.

Gwen found, to her dismay, that she had no more room for retreat. Her back was against the cold stone of the wall, and Rhys was standing toe-to-toe with her. He put his hands against the wall on either side of her head and glared down at her.

"Let me tell you why we cannot," he said in a low growl. "We cannot because I have spent every day of the past two years on fire for you. I have clasped my hands hard enough behind my back to draw blood and leave scars, all in an effort not to touch you. I have worn Connor and Jared down to the bone in the lists in an effort to tire myself so that when I was with you, I would have energy to speak of nothing more interesting than the condition of your damned herbs or the bloody weather."

"Then I wasn't boring you—" She shut her mouth at the look on his face and thought it a very wise move indeed.

"I cannot remain here one more hour when all I am allowed is to look at you."

She could only look up at him, mute.

"I cannot remain another hour near you and have nothing but speech with you."

He was leaving. She should have been prepared for it, but she found she wasn't.

"And above all else, I will not listen to one more bloody word about me being a noble, chivalrous, and unrequited champion!" he exclaimed.

"You made a good one," she offered.

"At the cost of two years of no bloody sleep at night!" he shouted.

She blinked. "You couldn't sleep?"

"I could not."

"But I slept very well."

"Did you?" he demanded.

"Aye," she said hesitantly, "I did indeed. Well, mostly. Surely your bed—"

"It wasn't the bed."

"Then your chamber—"

"It wasn't the chamber."

Gwen frowned. Perhaps lack of sleep had addled his wits. "I do not see—"

Without warning, she found herself enveloped in his embrace. Had there been any space between them before, it was there no longer. He could not have molded her to him any more successfully had she been nothing but the cook's finest pastry dough. Not that Alain's cook made a fine pastry dough, for it was always full of lumps and sand.

"Gwen," Rhys growled.

She blinked up at him. "Aye?"

She wondered what he had meant to say to her, then she realized he had merely been seeking her full attention. As if he didn't have it already. She was all too aware of his unyielding frame and the strength of the arms that held her captive against it . . .

And then he kissed her.

And she thought she just might faint.

Indeed she would have, if he hadn't had such a grip upon her. And it was surely no chaste kiss a champion might give his unattainable lady.

It was a kiss of raw possession.

All she could do was clutch his shoulders and cling to

him. It was devastating enough to have his mouth on hers once again after two long years of wondering if she'd imagined how sweet his lips were. Even more unfortunate, however, were the memories his present kiss brought to mind. He had kissed her thusly before, kissed her long and hard and so thoroughly she wondered if there possibly remained a part of her mouth he hadn't investigated. But that had come as a prelude to his claiming the rest of her body.

And her soul.

She felt tears begin to leak from her eyes, but she didn't bother to brush them away. Oh, how much they had missed! How many hours of loving, how many days of simple touches and soul-stirring kisses.

It would have brought her to her knees if she'd been able to get there.

He started to pull away, but she stopped him.

"Nay," she said against his mouth. "Not yet."

"Now do you see?" he rasped.

"Aye," she managed.

"I never forgot," he whispered, pressing gentle kisses against the corners of her eyes, tasting her tears. "Never once. Never for a moment. I don't know how you could have."

"Perhaps my imagination is my downfall."

"You should use it less."

"How else was I to survive?"

His only answer was another kiss, and then another, and then she began to lose track of where his kisses began and ended.

And when she thought she could truly bear no more, he merely rested his forehead against hers and drew in great, ragged breaths.

"I'll leave you Montgomery and the twins," he said quietly.

She pulled back quickly. "You'll *what?*"

"I'm taking John and leaving today."

Her mouth fell open. She was certain it was passing

unattractive to gape at him thusly, but the saints preserve her, it was all she could do.

"Think you I can remain?" he asked with a dry smile. "After that?"

"You're *leaving* me?" she demanded.

"Of course—"

"You unfeeling oaf!" she said, shoving him smartly. "You do that"—she gestured helplessly at the space now between them—"then merely walk away?"

He put his hands on her shoulders, ignoring her attempts to shrug them off.

"How else am I to raise an army?" he asked gently.

She frowned. "An army?"

"To take possession of Wyckham."

"Ah," she said, "then it comes down to this again."

"Saints, woman, how am I to care for you properly without soil to build a home on? Without soil to grow crops in? Without soil for our children to roam over?"

She closed her eyes briefly and prayed for strength. "It cannot be, Rhys—"

"You have no faith," he said. "Either in me or in love."

"I have a great deal of faith in both."

"Then you're failing to use your imagination. If you can imagine me content to live as your comrade-in-arms for two years, can you not imagine me capable of taking you for my own?"

She looked up at him. "And Robin?"

He took a deep breath. "Robin as well."

"Impossible."

"Difficult," he conceded. "But not impossible."

She shook her head. "I don't see how."

"Then stop trying to see. Trust me."

"But there are no grounds for consanguinity."

"As if that has ever stopped anyone before," Rhys said with a snort. "Eleanor divorced Phillip of France on those grounds, and she surely had no relation to him."

"But the sanctity of marriage vows . . ." She didn't bother to finish her thought.

She had kept her vows. Alain had not. Indeed, she wondered when he had first returned to his whores—the day after their wedding? A se'nnight later?

"You were mine first," Rhys said quietly. "Does that mean nothing to you?"

She bowed her head.

"A true vow is more than words spoken, Gwen. It must also be made with the heart."

She looked up at him, feeling her heart begin to break. "He'll never let Robin go."

"He might."

"He never will," she repeated, "and you know it well. And I cannot leave my son behind."

He was silent for several moments. "I would not ask you to choose between us, Gwen. I will find a way to free him as well." He cupped her face in his hands. "Will you trust me?"

She sighed. "Aye."

"I can ask no more of you than that."

"You'll leave today?"

"Within the hour. I've no doubts Alain expects it."

"And return when?"

"Within a year—"

"A *year?*" she demanded.

He lifted his shoulders helplessly. "Raising an army takes time, Gwen. I'll have to hire mercenaries, see to their expenses and training, retain men to see to their gear . . ."

"A year," she said in astonishment. "That is such a long time."

" 'Tis a far sight shorter than the rest of our lives," he pointed out. "You'll find something to keep yourself amused, I am certain of it. Perhaps you should take up minstrelsy."

She blinked, then smiled suddenly. "I could train with the twins."

"Absolutely not!"

"Then I can help you fight your war!"

She would have elaborated on her scheme, but he seemed determined not to hear any of it. And the longer he kissed her, the less appealing truly becoming a mercenary seemed.

At least for the moment.

"Lose sleep over me," he said, when he lifted his head. "Think pleasant thoughts of me. Trust me."

And before she could clutch him to her, he had crossed the chamber to the door.

"Rhys," she said, realizing just exactly what she stood to lose.

He turned and looked at her a last time.

"Wait for me," he said.

And then he was gone.

An hour later Gwen stood near the barbican and didn't bother to pretend to have business there. She was flanked by the twins, who stood in their usual poses with arms folded over their chests. Montgomery stood nearby, his shoulders having been pressed into service as a place for Robin to perch.

Rhys and John stood speaking together not far away. Gwen watched as Rhys and his squire mounted their horses and turned them out of the gates.

Gwen fully expected Rhys not even to mark her. He hadn't before in the two times she'd stood at gates and watched him go out to see to his business.

This time, though, he turned his head and looked at her.

No words were necessary.

Wait for me.

And so she would.

She had no other choice.

23

Rhys walked through the abbey's small outer garden, following a plump, slow-moving novice. He did not attempt to invite her to hasten. He had learned, over the course of his long life, that annoying the Lord's brides while at their duties would only earn him a thorough tongue-lashing. At least he only had his own tongue to guard. The saints preserve him had he been forced to guard John's as well. Unfortunately for them both, John seemed determined to prove to himself things that he could have more easily learned had he merely used his ears to their best advantage.

At present, however, the lad was safely ensconced with Rhys's grandfather in a nearby inn with their horses and all their gear. It had left Rhys free to proceed to the abbey unhindered and in disguise. Rhys could only hope his grandsire would be able to keep John free from trouble for as long as was required. He would have been unsurprised by any of either Sir Jean or John's antics. Perhaps it had been less than wise to leave the pair of them together.

Well, there was little he could do about it now. He adjusted his very fragrant cloak as his guide neared their journey's end. Rhys was ushered into a comfortable chamber where three chairs were occupied by three imposing women. There was the abbess, of course, with her assessing gaze fixed upon him. Rhys stared at her, amazed that such a beautiful woman should find herself in such a place. He shook his head. How strange were the twists of fate that drove women to such seclusion.

The abbess was flanked by women who Rhys knew were her second and third in command. They were no less unswerving in their appraisal of his person. He went down on one knee, as it seemed the prudent thing to do.

"My lady," Rhys said, inclining his head to the abbess. "God be with you."

"And with you, my son."

Rhys looked up in time to see the abbess dismiss her companions with a small wave of her hand.

"This one looks none-too-dangerous," she said placidly. "I think I am able to ascertain his business without your aid. There are other things more pressing than speech with a passing traveler."

Obviously the other women were accustomed to not arguing. They departed without sparing Rhys another glance and closed the door behind them. They wouldn't have recognized him anyway. He never came to this abbey twice wearing the same disguise.

"Rhys," the abbess said with a long-suffering sigh, "could you not have chosen a less fragrant pretense?"

"Swine herding is a very reputable calling, Mother."

The abbess rose and beckoned to him with a sigh. "Come give your mother a kiss, my love. But no hug, if you please."

Rhys laughed as he rose and bent to kiss his mother heartily on the cheek. "Surely you are happy enough to see me not to mind my smell."

She wrinkled her nose. "Could you not have chosen a friar as your disguise? Or a minstrel? They at least smell of smoke and ale, not pigs—"

"Mother!" Rhys laughed. "By the saints, your novices would be appalled could they hear you."

She only smiled as she drew him over to sit down next to her. "They fear me too greatly to trouble themselves over paying me any heed. They scuttle by and pray they don't attract my notice. Especially when it has been months since I've had word from my son, for that puts me in an especially foul humor.''

Rhys rolled his eyes. "I would have written—"

"But you feared to reveal my whereabouts. Aye, I've heard that excuse before."

He started to protest, but she waved away his words.

"You protect me well, and I am grateful for it. Now, tell me of your news and why you find yourself in France."

"Well—"

"Your grandsire says you have fallen in love with a girl you cannot have." She leveled him a very piercing look. "I wonder why it is you have not shared this with me."

"I wasn't sure you would approve."

"Is she so shrewish then?"

He shook his head, smiling. "Nay, she is passing sweet."

"Hard to look upon, then? Knock-kneed, cross-eyed, palsied—"

"Nay, nay," he said, staving off any more descriptions, "she is well formed and quite pleasing to the eye. I only feared you would disapprove of my looking above my station."

"Why?" she asked dryly. "Because you are but a knight?"

"Others would find that enough to deny her to me."

"You bear an honorable name, love. There is no shame in your heritage."

"Knight, healer, heretic." He smiled. "My father had an illustrious career, did he not?"

"Your father is a prince among men and braver than most. You have no reason to be ashamed of him. And if you doubt his courage, look to your grandsire. They are very much alike."

Rhys looked at his mother and wondered if she realized her mistake. "*Was*, Mother. My father was a prince among men."

"Hmmm," his mother agreed. "Very true."

It wasn't the first time she had made such a slip when speaking about her late husband. Rhys wondered if the solitude of the convent had begun to prey upon her mind. Did she believe Etienne was still alive?

There was reason, he supposed. His father had never received a proper Christian burial. That would be enough to cause some to wonder if he'd truly been laid to rest. Rhys had always assumed that he had no grave marker because of the slanderous label of heretic which had been placed upon him. It was enough to deny him entrance into any church's graveyard.

From time to time, however, Rhys wondered if it was because his father wasn't buried at all.

"Unfortunately, neither your father nor your grandsire bore any noble titles," his mother continued absently.

"Aye," Rhys agreed, pushing aside his foolish thoughts. His sire was dead. He'd been dead for almost twenty years. "A title would have aided me greatly."

"Ah, Rhys," his mother said, fixing her gaze upon him and smiling, "I daresay there is enough nobility in you for any woman. Now, tell me more about this girl. She is beautiful and her eyes are straight. What is the difficulty?"

"She's a baron's daughter."

His mother waited.

"And she's wed."

"Ah," his mother said. "I see."

"Hence my arrival in France."

His mother blinked. "Of course."

"I need gold. For bribes."

"What else?" she said. "You don't intend to steal her away?"

"'Tis a tradition, is it not? Grandfather stole Grandmother."

"And your father stole me."

"I, on the other hand, have been a dismal failure when it comes to this snatching of women."

"All the more reason to remedy it, my love."

Rhys sighed and leaned back against the chair. "I fear my only choice is to pay for what I wish to have." He looked at her and smiled grimly. "I've never succeeded at bribery before."

"Sword strokes are a much more direct way of solving problems," she agreed. "But the slaying of nobles is still frowned upon in England, is it not?"

"It was the last time I asked."

"She has a son, true?"

Obviously his mother was more versed in the events of his life than she admitted to being. He wasn't surprised. How she came by her knowledge of events outside her walls was a mystery, but her spies were thorough.

"Aye," Rhys said, "one she will not leave without."

His mother reached for his hand. "I cannot blame her. It fair broke my heart to let your grandsire take you away when he did, even though I knew I had no other choice."

"What else were you to do? My sire was dead."

His mother didn't argue that. "And it wasn't as if I could have traveled about with your grandsire. I do not regret my choice. It is a peaceful enough existence."

"Is it?" he mused. "Has Grandfather given up his spying for Phillip?"

"How would I know, love?"

"You would know, Mother, for he sends all his information through you. Peaceful existence, my arse," he said with a snort.

She only smiled. "I do what I can to uphold the family tradition."

"One I haven't carried on. Am I such a disappointment to Grandpère, then?"

"I daresay the king is more disappointed than your grandsire, but he will not press you. He knows you intend to make your home in England."

"A pity he cannot help me obtain the bride I want."

"I suppose he might, if you were to make it worth his time. Your father spent his share of time ferreting out details on the isle. Phillip wouldn't hesitate to use you if you were willing."

He shook his head. "I haven't the temperament for deception."

"So one sees by the lack of glee you take in disguising yourself when you come to visit me," his mother said dryly.

"Spying for the French king is something I cannot do, Mother," Rhys said with a sigh. "My lady has her feet firmly planted on English soil. Her land is there. Her mother is there."

"Her son is there," his mother murmured. "I envy her."

Rhys took his mother's hand and raised it to his lips. "At least I am free to see you when I will it, Mother. And I am still alive to do so. I cannot say what would happen should I follow in Father's footsteps."

She squeezed his hand. "True enough, my love. Very well, continue in your quest and may your efforts bear much fruit. I will keep your winnings safe, as always."

"The saints be praised for the crypt beneath your altar," he said with a smile. "I will appreciate it greatly."

"I am always happy to do what I can for the cause of love." She rose gracefully. "I will call for a bit of refreshment, then you will tell me of your journey here. I suppose the crossing was perilous, as always."

Rhys smiled to himself. If there was one thing his mother did not care for, it was setting foot on any kind of seagoing vessel. He half suspected that was why she found herself still in France after all these years.

Or perhaps it was because her vocation suited her. She had ample time to pray, to contemplate life's mysteries in her garden, and to offer succor to passing travelers. Phillip had seen to it all after Rhys's father's death, and Mary had accepted it willingly.

Who would have thought she would have become just as fine a spy as her husband?

Or was it that her husband was still spying and Mary only provided a convenient shield for his activities?

"Oh, by the saints," Rhys muttered in disgust. His

lady's overly active imagination had had a ruinous effect on his common sense. His father was dead. His mother was devious, but not so devious as all that.

Rhys watched his mother as she ordered her novices about and wondered, not for the first time, just where it was his mother had been born. She had told him "England, and leave it there, my love" more times than he could begin to count. His father had divulged no more, and his grandsire had been even more tight-lipped than either of them. Had her life been so terrible, then, that the mere mention of it was enough to grieve her so?

Or did she have kin who would likely want her back should they know where to find her?

"Sweet wine from the south," his mother announced, handing him a silver goblet. "Chilled, just as you like it, son."

Rhys almost asked for the entire bottle to silence his questions. His mother had her reasons for secrecy, and they were likely none of his business. That was enough for him. Besides, it wasn't as if he didn't have enough to occupy his mind at present. There was much to be done in preparation for the frequenting of tourneys. He would need to keep his eyes open for possible additions to his as-yet non-existent army. If that hadn't been enough to keep him occupied, seeing that John remained unscathed would be. Rhys drank deeply of his wine. The saints preserve him from a squire's arrogance.

"Mother, I need to have a message sent," he said. It was past time he wrote Gwen to assure her he'd reached France safely. "You have someone trustworthy?"

"Of course."

"Then might we retire to your chambers? They are, as I remember, much more comfortable than this."

His mother wrinkled her nose. "I believe first of all, my son, that you'll have a bath. While you're about that, I'll fetch the sister's habit you're accustomed to wearing."

Rhys scowled. "I have the feeling you only do this to see me in skirts."

She patted his cheek. "You would have made such a lovely girl."

"But such a tall one," he said.

"The sisters are more likely to look at the length of your feet than your height."

Rhys sighed. The indignities he suffered for a soft bed. But he would suffer them willingly, for he suspected it would be the last time he would feel goosefeathers beneath his back for some time to come. His mother, at least in her private chambers, was not one given to deprivation. The king had been most generous in his gratitude for Mary's continued service to his cause. Rhys had no qualms about enjoying the luxuries himself while he could.

It was several hours later that he sat at his mother's writing table, begarbed in a sister's habit, working industriously on the first of what he hoped were very few letters to his love. With any luck at all, it would take him half a year to earn the gold he needed and only a few weeks to acquire his army. He was counting on his reputation serving him well.

My love, he began, then shook his head and scratched it out. It wouldn't do to reveal too much of his heart. His mother's messengers were trustworthy, true, but one could not always count on a safe journey for any messenger. Better that he confine himself to less emotional matters.

My lady Gwennelyn, he began, *I am safely arrived here in France to find that the skies are passing gray and a continual drizzle falls wherever I go.* Rhys looked at his words with satisfaction. Should his missive be intercepted, no one would be the wiser as to where he currently loitered. There was drizzle aplenty this time of year. *My accoutrements, including my squire, seem to have survived the journey thus far fairly well. My horse only threw one shoe, which caused me grief, but that was remedied soon enough.*

Rhys paused, then sniffed. His mother's cook had obviously been at her work again. After the slop he'd eaten at Ayre for the past two years, almost anything would be an improvement.

He looked down at his letter and considered, then rose abruptly. He would eat first. It would give him something else safe to relate to his lady.

He left his mother's chamber, his mouth watering already. He walked down the passageway, ducking his head to appear less tall, and praying his mother's women wouldn't notice him. He would have to moderate his eating habits as well. It wasn't as if a traveling sister would devour her meal with the gusto of a starving mercenary.

One of his mother's more substantial sisters stood guard near the entrance to the dining hall. Rhys had seen the woman before and marveled not only at her stature, but her height. The woman looked at him, then quickly looked away.

Rhys sighed as he entered the dining hall. Regardless of what his mother said, he knew he did not make an attractive sister of the cloth. He couldn't blame the woman for not having wanted to look at him. Hopefully the rest of his mother's followers would feel the same way and he would pass his visit peacefully.

It would likely be the last time he had such luxury for some time to come.

24

"Damnation, not another child! How could I have let this happen?"

Gwen listened to the words in astonishment, as they were ones she had been thinking not a handful of moments before. These words, however, were coming out of a mouth she wouldn't have suspected. She pressed herself back into the shadows and looked at the man leaning down to suck a great mouthful of ale straight from the spigot.

"Bloody babe," Rollan snarled, spitting out the ale. "Bloody ale! Will nothing go aright for me this year? One heir was one thing." He took another large slurp of ale, swished it around in his mouth, and spat it out with a passion. "Now *another* one? I had planned that he should leave her be!"

So, Gwen thought to herself with a silent snort, had she. She'd managed to avoid encountering Alain and his bed at the same time for several months at a stretch, but unfortunately she hadn't been completely successful at it.

Now she had at least another four months of puking to

look forward to, which was why she found herself currently loitering near Master Socrates's cell, seeking something without specks to ingest. Perhaps this was a happy
chance, for how else would she have been nearby to eavesdrop on Rollan's private conversations with himself?

Rollan seemed to be finding the ale more palatable all
the time. In between great gulps he spewed forth more of
his innermost thoughts.

"Now there's another one who stands in the way of my
prize."

Gwen raised one eyebrow.

"I'll rid myself of the both of them. Nay, the three of
them. Alain and both his babes. I could push Gwen down
the stairs—nay, then I lose her as well, and that is not in
my plans."

The saints be praised for that, Gwen thought, with a fair
bit of alarm.

"I'll wait until she's birthed the babe, then I'll deal with
the three of them. And then *I'll* be known as lord of
Ayre," Rollan said, bending for another drink. He straightened, dragged his sleeve across his mouth, and turned himself toward the stairs. "I'll see Alain sent to Canfield this
afternoon, then be about my plans. Perhaps that little brat
Robin can take a tumble down the stairs. That would see
to one of them. . . ."

Gwen felt a cold chill go down her spine. Never mind
that her fondest wish was to go back to bed and remain
there for several more days. She would have to leave the
keep. Perhaps Alain could be persuaded to escort her to
Segrave on his way to Canfield. If he thought she would
be conveniently tucked away with her mother where she
could not trouble him, he might think more kindly about
it.

Gwen waited until she was certain Rollan had made his
way up the stairs before she followed. Her first task would
be to seek out Sir Montgomery and tell him of what she'd
overheard. Then she would brave Ayre's kitchens to prepare her husband something to sweeten his humor. Though
his palate was not overly discriminating—he never seemed

certain when something was tastier than something else except to remark that there was something odd about the fare—food was food when such a man's gullet was to be considered.

And then she would soon find herself ensconced in her mother's solar before Rollan could wreak any havoc.

Or so she hoped.

A fortnight later she found herself safely installed in her mother's solar at Segrave with a missive in her hands. It was a missive she had been waiting for nigh on to two months. She'd counted the days since Rhys had departed, allowing amply for the difficulties a messenger might encounter. She had received the anticipated epistle with joy and great relief.

And then she had begun to read it.

She currently reread the blighted scrap of parchment by light of her mother's finest tallow candles, and wished Robin were more deeply asleep that she might vent her frustration with a few words she had learned by frequenting the lists in her youth.

" 'A roasted goose with a savoury sauce of quince and onions'?" she quoted with disgust. "*This* is the drivel he chooses to write to me!"

Her mother only continued to stitch placidly. "What else is Rhys to say, my sweet?"

"He could say that he loves me! Or that he thinks of me morn and eve."

"Which he likely does—"

"Instead, I am forced to read in great detail about the mishaps which have befallen his gear, the dishes presented at his mother's supper table, and exactly what the elements are producing this time of year in France."

"Well—"

"These are things I do not care about!"

Joanna smiled. "Gwen, these are perilous times we live in. Messengers are untrustworthy. He has no way of telling who might read his words."

Gwen cursed under her breath. What she had wanted was a letter full of love. What she had received was a letter full of unimportant details. If she hadn't known better, she might have suspected Rhys's feelings had changed.

"He isn't exactly wooing me with his words," Gwen grumbled. "Perhaps he thinks I am already won."

"Perhaps he is trying to save your reputation, Gwen."

"And a simple word or two of love would ruin me?"

"He only thinks on your future, Gwen—"

"Nay, Mother, he's only thinking on his stomach! 'A sweet pudding accompanied by a delicate wine from the south.' " Gwen snorted in disgust. "Would that he were drinking the swill Alain's alemaster produces. I might have a decent bit of sentiment if that were the case."

Joanna shook her head with a smile. "Gwen, love, it would not serve you if the king thought you had committed adultery with Sir Rhys."

"I have been true to Alain, pox rot the man. Not that he has accorded me the same courtesy. And what do I care what the king hears? He doesn't think past the gold in his coffers."

Joanna set aside her stitchery with a heavy sigh. "Gwen, you accomplish nothing by pacing in my solar and complaining."

"I am not—"

"Aye, you are, and if I must listen to you go on thusly for another ten months, you will drive me mad." Her mother, however, smiled as she said as much. "And for all you know, it may take Rhys longer than that to complete his business, and then where will you be?"

"Hoarse," Gwen said shortly. She sat down across from her mother and tried to compose herself. "I am but restless."

"Then find something to do."

"What am I to do, Mother? Scurry off to the king and tell him my tale? Ask him to grant me an annulment?"

" 'Tis a bit late for that," Joanna said, looking fondly at Robin, who lay sprawled on the bed, sound asleep.

"I cannot choose divorce, either. I would lose Robin in

the bargain. And all my lands.'' She looked at her mother. ''You would lose your home.''

Joanna shrugged. '' 'Tis only by the good grace of Alain that I live here as it is. I can easily take my cook and go elsewhere.'' She seemed to brush aside any more thought about it. ''Just how is it your young Rhys intends to see you become his?''

''The saints only know. I believe he looks toward bribery.''

''Bribery for what?''

An annulment, Gwen started to say, then she stopped herself. Could an annulment be granted? Gwen supposed it could, though it would certainly turn Robin and her coming babe into bastards. Not a fate she would wish on them if she had any other choice. But to her, bastardy was far more tolerable than being at Alain's mercy. She shuddered to think the things Robin would learn at his father's hands.

Gwen glanced at her mother to find her regarding her with a searching look. And not for the first time, Gwen wondered how her mother viewed the situation. She hadn't had the courage before to even ask her, fearing what she would hear.

''Does it bother you, then?'' Gwen asked. No sense in not having the truth.

Joanna returned her look gravely. ''Though I cannot agree with divorce, given the Church's view upon the matter, I cannot deny that Alain was never the choice either your father or I would have made had it not been for his station.''

''And what of turning Robin into a bastard?''

''By an annulment?'' Joanna shrugged. '' 'Tis something that would haunt him, Gwen.''

''Would it be more grievous than what he would suffer being Alain's son?''

''And in return losing Ayre, Segrave, and everything else he would otherwise inherit? Only he could answer that, and 'tis a question he will not even understand for several years yet.''

''Rhys has Wyckham. He could give that to Robin.''

"If Rhys can liberate it from Alain's troops, and even then he will still be Alain's vassal."

Gwen sighed and buried her face in her hands. "Wyckham is his and the king holds the deed for him. But when you remind me of who his overlord would be, it sounds passing intolerable."

" 'Tis but the truth of the matter, Gwen."

"Would that I had wed with Rhys from the start."

"Aye. Both your sire and I wished it as well. But Rhys had no title and no lands."

Gwen looked at her mother. "There is more to life than land, Mother."

Joanna smiled. "Aye, I have always thought so, my love."

"Rhys has survived well enough without any."

"It does leave a man free to go where he wills," Joanna conceded.

Gwen rose and moved to kneel at her mother's feet. She took her hands. "Better that my children live with a man who loves them than a man who cares nothing for them, Mother."

"Or for you," Joanna agreed.

"Rhys could perhaps claim them as his own."

"Aye, he could," Joanna said carefully. "Though who will recognize that I cannot say. The king might choose not to."

"Then we'll go to France," Gwen said grimly. "If King Phillip knighted Rhys, then he must have a use for him somehow. Life might be kinder to us there."

Gwen's mother squeezed her hands. "Give your Rhys his year, Gwen, and see how events come to pass. You never know what the future will bring."

"Aye," Gwen said, rising, "there is truth in that." She paced to the window. "But I must do something. I cannot remain here for a year merely waiting."

"You could improve your stitchery."

"I could improve my swordplay," Gwen said, feeling the faintest twinge of excitement.

"Not in your current condition. Stitchery is safer. Or

perhaps a few new ballads learned on the lute.''

"The bow would not be too taxing. . . .''

"Gwen,'' her mother warned. "You carry a babe.''

Gwen sighed and resumed her seat. "My belly reminds me of that more often than I care to think about.''

If not swordplay, then perhaps preparation for the establishment of Rhys's household at Wyckham. Assuming there would be such a thing.

Nay, she would not doubt. Rhys would manage what her father had not been able to. She and Robin would find safety behind Rhys's strong arm.

As would the new babe. Gwen put her hand over her belly protectively. Oh, how she wished Rollan had never found her puking into her rosebushes. She likely could have escaped to Segrave and not have had Alain been the wiser about his future second child. She had little doubts Rollan would go to his brother with the tale, if only to lure Alain back to Ayre so he could be pushed down the stairs. Gwen was tempted to entertain that thought a bit longer. If Rollan were left to himself long enough, he just might solve all her problems for her.

But, for all she knew, if Alain met with a mishap, the king would wed her to Rollan before she could get word to Rhys, and then she would find herself in an even more intolerable situation. At least Alain spent most of his time at Canfield, engaging in the saints only knew what kinds of activities with the lady Rachel. For all the time she had passed with him, her husband might have been such in name only. It suited her well enough—and much more satisfactorily than if she'd found herself facing Rollan of Ayre in front of a priest.

Perhaps she would send the Fitzgeralds back to Ayre just to protect Alain. They were to have come with her to Segrave in her own train, but they begged leave to come more slowly that they might scout the surroundings for enemies. One did not argue with such intimidating men, so she had left them to their own stratagem. They should have arrived several days before, but she hadn't caught even a whiff of them as of yet. They could have walked from Ayre more swiftly than the pace they seemed to be traveling. Perhaps scouting was a more involved activity than she'd supposed.

"Gwen," Joanna said, interrupting Gwen's musings, "why do you not work some heroic design on a surcoat?"

Gwen shook her head. "He would not wear it, Mama." She sighed and put aside her worries. It did her no good to try to divine what Rhys's intentions were, for 'twas a certainty that he would do things in a way she wouldn't have chosen. That much she had learned about men in her short lifetime.

"I think," she said, looking about her for an appropriate amount of cloth, "that I will hem sheets."

"Sheets?" Her mother sounded surprised, and rightly so. It had been the last thing Gwen had ever cared to do.

"Sheets," Gwen said with a nod. "For a wedding bed."

And she prayed she would find the desired man in it. Rhys had said a year, and she prayed she would pass that time without incident. She hoped the time would go quickly. There would be the babe to see to, and Robin to tend as well.

Aye, she could pass a year and not mind it. There would be missives exchanged. Perhaps in time she might even convince Rhys that he could express a sentiment or two and not suffer from it.

It was certainly preferable to reading about what he had been eating.

Winter

THE YEAR OF OUR LORD 1206

25

January 1206

Letters, letters, ah, the joy of a well-received letter! A veritable hill of them lay on the rough wooden table. They had been read and reread scores of times, just for the sheer pleasure of seeing such words of love be put to paper. Indeed, what finer way could there be to pass an afternoon than perusing such correspondence with a flagon of ale at one's elbow?

Said peruser put a finger to his lips, as if he contemplated which pile of missives to attend to first. The decision wasn't truly a difficult one, as he had two new epistles to digest. It hardly mattered which he chose; each would be delicious in its own way. With a shrug, he reached for the missive nearest his cup of ale.

He read and smiled. It was truly astonishing how the passage of time had broken down the formality shown in the earlier letters.

Epiphany, 1206

Beloved Gwen,

*The siege is at long last ended, and I have managed to
frighten out of the count d'Auber more gold than he intended to spend, but he cost me six more months of my
life than I'd intended he should. With it I daresay I have
enough to satisfy even John's greedy hands, with ample
left over to send to Rome to sweeten the Pope's humor.
You will have your freedom and Robin as well, I am sure
of it.*

*Look for me in late spring. I'm bringing a handful of
lads home with me to secure Wyckham.*

> *Ever your servant,*
> *Rhys de Piaget*

Sir Rhys's letter was set aside carefully. Another sealed
missive from a different author was placed atop the table.
It bore no stains from hands of anyone but the author and
the one messenger. The wax seal was perfectly intact.

But the seal crumbled under the pressure of opening the
letter, for such opening was done with unseemly haste. But
that was of no import. No one would ever know how care-
lessly it had been loosened, for the missive would travel
no further.

The letter was read.

And the reader began to chuckle. In a few places the
words were actually amusing enough to cause him to
throw back his head and laugh. If nothing else, the author
of this less than pleasant letter had studied her equine anat-
omy and had used such studies to her best advantage. Very
inventive. A pity Sir Rhys would never read the like.

Still smiling, he set aside the letter and reached for a
clean sheet of parchment. He sharpened his quill, dipped
it into the ink, and tapped the feather a time or two against
his forehead to start his thoughts rolling in the appropriate

direction. Inspiration flowed through him and he prepared
to write.

My beloved Rhys,

*How I long for you! How I have lain awake nights
dreaming of you and your strong, manly arms about me!
Hurry, my love, and free me from this prison. I think of
no one but you, I desire no one but you. Bring all your
gold with you that you might bribe everyone in England
to have me. . . .*

Rollan paused, pursed his lips, and realized with a curse
that perhaps that was less subtle than he might have
wished. Gwen wouldn't have spoken of the gold. And he
began to wonder also if she would have used the term
''manly arms.''

Damn. He would have to start this one afresh.

With a sigh, he crumpled up what had been under his
quill and tossed it into the fire. He took another piece of
parchment and began again, doing his damndest to keep
in the forefront of his thoughts just how he'd worded all
the other missives he'd sent in Gwen's name over the past
three years. Imitating her fair hand had taken him a pair
of months to perfect, but it was trying to second-guess how
she would have gushed over the gallant Sir Rhys that had
given him the most trouble.

He did his best, then reread his latest offering. Satisfied
it oozed enough sentiment, he brushed sand over the ink
to hasten the drying. He rolled the parchment, tipped his
candle to drip upon the edges of the letter, and then pressed
a perfect copy of Gwen's seal into the warm wax. He rose
and left the inn's best chamber, found his messenger, and
sent the lad on his way with a small bag of gold. The sum
did not trouble him, as it came directly from Alain's cof-

fers. Rollan smiled pleasantly. His brother was such a trusting soul.

Intercepting the correspondence from both parties had been difficult, what with Gwen having spent so much time with her mother at Segrave, but Rollan had considered that nothing but an added challenge. Where gold hadn't been convincing enough, Rollan had used other means. Every man had his weakness. Susceptibility to bribery, wenches . . . poison. The list, he had discovered, was very long indeed.

He returned to his chamber followed by a serving wench bearing a heaping tray of their best fare. It was, unsurprisingly, better than what he would have found at Ayre. That was Alain's fault. One did not bed the cook's daughter under the cook's nose without finding some sort of retribution in one's bread from that point on. Rollan shook his head as he sat back down at his table. Discretion had never been his brother's strongest characteristic.

Rollan flipped the girl a coin and she scurried from the chamber. He'd been momentarily tempted to have her stay, then discarded the idea. He wanted to savor the final chapter of his finest scheme and such savoring needed to be done alone.

By now surely Gwen's feelings for Rhys had cooled past the point of rekindling. After all, she hadn't heard from the man in almost three years. What would she do when he arrived at the keep with his heart in his hands?

Fell him with an arrow, if Rollan's luck was running true.

He leaned back in his chair and smiled. And there he would be, ready to step in and comfort her.

Ah, but life was indeed very good.

Summer

THE YEAR OF OUR LORD 1206

26

June 1206
Segrave

She needed a change.

Gwen stared at the linen under her needle and cursed as she realized she was going to have to unpick half of what she'd done that morn. The pattern had become fouled hours ago, but she hadn't noticed. It was something for her wedding bed, a casing for a goosefeather pillow worked with all manner of flowers and beautiful stitchery. She did not even feel any guilt over not stitching for Ayre's beds. She suspected that if she ever returned to her husband's keep, linens would be the least of her worries. She shuddered to think on how the filth had multiplied in the three years since she'd set foot inside the gates.

It was hard to believe so much time had passed. Three years of stitching. Three years of waiting for word from a certain man. Three years of going from worried to hurt to angry. Nay, not angry.

Bloody furious.

It wasn't as if she hadn't heard of Rhys's escapades.

She had, in somewhat surprising detail and from the most unlikely of sources. Every time Rollan paused in his mischief-making to visit Segrave, he seemed to have a new adventure of Rhys's to relate to her. Where he came by his stories she didn't know, but she hardly doubted the truth of them. Rhys was certainly capable of holding scores of knights for ransom in tournaments all across the continent. He was certainly skilled enough to be sought after by any number of French lords to fight their battles for them. He was more than clever enough to spend ample time at the French court wooing whatever nobles found themselves there.

Or their ladies, if Rollan's gossip was to be believed.

What Gwen couldn't understand was why, with all his other skills, Rhys couldn't seem to find the ability to put ink on parchment and tell her of his successes himself. Was it because he was too busy on the battlefield? Or was he too busy in the bedchamber?

Or had he thought better of entangling himself further in the hopelessness of her situation?

She threw her stitchery into the basket at her feet and left her mother's solar, abandoning her mother and her ladies. A pity she couldn't have convinced Master Socrates and his granddaughter to come with her to Segrave. Perhaps she could have spent more time at their cooking fire and learned something of healing. Instead, they remained at Ayre and she was loitering at Segrave, wishing for a mighty change.

Not even her children were awake for her to amuse. Robin was asleep on her mother's bed, having exhausted himself thoroughly by a great deal of parrying that morn with Jared and Connor. The twins seemed convinced the lad couldn't help but profit from beginning his training so early. Gwen had been dubious until she had seen the great care the two men took of her son. Perhaps foisting the lad upon them so often while he was a babe so she could eavesdrop on Alain's conversations had been a boon. Surely there weren't two souls in the keep more willing and able to tend the boy than the Fitzgeralds.

She sighed and made her way down to the great hall. It was empty and that was tempting enough to entice her to stay and appreciate the quiet. But it wouldn't be enough. She needed the feeling of fresh air and perhaps a bit of sunshine.

The moment she opened the door, though, she could see something was amiss. Segrave was a calm place usually, filled with loyal knights who went about their business with a confident air. But now the inner bailey looked as if it were filled with an entire coopful of frantic hens.

Gwen ran merely because everyone else was running and she feared she might be trod asunder otherwise. She dodged mailed knights, half-mailed knights, and knights patting themselves frantically as if they wanted to assure themselves they were carrying all the weaponry they possibly could.

By the saints, were they under attack? She had wanted a change; she hadn't wanted a siege.

She wished desperately that she'd thought to dress more sensibly and perhaps belt her sword about her waist. Not even a knife resided up her sleeve. At least she had a pair of sewing needles in the purse at her belt. They would have to do.

She hastened to the barbican and ran up the steps. She burst out onto the small circular roof only to find Sir Montgomery leaning lazily against the parapet wall. He, at least, seemed none too worried about the goings-on.

"Well?" she demanded. "What by all the saints is the commotion about?"

Montgomery pointed off across the fields. Gwen followed his finger and squinted to make out what he evidently saw so clearly.

"Merchants," she guessed. "I can see the gleam of gems from here."

"What you see, my lady, is not the gleam of gems, 'tis the gleam of sunlight on armor."

She pursed her lips. "You imagine that."

"Think you?"

Indeed, she suspected he likely spoke the truth, for

Montgomery had very keen sight. If he said he saw armor, then armor he had seen.

"Friend or foe?" she asked.

"That would be for you to decide."

She frowned at him. "I've no head for riddles today. Is it Alain?"

"He's still in London, or so I've heard."

"Bending the king's ear and bedding the queen's ladies, no doubt," Gwen muttered.

"No doubt."

Gwen shielded her eyes from the sun with her hand and continued to watch the progress of the small group that came over her fields.

"They've a fair amount of haste," she noted.

"Aye, I'd imagine they would."

Gwen wondered where she could stick him to do the most damage. Montgomery only held up his hands in surrender.

"I had nothing to do with this."

"With what?"

"With the arrival of these lads today."

"Which lads?" she demanded.

He blinked. "Why, Rhys's lads, of course."

She wouldn't have been more surprised if he'd announced Saint George had come down to sit at her table and show her his knobby knees himself.

"Impossible," she whispered.

"Nay, 'tis him in truth."

"You can see him?"

"Aye," Montgomery said, backing carefully out of her reach. He smiled cautiously. "I daresay you're pleased by this."

"Pleased?" she gasped. *"Pleased?"* She spun away from him and leaned over to jerk open the door to the stairwell. "Down with the portcullis!" she bellowed. "Raise the drawbridge!"

"My lady!" Montgomery gasped.

She turned and pointed her finger at him threateningly. "You be silent!" she commanded. She turned back to the stairwell. "Well?" she demanded of its interior. "I don't hear any gears grinding!"

All movement in the barbican seemed to have stopped. Slowly a head peeked around the curve of the stairs and wide eyes peered up at her from inside a helm.

"But, my lady," a guardsman ventured, " 'tis Rhys de P—"

"I know bloody well who it is!" she exclaimed. "Now, do as I bid and secure the damned castle!"

The guardsman's mouth began to work silently. Gwen rolled her eyes. Was the man coming toward them going to have this affect on every blessed soul in the keep?

"I'll do it myself," she snapped, taking hold of her skirts and setting her foot to the top stair.

"Don't know that you'll make it in time," Montgomery said from behind her. "They've suddenly picked up their pace."

Gwen ran back to the wall and peered into the distance. Unfortunately, even she could see that the company was indeed coming toward the castle at a gallop.

"Oh, by the saints!" she exclaimed.

Montgomery had resumed his indifferent pose and was regarding her with an amused smile.

"No gate will keep him out," Montgomery said.

"This one will," she said confidently.

"Nor any drawbridge, I should think," Montgomery went on thoughtfully, as if he pondered some great truth. "I've heard tell he can scale an outer wall with his bare hands."

Gwen snorted the most derisive snort she could muster.

"And look how he's gone to the trouble of bringing his army with him." Montgomery smiled at her with wide, innocent eyes. "By the saints, lady, there must be something in this keep he wants very much. It would appear that he's come prepared to battle for it."

"What he wants he cannot have," she snapped, feeling the hideous sting of tears begin behind her eyes. "He's too bloody late. Three years too bloody late."

She slammed the door behind her and thumped down

the stairs as quickly as she dared. She made her orders clear to the gate guards, then hurried across the courtyard to the keep. The bailey was still a veritable hive of frantic knightly activity. Perhaps the men scurried to make themselves presentable.

Or perhaps they were seeking a hiding place so Rhys didn't run them through should they find themselves in his path.

Gwen gained the great hall, then turned and pushed the huge door to. Well, almost to. There were several pairs of hands preventing her from doing so. Gwen looked around the door and glared at half a dozen of Segrave's more sturdy guardsmen.

"Stand aside," she commanded.

They were all squirming. One brave one spoke up.

"No sense in barring his way, my lady."

"You fool, you would leave me at his mercy?" she demanded. "By the saints, I am your lady!"

"And he is Rhys de Piaget," another said in awe, as if he spoke of Saint Michael himself.

"All the more reason to lock him out. Now, stand aside!"

They didn't even blink.

She contemplated snatching one of their knives to aid her cause, but heaven only knew how that act might turn itself upon her. She grasped the keys on her belt and with the most hefty of them poked the nearest man. It made little impression, so she searched in her purse for her finest sewing needle. Armed with a very sharp needle in one hand and a heavy key in the other, she poked and prodded and bullied until she had said handful of knights flinching out of her way and right out the front door. While they were still twitching from various small and irritating injuries, she slammed the door home and struggled to heave the beam into its brackets.

There was no heaving to be accomplished. Gwen surrendered without a fight and put her back against the door. She braced her feet on an unslippery portion of her floor and prepared herself for the worst.

"My lady," a plaintive male voice pleaded from without, "we beg you to cease—"

"Begone, you coward!" Gwen said in her most commanding tone. "I've no fear of that black-garbed demon. I'll hold the hall against him myself!"

There was no formal reply, but Gwen could hear them conferring amongst themselves in frantic whispers. They were no doubt racking their pitiful brains for some other foolish ploy to secure her cooperation.

"My lady," the spokesman began again, "if you would—"

"I will not! Off with you all!"

"But, my lady, de Piaget is the captain of your personal guard—"

"Not anymore!"

They seemed to chew that one over for a few more moments. Gwen adjusted her back more comfortably and gathered her strength for the task of holding the door firmly closed.

"Perhaps he has been detained these many seasons," one of the men offered.

"Aye, by other more important matters!" another put in enthusiastically.

"Shut up, you fool," yet another guardsman said frantically. "Think you that will please her ears?"

"Aye, 'tis not what a lady wishes to hear," another voice said, obviously delivering some sort of cuff with his words. He cleared his throat. "My lady," he said loudly, "I feel certain Sir Rhys was perhaps held captive, or found himself detained unjustly at the French court . . ."

Gwen shut out the rest of his list of excuses. They were just words and she had long ago decided that words held little weight in matters of the heart. She hadn't always believed so. Indeed, hadn't words been what she had clung to for months after he had left?

Wait for me.

Aye, wait a year. Or, knowing Rhys, perhaps a bit longer than a year until he'd plundered every coffer on the continent to his satisfaction. One year. Not three.

There were several very audible gulps on the other side of the wood. Gwen dug her slippered heels more firmly into the floor. A pity 'twas stone and not dirt. She might have had better control that way.

Absolute silence surrounded her. She fancied she might have heard the echo of horses' hooves, but she couldn't be sure. Her heart was hammering too loudly in her ears to know for certain.

The timid knock against the wood almost sent her into a swoon.

"What?" she demanded in her haughtiest tone, praying it sounded less breathless than her own ears attested.

"My lady," a quavering voice said, "would you be so kind as to open up the door?"

"Nay, I will not."

"But my lady, he caught hold of the drawbridge 'afore it came all the way up, and flung himself over it—" a knight began.

"Then rolled himself under the portcullis 'afore it could slam home—" another interrupted.

"And he singlehandedly raised the portcullis and lowered the drawbridge so as his army could bring itself in behind him!" yet another finished breathlessly, as if this final act indicated beyond doubt Rhys's godlike prowess.

"I couldn't care less!" she exclaimed.

"Oh," yet another knight moaned, sounding as if he thought himself already a dead man. "We beg you, my lady. We've families, my lady. Small children still in need of their sires. I myself have a wife with a belly fair stretched to bursting, and if I weren't to be there to see to the feeding of that child, and my ten others—"

"Oh, by the saints," Gwen grumbled. She would just open the door and bid Rhys be on his way. Coldly. As a great lady of the realm would. She would show no emotion, raise not her voice, shed not a tear. She would remain perfectly in control of herself and the encounter.

She turned and calmly opened the door. With a regal wave of her hand she sent her handful of kneeling knights to their feet and on their way down the steps to the courtyard. She lifted her chin and looked down at the sight that greeted her. And had she not been so in control of herself and her emotions, she might have gone down on her knees herself and begged for mercy.

By the saints, 'twas no wonder her household had been scrambling for cover.

Some thirty-odd, grim-faced warriors stared back at her. Each was clothed in black from head to toe. Each wore armor that had been mended and repaired countless times. Helmets bore scratches and dents; cloaks were patched and travel-stained; saddles were scarred and worn. And then there were the faces themselves: hard, inflexible, seasoned. Mercenaries, the lot of them. A rougher group of ragtag knights she had never seen before in her life.

A terrifying group of men, to be sure.

Oh, and then there was John, of course. He made their tally a score and eleven, but even though he sported black as the rest of them did, his fresh scrubbed face and idiotic grin set him apart from the rest. Gwen glared at her brother-in-law, then turned her attentions back to the more intimidating souls.

One man nudged his great black destrier forward with his knees. He dismounted and thirty hands went to the hilts of their swords. The man who had dismounted held up his hand in peace, and his group of devils relaxed immediately. In spite of herself, Gwen was impressed. It would take a strong man indeed to command such loyalty from men whose loyalty likely could only be bought.

The man put his foot on the bottom step and stopped. Steel gray eyes stared at her from within the battered helm. Then large hands came up, jerked off the helm and pushed back the mail coif. Tousled black hair fell down around broad shoulders, shoulders that should have bloody well made an appearance long before now. Gray eyes twinkled merrily and a foolish grin graced lips that were the stuff of a giddy maid's dreams.

"Good morrow to you, *chérie*," he said, coming up the steps with a joyous bound and reaching up for her hand. "I came as soon as I could. I had expected to find you at

Ayre. Why were you barring your mother's gates? Did you
not recognize me?''

She'd promised herself she would not scream at him.
She'd vowed she would not shed a tear in his presence.
She'd been certain that she could dismiss the lout with a
mere flick of her wrist and that would be enough to satisfy
her.

But somehow, she found that remaining unmoved was
the very last thing she wanted to do. She pulled her hand
away from his. It was all she'd meant to do. Truly.

But somehow her fingers found themselves forming a
fist.

And then her fist did what it had been longing to do for
almost three years.

27

"Bloody hell, Gwen, why must you *always* do that!" Rhys exclaimed, stumbling back down the stairs. Several gasps accompanied his feet reuniting with the dirt of the courtyard. Rhys clutched his nose with both hands and looked around him.

Segrave's pitiful guardsmen who had been clustered about the great hall door all stood looking at him with their mouths agape. John was still atop his horse, gaping just as mightily. Rhys's army wore looks of astonishment, as well they should have. He had bested every last bloody one of them so thoroughly, they never dared gainsay him in anything. The sight of him being vanquished by a woman had likely scattered what wits remained the company.

Then he looked to his right to find the Fitzgerald twins staring not at him but at Gwen with looks of supreme satisfaction, as if they'd taught her the bloody maneuver themselves. Rhys was faintly surprised to see them there. Evidently they had somehow, in the past pair of years, managed to get themselves to Segrave intact. He had the feeling, based on the throbbing of his nose, that he might have been better off if they'd remained at Ayre.

And then there was the sound of a chuckle.

Rhys looked to the source. It was Montgomery, who stood to Jared's right with a finger or two covering his lips and his eyes watering madly.

Rhys wondered if he had time to humiliate his friend in the lists before finding out what Gwen was about. Montgomery only smiled and held up his hands in surrender.

"I wasn't the one to bloody your nose," he said with another grin.

There was suddenly much murmuring amongst his mercenaries, and Rhys turned and swept them all with a glare. To a man, they clamped their lips shut and suddenly found other things to look at besides him.

Rhys turned back around to face his errant lady and gave her the same glare he'd just dealt his men.

"*This* is the greeting I receive?" he demanded. He mounted the steps. "After three long years of driving myself into the dust, sleeping on my sword, risking my life in war and tourney alike?" He dragged his sleeve across his bleeding nose. "*This* is my greeting?"

"Nay, this is," she said. She looked at him so coldly, he felt as if a chill winter wind had blown through him. "Go to hell," she said distinctly.

And with that, she turned and disappeared into the hall, slamming the door home behind her.

If it hadn't been that he had truly seen Gwen with his own eyes, he would have believed he had just stumbled into the wrong keep.

He stared at the closed door, feeling more bewildered than he had in the whole of his life. By the tone of her missives he'd been led to believe she was anxiously awaiting his arrival. He'd expected tears of joy. He'd expected smiles and looks of love. He *hadn't* expected a fist in his nose.

"At least she didn't have a blade at her disposal," Jared offered suddenly. "Would have done you more harm than a little bruise."

"Especially after what I've taught her," Connor added.

"You? What did *you* teach her? *I'm* the one who taught her to approach coyly and blink her eyelashes rapidly at her opponent while slipping a dagger under his ribs—''

"But *I* taught her to feign a stone in her shoe, then catch him under the chin as he bends to see—''

"And *I* taught her to examine the embroidery on her sleeve as she slips a blade from its sheath strapped to her arm, then to bury it suddenly in his gullet—''

"Aye, a womanly move if ever I encountered one, which is why *I* showed her how to distract an enemy with a great baring of her teeth in a ferocious smile whilst she pulls a sharp stabbing needle from her purse—''

Rhys tried to ignore just what Gwen had been taught in favor of looking the twins over for new scars. Jared had a nick or two on his forehead, a bright red slash down one forearm which appeared to be rather recent, and a bandage wrapped around his hand.

Connor was missing part of his left ear.

"Did you allow her to sharpen that blade?" Rhys demanded.

Connor and Jared stopped their discussion and looked at him, blinking.

"Well?" Rhys asked. "Did you?"

Connor pursed his lips. "Didn't see any harm in it."

"I'd say your ear might have a different view of it," Rhys said.

Connor folded his arms over his chest and frowned at Rhys. "Had to keep the child busy somehow. She's been powerful irritated for these past pair of years."

"And as usual," Jared added with a grumble, " 'tis his fault. He never writes."

"I never write?" Rhys echoed. "Of course I write! I wrote! I wrote every bloody fortnight for almost three years and fair beggared myself to see the missives delivered!"

Connor and Jared both blinked several times, sure signs they were having trouble digesting what they'd just learned. Montgomery's mouth had fallen open in surprise.

Rhys frowned. Something foul was afoot.

He turned to his ragtag group of followers and dismissed them with a flick of his wrist. They'd been instructed to set up camp outside the walls and seek what sustenance they could in the village. Rhys waited until they'd gone, then tapped his foot until John had seen to the horses before he turned back to Montgomery.

"I have the feeling there are things we should discuss."

Montgomery continued to look at him in surprise. "You wrote?"

"And a bloody inconvenient thing it was, too. If you knew the places I've been in just the last year—"

"Gwen only received two letters," Montgomery said. "And those just in the pair of months right after you'd gone."

Rhys felt himself to be the one gaping now. "Just two missives?"

"Aye. If it hadn't been for the snatches of gossip we've heard over the past many months, we would have thought you dead."

"But I sent her scores of letters! And she responded!"

Montgomery shook his head. "I think perhaps you misread them. I'm surprised you didn't expect your reception, what with what she's been saying to you."

"*You* read the letters she sent to me?"

"She forced me to. Wanted to see a man's reaction, I suppose."

"But her letters were full of love!"

"Rhys, my friend, either you've lost all sense, or you weren't receiving what she sent to you."

Without another word, Rhys turned and strode off after John. Fortunately his squire seemed to be taking an inordinate amount of time to get to the front gates, likely because he would have rather stayed behind and eavesdropped, and Rhys was able to catch him easily enough. He rummaged about in his saddlebags, drew forth a bundle of missives, and turned to stomp back up to the keep. He entered the hall and stopped, realizing with a start that he had no idea where his lady might be hiding.

He'd been to Segrave, true, but that was many years ago. There was no one at the lord's table to ask where he

might find his lady. The first servant he approached took
one look at him and fled to parts unknown.

And then he heard the faint sound of cursing.

At least, he thought philosophically, there was something to be said for being out of favor. It certainly made
finding the curser a great deal less difficult.

He followed the sound up the steps and down the passageway. He stopped at a likely door and gathered his wits.
Clutching the proof of his devotion in hand, he pushed
open the door.

"And if that pompous horse's arse thinks he can—"

Gwen stopped in mid-curse and glared at him. Rhys
looked about the solar to see who else had been privy to
the slander. A handful of Segrave's ladies sat near the window, sewing industriously. Gwen was on her feet, and
Rhys suspected she had been pacing just as energetically.
Joanna sat in the largest and finest chair, holding a small
child in her lap. Out of the corner of his eye, Rhys noted
that Robin was in the chamber as well, staging a mock
battle with wooden figures. A gift from the Fitzgeralds, no
doubt. Rhys had received his own set to enjoy, though he'd
already been wielding a small sword at the time he'd received them. He'd treasured them just the same and had
plotted battles just as enthusiastically as Robin seemed to
be doing. Rhys lifted an eyebrow in surprise. The boy had
grown.

"We will have privacy," Joanna announced. "Ladies,
if you will."

Sewing was cast into baskets and five women filed reluctantly past him. Rhys scowled. They likely were re-
gretting not being able to be privy to more of the slander
they'd no doubt been enjoying those few moments past.

"Close the door if you will, Sir Knight," Joanna said
with a smile.

"Why?" Gwen said sharply. "I care not if the entire
keep hears what I have to say about him."

Rhys looked from one woman to the other and made a
hasty decision as to whom to approach first. He shut the
door behind him, then walked across the chamber to kneel

at Joanna's feet. He was painfully aware of his travel-stained clothing and the dust in his hair, but that couldn't be helped. He gave her his best smile.

"Lady Joanna," he said, bowing his head. "God's blessings upon you and upon yours. My grandsire and my mother send their greetings to you."

"How is Mary?" Joanna asked. "Still well-satisfied with her vocation?"

Rhys lifted his head and smiled at her. "Aye, my lady, she is."

"And you left your grandsire hale?"

"Stirring up as much mischief as he ever did. His only regret is that he could not come with me to present himself to you in person. He says you are the only sight worth making the journey for in the whole of England."

Joanna blushed and Rhys had to stop himself from smiling at the sight. Beautiful and charming. 'Twas no wonder men made excuses to pass by Segrave to tarry for a day or two. Joanna was indeed well worth the delay. She had to have been very young when she bore Gwen, for she was still an enormously beautiful woman and looked more of a sister to his lady than a mother. Rhys couldn't help but agree with his grandfather's words, though he himself would have made the journey merely for Gwen, no matter how she looked.

And she looked passing furious now. He turned to her and tried a smile to see how things would go for him.

She glared at him in return.

Ah, well, perhaps more conversation with the lady of Segrave would allow his love to cool her temper. Rhys turned his attention back to Gwen's mother. It was then that he had a good look at the girl-child sitting upon Joanna's lap. And then he felt his mouth fall open of its own accord.

The child was Gwen's. She could be no other. Already she resembled her mother as greatly as her mother resembled the lady Joanna. No one could mark those aqua eyes as belonging to any other line of women.

"Who is this?" he asked in a strangled voice.

"She's mine," Gwen snarled.

"Now, Gwen," Joanna said gently, "there's no need for that tone."

"No need?" Gwen echoed. She pointed at Rhys with a shaking finger. "He leaves me alone for *three* years, then comes bounding up my steps as if he had every expectation of me falling right into his arms!"

Joanna sighed. "You see, Sir Rhys, it has been a bit of time since Gwen received—"

"Three years!" Gwen bellowed.

"Three years," Joanna conceded, "since Gwen has had word from you. She was understandably worried."

"I wasn't worried," Gwen corrected. "I was bloody furious!"

Joanna sat back, embracing Gwen's daughter in her arms, and shrugged. She obviously had made her efforts toward peace and was now turning the matter over to him.

He sighed, said a quick prayer, and rose to his feet. Maybe if he blurted the truth out as quickly as possible, Gwen would actually hear him and forgive him before she cursed him any further.

Rhys held out the clutch of letters like an offering. "These are your letters to me. I was led to believe by them that you would be happy to see me."

"Then you didn't read very well what I wrote you," she returned. "And I certainly have none of your letters to me to show for the past three years."

"I wrote you every fortnight."

"Then you didn't send them."

"But I did!"

"Too much of whatever you were doing for the past three years has obviously addled your wits, Sir Knight, for I received nothing."

Rhys disentangled Gwen's last letter to him and opened it. " 'Beloved, I await your return anxiously,' " he read. " 'I am pleased to know you will be returning to England in May. My arms ache to hold you once again.' " He looked at her. "Your words."

Gwen frowned. "I didn't write that. In my last epistle

I spent a great amount of ink likening you to a horse's arse. And that was the pleasant part.''

Rhys pulled forth another letter and read to her from it. He stopped at the look of confusion on her face. "Not this one, either?" he asked.

She shook her head. "Nay."

Rhys looked down at his fistful of missives. "I believe, my lady," he said, feeling a chill run through him, "that we have been deceived."

"But my messengers were trusted men." Gwen looked at her mother. "Were they not?"

Her mother looked as shocked as Rhys himself felt. "Aye, so I thought," she said slowly. "But both sides of the correspondence were snatched. Who could manage such a thing?"

Rhys met Gwen's eyes.

"Rollan," they said together. There was no doubt in his mind and obviously no doubt in Gwen's.

"Devious," Joanna said quietly. "Aye, that I suspected of him. But to purposely set out to destroy your affection . . ."

"It would not surprise me," Rhys said grimly.

"But how can you be sure?" Joanna asked. "It could have been anyone."

"Who else would care?" Gwen asked. "Especially since we know what his true intentions are."

Rhys looked at her. "What intentions?"

"It was shortly after you departed for France that I overheard Rollan conversing with himself at the ale kegs," Gwen said. "It would seem that his plan is to become Lord of Ayre with me as his bride."

"A modest plan," Rhys said dryly.

"Aye," she agreed, "but an unpleasant one. I listened to him consider the merits of pushing everyone in his way down the stairs. I have no idea what he planned to do with you, but I'm certain 'twas equally as dire. Perhaps he planned to become both lord of Ayre and Wyckham.''

Lord of Wyckham. Rhys had become that when he reached a score and six, but somehow it had never seemed

to mean anything to him—likely because there was a
bloody army on his land, and it wasn't as if he'd been able
to take possession of it.

"How lovely that I am returned to oblige Rollan in the
carrying out of his plans," Rhys said, with a snort. He
looked at her with a frown. "You could have written me
to tell me of what you'd learned."

"I did," she said shortly.

Rhys sighed. He had no answer for that, and no way to
change what had transpired.

"Let us hope this is the extent of his treachery," Joanna
interrupted. "He hasn't seemed bent on destruction while
he has visited me."

"He also had the Fitzgeralds to face at every turn,"
Gwen said. "I doubt I would have tried anything with
them about, either."

Rhys looked at Gwen and frowned. "I wish I had
known."

"Would you have returned?"

"Aye," he said briskly. "I would have."

"And lost your time to tourney," Gwen said with a
sigh. She looked at him. "At least I assume you were
spending your time tourneying."

"Tourneying, hiring out my sword to whoever would
pay the most, warring." He shrugged. "Whatever it took."

"And you have earned what you need?"

He looked at her and attempted a smile. "Aye, and I
can only hope there is still a need for what I've earned."

She only returned his stare, but he thought he might
have seen a softening begin around her mouth.

"I would have come home sooner," he said again, "had
I known what Rollan was plotting."

She shook her head. "That wouldn't have served us,
Rhys, and no harm came of all Rollan's chattering to himself. Well," she added with a scowl, "no harm save three
years of simmering irritation toward you."

"Simmering?" Joanna echoed with a laugh.

Rhys thought it best to distract Gwen from thinking any
more on how angry she'd been. At least she appeared to

have cooled her temper a bit and was thinking kindly of him. "I did write you," he said, thinking that such a thing could not be said enough times. "And I spent a great deal of gold seeing the missives sent," he added, hoping that would impress her.

"Not gold well spent," Gwen noted.

"Well, nay, it wasn't." He shook his head. "I thought you were perfectly content to wait for me."

"And I thought you were bedding every noblewoman in Phillip's household."

He blinked. "Surely you jest."

"You are the stuff of legends, Sir Rhys. In the bed-chamber and on the battlefield."

"You can rest assured half of those rumors are false."

"Which ones?" she grumbled. "Tales of your swordly prowess?"

"Oh, nay," he said, feeling as if he might now have a chance to at least apologize for the fact that he had over-paid his messengers, "those were no doubt greatly under-exaggerated. My swordplay is much improved."

She scowled at him. "And your other weapon?"

"Dusty from disuse, no doubt."

Gwen's mother laughed out loud. She rose with the girl in her arms. "I will see to some refreshment for our poor, neglected Sir Rhys. Take the babe, Gwen."

Rhys watched Gwen accept the child and marveled again how much of a resemblance there was even at such a young age. Gwen held the child close and said nothing until her mother had left the solar.

"This is Amanda," Gwen said, lifting her chin as if she dared him to say aught.

"I see," he said, nodding. "A beautiful child."

"She has two years," Gwen added. "And three months. Alain was counting on another lad. He hasn't much use for a girl."

"Ah," he said, merely because he could say nothing else.

"I would not trade her," Gwen said fiercely.

Rhys took a few steps toward her, reached out, and

trailed a dirty finger down Amanda's cheek. "Of course you wouldn't. Alain is very shortsighted not to prize her."

He smiled at Amanda and received a sudden smile in return that smote him straight in the heart. Then, to his surprise, Amanda stretched out her arms to him. He took her, ignoring the tightness in his chest and the crumpling of letters in his hand.

This child could have been his, had things been different.

"And Robin you already know," Gwen said, beckoning to her son. "Robin, give greeting to Sir Rhys. He's been off in France these past years, fighting bravely against many knights."

Rhys looked down into huge gray eyes which found home in a solemn little face.

"Robin, a greeting," Gwen prompted.

"Good morrow, Sir Knight," Robin said, ducking his head.

Rhys looked at Gwen. "He resembles you less than Amanda does."

"He has my father's features," Gwen said. "And his eyes." She clutched Robin closer. "I only have him until he's seven," she blurted out. "And then his sire intends to send him to foster at court."

Rhys shook his head slowly. He hardly dared speak in front of the boy, but he vowed then that Robin would be in King John's clutches over his own dead body.

"And he is now almost five years?" Rhys asked.

Gwen nodded, her eyes suddenly swimming with tears.

"Two years is a very long time, lady," Rhys said softly. "And much can happen in that time."

"Men always send their sons off to foster."

"Not all men," Rhys assured her. "If I had a son, I daresay I would keep him home until he had at least twelve summers. 'Tis only then that a lad truly appreciates the adventure of making his own way. I daresay until that time he is better served by learning his craft under his father's hand. Wouldn't you agree?"

She held Robin even more closely to her. "Can it be done?"

He smiled. "I have several chests of gold in France which would agree that it could."

And then before he knew what would come next, Gwen had put her arm around his waist and buried her face against his chest. Rhys had barely the wits about him to put his free arm about her and draw her close before she burst into tears.

Well, a drenching was better than a sticking. Or another fist in his nose.

Or so he thought until Amanda saw her mother's violent weeping and set up a howl of her own. And then Robin began to use quite effective little fists to pummel him about his hips and waist.

"Oof," Rhys gasped as Robin made rather forceful contact with a tender part of his frame. "By the saints, lad, I'm friend, not foe!"

"You've made Mama weep," Robin said with marked disapproval. He did, however, leave off with his assault.

"Well, she bloodied my nose," Rhys offered.

Robin looked up and seemed to be weighing the sight of that against the sight of his sobbing mother.

"I think she's weeping because she's happy to see me," Rhys added, wondering what sort of logic would sway a five-year-old child.

Robin frowned. "How can that be when she struck you?"

"Ah, well, there was something of a misunderstanding between us, lad," Rhys said. "She was telling me of her displeasure, I'd say. I think she's forgiven me now."

Robin appeared to be taking this into account. Rhys had the most ridiculous urge to squirm. By the saints, this lad was too old for his modest years. Perhaps he'd seen more of Alain's mistreatment of his mother than was good for young eyes. His gaze was far too assessing.

"You aren't my sire," Robin announced.

"Nay, lad, I'm not," Rhys said, wishing mightily that

he were. "But I was at one time the captain of your mother's guard."

Robin nodded thoughtfully. "The Fitzgerald brothers told me tales of you," he said finally.

"Good ones?"

"Aye," Robin said, starting to look just a bit more interested. "They said you've a ruby the size of an egg in the hilt of your sword."

"I do."

"And that you've taken so many knights for ransom that you've lost count of the gold you've earned."

Lost count? Rhys smiled to himself. Saints, but he was intimately acquainted with every piece of gold he'd laid hands on the past three years.

"I've had my share of successes," he conceded modestly.

"All right, then," Robin said, seemingly approving of Rhys's person.

Gwen drew away, dragging her sleeve across her face.

"Sir Rhys is a very dear friend," she said, smoothing her hand over her son's hair, "and I've missed him sorely these past years."

Robin looked slightly confused. "But you called him 'unfeeling oaf' and 'blighted whoreso—'"

"Robin!"

The insults had rolled off Robin's tongue so easily, Rhys could only assume he'd heard them enough to have mastered them. Gwen turned a rather alarming shade of red and put her hand over her son's mouth.

"Aye, lad, I called him those and more," she said. "But there was this misunderstanding—"

"And you bloodied his nose for it," Robin said, escaping her silencing fingers. "But all is well now?"

"Aye, son."

Rhys felt the full impact of Robin's interest then.

"You'll show me your sword?" Robin asked. "And teach me swordplay? I have a wooden sword, you know. I give the twins splinters all the time with it."

"Better that than wounds that need to be sewn," Rhys

said, smiling down at the boy before turning to his mother.
"Connor seems to be missing pieces of himself."

"Very distractable, that one," Gwen said with a slight
frown. "Set him to boasting of his skill and his guard slips
completely."

Rhys found his sleeve being tugged on and looked down
at the tugger.

"A lesson in swordplay?" Robin asked. "Now?"

"Grandmother has prepared something for him to eat,"
Gwen said. "And then he will likely want a rest. He's no
doubt done many heroic deeds on his way back from
France and is weary from them. Perhaps tomorrow."

"Tomorrow." Robin sighed, as if the time required to
reach such a place was simply too great for him to fathom.

"Perhaps a short lesson this afternoon," Rhys said.
"And then your mother and I have much to discuss."

He disentangled his clutch of letters from Amanda's
hands, not exactly sure how they'd gotten there to begin
with and thereupon realizing that children took more
watching than he'd suspected, and handed them to Gwen.

"You might find these interesting," he said.

"I daresay I would," she agreed. "I only wish I had
like number to show you."

He looked down at her and wished greatly that a pair
of gray eyes would find something more appealing to observe than him so he could kiss Gwen properly. Painfully
conscious of Robin's regard, he could only smile grimly
at Gwen.

"I did write."

"I believe you."

Rhys wanted more than life and breath to draw her into
his arms and never let her from them again. He had spent
three years aching for her, dreaming of her, contenting
himself with the thought that she would in the end be his.
Every moment apart, every moment of thinking of her as
Alain's wife would only add to the sweetness of her being
his when he could manage it. He was tired of warring,
tired of racking his pitiful brain for ways to see her freed
from her marriage to Ayre, to see that she took her son

with her, to appease whatever clergy and royalty necessary to see his ends accomplished.

And now he stood a hand's breadth from the creature he'd dreamed about every waking moment for three years, and all he could do was hold on to her daughter and submit to her son's investigation of his person for possible warriorly accoutrements.

And look at the woman he loved more than life itself.

"Food now?" Robin prompted.

Rhys felt Robin slip his hand into his and Amanda's arm tighten around his neck.

"Aye," he managed, "food first. Then speech."

And he vowed in that moment to never let these three go.

No matter the cost.

28

Gwen wondered, as she chewed thoughtfully on a bit of roasted fowl, how it was that she could be so angry with a man one moment, then have such a rush of friendly feelings for him not a pair of hours later.

Such, she supposed, was the course of true love.

They sat together at her mother's table, sharing a trencher and a goblet. It had been her mother's doing to seat them thusly, and Gwen wasn't sure if she should be grateful for it or not. She'd wanted time to think on what she'd learned that afternoon. The thought of Rollan having possibly read all her missives left her torn between wanting to blush and wanting to murder him. Along with anger and embarrassment, she felt a chill. That Rollan should go to such great lengths to cool her feelings for Rhys only spoke of his determination and cunning. She had underestimated him.

How could she have been so blind? Rollan had visited Segrave many times over the past three years, and though Gwen had made certain never to be without a goodly portion of her mother's household nearby, she had never once suspected that he might be doing something so calculating. She had been waiting for him to push someone down the stairs, and he had instead been reading her letters. Always he came from a direction she didn't suspect. She would do well to be more on her guard. Perhaps with her and Rhys both watching him, he would succeed in making no more mischief.

"Shall we retire again to my solar?" Joanna asked, leaning in front of Rhys to look at Gwen. "We would be more comfortable resting there."

Gwen looked at Rhys. "Does that suit, or would you rather have speech with my guard?"

"To find out just how it is you damaged the Fitzgeralds so thoroughly?" he asked with a smile. He threw a look at the lower table, where Montgomery and the twins sat with John, indulging the young man by listening politely to his stirring retelling of his adventures. Either that, or John was retelling Rhys's glorious adventures. He shook his head. "I'm better off not knowing. And I would imagine that John would be slow to forgive me for robbing him of his audience."

Gwen nodded to her mother. "Aye, Mother. We'll be along presently."

Rhys looked at Gwen as her mother rose and made her way to the stairs. "Her will is still followed here?"

"Aye, my father commanded it."

"And Alain agreed to this?"

"We have, if you can stomach it, Rollan to thank for it," Gwen admitted grudgingly. "Whatever else his faults, he knows how to appreciate a fine meal. I imagine he feared Alain would offend the cook somehow, so he managed to convince his brother that Segrave was better left to itself."

"Kind of him."

"My mother had a hand in it as well, of course. Do you not remember the first time you and I came to Segrave after the wedding?"

Rhys shook his head, a small smile on his face. "I remember nothing save you, lady. I paid no heed to my surroundings."

She couldn't help but feel the pleasure of the compli-

ment, though she would be the first to admit she remembered little of the visit as well. It had been a brief stay and
Gwen had been mostly concerned with wondering how she
might avoid Alain's bed as often as possible.

"Then you may not have noticed," she said, passing on
those less than pleasant memories, "but my mother hid
her comeliest serving wenches in the village and installed
a stable lad as head cook."

Rhys laughed. "She didn't."

"Aye, she did. Even Alain noticed there was something
amiss with the fare. I daresay it wasn't hard for Rollan to
convince him that Segrave as a residence was not a desirable place. Collecting the rents is something, of course,
that he hasn't failed to do, but visiting seemingly doesn't
appeal."

Rhys looked at her thoughtfully. "Then Alain has not
troubled you in recent months?"

"I haven't seen him since Amanda was conceived."

"A blessing, to be sure."

"He fears my mother, I think," Gwen said. "And, of
course, he has no interest in a daughter. He sends Rollan
to investigate and bring him back tidings." She frowned.
"I have been a fool not to watch that one more closely.
Had I known what he was about, I would have added
something foul to his wine."

"Better to leave him trusting," Rhys said. "At least that
way the enemy is known."

Gwen sighed and rose with him. "Let us speak of something else for the night. I have no more stomach for thinking on Rollan's schemes."

As her mother had seen to putting the children to bed,
Gwen had nothing else to do but lead Rhys to the solar.
She was acutely aware of him following her up the steps
and down the passageway. She'd grown far too accustomed to the light step of her mother's feet, or the ever
rushing patter of Robin's as he ran here and there. Rhys's
solid footfall behind her was a pleasing sound indeed.

It was but moments later that she found herself sitting
next to her love in her mother's solar. Perhaps she should

have occupied her hands with some sort of stitchery, but the saints only knew what sorts of abnormal appendages would result on any kind of animal she embroidered.

"So, Sir Rhys," Joanna said, obviously feeling that stitchery was not beyond her, for she had intricate work under her needle, "why do you not tell us a tale or two of your travels. Since, of course," she added with a small smile directed her daughter's way, "we've had no word of them from you directly."

Gwen grunted in agreement, but said nothing. She'd said too much as it was. Rhys's ears were likely still burning from her curses.

"Well," Rhys said, settling back in his chair with a cup of wine, "I could perhaps begin with the tourney at Toulouse."

Gwen hardly cared where he began, for where he had ended was in the chair next to her. She leaned back and watched him as he spoke of his travels and felt for the first time in years that she might actually enjoy the evening, surrounded by those she loved.

Three years of warring had changed him—that and bearing the weight of almost a score and ten years on his shoulders. Gone were any of the soft lines of his youth. In his face were signs of the sorrows he had carried, but they showed mostly in the creases between his brow when he frowned while remembering this detail or that.

He looked at her now and then as he spun his tale and then he would smile. Gwen memorized the way the skin about his eyes crinkled and how the little dimple in his cheek appeared as if to celebrate his merriment. And the more she looked at him, the more she thought her heart just might break.

Ah, that he could be hers in truth.

"Gwen?"

She looked at him and couldn't stop the words from leaving her mouth. "I love you," she said.

He blinked, then another sunny smile burst forth from him. "By the saints, *chérie*," he said, reaching for her hand, "I think I should go away more often—"

"Do not," Joanna interrupted with a laugh, "lest you force me to take drastic measures. You did not have to endure her rampages for the past three years."

"I did not rampage," Gwen said archly. "I did but give vent to a bout or two of displeasure."

Joanna snorted delicately. "I cannot even speak of it, for the very thought gives me pains in my head yet again. Gwen, love, why do you not make your nightly rounds. Perhaps Sir Rhys would accompany you tonight."

Rhys looked at her and lifted an eyebrow in question. Gwen shrugged.

"I walk upon the roof to see that all is well." *And to see if anyone comes toward the keep in the evening when he might not be marked.* She should have known Rhys would come in the middle of the day, and anyone who thought to deny him entrance be damned.

His smile said that he guessed a bit of what she hadn't admitted. "You go alone?" he asked.

"Montgomery comes now and then. Usually the twins accompany me. It gives them a chance to intimidate my mother's guardsmen yet another time before retiring."

"I'm certain that pleases them," Rhys said dryly. He stood and held out his hand to her. "If I might have the pleasure this evening?"

"Don't be long, children," Joanna said as they walked out into the passageway.

"Aye, Mother," Gwen said, pulling the door shut behind her. "I've never heard that before."

"Perhaps she fears I will ravish you upon the roof."

Gwen looked at him. "Will you?"

"What else are battlements for," he asked with a smile, "if not for the ravishment of future brides?"

Just one night, Gwen thought. *Let me believe 'tis truly possible for just one night.* The roof limited greatly what sorts of things they could engage in, which was likely just as well, but at least she might feel his arms about her and imagine that she was to be his.

He took her hand and drew her along behind him up the steps. Gwen did not even make the pretense of walking the walls. She stopped in her accustomed spot and looked out over her father's land. It was Alain's land now, but she rarely thought of it that way.

"Do you always look south?"

Gwen put her hands on the rock and let the chill of it seep into her fingers. "Aye."

"Any particular reason?"

She looked up at him. "I was looking for someone to come."

He covered her hand with his own and looked down at her seriously. "There was no purpose in earning only a fraction of what I needed."

"Three years is a very long time, Rhys."

"We will have the rest of our lives together."

"And if something should happen to you, and we have no future together?"

"I am invincible, or hadn't you heard?"

"This is not a matter for jesting—"

He put a finger to her lips and shook his head. "I will make light of it no more, Gwen. But I will not think on giving you up before I can even call you mine. Trust me, my love. We will have many happy years together, and then what we have endured will seem but a small moment. Do not the past three years seem but a blink of an eye now we are together yet again?"

"Nay," she said shortly, "they do not."

He only laughed softly. "Ah, sweet Gwen, but I have missed having someone about me who is unwilling to humor me."

"I take it you have your army appropriately cowed, then?"

"Aye, they fear my temper."

"Which I do not, of course."

He reached out and tucked her hair behind her ear. "Is there nothing you fear, lady?"

"Losing my children," she said promptly. "And," she added, almost unwilling to say it lest it somehow come back to haunt her, "losing you. Or, even worse, never having you at all."

"I will see to it, Gwen."

How, she did not know, and the thought of it was enough to sour her humor. It was impossible. Even if she managed to free herself, how would she keep her children? Even Eleanor of Aquitaine, as powerful as she was, had been obliged to leave her children behind with her first husband. Gwen could not bear the thought of it.

"I don't see how," she said with a sigh.

"Then don't look. At least not now."

"But . . ."

He shook his head, then reached out and put his hands on her shoulders. Gwen immediately conceded the battle, deciding that speech was unnecessary, yea even undesirable, at the moment. Let the future see to itself—

Rhys bent his head and very softly, very tenderly kissed her on the mouth.

And the touch of his lips upon hers sent shivers down through her to the soles of her feet. By the saints, she had forgotten what a mere kiss from the man could do to her.

He wasn't wearing mail. She discovered that almost immediately, for he enveloped her in a formidable embrace from which she suspected there was very little hope of escape. Not that escape was uppermost on her mind. Never mind that 'twas passing chilly outside, or that her mother's guardsmen were likely all gawking at her—

"Gwen."

Gwen blinked and looked up at him. "Aye?"

"Stop indulging in so many thoughts."

"How do you know I'm thinking—"

"Your brow furrows. 'Tis quite attractive, of course, but leaves me wondering how well you are concentrating upon my kisses."

She sighed and closed her eyes. Let the morrow see to itself. Tonight was perhaps the only night for some time to come that she would have Rhys to herself, and she would not ruin that time.

And so she gave herself over to the sweetness of his kiss. She sighed at the pleasure of having his hands sliding softly over her hair. And when he cradled her close, merely running the flat of his hand over her back time and time again, she closed her eyes and rested her cheek against his chest. Ah, that such comfort could be hers in truth.

"I will see to it," he murmured.

Gwen sighed, too content to argue with him. She concentrated instead on how it felt to be in Rhys's arms again. She listened to his breathing, felt the warmth of his body seep through his clothes and warm her, and heard the echo of his voice rumbling deep in his chest. And she realized in that instant how much more she had missed him than she'd been willing to admit. Even though they had not shared such embraces while he was her captain, at least he had been ever near her.

Three years had been a very long time.

"Would you care to hear an item of interest?"

"Hmmm," she agreed, settling more comfortably into his arms. "As you will."

"It would seem," he said conversationally, as if he discussed nothing more important than what they stood to eat for supper the next day, "that Lord Ayre is out of favor with our good Lackland."

"Is he?" Gwen asked. She almost smiled. Standing there as she was in Rhys's arms, feeling as if it were the one place she truly belonged, it was easy enough to speak of Alain. Where she was at present, he could not touch her.

"Aye, he is," Rhys continued, as easily as if he somehow shared the same feeling. "It would seem he made the grave mistake of deflowering the king's cook's daughter."

"Poor girl."

"And, as usual, he was caught while at his work."

"How inconvenient for him," she remarked. "I would say he spends far too much time in the kitchens."

"I couldn't agree more. Unfortunately, this is the cause of John's understandable irritation. Having caught wind of the turn of events while I was still in France, I managed to procure His Majesty a fine new creator of delicacies, so I am, oddly enough, in the king's good graces."

That was enough to make her look at him. "How in the

world did you manage to unearth that tidbit?"

He smiled modestly. "I can take no credit for it. My grandfather had been talking with an old friend who had quite recently been in London listening to the king rage on. My grandsire met me at the dock with a new cook saddled and prepared to venture forth from France."

"And this man was willing to come to England?"

"My grandsire can be very persuasive when he wants to be."

Gwen felt her contentment begin to slip away. She rested her head against Rhys's chest and looked out over the fields. "Even if you manage to convince John, Rhys, how can you hope to convince any clergy? I have two children I will likely lose."

"Nay, love, you will not. If they will have me, I will claim them as well."

"They would have you, but how will you convince Alain to give them up? He will want his heir. He cares nothing for Robin save that."

"He can sire another on Rachel. Or acknowledge one of the handful of bastards he has scampering about here and there."

She stiffened, then pulled away. "He has bastards?"

"Aye, Gwen," Rhys said patiently, "he has bastards. Robin would likely be better off as my son, for he will have no one crowding his hall to fight him for his inheritance."

"You uncover too many things," she said slowly. "I think I would rather know less about Alain's activities."

" 'Tis all done to aid me in my goal, which is to have you. Now, come," he said, bending to kiss one, then the other ear that seemed to have escaped with his help from their covering of hair, "and let us descend before you grow chilled. I don't wish to ride off to Wyckham knowing I've left you here ailing from the ague."

"Ride off to Wyckham," she repeated. "Without me?"

"Well—"

"You will *not*," she said distinctly, "leave me behind again. The saints only know when I'd see you next."

"Gwen—"

"Nay," she said. So much for any more kissing. For all she knew, Rhys intended to distract her so thoroughly that she would forget what he was about until he'd already ridden out from her gates. She took his hand and pulled him toward the tower door. "I'll come along."

"It would mean stopping at Fenwyck."

She stopped and considered. Passing any time whatsoever with Geoffrey of Fenwyck was enough to make her rethink her choice. He would look at her ears. She'd only seen him a handful of times since her imprisonment in the piggery, and each time he had stared most rudely and thereafter favored her with a smirk she couldn't help but interpret as slanderous.

She had always returned the favor by looking quite pointedly at the gap in his front teeth.

But her alternative was watching Rhys ride off again. Humiliation, or letting her love out of her sights. Saints, but it was a difficult choice.

She turned toward the door, her decision made. "We'll start off tomorrow that the journey might end that much sooner," she said grimly. "I'll bear it."

He laughed softly from behind her. "I'll need a day or two to rest and prepare the men, Gwen."

"A day or two?" The thought of putting off the torture even that long was tremendously unappealing.

"We're heading toward possible war."

"With Fenwyck?" she asked darkly.

He tugged on her hair gently, then reached over her and pulled the door to the stairwell open. "Of course not. A mere glare from you will subdue Geoffrey. I am thinking on Wyckham."

"Then perhaps we should talk a bit and enjoy some quiet, what with both of us heading into battle."

"My thought exactly," he said dryly.

"Besides," she said, starting down the steps, " 'twill give me time to sharpen my sword."

She only managed to reach the bottom of the stairs before Rhys pulled her into his arms again. She shook her head.

"No more."

"Aye, more," he said, smiling.

"You think to distract me—"

"Actually, I was just thinking about kissing you, but if distraction happens as well . . ."

Let him try, Gwen thought to herself as his mouth came down on hers. And then as he kissed her, she suspected that he might very well succeed, at least for that night. There was no harm in that, she supposed. The morrow would bring a return to her concentration, and then she would prepare for their journey north. A new wimple would perhaps distract Geoffrey from his observation of her e—

"Gwen," Rhys said in exasperation.

She blinked at him. "What?"

He took her by the shoulders and turned her away from him. "Do all your thinking now, lady, for I vow I will not share you once we are wed!"

He sounded as if he expected it to come about. Gwen nodded and let him direct her down the passageway.

If he believed it so fully, how could she do anything else?

29

Rhys walked along the dusty path into the village, praying he wasn't being foolhardy in taking Gwen from the keep with only Montgomery, the twins, and John as guardsmen. It wasn't as if he was expecting any mischief, but then again he had no idea of Rollan's whereabouts. Joanna seemed to think Alain's brother to be harmless, but Rhys knew better. That he should voice his schemes aloud, even if he thought it was in private, indicated to Rhys how certain Rollan was that he would find success. It was enough to make a man look behind him before he considered descending any steps.

"—Don't you agree, Sir Rhys?"

Rhys looked down at the small boy who walked next to him. "Forgive me, lad, I didn't hear you."

"An arrow through the eye," Robin said patiently. "That would fell a dragon, wouldn't it?"

"Well," Rhys said slowly, "I suppose an arrow through the eye would be as effective as anything, but it doesn't seem very sporting, does it?"

"But the fire," argued Robin. "The beastie'd burn my fingers should I try to get closer than that!"

"And I suppose chain mail would be little protection

against such heat," Rhys agreed solemnly. "Passing warm, I should think."

"Two-fisted thrust through the underbelly," a voice grumbled from behind them.

"Nay, brother, better a slash made to lop off the head. Solves the problem of fire from the nostrils."

"Dodge *under* the fire," Connor insisted, "and come up under the belly."

"And be squashed in the process?" Jared demanded. "Have you lost all sense?"

Rhys heard Gwen sigh lightly next to him, and he wondered if she'd been privy to these kinds of arguments for the past three years. He met her gaze and saw the amusement lurking there.

"A day of leisure?" she asked dryly.

"Matters of war, Mama," Robin said importantly, "are always a ripe subject for glorious discussion."

Rhys looked over his shoulder at Connor. "Did you teach him that?"

"Nay, *I* did," Jared said proudly. "A quick study, that young one. As eager as you were."

"Aye," Connor agreed, "he'll make a fine warrior, he will."

"So," Robin continued, "I think it must be an arrow through the eye." He looked back at Connor and Jared, seemingly to check to see if they approved of his line of thinking. " 'Tis the only way."

"Thinks for himself," Jared noted.

"*I* taught him that," Connor boasted.

Rhys began to wonder if he'd brought too many guardsmen with him that day. John would have likely been enough. At least he was watching his surroundings instead of chattering them to death.

Gwen cleared her throat pointedly. "And what of the maiden? Shouldn't you be giving consideration to her rescue?"

"She *is* the point of the entire exercise," Montgomery agreed from where he walked in front of Rhys. "Not that you'd know it in this company."

Gwen snorted and looked up at Rhys. "This is the company you left me with. You can imagine the reaction I've had to whatever lays I've struggled to compose."

"Not nearly enough blood," Connor complained, "though 'twasn't for a lack of my trying to aid her."

"Her accounts of battle have improved, though," Jared conceded. "That was *my* doing."

"The dragon, Sir Rhys," Robin said, tugging on Rhys's hand. "*He* is the interesting part."

"The saints preserve me from the child," Gwen muttered under her breath. "And to think I spent all these years spinning him tales of bold rescues. I had no idea what part he was listening to the more!"

Rhys listened to the confusion going on around him and found the sound of it sweet indeed. The feeling of a small boy's hand in his and the sight of his lady's daughter riding in Montgomery's arms was delightful as well.

But the most wonderful thing of all was knowing that his love was by his side. Every time he caught sight of her, he smiled. Every time he heard her laugh, he wanted to laugh as well. And every time he thought about what it would take to have her as his own, he wanted to drop to his knees and pray for success. Gold he had. Determination he possessed in abundance. But a plan that would guarantee victory?

It was the one thing he needed, and the one thing he lacked.

"You, there! Cease!"

Montgomery's shout startled Rhys from his uncomfortable thoughts. And almost before Rhys could think about what he needed to do, he found himself leaping ahead of the company. He caught the strap before it came down another time.

A young boy lay in the dirt at Rhys's feet, cowering. A very large man held the leather strap in his beefy fist. He jerked it free of Rhys's hand and glared at him.

" 'E's mine," a man snarled, "and I'll beat 'im as I see fit."

Rhys pursed his lips in disgust. "And what could a child

of such tender years have done to merit this?''

"Didn't work 'ard enough," the man said. "There's no place for a sluggard at my board."

Rhys looked at the man, noted the substantial arms and broad chest. A blacksmith, perhaps, or a mason. Not a pleasant soul, if the coldness in his eyes was any indication. Certainly not a man Rhys would want anywhere near any of his children.

Rhys ignored the man's growling and reached down to pick up the boy where he had fallen in the dirt. There was blood on the back of his ragged tunic. Rhys pulled the boy behind him.

"How much do you want for him?" he asked bluntly.

The man's eyes took on a calculating look. "More than you're willing to pay, likely."

"Think you?" Rhys asked. "Shall it be a piece of gold or two, or would you rather barter with my fists?"

"Or my sword!" John interjected, bouncing on the balls of his feet as if he itched to show his prowess.

"Or his sword," Rhys agreed, folding his arms over his chest.

"Take more than a piece of gold to replace the labor I'll lose," the man said. "Not that I ever wanted him anyway, but 'e's a strong lad."

"For a sluggard," Rhys agreed dryly.

"What was I to do with 'im?" the man demanded. "Ayre's young lord came through 'ere one day and took me sister home for his pleasure. Damn 'er if she didn't return a'carryin' this whelp. Was I to turn 'er out, I ask ye?"

"How kind," Rhys remarked.

"Someone had to work for their keep," the man continued. "And it weren't to be 'er. Lazy wench."

"She's sick," the boy whispered. "Not lazy."

Rhys found himself pushed aside by Gwen before she knelt down before the child.

"Your mother is ill, lad?"

His eyes filled with tears. "Aye, lady. Near to dying, I'd say."

She took his hand. "Where is she?"

He nodded toward the hut.

"Show me."

Rhys watched her go inside and wondered at the wisdom of it, but he suspected there was little he could do to stop her. When his lady was determined about something, the saints preserve any soul who thought to stand in her way.

He found that he had nothing to say to the man, so he merely stood there and stared, his arms folded over his chest, and waited.

Gwen returned in time, bringing the boy along behind her. Rhys opened his mouth to ask her what had transpired, but she seemingly had no desire for speech with him.

"His mother is gone," she said shortly to the boy's uncle. "How much for the boy?"

"Three pieces of gold," the man said promptly. " 'E is me nephew, after all, and dear to me—"

"By all the saints," Rhys exclaimed, "you were nigh onto driving the life from the lad!"

Gwen removed Rhys's purse from his belt before he could protest, rummaged around in it, then handed the man four pieces of gold.

"Gwen—" Rhys gasped.

"Here is an extra piece to make certain you do not change your mind. The boy is mine now," Gwen said to the blacksmith. "If you come within ten paces of him again, I will kill you."

The man looked at his gold, then at her. And his eyes took on a calculating look she didn't care for in the slightest.

"Or perhaps Sir Rhys will merely use you as sport," she conceded. "You've no doubt seen his band of mercenaries camped yonder. He is, of course, the fiercest of the lot and more merciless than the rest. I doubt his finishing of you would be nearly as swift as mine would be."

The man looked at Rhys appraisingly. Rhys mustered

up his fiercest look. No sense in not living up to Gwen's boasts.

"You know," she continued, lowering her voice as if she had a delicious secret to share, "I've heard the sound of screaming soothes him." She smiled pleasantly. "I wouldn't want to know the truth of the matter myself, but perhaps you're made of sterner stock than I am."

Rhys smiled at the man. The man took one last look at Rhys, then immediately turned and went inside his hovel.

"Montgomery," Gwen said softly, "if you would be so good as to see to the mother's remains?"

"Aye, lady," Montgomery agreed.

"Twins, you will see to my children?"

Amanda and Robin were summarily deposited upon broad, Viking shoulders and carried back toward the keep.

"John, go after them and inform my mother we come and we've a lad in need of tending."

John looked at Rhys as if to ask if he should be obeying his sister-in-law.

"I wouldn't argue," Rhys advised.

John trotted off obediently.

Gwen drew the boy alongside her. "Rhys, this is Nicholas. Nicholas, this is Sir Rhys."

Rhys looked down into a dirty little face belonging to a lad who could be no older than Robin, or so Rhys guessed. His hair was filthy enough that Rhys could not divine its color, but the boy's eyes were pale. And filled with tears.

"Oh," Rhys said, his heart breaking a little within him. "Poor lad." He looked at Gwen. "Are we keeping him?"

"Aye," she said, and he was almost surprised by the vehemence in her voice, "we are."

Rhys had another look at the lad. Though the child's uncle claimed the boy had been sired by Alain, Rhys could not see it. The child looked nothing like Ayre, and that was likely why Gwen wanted him so badly. Then again, his lady had a tender heart where children were concerned.

"Well," Rhys said, "if you wish to have him."

"Don't you?"

Rhys met those pale gray eyes and saw the despair there.

If humoring his lady hadn't inspired him to acceptance, the sight of a half starved, sorrowful little one certainly did.

"Aye, I will take him gladly," Rhys said firmly.

"I suspect," Gwen said, "that that isn't the last time you'll say that."

Rhys looked at her in surprise, but there seemed to be no hidden message in her gaze. He surmised that she was pleased with him for his choice, and he accepted that with a smile. Then he looked at Nicholas.

"Do you care to come with us?"

Nicholas looked as if the very thought and the hope it engendered might break him into pieces.

Rhys smiled and took the lad's small grubby hand in his own. "Answer enough, I suppose. Let us seek out something for you to eat. I suspect you could use something substantial."

Rhys found his other hand taken by his lady. So much for their leisurely walk. Perhaps 'twas just as well. He needed to make final preparations for their journey north. Joanna seemed determined to come with them, and he welcomed not only the protection from scandal she would provide, but the handful of men she intended to bring along. He was glad of the aid. Perhaps he might even have a bit of help from Fenwyck.

Assuming, of course, he could keep Gwen and Geoffrey from killing each other.

The saints preserve him from the pair of them long enough for him to battle what he truly needed to.

Gwen stood at the doorway of the kitchens and smiled at the sight before her. By his words, Rhys had seemingly intended to go straight to the lists after they had returned to the keep. Somehow, though, he had found himself seated at a table in the kitchens with Robin at one elbow, Nicholas at the other, and Amanda on his lap. Robin was talking as quickly as his chewing would allow, Amanda was investigating Rhys's purse for anything interesting, and Nicholas was staring at the three of them as if he couldn't believe where he was.

It was where he belonged, though. Gwen thought back to what she'd learned that afternoon and had to shake her head.

She'd had but a handful of words with Nicholas's mother, but they were enough to identify Nicholas's father and how the event had come about. The poor girl had found herself carried back to Ayre from Segrave to be used for Alain's pleasure. The thought of that had set Gwen's teeth to grinding, but she knew she shouldn't have been surprised. It had been on the day of Lord Alain's nuptials, very late that evening, the girl had found herself meeting her fate, as it were. The man had been, however, so into his cups that he could hardly manage to keep his feet.

As Gwen had bent to hear the man's name whispered in her ear, she had fully expected for it to be Alain's.

It hadn't been.

Gwen looked at Rhys, then at Nicholas, searching for the similarity of features. It was there, but only if one looked very closely and if one knew what to look for. Perhaps things would change as the lad grew.

Gwen wondered if she should perhaps have been jealous of Nicholas's mother. To have Rhys in her arms for even a night . . .

But nay, Gwen had had him as well, and she had been his first. With any luck at all, she would be his last.

It was enough that Nicholas was found and rescued. Perhaps she would tell Rhys in time, for she very much suspected he wouldn't notice it himself. For all his skill, he was powerfully unobservant about some things.

"We go Fenwyck?" Amanda was asking Rhys.

"Well . . ." Rhys began slowly.

"We come," she said firmly, seeming to sense Rhys's hesitation.

"But—"

"We *come!*" she announced, her chin jutting out stubbornly. She turned a sunny smile on Nicholas. "And bring *him.*"

Gwen put her hand over her mouth to hide her smile. Rhys might have bested the most formidable knights France had to offer, but he stood not a chance against Amanda of Ayre.

Rhys sighed, defeated already. "If you wish."

Gwen left the kitchen and made her way up to her mother's solar to begin her own preparations. Perhaps she would take an extra wimple or two. Tight ones that would bind her ears more closely to her head. There was no reason to give Geoffrey more to mock her about than he would find on his own. She also packed her sharpest sewing needle and strapped her knife to her forearm. No sense in not being prepared.

She had little desire to halt at Fenwyck, but she could see the wisdom of it. Her father and Geoffrey's father had been comrades, if not friends, and her mother was certainly still in Geoffrey's good graces. It would give them a chance to rest before they continued on to the inevitable skirmish at Wyckham. And for all Gwen knew, Geoffrey might find Rhys a more tolerable neighbor than Alain's troops and be willing to help with the removal of her husband's men.

She also knew that Rhys had hopes that Geoffrey might speak kindly of him to the king. Gwen had little confidence in such a thing, but perhaps in this case Rhys was using his imagination more than she did. All she could imagine up in her heart was a score of ways to humiliate Geoffrey before he returned the favor.

By the saints, she did not relish the thought of the journey. And to think she had considered three years of waiting for Rhys to be disturbing.

She put her hands over her ears in one last attempt to train them, and continued on her way to her mother's solar.

30

Rhys thought he actually might have to use his sword on Geoffrey of Fenwyck this time.

Assuming, of course, that Gwen didn't get to the man first.

Rhys sat on his horse just inside Fenwyck's gates—and he knew he was damned fortunate to even have gotten that far—and struggled to remind himself of all the reasons why taking his sword and heaving it through Fenwyck's heart would be ill-advised. He would be killing one of John's favorite, if not double-crossing, barons. He would be killing one of Gwen's childhood acquaintances—though he was certain they all still remembered her time in the piggery and Gwen would feel no regret at all if she never had to look Geoffrey in the face again. Unfortunately Rhys had to admit that he would also be killing a potential ally who could very possibly help him convince John that gold in his coffers was reason enough to aid Rhys in further bribing the necessary clergy to see Gwen's liberation accomplished.

But at the moment, all Rhys could do was stare at the way Fenwyck was slobbering over Gwen's hand and imagine up in his heart a score of very painful ways to end the man's life.

Gwen looked about her in a panic. Her mother only shrugged and smiled. Gwen searched for Rhys. She met his eyes and he could hear her thoughts as clearly as if she'd been shouting them at him: *Get him away from me!* She had vowed she would do all in her power not to offend, that Rhys might fare better with Geoffrey, but Rhys could tell she was using every smidgen of control she possessed not to draw her sword and do damage with it.

Unfortunately, he felt the same compulsion. In truth he couldn't blame Geoffrey for the less than friendly welcome. One did not travel with thirty ill-mannered mercenaries and expect to find gates flung open in welcome. But by the saints, it wasn't as if Gwen's mother hadn't brought several of her own guardsmen wearing her late husband's colors. She had even sent a man ahead with tidings of their impending arrival. Geoffrey had known who had come knocking. It had been a discourtesy directed at him personally, and Rhys was swallowing a great lump of pride to ignore it. Never mind that he would have left his men outside the gates in any case. That Geoffrey had come close to denying him entrance as well was the true insult.

But there he sat, contemplating his next action—and that action would have to come quickly, before Gwen had a good look at Geoffrey and his pleasing face. Rhys knew Gwen's heart was true, but 'twas rumored that the sight of Geoffrey had made more than one strong-minded maid lose her resolve. At least that was the rumor, and it was one Rhys couldn't be completely sure that Geoffrey hadn't started himself.

Of course none of Geoffrey's supposed charm would have mattered had the man been every day of fifty and as corpulent as Gwen's former guardian. Unfortunately, Geoffrey was fair-haired and fair featured and damn him if he didn't look as fit as if he trained regularly with his men—which Rhys suspected he did. He was also a widower and surely the most sought-after of nobles in the realm. Why some clever father hadn't ensnared the man for a son-in-law before now was surely a mystery. Rhys could only regret the oversight as it surely left him with trouble he didn't need.

Such as all that slobber on the back of Gwen's hand.

And now on her palm!

"Ahem," Rhys said pointedly.

Geoffrey looked up narrowly. "Something stuck in your throat, friend?"

There was little warmth coming from Fenwyck, and Rhys understood why completely, as he had little to return. Geoffrey obviously still had very vivid memories of their last encounter. Rhys dismounted in the muddy courtyard and in the next heartbeat had Gwen's hand disentangled from Geoffrey's. He congratulated himself on limiting his actions to that when he would have rather been clouting the randy whoreson on the nose.

"I daresay the lady Gwennelyn needs a cup as well," Rhys said, pointedly tucking Gwen's hand into her own belt. "Long ride, you know."

Geoffrey deftly untucked Gwen's hand and slipped it into the crook of his arm. "How right you are, *Sir* Rhys."

The emphasis was, of course, on Rhys's lack of station. Rhys had to remind himself that he was indeed lord of Wyckham. Never mind that he was no baron as Geoffrey was with numerous holdings to his name. He was a lord and would inform Geoffrey of it at his earliest convenience. It would do little to impress Fenwyck, but Rhys suspected he himself would have his pride eased a bit.

"Here I have kept our lady outside when I could have been looking after her more carefully inside the house," Geoffrey continued. He looked at Rhys coolly. "I'm certain you'll want to take your ease in the garrison hall. After," he added with a look at Gwen's guard, "you see to your men."

Rhys gritted his teeth. It wasn't as if he was Fenwyck's equal in station, but he was certainly above the garrison hall.

"Rhys," Gwen began.

"Never fear, lady," Geoffrey said smoothly. "I will see

to you. And to your lovely mother. Lady Joanna, 'tis ever a pleasure to see you."

"But—" Gwen protested.

"You will come to no harm in my care."

Gwen was still spluttering as Geoffrey led her and her mother away.

"Montgomery!" Rhys shouted, spinning to look for his friend. The sooner his business was seen to, the sooner Gwen could be rescued. "Montgomery," he said again, "see to the men!"

Montgomery had already swung down and seemed to be preparing to do just that. He stopped and stared at Rhys. "All but them," he said, pointing to the Fitzgeralds. "I'm not going near that pair."

Rhys supposed he couldn't actually blame him. He wasn't looking forward to it overmuch himself, but the twins would have to be tended eventually.

Rhys walked over to where the Fitzgeralds lay strapped to their horses, completely oblivious to their surroundings. He could only assume they were still exhausted from all the puking upon flora and fauna they'd done during the first few days of the journey.

The Fitzgeralds did not travel well by horse.

In fact, he suspected the Fitzgeralds did not travel well by any means other than their own two feet.

He approached Jared's horse, then laid a hand on the man and shook him gently.

"Jared," he called softly.

Jared lifted his head, moaned, then vomited down the front of Rhys's tunic.

Well, at least one of them was awake. Rhys loosened the ropes binding Jared to his horse and made a token effort of catching the larger man as he fell facefirst down into the mud. Satisfied Jared would eventually find his feet now said feet were on solid ground, Rhys turned his attentions to Connor. At least with this twin he managed to avoid finding himself in Connor's sights, as it were. Connor fell off his horse into Rhys's arms. Rhys let him slip down gently into the muck.

"I imagine there's supper inside when you're up to it," he announced to both fallen warriors.

Groans were his only answer.

Rhys looked about him for his squire only to find John standing a healthy distance away. It was, to be sure, the first time the lad hadn't been within arm's length for years.

"See to their mounts and ours," Rhys instructed.

"And them?" John asked, looking powerfully afraid he might be asked to act as nursemaid.

"You could help them up when you've tended their horseflesh. I'd leave them be until then."

John didn't have to hear that twice. He was heading toward the stables with four horses in tow before Rhys could give him any more instructions. Rhys turned back to his fallen comrades and wondered if he shouldn't perhaps at least remain with them a bit longer. Then he noticed that Jared was feeling the mud tentatively with one hand. A bleary blue eye opened and stared at the soil closest to it with something akin to astonishment, as if the man couldn't quite believe he was on the ground and it wasn't moving. He gurgled something that Rhys could only assume was some sort of prayer of gratitude.

Connor seemed to be making the same patting motions with his hand and Rhys relaxed. They would realize soon enough that they were no longer atop their steeds. As he was certain they hadn't eaten in days, or rather they had but they hadn't enjoyed the benefits of the food for days, there was no doubt there would be seeking Fenwyck's table soon enough. All that remained was for him to put on less fragrant clothing and find his own place at Fenwyck's table.

Sitting in between, of course, Fenwyck's lord and his quarry.

"I need him alive," Rhys repeated to himself as he crossed the courtyard. "Unmaimed. Coherent."

He had the feeling he would be reminding himself of those things quite often in the near future.

• • •

It took him longer to clean himself up than he would have liked. At least an hour had passed before he entered the great hall, let his eyes adjust to the gloom, and saw what he'd feared he might.

Geoffrey sat between Gwen and her mother looking as smug as if he'd just, well, managed to seat himself between the two most beautiful women in the realm. Joanna was lovely, as always, and Gwen was so fair Rhys thought he might expire on the spot just from the sight of her. Expiring, however, seemed to be the last thing on Fenwyck's mind. Fawning and petting seemed to be more in his thoughts. He had obviously matured when it came to how he chose to treat women. Rhys had liked him better before.

And he hadn't liked him very much then.

"Swordplay?" Geoffrey's gasp of surprise echoed in the great hall. "With these soft fingers? Lady, you jest with me! Lady Joanna, tell me your daughter—and I can hardly believe that she is actually your daughter, for you are far too young for such a thing to be true—"

Rhys rolled his eyes in disgust.

"Tell me that the lady Gwennelyn jests about wielding a blade. Such a delicate maid about such an ugly business!"

Rhys saw more finger fondleage than he would have liked as he looked at the table. He was half tempted to vault over it and land in Geoffrey's lap. With any luck a weapon of some sort might come loose in the vaulting and Geoffrey would find himself accidentally, and surely regrettably, impaled in some strategic spot. Not a fatal wound, though. Rhys did have a use for the man eventually.

He cleared his throat purposefully as he approached the table.

Geoffrey looked up and a dark scowl came over his features. "I believe, Sir Knight, that you—"

"Were captain of my lady's guard," Rhys said as he rounded the end of the table, "and am now lord of Wyckham. If I am not welcome at your table, I will at least stand behind it and offer my lady the security of my presence."

Geoffrey looked at him in surprise. "Wyckham?"

"As of his twenty-sixth year," Joanna said smoothly, "which is a wonderful thing, is it not?"

Rhys suspected Geoffrey was thinking it to be anything but that.

"Surely he can sit with us," Joanna said, giving Geoffrey a smile that would have knocked any breathing man to his knees, "don't you think, my lord Fenwyck?"

Geoffrey was not unaffected. He blinked as if he'd been stunned by a sharp blow to the head. Rhys took the opportunity to slip into a chair next to Gwen before Geoffrey could gainsay him. Geoffrey finally roused himself from his stupor and turned back to Gwen. "Ah," he said, "swords . . . wasn't it?" he asked, blinking stupidly.

"She's quite the swordsman," Rhys said, leaning over Gwen to look at Geoffrey. "Perhaps you would care to face her over blades." *And perhaps she will cut off something important, and it will distract you enough to keep your mind off licking her fingers for a bloody heartbeat or two!*

"Tempting," Geoffrey managed. He looked at Gwen and seemed to focus again on her. "What an afternoon that could turn out to be."

Gwen was looking more tempted by the thought of skewering Geoffrey on her sword than was good for her, so Rhys distracted her by removing the trencher she was sharing with Geoffrey and placing it between himself and his lady. He took his own freshly dressed slab of bread and tossed it in front of Fenwyck's lord.

"You look to have a hearty appetite," Rhys said shortly.

"Aye, I do," Geoffrey said, seemingly finding the energy to dredge up an appreciative glance for Gwen. "For many things."

Gwen was beginning to look as nauseated as the Fitzgerald brothers.

"I do as well," Rhys said. "But since the lady Gwennelyn is in *my* care, I am careful not to overindulge. I would suggest, my lord, that perhaps you follow my example.''

Fenwyck looked at him and apparently finally realized Rhys had taken a place at the table. He glared. ''I think I can choose my own meal well enough, friend.''

''In this instance, I think you would be wise to take my advice on the matter.''

''And who are you—''

''I am her—''

''Oh, by the saints,'' Gwen exclaimed, ''will you both cease!''

''Please do,'' Joanna agreed.

''We need him alive and unirritated,'' Gwen muttered under breath. ''The saints help me remember it!''

''I think you both should keep yourselves to your own trenchers,'' Joanna continued, obviously striving for a lighter tone. ''Perhaps Gwen and I would be safer eating directly off the table.''

''Best wash that hand first, Gwen,'' Rhys grumbled.

Fenwyck scowled. ''Our good Sir Rhys is powerfully protective for being just the captain of your guard, my lady Gwennelyn.''

''As I said before, I am no longer captain of her guard,'' Rhys said, resurrecting thoughts of a sharp weapon through some part of Geoffrey's form.

''Then what interest do you have in the girl?'' Geoffrey demanded. ''A simple knight does not—''

Gwen slapped her hand down on the table so forcefully that Rhys, as well as Geoffrey, jumped. She glared at Geoffrey.

''He is my love,'' she began angrily.

''Your *what?*'' Geoffrey gasped.

Rhys watched as Gwen reached for his hand and clasped it between both her own. At least 'twas better that both her hands rest there than be free to be captured by Geoffrey's.

''I love him,'' Gwen said distinctly, ''and he loves me.''

Geoffrey's mouth worked, but no sound issued forth.

Rhys thought, however, that Geoffrey's eyes might fall from his head at any moment.

"We plan to wed."

"You plan to wed," Geoffrey echoed in disbelief.

"And then we'll likely need your aid, though I've no mind to beg you for it. Perhaps Rhys isn't a baron with your lands and power, but he is a good man . . ."

Rhys listened to her list his virtues and watched the realizations enter Geoffrey's eyes. Rhys was now, whether he liked it or not, the lord of land that bordered Fenwyck. Rhys would be, whether Geoffrey cared for it or not, Gwen's husband.

Geoffrey seemed to be having a great deal of trouble swallowing it all.

"And you would actually have this," Geoffrey pointed at Rhys and looked at Gwen in disbelief, "this . . ."

Later Rhys knew that if Fenwyck had finished that thought, he would have been recovering from a potentially fatal wound, but the man was spared by a commotion at the door. Rhys turned his attentions there, fully expecting to see the Fitzgerald twins stumbling inside, perhaps covering others with the contents of their poor bellies.

Instead what he saw was a man so exhausted, Rhys marveled that he was still moving. The man fell to his knees in the rushes, panting. Rhys found himself on his feet and walking around the table almost before the thought of doing so took shape in his mind. Geoffrey had obviously had the same idea, for they collided on their way to the door. Rhys growled at Fenwyck, received a growl in return, then continued on his way, Geoffrey keeping pace with him. They approached the man together.

"My lord," the man said, panting, "there is a fire. *Was* a fire."

"Fire?" Geoffrey demanded. "Where?"

The man bowed his head and continued to suck in great gulps of air. "A fire," he gasped. "Too great to stem."

"Where?" Geoffrey asked again. "Fenwyck?"

"Aye," the man rasped, "there, too."

"Damnation!" Geoffrey bellowed.

"The rain quenched it," the man wheezed, "but not before it burned a field or two of yours, my lord. I saw the fires from a distance and rode to see. A great amount of smoke."

"Aye, well, that's a fire for you," Geoffrey said impatiently. "Who set the bloody blaze?"

"Didn't recognize them," the man answered. "But there were a handful of them riding hard away from the keep. There's nothing left of that now."

Geoffrey frowned. "The keep? What keep?"

"Nothing left of any of the fields surrounding the castle, either," the man continued. "The fire burned itself out there."

"By all the sweet saints above," Rhys exclaimed, unable to help himself. "Where is the bloody fire?"

The man looked at him and blinked.

"Why, Wyckham, of course."

31

Wyckham.

Gwen heard the man's words, saw Rhys reel as if he'd been struck, then watched as he began to weave. She thought he just might faint.

"Wyckham?" he repeated, but the man didn't answer him. He turned to look around him, as if he searched for aid. His gaze fell upon Gwen. "Wyckham?" he asked again, as if he simply could not take in what he'd heard.

Geoffrey waved him aside. "Your problem, friend, not mine. Now, Edlred, what is this of damage to my fields?"

Rhys stumbled toward the door. Gwen leaped up from the table and rushed after him. Geoffrey caught her by the arm and stopped her.

"I daresay it may rain again, lady. Perhaps you would be better served—"

"Let me go," she said, jerking her arm from his. "He's going to go see the ruin. I can't let him go alone."

"Of course you can—"

"You fool, that is his land!"

"I know, but—"

"The fire was purposely set. The saints only know who has been left behind to harm him!"

"Now, Lady Gwennelyn . . ." Geoffrey began.

"Mother," Gwen called, "please rescue me from this imbecile! I must go after Rhys."

She managed to get out the door and into the courtyard before Geoffrey caught up with her again. Gwen ignored him and looked about her for the stables. She watched in consternation as Rhys ran from the stables, pulling his mount along behind him. He vaulted into the saddle and spurred his horse through the gates. It took her no time at all to confirm her decision. He couldn't go alone. If he did, the saints only knew what might happen to him.

Gwen ran across the courtyard and was almost plowed over by John, who didn't wait to leave the stables before he had mounted his own horse. She caught her breath, then made her way down to the proper stall. Fortunately three years at Segrave had done more than just provide her with sheets for another marriage bed. Though the twins had been of no use when it came to equine endeavors—and now she understood why—Montgomery had been susceptible to bullying and had therefore taught her a great deal about horses. She'd even come to the point of being able to saddle one with moderate skill.

She put all her skills to good use now. It took her longer than she would have liked, but Geoffrey was of no help— not that she would have asked him anyway. He was far too busy ordering his lads to see to the saddling of mounts for himself and several guardsmen. The only thing that remotely cheered her was the sight of Montgomery retrieving his horse. At least she would have companionship she could bear.

"How far is Wyckham still, do you think?" she asked him as they left the stables together.

"A good day's ride," Montgomery said grimly. "Far enough that we should take along provisions."

Gwen found her way blocked again by Geoffrey. He frowned at her.

"This is very ill-advised, lady," he said. "He will likely collect his mercenaries on his way, and I think it imprudent that you be amongst such company."

"And yours is any safer?" she demanded.

He seemed to be searching for some return for that. Gwen was certain it would take more time than she had at her disposal, so she tried to push him aside.

"Out of my way," she commanded. "I've things to do."

He remained stubbornly in front of her. "I don't understand how the land came to be his," he said.

"It was my sire's," Gwen said shortly. "It became Alain's upon my marriage to him. Alain's father Bertram commanded that Alain give it to Rhys upon Rhys's twenty-sixth year as reward for his faithful service."

Geoffrey grunted. "Then I suppose 'tis more than simply Sir Rhys boasting to impress you."

"Get out of my way," she said distinctly, "lest you force me to draw my blade and use it upon your sorry form."

"The saints preserve me from that," he said as he hastily stepped aside. He cleared his throat. "I'll come as well."

She paused and looked at him. She didn't want to converse any more with him, but she would be the first to admit that he was, after all, a powerful man with many knights at his disposal. And she had promised Rhys she would be agreeable to the wretch.

"Why would you come?" she asked reluctantly.

"I'll need to see what's been done to my fields."

Of course. It wasn't as if he would come along to help Rhys. "Do as you like," Gwen said, tugging on her horse. "I could not care less."

"Of course you couldn't. Provisions!" Geoffrey bellowed at one of his men as he halted in the courtyard. "See to them and follow us as quickly as may be."

Gwen found her mother in the small group gathered near the keep and wasn't surprised to see the children there with her. Robin looked to be itching to go, that much Gwen could surmise by the firm hold Joanna had upon his small person. Amanda was clutching her grandmother's skirts. Nicholas stood a few paces back, looking very uncertain.

Gwen spared a brief moment to hug all three little ones, then thank her mother for their care.

"Back soon?" Amanda asked, looking worried that such might not be the case.

"Aye, love," Gwen said, bending to kiss the small, plump cheek. "Very soon. We must fetch Sir Rhys, then we'll be right back. Watch after the boys until then, aye?"

Amanda looked at Robin and turned her nose up. She espied Nicholas and immediately released Joanna's skirts and advanced upon her prey. Satisfied that the children would survive her absence, Gwen mounted her horse and left the bailey.

She soon found that Geoffrey seemed determined to ride beside her, so she did her best to concentrate on the view before her. It was either ignore him or say something she would regret. With the morning Rhys had had already, she knew he wouldn't appreciate her damaging his chances for flattering Fenwyck.

"How odd that someone should set fire to the land."

"Odd?" she echoed. "You fool, 'twas deliberate!"

He looked at her narrowly. "I am no fool, lady—"

"You misunderstood what your man said, then, and if that doesn't make you a fool, I don't know what does." She looked pointedly at the gap in his teeth for good measure. By Saint Michael's crossed eyes, what had possessed Rhys to think this oaf could possibly be of any aid to them? He was rumored to know of all that passed in England. How could he not know of the business at Wyckham?

Geoffrey scowled. "Very well then, lady, if you are so wise, who was it who set the fire? Alain?"

"His troops were upon the land, daring Rhys to take it from under them."

That, at least, seemingly captured Geoffrey's attention. "In truth?"

"Alain said as much to Rhys three years ago. Hence his long journeying in France to obtain an army."

"Surely Alain would not do such a thing," Geoffrey said, though Gwen suspected by the hesitation with which he spoke that he believed it readily enough.

"I doubt 'twas his idea, either to encamp upon it, or to burn it. He hasn't the imagination for something this foul."

"Who then?"

"Rollan, of course."

Geoffrey did not look at all surprised. "I am always amazed by the depth of Rollan's spite. How Bertram sired such a knave is a mystery. Alain is almost as disagreeable."

"I thought you found Alain's company quite to your liking." She glared at him. "You never spared any breath on my behalf at Segrave when he would disparage me."

He shrugged. "You were insufferably smug. Why would I have wanted to defend you?"

"Me?" she gasped. "Smug?"

"Aye. Forever were you about some mischief at my expense."

"I only reported upon the mischief you combined."

"Smugly," he agreed.

"At least I had a large enough store of wits to warrant such arrogance."

"And large enough ears," he said with a nasty smile that reminded her of all the reasons she truly did not care for the man riding next to her.

"At least my ears do not show when I open my mouth," she countered. "I can hide them with a wimple."

He glared at her and she returned his glare. She would have truly given him full measure of her irritation, but the smell of smoke was faint in the air and the sight of it was clear on the horizon. That was enough to persuade her to cease her journey down this path of insults. Best to do so anyway before she completely humiliated Geoffrey. He would, of course, never best her. She had imagined up in her mind countless encounters with the man and in every one, she had come away the victor. It would be no different this time and that would only serve to perhaps convince him that Rhys did not deserve his help. Gwen gathered all her strength of will and held her tongue.

"What does he think to do?" Geoffrey asked, obviously

having come to the same conclusion that fighting was pointless. "Stand on his soil and stamp out the remaining flames himself?"

"He'll grieve," Gwen returned shortly. "What else can he do?"

"Retaliate?"

"How? By attacking Ayre?"

Geoffrey chewed on that, but said nothing.

Gwen turned away and concentrated on the smoke in the distance. She should have known Geoffrey would be of little aid. They would have to invent a new scheme. Perhaps there would be something left behind, something that would point to who had done this thing. Then they would go to the king and give him the tale. Perhaps it would be enough to convince him that Alain was an unfit lord for all her lands and that they should be given to another.

Rhys, for instance.

It was dusk when she finally caught up with him, though they had left Fenwyck in the late morning. Gwen had hated to use her mount thusly, but it was either that or lose Rhys's trail.

She dismounted and left Montgomery to deal with their small company. Rhys stood some paces away, alone and unmoving. She approached quietly. Rhys continued to stand as still as stone. Gwen half wondered if he'd even marked her arrival. Then she stopped at his side and looked up at his face.

His cheeks were wet with tears.

She slipped her hand into his. When he gave no sign of noticing even that, she took his hand in both of hers and merely stood next to him silently, wishing she could take away his grief.

"Oh, Rhys," she said softly. "I'm so sorry."

Without warning, he pulled her in front of him, wrapped his arms around her, and buried his face in her hair.

His shoulders shook, but only once.

Gwen put her arms around him and held him tightly.

"I'm so sorry," she repeated. It was all she could think of to say.

She wasn't certain how long they stood there thusly, with his silent tears slipping across her temple and down her neck. It could have been hours. Finally, though, he lifted his head and looked down at her. She could scarce see him for the lack of light, but what she could see was the bleakness in his gray eyes.

"Will you know what frightens me the most?" he whispered.

She waited, mute.

"If they—Alain and Rollan—can do that to land that I loved a great deal, what might they do to what I love the most?"

She swallowed, hard. "I've thought on that as well."

He gripped her by the shoulders. "You will not leave my sight, do you hear me? Not for a moment. The saints only know what either of them will think to do next."

"As you will, Rhys."

"And the children," he continued. "You'll keep them near, and I'll see to you all."

"Of course, Rhys."

He dragged his sleeve across his eyes and swept the landscape with a disbelieving glance.

"Am I the only one here who cannot believe what I'm looking at?" he asked. He looked down at her. "Alain did this, don't you think? Have I lost what little wits still remain me? Could someone else have wrought this to spite me?"

She shook her head. "You know it was Alain and Rollan together, Rhys."

"I wish I had proof."

"They might confess it, given enough incentive."

Rhys laughed shortly, without humor. "What am I to do? Use hot irons?"

She shrugged. "Perhaps Geoffrey will offer his aid."

Rhys sighed, and it sounded as if it had come straight from his soul. "We couldn't be that fortunate. Besides, it doesn't help us now. Gwen, I don't see how we can survive here. We've nothing left of the crops and 'tis too late to replant this year. And we would have to rebuild the keep.'' He looked at her bleakly. ''I don't have the gold for this.''

''We'll live in a tent, then.''

He laughed bitterly. ''Oh, aye, and freeze our sorry arses off in the winter. What kind of protection can I offer you in a tent, my love? I want walls about you so strong that not even John and his armies can breach them. I want no thief coming in to steal you away, or to make off with Robin or Amanda.''

''Or Nicholas,'' she added.

He smiled faintly. ''You've become fond of that lad.''

''Aye,'' she agreed, ''I have.''

''The three of them, then,'' Rhys said. ''And most important, you. I'll not leave you unprotected.''

Gwen looked around her and could see that indeed restoring Wyckham to anything livable would be an undertaking of immense proportions. And it would only be done at great expense. But how much less dear would improving the land she was thinking of be?

''Rhys,'' she said slowly, ''there is another choice.''

''Another choice? What?''

''I never thought to speak of this before, as my sire always told me the land was worth nothing.''

He waited.

''I have land that is mine,'' she continued. ''It remained mine even after wedding Alain.''

He started to frown. ''And?''

''And I never thought it was of any value. It is another week's hard ride north of here—at least so I've been told. My sire thought that perhaps I might will it to an abbey at some point in my life, so he left its disposal in my hands. I think it must be quite a barren and wild place, for it borders those barbaric northern lands.''

''Barren?'' he asked with a dry smile. ''Can it possibly be any more desolate than this?''

''The saints only know.'' She sighed. ''I should have

perhaps told you sooner. I just never thought it would be of any use to either of us.''

"Land is land.''

"Is it?'' she asked, nodding to the scorched field next to her. "This may look rather inviting after your first view of Artane.''

"Artane,'' he mused. " 'Tis a good name, I suppose.''

"Sounds a bit on the bleak side to me, but 'tis perhaps worth a look.''

"Perhaps it will be so bleak no one will trouble us.'' He laughed suddenly. "John, Alain, and the whole of England on one hand and barbarians from the north on the other. By the saints, lady, our life together is destined to be a troubled one.''

"I was actually thinking it might be just the place for us. Perhaps we will go north and everyone will forget of our existence.''

He looked down at her and pursed his lips. "When I have snatched the most beautiful woman in England and carried her north to some bleak wasteland to ensconce her in a keep I cannot afford to build? Somehow, Gwen, I think forgetting about us is the last thing anyone will do.''

"If the king thought you might be willing to defend his borders, perhaps he would build you a keep.''

"And likely install a permanent garrison there to keep me in check. Many thanks, but I'll find a way to build it myself.''

She shook her head. "Not another handful of years on the continent warring, Rhys. I cannot bear that.''

"There may be no other way.''

"We'll find one,'' she insisted. "Either that or you will take me with you and I will be the one to guard your back.''

He looked as panicked as if she'd suggested she would be the one to single-handedly defend the English border.

"We'll find another way,'' he agreed promptly. "Wonderful idea. Wish I'd been the one to think of it.''

She patted him on the back and smiled up at him. "Then

let us see to our journey north. We'll likely want to return to Fenwyck for stores before we go."

He nodded with a smile, then she saw him look at his land again. His expression sobered.

"This is still mine," he said softly.

"Aye, and you've earned it. It will recover, Rhys. I've always heard there was good soil here. You'll see the day when it's well planted and the keep rebuilt."

He sighed, bent his head, and rested his forehead against hers.

"Thank you."

"For what?"

He smiled at her. "For the hope." He raised his head. "Come, lady, and let us see what bleak bit of ground your wily sire left to you. And let us hope Alain hasn't been there before us."

Gwen watched him for the rest of that day, and then the pair of days that followed after they returned to Fenwyck to prepare for their journey. And despite the size of his loss, he seemed to be taking it remarkably well.

When he thought people were watching him, of course.

It was those unguarded moments that broke her heart, those moments when he seemed to think he was unobserved. It was then that she saw how deeply Alain's desecration had wounded him. It was hard enough to have been denied Bertram's gift for so many years, but to watch that gift so senselessly destroyed was surely another matter entirely.

It was at just such a time that he caught her watching him from behind a tree in Geoffrey's garden. He had been sitting in the sunshine on a bench, his hands dangling between his knees and his head bowed. Gwen had been sure she'd made no noise, but evidently his hearing was better than she credited it for being, for he lifted his head and looked straight at her. His expression of grief didn't change, but he did hold out his hand for her.

She emerged from her hiding place and came to sit next to him on the bench.

"I'm sorry," she said. "I can't seem to say anything else."

"I wasn't thinking on the land."

She blinked. "Then what?"

"You," he said simply. "And how much worse it would hurt if something happened to you." He smiled sadly. "I thought I knew how much I loved you, Gwen, until this happened. All I could think about as I stared at those ravaged fields was how much worse I would feel had it been you to suffer such an injury."

"I won't."

"Aye, you won't," he said calmly, "because you will never be in a position to be harmed thusly. I cannot believe I left you for three years in the company of those puking Vikings."

"The Fitzgeralds are remarkably skilled when they've both feet on *terra firma*."

He looked unconvinced. "We will also make do with the gold we have," he continued, "that I need not tourney in France again. If I must kneel and lick John's boots for a keep of my own, then I will do so. I daresay he won't be coming north that often to see how his garrison fares."

"With any luck, he won't."

He rose and pulled her up with him. "Why don't you go rest for the afternoon. We've a long ride before us on the morrow."

"I feel fine—"

"And cease with your spying upon me, Gwen."

"I haven't been spying."

He lifted one eyebrow as he pursed his lips. "Yesterday you had cobwebs in your hair, and today you've enough twigs therein for a bird's nest."

She would have argued, but he suddenly took her face in his hands, bent his head, and kissed her. It was a sweet, gentle kiss that completely distracted her from what she'd been intending to say.

He lifted his head and smiled down at her. "Agreed?"

"Agreed," she said, hoping that he didn't realize she would have agreed to near anything at that moment.

"Then come, my love, and let us be about the rest of our day. I, for one, am actually relishing a small journey north. We never know what we'll find."

They started back to the keep only to find Geoffrey in their way. Gwen glared at him and he glared back at her before he turned his attentions to Rhys.

"I'll help," he said shortly.

Gwen almost fell down in shock. Even Rhys seemed greatly surprised by the offer.

"You will?" he asked.

"I have little love for Alain."

"And that is your reason for helping?" Gwen demanded. "What if it wasn't Alain who did the deed?"

"I am willing to at least consider the notion that he was behind it. And if I discover that 'tis the truth, indeed, I will not hold him guiltless."

Rhys seemingly had no hesitation about Geoffrey's motives. "Good," he said shortly. "I'll need all the aid I can have."

Gwen was still unconvinced. "That is all?" she asked. "You've no other reason to aid us?"

He looked at her and for the first time ever she had a small smile of camaraderie from him. "He bedded my cook's daughter the last time he was here. Haven't had a decent meal since."

Rhys laughed shortly. "Poor Fenwyck. 'Tis nothing more than you deserve for inviting him to visit."

"I *didn't* invite him," Geoffrey grumbled. "He caught me in a hospitable moment. I should have listened to my first instinct, which was to raise the drawbridge against him."

"And yet you let us in," Gwen said suspiciously.

He smiled. "You and your mother both at my table? Only a fool would deny himself such beauty."

He'd made no more mention of her ears, and he didn't seem to be looking at them overmuch. Gwen felt Rhys elbow her in the ribs and decided that perhaps 'twas time to call the battle a standoff and leave it at that. It was likely as close as Geoffrey would ever come to an apology for his slandering of her while she was young. She could perhaps forgive a little. Besides, Geoffrey had seemingly cast in his lot with Rhys.

Perhaps things had begun to turn their way at last.

32

A se'nnight later Rhys sat atop his horse and shook his head, unable to believe what he was looking at.

Artane was not at all what Rhys had been expecting.

For one thing, the only thing that could even remotely be termed empty was the remnants of a keep that rested atop a ridge that had a commanding view of both ocean and land. The keep was nothing more than a wooden shell that consumed only a fraction of the space that could have been allotted to such a dwelling.

What a crafty old whoreson William of Segrave had been.

He looked to his right to see Gwen wearing a look of complete astonishment. It was the same look she had worn for the past three days, the three days during which they had traveled only partway over her land. She'd been certain they would arrive to find it nothing but wasteland. She had apologized in advance scores of times while they had made their preparations to come north. While Rhys had been organizing his men, Gwen had been interrogating her mother—with no success. Either Joanna had not been able or hadn't wanted to divulge any details. Now Rhys understood why. What a surprise it had been, and an exceedingly pleasant one at that.

"You were so right," Rhys drawled. "Pitiful, barren bit of soil this is."

She looked at him, still gaping. "I had no idea!"

"I imagine your sire did," Rhys said, feeling his smile turn into a grin. "By the saints, Gwen, the man had a fine instinct for a good jest."

"It is *enormous*," she managed.

"Aye," he said in wonder, "such vastness I've never seen outside the Aquitaine. Not quite as lush, of course, but the soil seems workable enough."

"We can only hope Alain went straight home and didn't see this."

"He wouldn't have bothered."

"Rollan might have made the effort."

Rhys shook his head. "My scouts have seen nothing, and believe me they would love to capture him. And then Alain would have spent the rest of his life wondering what had happened to his brother, for he never would have seen him again."

Gwen shuddered. "I wonder about the company you keep, Rhys. How does your mother feel about this?"

"She's praying mightily for their souls and mine, believe me."

"I don't doubt it." She looked toward the shore. "Shall we go up the hill and see the view?"

"Aye, gladly."

It was a perfect place for a keep. Rhys had known it from the moment he'd seen the bluff, but setting foot on the crest of the hill reconfirmed it. The knoll stretched down to the sea in hills of sand that no army would be able to wade through with less than great difficulty. Behind them, a rocky cliff separated the top of the hill from the floor of the land. Beyond that was land that had lain fallow for the saints only knew how long. Rhys suspected it would yield plentifully when it was finally planted.

"Listen," Gwen breathed.

At first it was hard to hear anything but Robin's and

Nicholas's shouts of delight as they rolled themselves down the hillside. Rhys spared a brief moment to be glad that Joanna had kept Amanda behind. He had visions of cleaning sand out from behind her ears for days. At least the boys he could merely dunk in a barrel of rainwater and consider them washed.

Once the boys had rolled away far enough, Rhys found he could listen in peace. And it was then that he noticed the sound of the waves against the shore.

Gwen slipped her hand into his and stared out over the sea.

"Bliss," she whispered. "Surely my father must have come here and known it would please me."

"I suspect he did, my love," Rhys said quietly. "And if not him, surely your mother knew."

She looked up at him and her eyes were full of wonder. "Will you build us a keep here? Right on this spot where we may hear the sound of the sea?"

He smiled and reached over to push strands of hair back out of her face. "If you do not mind my building a castle on your land."

"Count it as my dowry. That will soothe the wagging tongues on both sides of the sea. Think on your reputation should you marry me merely for love."

"It would ruin me, certainly," he agreed.

"Then will this suit?"

"Aye, love," he said, "it will suit very well indeed."

"Then let us wander our land a bit and plan where the keep should go. Two baileys, don't you think? It should be much larger than Segrave, and we certainly should make Ayre look like a hovel. And then we must have a garden. I wonder what will grow this far north. We must needs question the friars at that abbey we passed on our way here."

"Seakirk," he supplied.

"Aye, there," she said, pulling him along with her as she walked the top of the hill. "They will surely know what we can grow successfully in this wasteland."

Rhys heard what she said and had to smile at her plots

and schemes for growing this herb and that, but at the same time he could hardly concentrate. It was so much more than he had expected. By the saints, it made Wyckham seem as large as a modest abbey pleasure garden. To think this all belonged to Gwen. No matter if she held it in her name for the rest of her life. If she would just be kind enough not to flinch when he built the most modern keep England had ever seen on her soil, he would be content.

"What do you think?"

Rhys realized she had stopped and was looking to him for some kind of response.

"Ah," he stalled, "very nice. Truly."

Her eyes narrowed. "You were not attending me."

"I was—"

"You were not. Roses, Rhys. We must see if roses will grow here. I've seen the ones brought back from the Crusades. Aye, I will have them here to please the eye as well as serve their medicinal purpose."

And off she went again, listing in detail the herbs she would need planted and then the flowers she would have for their beauty alone. But all Rhys could think about was stone, and a great amount of it. He would construct walls so thick, they would never be torn down. Gwen would be safe here, safe from Alain and safe from Rollan.

Rhys wondered just how much William of Segrave had known about his future son-in-law's character. Had he kept this whole plot of land secret for a specific purpose?

"—trees, don't you think?"

Rhys blinked. Then he winced at her glare. "My apologies, lady. I was thinking of stone."

"As in a wall around the garden? A fine idea, Rhys. You'll see to it, won't you?"

He bent his head and stole a brief kiss. "I'll see to it all, my love."

Gwen groaned suddenly. "Those lads will drive me daft. Robin! Nicholas! Do *not* go out into the sea thusly! Know you nothing of the beasties therein?" She stalked off to where she could no doubt be better heard bellowing her displeasure, casting an "I'll be back presently" at Rhys.

He watched her go, then turned his attentions back to the soil under his feet and the vastness surrounding him. He could see for miles. No army would come upon him unawares. No ships could attack without him having marked them well in advance. It was, undoubtedly, the perfect place to build a keep, and Rhys could only shake his head in wonder that John had not appropriated the land for the crown already.

And if the land was to be inherited by Gwen only, perhaps Rhys could go down on both knees, kiss John's crooked toes, and beg for fealty straight to the crown for it. As appealing as Wyckham was, it came with Alain as liege-lord, something Rhys was not relishing. Perhaps John would accept his sword, and his loyalty, for Artane and count himself fortunate to have someone trustworthy guarding his northern border.

Rhys stood with his feet firmly planted on goodly soil, heard the crash of the waves against the shore and the screaming of gulls as they wheeled in the air, and thought he just might weep from the wonder of it all.

This land could be his. And all he had to do to have it was win the one thing he wanted more than life itself.

Gwen.

And though there was no time like the present to begin, he found that he couldn't force himself to go confer with his mercenaries quite yet. Nor could he chase after his lady and join in the scolding of the two very wet lads who cavorted happily along the shore. All he could do was stand where he was and breathe deeply of the salt air and listen to the rumbling roar of the sea.

Land.

And Gwen to share it with.

Now all he had to do was see that it happened.

They camped on top of the hill for two days. Rhys could have stayed there forever, and so could the boys if their moans of frustration at leaving were any indication. Well, perhaps calling it two sets of moans wasn't exactly the way of it. Robin complained quite loudly. Nicholas bore up stoically under the burden of loss, though Rhys suspected he was every bit as disappointed as Robin was. As Rhys watched them have a final run down the hill, he vowed again that he would make certain Gwen kept her son.

Robin could be claimed as his. So could Nicholas. Considering that Gwen's annulment would make Robin a bastard as well, what was the difference between the two lads? Besides, Gwen had taken a great liking to Nicholas, and Rhys had to admit that he was growing fond of the lad as well. A man could do worse than to acquire a bride and two sons at the same time.

They returned as quickly as the horses could manage. Rhys could have traveled more quickly with just his mercenaries, but he didn't mind the slowness of the pace, for it gave him ample time to observe his surroundings and discover the lay of Gwen's land.

But he was relieved nonetheless to see Fenwyck in the distance. The sooner Gwen was free, the sooner the keep could be started. Rhys knew there was a wedding that would take place also in that time, but he'd spent so many years not thinking about it that it had become a habit. He would give it some thought after he'd secured John's and the archbishop's blessing.

He prayed he had enough gold for the like.

After seeing to the men and spending a few moments in the garden submitting to young Anne of Fenwyck's and Amanda's demands that he serve as a horse for their pleasure, Rhys finally made his way into Fenwyck's hall for a cold cup of ale and a bit of peace for thinking. He was unsurprised to see Fenwyck's lord hovering over Gwen like a persistent cloud.

"What I wouldn't give for a substantial gust of wind," he muttered as he accepted a cup from a servant. He car-

ried it to the high table and made Geoffrey a small bow.
"If I may sit?" he asked.

Asking permission would be another thing he would be
bloody happy never to do again.

Geoffrey looked at him with something akin to reluc-
tance. "I suppose if you must."

"Now, Geoffrey," Joanna chided gently from where she
sat on his left hand. "You've behaved so nicely the past
fortnight."

While I was away, Rhys noted wryly. He reached over
and pulled Gwen's hand from Geoffrey's. No traces of
spittle. So it would seem that Geoffrey of Fenwyck would
keep his head for another few days.

Geoffrey tried to pull her hand back, but Rhys held on
to it more firmly.

With a disgusted snort, Gwen retrieved both hands and
tucked them under her arms.

"You would think I was a roast fowl," she said.

"Give me your hand," Geoffrey said, "and I'll nibble
it to see—"

"Do and your life will end." Rhys couldn't believe the
words had come out of his own mouth, but there they were
and there was no taking them back now. Perhaps he'd
exhausted his store of patience more quickly than he'd
thought.

Joanna laughed. "Oh, by the saints, cease." It was the
same exasperated tone Rhys had heard her use with Robin
and Nicholas several times already that day. "If you cannot treat each other with kindness and respect, then please
take yourselves out to the lists and solve your differences
there."

Gwen looked as disgusted as her mother sounded, and
Rhys began to feel as immature as Robin himself. He felt
somewhat better, however, when she turned the same look
of disgust on Geoffrey.

"Harumph," Rhys said. "Well, then."

"Indeed," Geoffrey said, sounding equally as disgruntled.

"Rhys," Joanna said, leaning forward to look at him,

"what are your plans now, love? Are we for Segrave, or will you have us remain here?"

Rhys felt, unaccountably, a rush of pleasure go through him. Never mind that he was not Gwen's husband, nor Joanna's son-in-law. That she should accord him such a courtesy despite his lack of rights was a sweet thing indeed.

"Well, my lady," he said, "I plan to send a messenger to my grandfather today. I must needs travel to London to meet him there and grovel before the king, but I daresay 'tis best neither you nor my lady accompany me there."

"In case you lose your head?" Gwen asked grimly.

He smiled briefly. "I will lose nothing and will instead come away the victor, you'll see. All you must do is trust me."

"And remain here?" Gwen shot Geoffrey a frown.

He held up his hands innocently. "I have said nothing to you, my lady Gwennelyn, neither about your ears or your height."

"My height?" Gwen echoed. "What is amiss with my height?"

Geoffrey very quickly, and very wisely, took hold of a leg of roast fowl and began to chew industriously upon it.

Gwen turned to Rhys and glared. "Are you to leave me here then to face this?"

"I will travel more quickly alone," Rhys offered.

"Best be quick about it," Geoffrey said from behind his joint. "I may need a rescue." He shook his head. "I cannot believe you intend to make off with this girl."

" 'Tis a family tradition," Gwen said, "though you would have to admit that he's been a failure at it so far." She looked at Rhys with one eyebrow raised. "You said so yourself."

"Do you hear me gainsaying you?" he groused. "My sire would be appalled. My grandsire *was* appalled. He snatched his lady as she was being garbed for a wedding to another. He thought I'd had more than ample opportunity to make off with you before you made your vows."

"Did you remind him how many guardsmen filled Ayre's courtyard?" she asked.

"He remained quite unimpressed. Something about spending several se'nnights recovering from wounds inflicted by a score of sewing needles. Fair ruined his nuptials, or so he claimed." Rhys grimaced. "I think my grandmère's ladies were aiming for a most strategic target."

"By the saints," Geoffrey gasped, crossing his legs quickly. "I marvel at your grandsire's courage."

"Well, since you're here sitting with us," Gwen said to Rhys, "we can assume that he recovered."

"Aye," Joanna agreed, "and now tell us how it is you intend to proceed. It concerns me that you go to London with gold and no guard to speak of. Do you not fear John will take your offering and give you nothing in return?"

Rhys had very unpleasant memories of Hugh of Leyburn accepting his purse and then laughing in his face. Short of heaving a chest of gold at King John's head and hoping it knocked the man so senseless he could do nothing but say aye to whatever question was put to him when he awoke, Rhys wasn't sure how to proceed.

Rhys looked at Geoffrey. "You have the king's ear."

Geoffrey frowned. "From time to time."

"Perhaps you might be persuaded somehow to suggest a few ways it could be bent my way."

Geoffrey scowled. "Now, why would I want to do that? Especially when the one you intend to steal away is the one woman in all of England I would choose to wed were she free?"

Rhys turned over in his mind all the reasons why Geoffrey would want to help him, the most important being that if he didn't, Rhys would do him bodily harm. Gwen saved him from having to admit that.

"You should do it because I love him," Gwen said.

Geoffrey pursed his lips. "I suppose I can think of worse justifications for sedition."

"Especially since I wouldn't wed with you if you were the only male left in England," Gwen muttered.

Rhys watched Geoffrey scowl at her, then return his attentions to his leg of fowl.

"Alain is a powerful man," he said between chews.

"And you are no less powerful?" Joanna asked. "Come, my lord Fenwyck, you are too modest."

Rhys would have snorted loudly at her flattery, but Geoffrey actually seemed to believe what she said. He sat back, not about to ruin the spell his lady's mother was weaving. Joanna spent a goodly amount of time pointing out to Geoffrey all his good points while at the same time listing all Alain's bad points so thoroughly that even Rhys began to believe that perhaps Geoffrey could succeed where Alain never could have.

"So true, so true," Geoffrey agreed finally when Joanna had seemingly exhausted a very deep well of flattery. He stretched like a satisfied cat. "I suppose that along with alerting the king to Alain's damage to my land, I might also speak kindly of you, Rhys. I feel quite certain he will listen to me."

Rhys felt nothing of the kind, but he supposed a little help was better than no help at all. Perhaps Geoffrey could distract John while Rhys snuck up behind him and clouted him over the head with several bags of gold. Perhaps the clouting would render the king's reason a bit unusable, but not affect his hands so much that they couldn't sign a handful of documents Rhys would have prepared.

"I'll think on it more," Geoffrey announced, "and let you know my plans within the se'nnight."

Rhys sighed. It was longer than he wanted to wait, but when he'd already been waiting for Gwen half his lifetime, what was another week?

But as it happened, his decision was made for him much sooner than that. He and Gwen hadn't been returned to Fenwyck but two days when a messenger came running across the lists to him, a missive clutched in his dirty hands. There was no seal, which aroused his suspicions immediately, but seals were certainly no guarantee of authenticity. If anyone would know that, it would be him. How many letters had he received under Gwen's seal only to learn later that they were forgeries?

I, Jean de Piaget, write this by mine own hand this last day of June, the Year of Our Lord 1206, to Rhys de Piaget. Greetings to you, Grandson, and may the good graces of our Lord be upon you.

There is trouble afoot and I fear it travels to your mother's doorstep. Meet me there, if you will, and come with all haste. You know the swiftest way there, though I would not think it strange if you were to pause in London and obtain some trinket to sweeten her humor. You know how foul-tempered she will be otherwise.

Let not all you've worked for be snatched away from you whilst you sleep, Grandson.

Jean de Piaget

Rhys pursed his lips and handed the letter to Montgomery. "What think you?"

Montgomery read it and looked up. "I think your grandsire wastes ink overmuch worrying about your mother's temper."

"You don't know my mother."

Montgomery smiled. "I know what you've told me, and she doesn't seem a woman given overmuch to bouts of ill humor."

Rhys folded the missive. "I'll leave before dawn on the morrow."

"But, Rhys," Montgomery said, aghast, "you cannot believe this is genuine. There was no seal, no guarantee—"

"It was from my grandfather," Rhys said, knowing it could be from no other. Not even his mother knew the combination of items and cities he and his grandfather had discussed between themselves. Trinkets from London, cloth from Paris, and fresh fish from Calais. Simple, foolish things, but a guarantee of authenticity.

As much as anything could be guaranteed.

"I'll leave the twins behind with you," Rhys continued.

"I'm certain they will be grateful for that," Montgomery said dryly.

Rhys couldn't smile. That his grandfather should have investigated enough not to only find him but to send a missive along as well could only mean there was serious trouble afoot indeed. Was the abbey near to being overrun?

"Fenwyck's garrison should be enough to keep Gwen safe, and I'll make certain Geoffrey knows you have the keeping of my lady," Rhys said, pushing aside his worry. He could only ride so fast, and it wasn't as if he made for France from Ayre. He had a good fortnight before he would even reach London, then another fortnight to reach his mother's. This was not how he intended to pass his fall.

"Go freely, my friend," Montgomery said. "I will keep watch over your lady."

"I fear Geoffrey more than any ruffians."

"As well you likely should."

"I want you to mark every drop of spittle he leaves on her hands," Rhys growled. "The saints preserve him should he place any in other locations."

Montgomery laughed. "Poor man. I suspect he knows that already and is appropriately cowed. I suspect you'll return to find your lady safely unmolested."

"For his sake," Rhys said with a sigh, "I certainly hope so."

It took him all of that day to arrange matters to his liking. Gwen had demanded to come along, and it was only by threatening to bind her to a chair and leave Geoffrey with any tools of liberation that she relented and reluctantly agreed to stay behind. Rhys didn't trust her word, and he suspected he had good reason not to based on the glint in her eye, but a quickly exchanged look with Joanna at least allowed him to rest easier knowing that Gwen's mother would do her best to stop Gwen from following him.

He planned to take fifteen of his most ill-tempered mercenaries and leave the others behind to guard his lady. Where Joanna and the Fitzgeralds failed in convincing Gwen to remain at Fenwyck, perhaps the lads would succeed.

It was near dawn when he and his company were finally prepared and waiting in the courtyard. He surveyed whom he was leaving behind that he might call up the memory to give him courage when he needed it.

Geoffrey seemed to think that remaining at Fenwyck with Gwen might be more than his frail powers of restraint could bear. He promised to meet Rhys in London in six weeks' time to have speech with the king. By then Rhys hoped he would have finished his business in France, rescued his mother and his gold, and returned to London prepared to haggle with the king over Gwen's hand. Perhaps Geoffrey would have reached the king first and filled his ears full of Alain's treachery. Rhys suspected he would need all the aid he could muster.

Joanna wished him godspeed and good fortune. Geoffrey stood next to Gwen's mother, his hands in plain sight in front of him and a look of innocence on his face. Gwen's guard, augmented by grim mercenaries, looked equal to the task of keeping her in line. Nicholas stood near Gwen with his hand on the hilt of the dagger Rhys had gifted him earlier. Rhys had bid him look after Gwen, and Nicholas had taken the instruction to heart, though Rhys suspected the lad knew nothing more about wielding the blade than what Robin had showed him. He would remedy that when he returned.

Of Robin there was nothing to be seen. He'd asked to come along, been flatly refused, and gone off in a temper. Rhys tucked away a thought to remind himself to glance up at the walls before he left them, just to make certain Robin wasn't about to fling something at him in retaliation. Rhys sighed. He would bring the lad back something from

London to sweeten his humor. He could do no more than that.

Amanda wept and clung to him, begging him not to leave. By the time Rhys had hugged her to her satisfaction, the neck of his cloak was drenched and he was near to weeping himself. By the saints, no one had warned him children could have such a detrimental affect on his heart.

He started to bid farewell to his lady only to find that she had flung her arms around his neck as well. She kissed him full on the mouth before the entire company, then stepped back and shooed him away.

"Off with you then," she said with a frown. "Why are you dawdling here when there is gold to be fetched?"

He laughed and kissed her for good measure, grateful for confidence shown when she could have been continuing the berating she'd given him earlier for going without her. He mounted quickly and set off before she could change her mind and curse him yet more.

If they rode hard, they could make Dover in less than a pair of fortnights. He started to worry about how long it would take to accomplish everything else, then stopped himself. It would take as long as it took; there was little he could do to hasten things along unless he sprouted wings.

Gwen would be his before the chill of winter had fallen, surely.

Or so he prayed.

33

"Where is Robin?"

Amanda looked up from where she was digging enthusiastically in Geoffrey's garden with Anne and smiled a toothy smile. "Gone," she said cheerfully.

Gwen looked about frantically. She could hardly believe she'd been preoccupied enough with Rhys's having left not to have made a more continual effort to ascertain her son's whereabouts. She'd seen Nicholas several times the day before and assumed that he was alone only because he and Robin had had another fight. The two scrapped like puppies one moment, then were inseparable the next. Nicholas had been often out of her sight, which had led her to suppose that he'd been with Robin. It was hardly unusual for her not to have seen her son for a day or two, especially when he was at his training with the twins. He had of late gone through periods when he liked to pretend he was already a knight and that had precluded, she had come to learn, many unmanly things—such as visits with one's mother. She trusted the twins with her life, so she had reasoned within herself that she had no need for concern.

It was, however, that morn that she realized she hadn't

seen Robin with either the twins or Nicholas in quite some time.

Gwen spotted a blond head peeking out from between a cluster of bushes and she strode over immediately.

"Nicholas?"

The blond head lifted and she was greeted by the sight of two very guilty-looking pale eyes.

"Aye, milady?" he said, his voice but a whisper.

"Where is Robin?"

He swallowed, but not very well. He looked as if he were trying to ingest a large boot.

"Is he here in the keep?"

He blinked at her and looked horribly uncomfortable, but he couldn't seem to form words.

Gwen took him by the hand and led him over to a bench. There was trouble afoot, and she had the feeling her son was at the bottom of it. She had a fairly good idea that if she managed to catch him, she would be more than tempted to acquaint his bottom with the flat of her hand a time or two. She doubted she would do it, but it would be tempting. How Robin managed it she wasn't sure, but the lad could talk his way out of a scolding with nothing more than a few contrite looks and a solemn promise never to commit mischief again.

"I didn't want to lie," Nicholas blurted out suddenly.

Gwen looked at the lad. Obviously he had a more developed sense of guilt than her son did.

"You lied?" she asked sternly. No sense in letting him believe such behavior was permissible.

And then Nicholas broke down into such heartwrenching sobs that Gwen immediately regretted her frown. She drew the boy onto her lap and rocked him while he wept as if he'd never stop. Soon Amanda and Anne had joined the little group. Amanda kept patting Nicholas soothingly. Anne merely stood by, clutching her hands together and watching with wide eyes.

"Oh, Nicholas," Gwen said gently, "it can't be as bad as all that."

"He's gone to France!" Nicholas wailed.

Gwen realized then that it certainly could be as bad as all that. She felt a chill steal over her.

"Did he go alone?"

"Nay," Nicholas wept, "he went in Sir Rhys's company!"

"Well, that isn't as bad as it could be." As if the thought of her son traipsing about with almost a score of mercenaries wasn't bad enough. "Does Sir Rhys know of it?"

Nicholas stopped wailing long enough to look at her, aghast.

"Of course not, milady! He would never have agreed to such a thing."

"True enough."

She almost set Nicholas aside to run to the keep and send someone after Rhys to fetch Robin, then she thought better of it. He was already a day out, more than that if he'd started at dawn that morning. The company could be caught, true, but was that the best thing? The thought of Robin riding into possible war with Rhys was enough to make her wish to ride out herself to catch them, but was war what Rhys would find waiting for him? For all she knew, Rollan was behind the entire scheme and Rhys was riding off on a chase that would lead nowhere. Should Alain and his brother decide to visit Fenwyck, wouldn't the best place for Robin be anywhere else?

The more she contemplated that, the more she began to think that might be the best plan. Rhys would care for Robin as if he'd been his own son. It wasn't where she would have chosen to have her firstborn, but the choice apparently wasn't hers.

"How did Robin manage this?" she asked Nicholas with a sigh.

"He bribed one of the mercenaries."

Unsurprising. "With what?"

"Your cloak brooch, milady. I begged him not to, but he wouldn't listen."

"Of course not," Gwen said, pursing her lips. Stealing and bribery. Where, by all the saints, had he come by such unwholesome ideas? Too much time listening to her mother's minstrels, obviously.

"He made me swear I wouldn't tell, swear it by the Holy Rood, lady," Nicholas said. "Then he told me if I kept his secret, he would pretend we were brothers."

Gwen watched Nicholas's eyes well up with tears, and her heart broke at the sight of it.

"I suppose he won't want to now," Nicholas said, dragging his sleeve across his eyes.

Gwen gathered him close and hugged him. "Nicholas, love, by the time Rhys is through shouting at him, he will have so few wits left he will have forgotten about what he made you promise."

"Think you, my lady?"

"Aye, lad, I do. But surely he doesn't think to travel all the way to France undiscovered."

"He's very clever," Nicholas said, his tone tinged with awe.

"*Devious* and *disobedient* are words I would more readily choose, but I suppose you have it aright." She patted him on the back. "Come, lad, and let us seek out the shelter of the hall. Rhys will see to Robin well enough after he's done scolding him. No doubt it will be a grand adventure for him and he'll have many tales to tell you when he returns."

And the first one would likely be how loudly Rhys had shouted at him for his stupidity, but that was one Gwen would gladly listen to. She knew she likely should have been sick with worry, but if there were anyone who could keep Robin safe, it would be Rhys—if he survived the pains in his chest just seeing the lad attached to some mercenary's saddle would give him.

Gwen started to shepherd her little group back to the hall, but the girls had a different idea. Nicholas was pressed into service as a horse and he submitted willingly. Gwen suspected by the long-suffering look on his face that he thought it a just penance for the grievous sins he'd committed.

She closed her eyes and sent a prayer flying heavenward

that her son would be safe and that Rhys wouldn't strangle him when he'd found out what Robin had done.

And then she said one for herself that sometime in the near future her life would arrange itself as it should. No wars. No fighting. Nothing more to do than sit in her solar with a bit of cloth under her needle and worry about what might find its way into the stew at supper.

It was over a month later that she had finally managed to at least make herself a place in Fenwyck's solar. The day was fine, the light was bright, and the children played at her feet. Her mother had somehow managed to unearth a minstrel from the surrounding countryside, and the lad sang skillfully. Sweet music, fine wine at her elbow, and those she loved surrounding her. The only things lacking were her son fingering his wooden sword purposefully and her love himself sitting across from her, snoring in the sunlight.

The vision was so powerful, and so disturbing, that she set aside her embroidery and rose.

"My lady?" Nicholas asked, looking up immediately.

She smiled as best she could. "I'm just a bit restless, lad."

"A walk in the garden, love?" Joanna asked, looking up with a smile.

"Aye, Mother. It will do me good."

"I'll watch over the girls," Nicholas volunteered.

"What a patient lad you are," Joanna said with approval. "A fine, knightly virtue that is, to look after those weaker than yourself."

Nicholas looked as if he'd just been recognized by the king himself. "Think you, my lady?"

Joanna nodded at him, then looked at Gwen. "A good lad, this one. You were fortunate to find him. I wonder if Rhys understands how fortunate."

Gwen pursed her lips. "He's a man, Mother, and as unobservant as they come. He'll realize his good fortune in time. For now, though," she said, laying her hand gently on Nicholas's head, "I am merely grateful for a good lad who is so patient with the ladies about him."

Nicholas smiled gamely. "The girls think of new animals for me to be each day, you know," he admitted. "I learn to be one kind well enough to make them happy, then they change their minds." He considered for a moment, then looked up at her. "Are all women thusly, my lady?"

Joanna laughed. "You've spent too much time with Robin, love. The girls are merely clever, not fickle."

Nicholas appeared to be digesting that. Gwen smiled and bent to kiss the top of his head.

"I thank you for your goodness to the little ones. They love you for it."

By the way he straightened his shoulders and took on a more purposeful expression, Gwen assumed that comment was enough to make him happy. She suspected he would have crawled to London and back on his hands and knees if Amanda and Anne had asked it of him. The lad was starved for any kind of affection, and Gwen was only too happy to see it given to him.

She made her way down to the great hall, wondering if perhaps the twins might be found and persuaded to train with her a bit. Rhys had absconded with her sword and replaced it with a completely useless blunted piece of steel. Fortunately the Fitzgeralds had recovered from their *mal de cheval* in time to discover with whom Rhys had hidden the blade and exerted their considerable charm to take possession of it. Gwen couldn't decide if they thought she should have her sword because it was a challenge to avoid being nicked, or if it was because they thought her skill was improving enough that they no longer needed to worry about their tender skins. She liked to believe it was the latter.

Hisses and angry gestures drew her attention. She looked to the hearth to find Geoffrey and Montgomery quarreling fiercely, albeit quietly. The moment they saw her, they both assumed such false looks of innocence that she knew whatever they discussed involved her intimately.

It was definitely something to be investigated.

She strode over to them, stopped a pace away, and put her hands on her hips. That posture always intimidated Robin. Perhaps it would work here just as well.

"What is it?" she demanded.

"Nothing," they answered in unison.

Gwen saw a hint of parchment poking up from the neck of Geoffrey's tunic. Without giving it further thought, she leaped upon him, wrenched it free of his clothing, and stuffed it down the front of her gown. Both men turned on her as one, their fingers flexing and their mouths working soundlessly.

"Good morrow to you," she said, turning to walk away.

"My lady," Geoffrey pleaded, "I beg you return that."

She turned back around. "I think not."

" 'Tis a small thing, truly."

"Then what does it matter if I know of it?"

Montgomery took a step backward and shook his head. "I hereby remove myself from this disaster." He looked at Geoffrey. "The full weight of Rhys's displeasure will rest upon you, my lord."

Gwen didn't wait to hear more. She pulled the missive free and managed to read the entire thing save the signature before Geoffrey ripped it from her hands.

I, Jean de Piaget, write this by mine own hand this last day of July, the Year of Our Lord, 1206, to Rhys de Piaget. Greetings to you, Grandson, and may the good graces of our Lord be upon you.

There is trouble afoot and I fear it travels about France at will. I have gathered up your treasure and will bring it to Ayre. Meet me there with all haste.

Let not all you've worked for be snatched away from you whilst you sleep, Grandson.

Jean de Piaget

"We must go at once to Ayre," Gwen announced.

Montgomery held up his hands. "I will have nothing to do with this—"

"Of course you won't go to Ayre," Geoffrey said firmly. "This could be a forgery."

"You fool, the first missive was obviously a forgery!" Gwen exclaimed. "It begins as the last with Rhys's grandfather smelling trouble. It is perfectly logical that he would bring all Rhys's gold to Ayre to keep it from being snatched in France."

"Now, lady—" Geoffrey began.

"And so we must away for Ayre," she said, glaring at him. "What would you have—Rhys's grandfather delivering the gold straightway into Alain's hands? Or Rollan's? Come, Montgomery. We will see to the gathering of the men and be on our way immediately."

"Oh, nay," Montgomery moaned. "My lady, I beg of you, nay."

"Then I'll go myself—"

"You will not," Geoffrey announced. He folded his arms over his chest and looked at her sternly. It would have worked a bit better, perhaps, if he had been as tall as Rhys. Gwen hardly had to tilt her head backward much at all to meet his eyes, though she did concede that his breadth was somewhat intimidating, as was his steely expression.

And then there were those uncomfortable memories of her time wallowing in pig manure thanks to Geoffrey's ingenuity.

"You have no business traipsing across England to rescue Rhys's gold for him," Geoffrey continued firmly. "I can easily send men to do the deed in Rhys's stead."

"But—"

"I will go myself," he added, then he stopped and frowned. "Saints above, what possesses me to say the like is something I'm certain I'll never understand. I'm equally as certain I'll regret it."

"But it must be done soon—"

"In a day or two," Geoffrey said. "I had planned to

meet Rhys in London in a fortnight just the same."

"But you must meet him in London as promised," Gwen argued, "else he won't know what has transpired. He would return here to Fenwyck and find us gone."

Geoffrey sighed heavily. "Very well, I will go to Ayre and send someone else to London to alert him as to what has transpired. He will come to Ayre instead of Fenwyck, and we will have this tale finished with Alain."

"And another messenger sent to Dover."

"But—" Geoffrey protested.

"Lest your messenger in London miss him!"

"Very well," Geoffrey said with a heavy sigh. "Two messengers in two places. And let us hope Rhys does not slip past the both of them. I will have the lads set out in a day or two. Now I will have to see to the running of the keep in my absence." He looked at her. "You would be a good choice for that."

Two days? Rhys's grandfather could already be a handful of miles away from Ayre and nigh onto walking into a trap in that time. Two days was too long to wait.

"Chasing after Amanda and Anne together will occupy your time quite nicely," Geoffrey added. "And perhaps seeing to a bit of my mending."

It was an enormous effort not to wallop him strongly on the head. It was, however, tempting to make several alterations to his clothes.

Perhaps if she filched a horse and left at dusk she could be well on her way before anyone discovered her absence. The twins could be left in charge of seeing to the children. They were as much under Amanda's sway as Nicholas was, but perhaps with a stern lecture from her they might realize how necessary it was to keep the children in check. Nicholas would be there to entertain her. Her mother would oversee the care of the children and Gwen's guard both. Indeed, Gwen suspected she likely wouldn't be missed overmuch.

"And a day or two overseeing the kitchens as well," Geoffrey said, obviously captivated by the thought of all the things a woman could do for him that hadn't been done since his lady had passed.

It was obvious what she had to do. Fortunately she had given much thought, if not practice, to her mercenary attributes over the past few years. One never knew when a vice might come in handy.

"Of course, I'll stay behind and see to all those tasks," she lied enthusiastically.

Geoffrey blinked. "You agree?"

"Geoffrey, 'tis obvious you have given this much thought and I must submit to your superior wisdom in the matter. What good would I be as a mere woman?"

"What indeed?" Montgomery muttered.

Gwen shot him a warning look, then turned a bright smile on Geoffrey. "My place is at the tapestry frame and cooking fire, my lord, as you suggested."

Montgomery began to choke. Indeed, he seemed determined to cough the life out of himself. Gwen pounded him very forcefully on the back until he held up his hands for mercy.

"Rest assured," Gwen said to Geoffrey, "that your keep will be in capable hands while you trot off on the rescue. Rhys will be most grateful to you."

"Well," Geoffrey said, sounding quite frankly amazed, "I'm happy to see your good sense."

"I'm quite certain you are."

Geoffrey looked at Montgomery, then back at Gwen. "I should perhaps begin preparations," he said.

"I couldn't agree more," Gwen said pleasantly. She shooed him away. "Take no more thought for your keep, my lord. I'll see to it all."

Geoffrey walked away, still looking the faintest bit unsure.

"I remain unconvinced," Montgomery said hoarsely.

"Silence, or I'll let you choke the next time."

Montgomery frowned at her. "Lady Gwennelyn, Rhys left me with specific instructions to keep you here."

"And what makes you think I intend to leave the keep, good sir?"

"Have you any idea how long I've known you, lady?"

"I've matured."

He snorted. "You've grown more cunning. Now, to assure myself that you truly intend to do as you should, I think I will require some sort of swearing from you."

"My father taught me never to swear."

"Vow it," he said in exasperation. "Vow by the Rood you will not go to Ayre to get Rhys's gold."

"Need I remind you that I am your lady and 'tis your duty to obey me in all things?"

His frown turned into a glare. "And need I remind you what will happen to *me* if aught happens to *you?* You could be the bloody queen of the whole realm, and I'd still say as much to save my sorry neck. Saints, lady, whom do you think I fear more?"

She couldn't blame him, actually, though it galled her to do so.

"He isn't my lord yet," she groused.

"I'll leave you to convince him of that when he returns. Now, for my own sweet soul's salvation, please swear by the Rood that you will not leave Fenwyck to attempt this foolishness."

Her dilemma was clear. If Rhys lost his gold, he would never be able to bribe John, they would never marry, and she would take a blade to her breast; her soul would be consigned to hell. If she swore by the cross that she wouldn't leave Fenwyck when she fully intended to do so, her soul would be consigned to hell.

Her choice was singularly simple.

Surely God wouldn't hold a little lie against her when it meant so much to a man who had served Him so faithfully for so many years.

She met Montgomery's eyes unflinchingly and gave him the most innocent look she could muster. She'd convinced him to help her do several things he hadn't approved of over the years; there was no reason she couldn't convince him now of her sincerity. "I vow," she said solemnly, "by the Rood that I will not leave Fenwyck to attempt this foolishness."

He looked at her closely. "Are you lying?"

She did her best to gasp in outrage. "Sir Montgomery, you doubt me?" It obviously hadn't been as believable as she might have liked, for he didn't look convinced.

"May heaven have mercy on my soul." He looked at her once more before he walked away. "Assuming that's where I go after Rhys is finished with me. Saint Michael, please let it be a quick and painless death. . . ."

Gwen dismissed the future location of Montgomery's soul and concentrated on what she would need to accomplish before the day was through.

Dawn was rapidly approaching. Gwen knew that because she hadn't slept for the whole of the night. She'd wondered repeatedly if she might have been better off having brought someone with her, but whom could she have trusted? Montgomery had threatened at the evening meal to tie her to a chair, and such a plan was heartily seconded by Geoffrey. Nay, leaving alone had been her only choice.

She had just resaddled her mount when she heard the unmistakable sound of footsteps coming from the woods to her left. So soon? In the back of her mind she sincerely hoped it was someone from Fenwick and not one ruffian in a band of many. The saints preserve her from that kind of test of her mettle.

She loosened her sword in its sheath and moved back into the shadow of the trees. The footsteps continued to approach stealthily, and she was impressed by the lightness of the footfall. For a man to move that silently took concentration and skill. At least her visitor wasn't Geoffrey. He ever moved through the undergrowth with the grace of a wounded boar.

The moonlight glinted off blond hair.

"Nicholas!" she exclaimed, putting up her sword.

"My lady," he said, running to her and throwing his arms around her. "I feared for your safety!"

She lifted his face up. "Did anyone see you?"

He shook his head.

"How did you reach me so quickly? Did you make off with a horse?"

"Nay, my lady. You haven't traveled very far. Indeed, I think you may have gone in a very large circle. Fenwyck is quite close."

Damn. Gwen took his hand and pulled him to her horse. "We'll have to ride doubly hard now, lad. I wish I'd brought some kind of map."

"I can help," he offered as she pulled him up behind her. "Sir Rhys taught me how to tell the direction from the sun. And I remember that we came north to Fenwyck, so we must needs go south to Ayre."

She couldn't argue with the logic of that, and she certainly wasn't about to send a perfectly capable navigator back to Fenwyck. She put her heels to her mount's side and followed Nicholas's directions.

And she sincerely hoped her rescue finished more successfully than it had started.

34

Rhys stood in the clearing, waiting until his breath returned. It had been an exhausting morning, what with the shouting he'd done and the subsequent necessity of having to plant his fist in Jacques de Conyer's face so many times. Damned hard on a man's knuckles.

And now this. Rhys folded his arms over his chest and frowned at the second culprit. He also wondered, in passing, why it was he hadn't realized until now that he'd had an additional member in his company. No wonder Jacques had volunteered to ride behind the company the entire way to France.

Rhys looked down, wondering just what it would take to convince the little fiend of the seriousness of what he'd done. And damned that Robin of Ayre if he didn't fold his own scrawny arms over his chest and frown right back at Rhys as if he'd been the one wronged.

"You stole," Rhys growled, deciding that to be a fine place to begin. "You stole your mother's brooch."

"Mama says mercenaries always steal," Robin informed him.

Rhys scowled, momentarily stymied. Robin had a point with that one. Rhys wondered if he perhaps should save his shouting for Gwen. What was she doing teaching this lad such things?

"You lied, then," Rhys said, grasping for another of Gwen's mercenary vices.

"I did not!" Robin argued hotly. "I bribed Sir Jacques forthrightly."

Rhys could hardly believe the lad before him hadn't yet reached his sixth year. The saints preserve him once Robin truly found his tongue.

"Then," Rhys said, scrambling for something to chastise him for, "you didn't tell your mother where you were going."

"She wouldn't have let me come."

"Neither would I!" Rhys exclaimed.

Robin thrust out his chin. "You may have need of me."

"What I have need of is a handy stump where I might sit comfortably when I turn you over my knee and blister your arse!"

Robin looked properly horrified by the prospect. He gulped, then put his shoulders back. "If you must," he said, his voice only quavering the slightest bit. "Or perhaps you could just bloody my nose and call it good."

Rhys stared down into the earnest little face and tried not to laugh. Saints, but this lad was cheeky. And Rhys had to admire the boy's determination to help. It reminded him so sharply of Gwen, he almost caught his breath. And with the next heartbeat he wanted more than anything to hug Robin fiercely and thank him for the loyalty.

But the saints only knew what sorts of antics that might encourage, so Rhys put on his best frown and tried to think of a suitable punishment.

"You disobeyed me," Rhys said, "and surely that merits some sort of penalty."

"You didn't say that I *couldn't* come," Robin pointed out.

"What I *did* say was that I expected you to stay behind and look after your mother."

Robin looked down at his feet. "You aren't my father."

He ducked his head even harder. "I don't have to obey you."

Rhys was surprised by how much the words hurt. In truth, he wasn't Robin's sire. But he would have given much to have been the like.

"I see," he managed finally. "I suppose, then, 'tis good to know what you think—"

And then he suddenly found himself clutched about the hips by a small boy who had broken down into sobs.

"I wish you were!" Robin cried. "I wish it more than anything!"

If the former hadn't left him with tears in his eyes, the latter certainly did. Rhys hefted Robin in his arms and hugged his fiercely. He suspected most, if not all of his company watched him, but he cared not what they thought. He patted Robin on the back and said a few of those soothing words Gwen always said to Amanda when she was weepy. And when Robin had stopped wailing loudly enough to alert everyone in France to their arrival, Rhys set the boy down, took him by the hand, and led him out of the middle of the clearing.

He squatted down in front of Robin and used his sleeve to briskly dry away the boy's tears.

And he fought his smile when Robin reached out and did the same for him.

"Father and son we aren't," Rhys began, "but perhaps we would choose differently if we could. In any case, I think you are a good lad, and I would certainly be proud to call you mine."

Robin looked as if Rhys had handed him two dozen new blades of the finest Damascus steel and the skill with which to wield them all.

"Would you?" Robin breathed.

"Aye," Rhys said simply. "But I fear then that I would expect certain things from you."

The glow dimmed a bit. "You would?"

"Aye. I should hope that you wouldn't steal again. 'Tisn't an honorable thing for a knight to do."

"But a mercenary—"

"I speak of knights, Robin. An honorable knight does not steal. Neither does he lie."

Robin chewed on that.

"He protects women and little ones and he most certainly doesn't put worms down his sister's gown." Rhys knew he was making an impression on the boy; no sense in not clearing up a few other things while he was about the task.

Robin looked crushed. "He doesn't?"

" 'Tisn't chivalrous, Robin."

"Oh," the lad said, seemingly considering the consequences of committing to a life of such goodness. Evidently he found it not too taxing a burden, for he put his shoulders back and sighed. "No more worms. No more snakes. No more spiders."

Poor Amanda, Rhys thought to himself.

"But about the other," Robin said, looking up suddenly. "You plan to steal my mother, do you not?"

Rhys found he had no answer for that.

"And you didn't tell my father, did you?"

Rhys shook his head, still speechless.

Robin regarded him for several moments in silence, then shrugged. "Perhaps it is because you are protecting women and little ones. Is that the most important part of being a knight?"

No lying and stealing, my arse. How did one explain to a six-year-old boy the finer points of life? Or love? Rhys shook his head. Perhaps he was committing the same crimes he'd forbidden Robin to indulge in. Lying and stealing were acceptable mercenary traits, and they certainly were serving him well in his present endeavor. But he was also almost a score and ten and pressed to use whatever he could to have his dreams.

Saints, but children were greatly skilled at making a man question his own actions.

"Robin," he said, taking a deep breath, "I am not going to steal your mother."

"You aren't?" Robin looked crestfallen.

"Nay, lad. I'm going to win her fairly."

"By bribing the king?"

"Knights also do not eavesdrop, lad."

Robin frowned and fell silent.

"I will do what I must, for she needs to be rescued from your sire. Perhaps in this case I will be forced to use bribery, but 'tis not a thing I do lightly, nor do I do it often. Neither should you."

"I did not bribe Sir Jacques lightly," Robin pointed out. " 'Twas necessary that I be here with you. To guard your back. But," he added with a sigh, "I suppose I won't escape a bloodying of my nose just the same." He stepped back, clenched his fists down by his sides, and closed his eyes. "I am ready, Sir Rhys."

Rhys put his hands on Robin's shoulders, turned him around, and pointed him to the horses. "A better punishment is seeing to the horses for a se'nnight. Your nose is safe."

Robin threw him a grateful look, then bolted for the other side of the camp. Rhys suspected the joy would only last a pair of hours until he'd had his fill of shoveling horse manure, then the lad would return and beg for a boxing of his nose.

That gave him at least another pair of hours to decide how he would keep Robin out of harm's way. They hadn't had any trouble thus far, but they'd also been riding hard since they'd landed. The saints only knew what they would find when they met his grandsire at Rhys's mother's abbey. Rhys couldn't credit Alain with stirring up mischief in France, so that left Rollan. And Rhys knew he couldn't put anything past Ayre's younger brother.

Well, all they could do was make for Marechal, where he knew his grandfather currently loitered, and hope to find all well there.

Rhys took a final look about camp and, satisfied that all was going according to plan, took himself off for a walk in the woods. It wasn't to say that he didn't trust the men he paid so dearly for. He told himself he would ease through the surrounding forest simply because it soothed him to do so. He was a good scout, and three years of warring had certainly improved that skill. He'd never once been caught unawares, though he'd certainly run afoot of many others during their naps.

He waved off his guard and made his way carefully through the trees. After all, what need had he for someone to watch his back? He could watch it well enough himself.

He contemplated his well-earned prowess for perhaps another quarter hour. Aye, he was a fine tracker indeed.

And that was the last thought he had before his world unexpectedly went black.

"Ye fool, ye were supposed to wait till *after* the gold was fetched!"

"Ouch! Quit yer wackin' of me!"

"Aye, leave off, François, before I takes to wackin' the both of ye! We wasn't supposed to touch the bugger a'tall!"

Rhys opened one eye a slit. He would have liked to believe it was because he was being stealthy, but in truth it was because of the blinding pain in his head. By the saints, what had they felled him with, a boulder?

"If Jean-Luc wasn't so bloody greedy—"

"If François wasn't so bloody violent—"

"And if the both of you wasn't so bloody stupid, we wouldn't find ourselves in this fix!"

Rhys opened both eyes, certain the argument was heating up enough that he wouldn't be noticed. He found himself tied to a tree, watching three characters of less than sterling quality standing toe to toe, shouting and clouting each other. Taking in the dirty hands and faces, torn clothing, blackened eyes and teeth led him to one conclusion: Rollan was behind this.

That led him to another conclusion which was even more startling than the first: Rollan knew at least one of the secrets Rhys and his grandfather shared. And if he knew about their agreed-upon signals to be used in missives, what else did he know about?

The thought was enough to chill Rhys to the bone.

"We *was* just supposed to watch him," the third of the group reminded the others. "And keep our ears open to his mama's whereabouts."

"Aye," said François, giving who Rhys assumed was Jean-Luc another substantial blow to the side of the head. "That's what we was supposed to do, idiot."

Jean-Luc rubbed his ear in annoyance. "Pierre, tell him to stop a'cloutin' me. I'm having pains in me head."

Pierre, the obvious leader of the trio, rolled his eyes in exasperation. "François, leave off. We needs Jean-Luc to do the navigatin' for us. Remember, he's to remember where we's been so we can tell Lord Rollan."

The saints preserve you, Rollan, Rhys thought dryly, *if this is the one you've put your trust in.* Jean-Luc was still rubbing his ear and shaking his head. Perhaps he was afraid François had jarred something loose.

There was a crash in the undergrowth behind Rhys, and he quickly closed his eyes as all three swung about to look at him, their mouths agape.

"A beastie," François whispered in horror.

"Aye, run!" Jean-Luc gasped. "Run for our lives!"

The sound of two forceful slaps echoed in the little clearing.

"Oof," François said. "Thanks be to ye, Pierre."

"Aye," Jean-Luc agreed, "most needful. I'm feeling much better now."

Rhys leaned his head back against the tree and listened to the three resume their discussion of just what it was they were supposed to have been doing. Other than capturing him, of course. It seemed to entail a great deal of instruction from their employer, the mighty Rollan of Ayre. Then they spent ample time discussing what he'd promised to do to them if they failed. The more they discussed that, the more panicked François and Jean-Luc became, which necessitated a handful of slaps which Rhys could only assume had been delivered by Pierre.

Rhys wondered if his mercenaries were clustered about in the underbrush, stuffing their cloaks in their mouths to stifle their giggles.

He had just determined to open his eyes to see if that were the case when he felt the ropes binding his hands begin to be sawed asunder. Once that was accomplished, the hilt of a knife was pressed into his palm. And immediately after that, a small body launched itself into the clearing and dived for Rhys's sword.

Rhys watched in horror as Robin drew the blade and brandished it. He came close to severing Pierre's arm off above the elbow.

Like mother, like son, Rhys supposed.

Fortunately the three in the clearing were so appalled by the sight of a small boy waving about a blade he obviously couldn't control, they could only stand there and gape, which gave Rhys time to get to his feet, clear his head, and take the sword from Robin. He glared at his captors.

François and Jean-Luc dropped to their knees and clasped their hands before them.

"Nay," Jean-Luc pleaded, "don't take me life, Sir Rhys!"

"Aye," François said, bobbing his head in agreement. "We've heard tales of ye!"

"Fierce."

"Merciless."

"And do ye know," Jean-Luc said, turning to François suddenly, "that he bathes quite regular. Heard the rumor meself at that inn near Conyers—"

A muffled laugh or two from the trees made Rhys grit his teeth. Once his head stopped paining him thusly, he would knock a few other heads together for their trouble.

"Yield!" Robin shouted suddenly to Pierre, brandishing his own wooden sword as if it were a mighty weapon of death.

Pierre clutched his bloody forearm and glared down at Robin. "I should cut ye to ribbons, ye little demon—"

Well, there was no excuse for that kind of talk. Rhys leaned over and planted his fist in Pierre's face. Pierre crumpled like a handful of fine silk.

"I could have taken him," Robin pointed out.

"You had him, lad," Rhys assured him. "Distracted him very well. Kind of you to allow me to finish him off."

"Harumph," Robin said, resheathing his own sword with gusto. "Perhaps my mama will make up a tale about it."

"I'll be certain to relate to her all the important points," Rhys said. "Now, let's tie up these other two and see what kind of tidings we can have further from them. I daresay you'll want to remain for the questioning."

"Of course," Robin said, folding his arms over his chest and looking at the two culprits. "Perhaps we could use worms. Or a handful of spiders down their tunics."

Almost six summers. Rhys suppressed his smile as he did the honors of securing Robin's prisoners. So Rollan was spying on him to ascertain his mother's whereabouts. Interesting. Rhys could hardly see what good that would do the man, short of a kidnapping. Did he have no idea of Rhys's mother's secure haven? Or the lengths to which her women would go to see her protected? There was surely some benefit to being Jean de Piaget's daughter-in-law, and, no doubt, another soul following in the de Piaget tradition of spying for the king. Nay, there had to be more to the tale than was being told.

And he would have it all, just as soon as he'd discovered which of his men had been lurking in the bushes, chuckling. After they'd been properly rewarded for their humor, he would turn his mind to the other riddle. He hoped it didn't have as poor an ending as he suspected it might.

With Rollan of Ayre, one could just never be sure.

35

It had been four days. Four days was long enough to wait. And it wasn't just that to annoy him. He'd been loitering about the countryside for well over a month before that, waiting for the effects of his work to come to the fore. The missives had been sent and the journeys begun. Now the time for action had come and where did he find himself?

Waiting for his brother. For four days, no less. Rollan grumbled under his breath as he mounted the steps, narrowly missing being trampled by a pair of foul-smelling knights on their way down to the great hall. Had he not been so adept at hugging walls while eavesdropping, he likely would have tumbled to his death.

By the saints, he hated Canfield. He couldn't understand how Alain bore the place. Rachel wasn't even in attendance, but that hadn't stopped Alain from being entertained nonetheless. Why Alain couldn't have entertained himself thusly at home, Rollan didn't know. What he did know was that he himself had been mightily inconvenienced, and he was less than happy about it.

Of course those four days had given him ample time to contemplate his finest bit of mischief. He'd spent several cups savoring the fact that he had actually sent Rhys to France thanks to a perfectly crafted forgery using the password known only to Sir Jean and Rhys himself.

Or so they thought.

Then he'd enjoyed the knowledge that Gwen had gone dashing off from Fenwyck after she'd received the other forgery Rollan had so carefully concocted. And bless the girl if she didn't do just as Rollan suspected she would by sending messengers to both Dover and London to instruct Rhys to come straightway to Ayre upon his return to England.

Rollan couldn't have planned that better himself if he'd been the one to do so.

Which, of course, he had.

Now the last task that lay before him was to convince Alain that returning to Ayre as quickly as possible was the only course of action left to him. Rollan could almost envision the scene that he was certain would greet his eyes eventually. Alain, comfortable at home and determined to act on the thoughts Rollan had placed in his head. Gwen full of fervor, determined to rescue Rhys's gold. And Rhys himself, likely purple with rage over having been duped.

It could, Rollan conceded modestly, quite possibly be the most ingenious scheme he had ever set in motion.

Now to see to Alain's part in it. Rollan walked down the passageway to the chamber he knew his brother occupied during all his stays here and threw open the door. He was hardly surprised by the sight that greeted him, so he walked to the footpost of the bed and looked down at his brother who lay sprawled in a tangle of sheets.

"Perhaps you didn't receive the messages I sent up," Rollan said.

Alain looked at him blankly. "Messages?"

"I've been waiting to speak to you for several days, brother," Rollan said, dredging up what little patience he still possessed after days of drinking the swill that passed for ale at this keep. To think he might have been dining so deliciously at Segrave. Gwen and Rhys were no longer there to see him denied entrance. Even though Joanna also had gone with them, her seneschal wasn't overly opposed to Rollan. Rollan was, after all the one who kept Alain far from their doors. Surely that would have earned him a meal or two.

Alain frowned. "What about?"

"I have tidings I'm certain you'll be interested in."

Alain waved with a kingly gesture. "Give them to me now."

Rollan would have preferred to speak to his brother in private, but 'twas obvious Alain had no intention of moving.

"Very well," Rollan began slowly, wanting to make sure his brother didn't miss anything. "It would seem that the lady Gwennelyn is returning to Ayre."

"Thought she was still in the north. Likely trying to get the stench of smoke out of her clothes." Alain smiled widely, obviously waiting for some response to his cleverness.

Rollan would have preferred also to have their activities at Wyckham remain secret, but it wasn't as if a simple castle whore or two would have made sense of it. Rollan laughed to soothe his brother's ego, then recaptured his sober look.

"Gwen is returning to meet Sir Rhys."

Alain looked more perplexed than usual. He sat up and rearranged a pillow or two behind his back. "Meet him at Ayre? I thought they were together at Fenwyck."

"Our gallant Sir Rhys has been in France, collecting his gold."

"He'll need it," Alain said. "It will take every last bloody piece to rebuild Wyckham."

"I daresay he doesn't intend to rebuild it," Rollan corrected. "He intends to use it to buy Gwen's freedom."

Alain looked as if he'd been plowed over by a team of horses. "Her freedom? From me?"

Rollan suppressed the urge to clap his hand to his forehead and groan. Truly, the depths of his brother's stupidity amazed even him at times, and he'd lived with the fool his entire life.

"A new scheme," Rollan lied. "I just learned of it myself."

"But how?" Alain asked. "Divorce?"

Rollan shook his head. "More likely an annulment."

"But," Alain protested, "that would say that I had never bedded her."

"But we know you have," Rollan said.

"But others would think I hadn't!"

"You have two children, Alain."

Alain thumped the pillow in frustration. "What does that matter? An annulment means I have not bedded her!"

Rollan sighed lightly. "A blow to your pride, of course."

"Annulment," Alain said in disbelief, as if he hadn't heard anything Rollan had said. "I can hardly believe it."

"Seeking to obtain such a thing would be gold wasted if you ask me," Rollan said. "I thought perhaps you might find a better use for it than seeing it wind up in some London coffer."

"Always could use more," Alain conceded.

"My thought as well," Rollan said. "Which is why I suspected you would want to make for Ayre as soon as possible. They should be there together by the time you reach the keep. Catching one's wife in the act of adultery should surely be enough to see her disgraced."

Alain blinked. "Will I lose her lands?"

"With the love the king bears you?" Rollan said soothingly. "Surely not, my lord. And think on this: you would be free to wed where you will." Rollan looked at the three very voluptuous serving wenches curled up in Alain's bed like so many puppies and smiled faintly. "Or perhaps not. You have an heir. You would simply be ridding yourself of an annoying wife."

"Rid myself of Gwen," Alain said, obviously finding the idea to his liking. He smiled brightly. "I'll do it."

"Now?" one of the women complained.

Alain frowned, distracted by the ample flesh on display. "Hmmm," he said, scratching his head thoughtfully, "perhaps later."

"Ah, but it must be now," Rollan interjected. "Immediately. Before de Piaget and the lady Gwennelyn flee the keep. Why they could be romping betwixt the sheets even as we speak. You'll want to catch them at it."

Alain shuddered. "Don't know why he'd want the acid-tongued wench."

"Who can explain a man's tastes?" Rollan asked pointedly.

"Who indeed. Let's be off," Alain said as he threw off the sheets, scattering his collection of bedmates. "The sooner, the better."

Rollan leaned against the footpost and watched his brother dress.

"You'll want to insult de Piaget, of course," Rollan remarked casually. "Enough to make him challenge you."

Alain froze. "Challenge me?"

"Can you not see the wisdom in it? A mere knight attacking a lord of the realm?"

"Ah," Alain said, nodding. Then he frowned. "But he will best me."

Rollan laughed softly. "Brother, you give yourself too little credit. The tales of his prowess are greatly exaggerated. Besides, you'll catch him fully sated from being abed with your wife. I daresay he'll have little strength to stand against you."

"You've quite the head for strategy," Alain said.

"That I do."

Alain paused. "Should I have my sword sharpened before we go?"

"Use the crop instead," Rollan advised. "Then finish him with a dull blade. More entertaining that way."

"I believe you're right, brother."

Rollan turned away and left the chamber before he had to watch his brother give very thorough kisses of parting to his afternoon's entertainment. Alain did not deserve Gwennelyn of Ayre. Rollan suspected that he should be very grateful that his brother had found her so unpalatable. The thought of anyone touching her set his teeth on edge.

He descended the steps to the great hall and contemplated the feelings coursing through him. He was surprised to find that amid the rage, there was actually a bit of something soft. He thought again about Gwen and the softness increased.

By all the bloody saints above, could that be love?

He came to a halt, fair frozen in place by the horror of the thought. He'd felt many things over the course of his life for Gwennelyn of Ayre, but love had certainly never been among them. He put his hand to his head. He wasn't feverish. He'd just celebrated the anniversary of his birth, so 'twas possible that the aftereffects of that celebration had wrought this unpleasant change in him.

"Murder," he said, rolling the word on his tongue. "Mayhem. Mutilation." His three favorites.

Ah, there were the stirrings of ruthlessness he felt so comfortable with. That softness had been but a moment's weakness. He would have Gwen, to be sure. And he would find ways to make her suffer while he took her. After all, she had spurned him once, leaving her bloody needle marks in his belly. She should pay for that.

But first Alain. The current lord of Ayre should surely make a stand at his own keep—the keep should have been his, Rollan of Ayre's, by birth. It would be his by death. If that death happened to be his brother's, what could he do but grieve over the deed?

And when his brother was killed by a mere knight, what else could Rollan do but take up a sword to defend his fallen brother's honor? And if that sword happened to end Rhys de Piaget's life, what could anyone do but count it a meet revenge?

Rollan planned, of course, to use a crossbow. There was no sense in getting any closer to de Piaget's sword than necessary.

And when Alain was dead and Rhys slain in recompense for the deed, there would be Gwen, alone and in dire need of a protector.

And who better than Rollan of Ayre to be that protector?

He continued on his way to the hall door, whistling cheerfully. Ah, but familial mayhem was enough to brighten any man's day.

36

"Sir Rhys says thievery isn't a proper knightly activity."

Gwen clutched the stall door and gritted her teeth. Much as she had grown fond of Nicholas over the past fortnight, she thought that if she had to hear one more quote from that unwritten tome *De Piaget's Knightly Wisdom*, she would go mad. How Nicholas had memorized so many entries she wasn't sure, but obviously he'd made good use of his short acquaintance with the gallant Sir Rhys. She took a deep breath.

"So true," she agreed. "But at the moment, neither of us is a knight and both of us are very hungry."

Nicholas considered that for a moment before looking up at her with a small pucker forming on his brow.

"We could not merely beg a meal?"

"From Ayre's cook?" She shook her head. "Nay, lad, 'tis better that no one know we've managed to breach the defenses of the keep. I fear a snatching is what we must resort to. Besides, they would expect nothing less of us dressed as we are in our mercenary garb."

Nicholas looked less than convinced. "My lady," he said slowly, "they cut off hands of thieves. What if they mistake us for thieves instead of fierce mercenaries?"

He had tucked his hands under his arms protectively, as if he could already feel the knife severing hand from arm. She looked down at her own disguise, then at his. They were both liberally smudged with soot and other unmentionable substances and to be sure the clothing Nicholas wore would have done any ragtag mercenary's lad credit. Her own clothing was something she'd filched at Fenwyck, and she felt confident that almost three weeks' worth of travel had added authenticity to her own appearance. Surely they would be taken for what they pretended to be. Besides, she was hungry enough not to care. She'd packed only enough food for herself. To be sure Nicholas was a slight lad, but he was a lad after all and seemingly trying to make up for nigh onto six winters of poor fare at his uncle's cooking fire. As far as she could see, she had no choice but to take her chances at pilfery. Though she anticipated that Rhys would arrive at any moment, thanks to the messengers Geoffrey had sent, she was certain she would be in a better state to greet him having had something to fill her belly.

"Come, Nicholas," she said, reaching for his hand. "No harm will come to us. We're far more likely to starve to death than to be branded as thieves."

Nicholas smiled gamely and took her hand. "I'll protect you, my lady, should it come to that." He patted the spare knife Rhys had given him and put his shoulders back. "Sir Rhys would wish it of me."

Gwen shook her head as she crept with Nicholas from the stall. It was no wonder Rhys had such a following of mercenaries. If he hadn't beaten them all into submission, he surely would have charmed them into following him. It was certain he had made a loyal follower out of Nicholas. She could only hope Robin was being so obedient. She had no doubt her son had been discovered long before now, and she wished mightily she could have seen Rhys's reaction to it. Robin must have hidden himself all the way to France. Gwen didn't doubt Rhys would have turned around and brought the lad home had they still been on English soil.

And turn around he would, once he discovered the false-
ness of the missive he'd received. It had to have been
Rollan behind it. She was certain he had lured Rhys to the
continent so he could be at Ayre to receive the gold. She
hadn't seen him as yet, but she hadn't ventured out of the
stables either, preferring to wait a day or so before making
the attempt. Just getting inside the gates had been hard
enough on her heart.

"Bloody hell!"

Gwen paused. That sounded uncomfortably like Geoffrey of Fenwyck. That did not bode well.

"Turn the other way, you puking fool!"

Gwen came to a dead stop at the entrance to the stables
and looked out into the courtyard. There stood Geoffrey
of Fenwyck, his guard, Montgomery, and fifteen grim-
faced mercenaries.

Oh, and the twins strapped, as usual, to their horses.

"Oh," she said.

"Nay, Connor, not you, too! And do not fall upon me!"

Gwen would have laughed, but Geoffrey of Fenwyck
had just caught sight of her, and she thought better of her
reaction.

"You!" he said, shaking the more substantial items off
his very damp sleeve and pointing at her. "This is all your
fault!"

Evidently the twins had braved the journey south, but
not survived it any better than their trip north. Geoffrey
looked to have not weathered the ensuing results very well.

"Told you not to stand between them," Montgomery
remarked.

Geoffrey snarled a curse at Montgomery, then removed
himself from between the two fallen Vikings.

"You could at least roll them over so they don't
choke," Montgomery said. "Then again, maybe I'll do
it," he added at Geoffrey's look.

Gwen folded her arms over her chest and waited for the
inevitable eruption.

"You *swore* you would stay behind!" Geoffrey shouted
at her.

"Swore by the Rood, too," Montgomery said with a grunt as he heaved a Fitzgerald onto his belly in the dirt.

"I've never been tempted to beat a woman before," Geoffrey growled, "but I vow that the thought grows more appealing by the moment. Especially now. Look at me!"

Gwen looked. And she suppressed the urge to hold her nose closed.

"What did you feed them last eve?" she asked.

"Does it matter? They bloody can't look at a horse that they aren't puking!" He flexed his fingers. "Yet another thing to hold you accountable for—"

Gwen found herself suddenly standing behind a bristling, knife-wielding six-year-old.

"N-not while I l-live," Nicholas said, brandishing his blade. "You'll n-not t-touch her!"

Gwen realized then that Nicholas wasn't bristling, he was shaking with terror. She couldn't help but smile at his bravery. Even Geoffrey seemed impressed. He folded his arms behind his back and looked down gravely at the boy.

"Think I should leave her be?" he asked.

"If you v-value your l-life," Nicholas said, stabbing the air in front of him meaningfully with his knife.

"And what think you of her lying her way from Fenwyck to come here?" Geoffrey asked.

Nicholas stopped stabbing and merely pointed his knife at Geoffrey. "Sir Rhys wouldn't have approved—"

Geoffrey looked at Gwen with one eyebrow raised.

"—but since we're posing as mercenaries and not knights, it's all right."

"Mercenaries," Geoffrey repeated.

Montgomery laughed. "Lady, isn't such a thing what got you into trouble initially?"

Gwen scowled at the two of them. "I did what I had to. And now I'll thank you both to leave me in peace to continue my labors. I can only pray you haven't spoiled my ruse beyond repair."

Geoffrey clapped a hand to his head. "By the saints, I think I should let Rhys have you. I don't think I've the stamina for your schemes."

"As if the choice were yours," she said tartly. She put her hand on Nicholas's shoulder. "Come, lad, and let us see if we can filch supper, then we'll return to our post and wait for the proper moment to recover Rhys's gold."

"Oh, nay," Geoffrey said, shaking his head. "You'll not continue along this path. Montgomery and I will see to the unraveling of this mystery."

"Rollan will never reveal himself with you here," Gwen argued. " 'Tis better that I see to it."

"How, by holding a handful of sewing needles to his throat?"

"I can wield a blade well enough," she said through gritted teeth. "Shall I demonstrate on your sorry form?"

"If I might venture an opinion," Montgomery began.

Gwen threw a curt "Nay, you may not" at him only to realize Geoffrey had said the same thing.

"My lord, my lady," Montgomery continued, "surely we can settle this amicably."

"He has insulted my skill," Gwen said stiffly.

Nicholas patted her hand that still clutched his shoulder.

"My thanks, lad," Gwen said, "but I think I'd like to repay him myself. There are several other things I should like to avenge myself for as well."

"What?" Geoffrey demanded.

"Numerous tweakings of my plaited hair while I was a child," Gwen said, drawing her blade.

Geoffrey snorted in disgust. "What a pitiful reason."

"Very well, then," Gwen said, pulling Nicholas behind her, "there are other things I might seek satisfaction for."

Geoffrey only glared at her.

Gwen took a deep breath. "The locking of me in the piggery."

"Ha," Geoffrey said, "I *knew* you hadn't forgiven me for that."

"I could have been trampled to death!"

"Snuffled thoroughly, more likely," Geoffrey returned. "Besides, the sow was away from her piglets at the time. You were perfectly safe."

"What about threatening to toss me in the dungeon?"

He smiled just as wickedly as he had when he'd threatened it. "Many thanks for the reminder. Perhaps you would care to see the inside of Ayre's."

Gwen glared at him and fingered the hilt of her sword. Geoffrey folded his arms and looked at her with what she could only term a smirk, as if her skill was too paltry to cause him any distress or concern.

"Make way for the lord of Ayre!"

Gwen jumped. The announcement even produced something of a start in Geoffrey. He whipped around to look at the gate guard who had bellowed those words. Gwen contemplated a quick duck back into the stables to protect what anonymity she still had, then found she was far too late.

She had counted on Rollan. She hadn't anticipated having to face her husband as well. She put her shoulders back. Perhaps 'twas best she confront Alain and Rollan together. At least she would have the support of her small army, though she had to admit Geoffrey looked none-too-enthusiastic about the prospect. At least Rhys's mercenaries were looking appropriately fierce.

The herald's words had hardly died away before Alain himself rode through the gates and came to a halt. He was surrounded by a handful of guards and trailed by his brother.

"Well, this is interesting," Rollan drawled. "Sister, are you felling your guardsmen again?"

Gwen wished desperately that the Fitzgeralds were doing something besides moaning in the muck. They surely would have added to her air of invincibility.

Alain was looking at her and blinking. "You're not abed," he said.

"Nay, my lord, I am not," she agreed.

Alain looked at Rollan. "I certainly wouldn't want to bed her now. She smells."

Gwen wished she'd thought of her disguise on her wedding night.

"Where's de Piaget?" Alain asked.

"Ask your brother," Gwen said. "I imagine he knows."

Alain scratched his head. "Rollan said he would be—"

"Ah, aye," Rollan agreed. "Off doing some chivalrous deed, no doubt."

"But he's supposed to be here," Alain argued. "Bedding *her*. Though why he'd want to, I don't know."

Gwen smiled at her husband. "Oh, you won't have to wait long for him. I imagine he's on his way here by now. I don't know that I'd want to meet him, though. I doubt he'll be all that happy when he arrives."

Alain looked faintly panicked. "Then perhaps we should raise the drawbridge. Just in case."

"Riders approaching!" another guard shouted.

"It can't be him," Alain said, fingering his crop nervously. "I didn't see him on the road."

"I did," Montgomery offered.

"And you know what fine eyes Sir Montgomery has," Gwen added, finding that a great sense of relief had already begun to wash over her. Though she was certain she could have bested Alain on her own, having Rhys there beside her would be a boon indeed.

"No device on them!" the guard shouted down. "But dressed in black they all are!"

Alain gulped audibly. "Raise the drawbridge," he called nervously.

"That won't do any good," Gwen said confidently. "I tried that before."

"He won't scale *my* walls," Alain boasted, but he didn't look all that convinced.

Gwen raised one eyebrow, then shrugged and positioned herself where she could see the barbican. And as the drawbridge began to rise, she began to wonder if Rhys actually would manage the feat.

But then she saw a leg swing over the end, followed by the rest of a black-swathed body which rolled swiftly down the span toward the gatehouse.

"Down with the portcullis!" Alain squeaked.

It was too late. Rhys was standing inside the gates before Alain's command had reached the gatehouse. Rhys looked at the guards and snarled, "Lower the drawbridge."

The men began to crank furiously, in direct disobedience to Alain's direction.

"Traitors," Alain complained as Rhys's men swarmed into the bailey. Gwen smiled pleasantly at Alain.

"Told you so."

Gwen turned back to look at Rhys. He spared her a glare, and she suspected that he was less than pleased to see her there. She searched through the ranks of his men and felt an almost overwhelming sense of relief to see Robin waving merrily at her from where he sat before John on John's horse.

One loved one safe. Now if Rhys could just manage to avoid any stray arrows from Alain's guardsmen.

Another man had seemingly joined Rhys's company, and Gwen marveled at the white in his hair. The resemblance to Rhys was very strong and Gwen wondered if that might perhaps be his grandfather. She smiled at the man and received a sunny smile in return. At least Rhys's gold was safe. Or so she supposed.

She looked back at her love and wondered, by the fierceness of his expression, if she might have relaxed too soon.

Or perhaps he was reserving his stern look for Alain and his brother.

Gwen took a firmer grip on her sword. She'd sought Rhys out at one time in her life, ready to offer her sword to guard his back.

Perhaps that promise would be called upon after all.

37

Rhys knew he shouldn't have been surprised by what he was seeing, but he was. He distinctly remembered a very serious discussion he had had with his lady about the importance of remaining safely at Fenwyck. When he'd encountered Fenwyck's messenger at Dover, however, he'd begun to worry that perhaps Gwen might have decided that a quick journey to Ayre was called for. He couldn't have been so fortunate as to have had her not read the second missive. Rhys shot Rollan a look of promise before he turned back to his lady. Obviously she had as much regard for the sanctity of his word as did her son. He sighed. He was doomed never to be taken seriously. He looked at Gwen and frowned, just to let her know where his thoughts were leading him.

She was dressed, and this came as no surprise to him, either, in what she deemed mercenary garb. She was brandishing her sword as if she fully intended to use it. Well, at least she hadn't done any damage to any of her keepers yet. Nicholas had also been subjected to a liberal sooting and held his knife in front of him as if he expected to be attacked at any moment.

Rhys looked at the men in whose care he'd left his lady

and had no doubts of their inability to control her. Geoffrey didn't look overly happy to see him, though Rhys suspected that look came more from wanting Gwen for himself than any remorse for a failure to keep her at Fenwyck. Montgomery was only shaking his head, smiling dryly. Rhys could hardly wait to hear what he had to say about the situation.

And the Fitzgeralds, of course, were lying facedown in the muck, conveniently senseless.

And then there was Alain watching the group just as Rhys was, with his entourage of guardsmen and Rollan slinking along behind him as usual. Rhys wondered how long Ayre's lord had been facing off with his wife.

And he shuddered to think what would have befallen Gwen had Geoffrey's messenger not found him. He would have traipsed back merrily up to Fenwyck, fully expecting to find things as he had left them, only to realize he should have stopped at Ayre.

"You were to be here already," Alain said pointedly.

Rhys blinked, then realized he was the one being spoken to. "Was I?"

Alain shot Rollan a look of irritation. "This isn't working out as you planned."

"Keep to your path, my lord," Rollan advised.

The saints preserve us all, Rhys thought. He found that Alain was looking at him with his customary look of disdain. Alain scowled and huffed and seemed to be searching for something to blurt out. Evidently he stumbled upon something, for his frown was replaced with a look of triumph.

"Can you not choose some sort of device?" he demanded.

"I plan to," Rhys answered calmly. "When my hall is built." Indeed, he'd already given it much thought. It would be a black lion rampant in deference to his own pride in his skill. And there must needs be something to honor his lady. He had not decided finally upon that as yet.

"Well," Alain said, obviously struggling for something

else to say, "you look foolish without a device." He looked at his brother for approval.

Rhys watched as Rollan rolled his eyes. What mischief were these two about? Rhys looked back at Alain. He was obviously waiting for some kind of reaction.

"Foolish?" Rhys asked.

"Aye," Alain said. "Quite foolish."

"I think he looks sinister," Gwen put in.

Alain glared at her. "I didn't ask for your opinion." He turned back to Rhys. "And look at your hair. Unfashionably long."

"Oh, by the saints," Rollan groaned.

Alain turned a glare on his brother. "I'm doing well enough on my own, without *your* aid. I've just begun to point out his flaws."

Rhys folded his arms over his chest and tried to maintain a serious expression. He could hardly believe what he was hearing. "Are you trying to insult me?"

"See?" Alain said smugly to his brother. "*He* caught on readily enough."

Rhys wasn't sure if he should laugh or truly be offended that Alain couldn't think up anything more clever. He shook his head.

"Why would you want to offend me?"

"So you'll challenge me," Alain answered promptly. He looked him over critically. "I suppose you're just as weary from your travels as you would be from spending a fortnight in my wife's bed."

Rhys shook his head, certain he was hearing things.

Alain waited expectantly. "Well? Are you going to challenge me?"

"Why would I want to do that?"

Alain looked at him as if Rhys had just lost his mind. "Surely several reasons would be readily apparent."

"Oh," Rhys said, nodding. "The complete destruction of my land, perhaps?"

"That would do for a start."

Rhys smiled. "Somehow I think I'll leave our beloved

monarch to take his revenge for that. He was none too pleased to learn of it.''

"You told the king?" Alain demanded. "When?"

"When I was in London on my way back from being ambushed in France." Rhys smiled at Rollan. "Hire less greedy thugs the next time, my friend. These could hardly wait to get their hands on my gold.''

Alain threw his crop at his brother. "Fool!" Then he looked down at his empty hand. "Damn," he said, looking rather stunned. "Now what am I to use upon him?"

Rollan sighed deeply and gently threw Alain's crop back to him. "Here, my lord. Now you are fully prepared for the task at hand.''

"Oh, by the saints!" Gwen exclaimed. "Will someone fetch me a chair of some kind that I might sit through the rest of this absurdity?"

Rhys shared her sentiments fully.

"Aye"—Alain nodded—"the challenge. Well, Sir Rhys, get on with it. A good thing you've already dismounted before you deliver it.''

"Easier for you to wield your crop that way?" Rhys asked, amused.

"Aye," Alain said. "And then to finish you with a very dull blade.''

"It doesn't seem quite sporting, does it, for me to be on my feet and you on your horse?" Rhys asked. "Perhaps you should dismount as well.''

Alain swung down, obviously before he realized what he was doing. He looked so appalled at his own actions, Rhys almost felt sorry for him. He could hardly believe he pitied the man who had caused him so much grief, but then again, Alain was only the figurehead. Rhys felt certain if he dragged the entire affair out long enough, Alain would reveal all of Rollan's machinations.

"So I am to challenge you," Rhys said conversationally. "First for insulting me, then for Wyckham? Or is it the other way around?"

Alain blinked in confusion, then suddenly nodded. "Aye," he said, weighing the crop in his hand.

"And then you'll kill me."

"A knight doesn't insult a lord and come away un-scathed."

"Why do you care if I live or die?" Rhys asked. "Surely Wyckham isn't that important to you."

"Isn't Wyckham," Alain said, waving off the guards-men who had begun to cluster around him. "It's all of her lands."

"All of them, hmmm?" Rhys asked, exchanging a pointed look with the captain of his mercenary company. Robin was safely taken care of by John and the rest of his men had taken up positions behind Gwen and Nicholas. His grandfather was sitting apart watching the proceedings with a smirk. Rhys shot him a warning look, but Sir Jean only lifted a shoulder in a half shrug as if to say he did not feel himself in any danger.

"Aye, all her lands," Alain said. "You see, if you live and manage to buy an annulment—"

"Or a divorce," Rollan interrupted.

Alain shot him a look of displeasure, then turned back to Rhys. "If you have an annulment from the king," Alain continued, "I might lose her lands. But if you're dead, then she'll have nowhere else to go." He looked at Rollan and he frowned. "That can't be right, for that leaves her still with me. How do I marry where I will if I'm still shackled to her?"

"Perhaps *you* could divorce *her*," Rhys suggested. "Consanguinity, or some other such rot."

Alain looked at him in surprise. "Aye, that would work well enough. And then surely the king would allow me to keep her soil."

"After your work at Wyckham?" Rhys asked doubt-fully. "I wonder."

" 'Twas Rollan's idea," Alain answered promptly. "I'll tell that to John myself."

Rhys looked at Rollan to find him staring intently at his brother, as if he willed him to close his mouth. So, it was as they had suspected. Rollan was behind the treachery.

Rhys spared Rollan a brief glance filled with promise of retribution, then turned back to Alain.

"You realize," Rhys said slowly, "that no matter whose idea it was, John will hold you responsible."

"He will not," Alain disagreed.

"Won't he?" Rhys asked. "You are lord of Ayre, not Rollan, and he will surely blame the damage to Wyckham and Fenwyck upon you." He looked at Alain thoughtfully. "I wonder what other ideas of Rollan's John will hold you accountable for."

A look of panic began to descend on Alain's features.

"Indeed," Rhys continued, "I suspect that might be Rollan's plan." He looked at Rollan to see his reaction to that statement. And if he'd been made of less stern stock, he might have stepped back a pace at the look of pure hatred Rollan was sending his way.

"My lord," Rollan said, still glaring at Rhys, "he spouts nonsense. You know my loyalties are to you—"

Alain cut him off with an impatient motion of his hand. "I don't think I understand," Alain said to Rhys. "His plans only include you."

"Do they?" Rhys asked.

"Aye. You are the one who wants all my land."

Rhys shook his head. "I don't want your land. I want your wife."

Alain blinked, as if he wasn't quite sure to what to do with such a blatant admission. "You must want the land."

"I have enough."

The lord of Ayre was obviously becoming more confused by the moment. "But I must kill you, or so Rollan says. And you must challenge me that I might kill you fairly. That is the only way to keep Gwen's lands and rid myself of her as well."

"My lord," Rollan put in.

"Silence!" Alain commanded. He slapped his crop into his hand and frowned at Rhys. "I suppose if all you wanted was the wench, that would still be enough reason to challenge me."

"I would think it would just be easier for me to buy a

divorce,'' Rhys said, ''but no doubt Rollan has other ideas about that as well. You might want to think on what those could be.''

Rollan laughed, but even Rhys could tell it was somewhat strained. ''He babbles foolishness, brother. Have at him and let us be done with this.''

Alain fingered his crop nervously. ''He doesn't look all that weary to me. He was to be much wearier before I fought him.''

''And even if I were,'' Rhys added, ''do you truly think you could best me?''

''Boastful whoreson,'' Rollan hissed. ''Take him, Alain, and repay him for his cheek.''

''Rollan knows you won't come away the victor,'' Rhys said. ''I daresay he expects you to suffer a fatal wound as well. I wonder just how long he's been envisioning himself as lord of Ayre.''

'' 'Tis a lie,'' Rollan said. ''I have no other purpose than to serve . . . my brother,'' he finished with an audible swallow.

Rhys could understand why. Perhaps the light had been slow in dawning on Alain, but apparently he'd finally seen it. He turned to his brother, his mouth hanging open.

''You want what I have,'' Alain said, sounding stunned.

''Now, brother—''

''You want my land!''

''And your title,'' Rhys suggested.

''Gwen, too, I'd say,'' Geoffrey interjected from behind Rhys. ''I've seen the way he looks at her.''

Alain strode over to where Rollan still sat atop his horse. ''You intended to see me slain!'' he roared, striking what he could reach of his brother with the riding crop.

''Or at least out of favor with the king,'' Rhys prodded. ''That would likely be a worse fate—''

''Aye, 'tis true,'' Rollan spat, lashing out at Alain with his foot. ''I wanted you dead.''

''You traitor!''

''You imbecile!'' Rollan returned. ''Saints, Alain, you've not even a pair of wits to mate and produce enough intelligence to govern Ayre! Who do you think has seen to everything until now? You?''

"Traitor," Alain said, continuing to beat at his brother with the crop. "You liar! You led me to believe you wanted naught but my glory!"

Rhys watched as Rollan's mount began to buck, having received the brunt of perhaps one too many of Alain's blows. Rollan fought to maintain his seat, jerking back on the reins to try to control his stallion. The more the beast reared, the closer in Alain moved. Rhys would have called out a warning, but it was obvious the current lord of Ayre was beyond reason. He seemed to be viewing the mount as an extension of his brother, for he lashed it savagely.

And then whether by fortune or design, Rollan caught his brother in the head with his foot and sent him down to his knees. Before any in the company could move to pull Alain out of the way, the stallion had taken his own revenge with his hooves, slashing and then stamping until Alain was no longer moving. It was only then that Rollan regained control of his horse and urged him away a few paces.

"Merciful saints above," Gwen whispered from behind Rhys. "Is he dead?"

"Only if he's fortunate," Rhys said quietly. There wasn't enough left intact of Alain for life to have been a possibility. Rhys looked up at Rollan.

Rollan looked more shocked than Rhys had ever seen him. He stared in horror at his brother, then looked about him at the gathered company.

"I never meant—" he began, his hands fumbling nervously with the reins. "I mean, I never meant to be the one—"

"Seize him!" Geoffrey exclaimed.

Rollan seemed to gather his wits about him. "Nay," he shouted suddenly, gesturing furiously at Rhys, "seize *him!*" He looked for the captain of Alain's guard. "He is the one who has caused this tragedy!"

Rhys felt his mouth drop open. "Me?" he gasped.

"Aye," Rollan said, recapturing his coolness. "Captain,

bind him and put him into the dungeon. I will see to the lady Gwennelyn until the king can be told—''

Alain's captain, Osbert, did not need to be told more than once that he could have a go at Rhys. Rhys had faced the man numerous times in the lists, merely as exercise of course, but even so the encounters had never been friendly. Rhys suspected Osbert was relishing the thought of doing him harm with a clear conscience.

Rhys held up his hand. "Osbert, you saw with your own eyes—"

"—You goading my lord," Osbert finished with a snarl, drawing his blade with a flourish. " 'Tis as Lord Rollan says. All your fault."

Rhys groaned silently. Alain's captain was no brighter than Alain himself had been. There was no point in trying to reason with the man, especially since Osbert's blade was already coming his way with a goodly amount of enthusiasm.

At least Osbert was the only one of Alain's guard who had drawn his weapon. Perhaps the afternoon's events could be sorted out sooner than Rhys had hoped.

And then he found himself with no choice but to draw his own blade and concentrate on the man who came at him, salivating at the prospect of doing him in. It took three strokes to disarm Alain's captain and a fist under the chin to send him slumping to the ground, senseless. Rhys looked at the rest of Alain's guard. Not a one moved. Indeed, they seemed to be finding many things more interesting than him to look at.

Such as the rump of Rollan of Ayre's horse as it galloped out the gates.

"Someone should go after him!" Geoffrey exclaimed.

Rhys shook his head. "Let him go. We'll send word to John and let him see to the matter. Perhaps 'tis best that Rollan live with what he's done for a bit."

"A fine new lord of Ayre in that one," Geoffrey muttered. "Escaping across the countryside."

"The title is Robin's, my lord," Rhys said with a sigh, "as you would realize if you thought about it long enough.

We can only be grateful Gwen's lands will go to someone with the sense to see to them."

"Why, thank you so very much," John said, lowering Robin to the ground. "I could have taken them over. And I daresay I would have dowered my sister-in-law very well that she might make a fine match of some nobleman."

Rhys shot his squire a dark look, then turned to look at the freshly made widow of Alain of Ayre.

She was staring at Alain as if she could hardly believe her eyes. Then she walked over, took off her mercenary's cloak, and covered him with it. She turned to look at Rhys.

"This isn't how I would have had it finish."

He nodded grimly. "Nor I. But 'tis done and we must make the best of it. The king will have to be informed."

"I'll see to it," Geoffrey volunteered.

"Later, if you will. I have need of you presently."

Geoffrey looked a bit surprised at Rhys's tone, but Rhys didn't spare that much thought. He had two things to accomplish, and the sooner they were done, the better he would like it.

And once those were done, they would ride like demons for Artane and pray John was too lazy to come after them. Rhys hadn't spared Rollan out of the goodness of his heart. A good chase would keep the king busy, and Rhys could only hope a murderer would interest the king more than a disobedient vassal.

For he fully intended to do exactly what the king had expressly forbidden him.

He looked at his lady and fingered the hilt of his sword. "We have business together, lady."

And it was business best seen to while they still had the freedom to do so.

38

Gwen wondered if Rhys now planned to use his sword on her. The way he'd said *business* had left her wondering just what he intended. With the severity of his frown, it could have been anything from a lengthy kiss to an encounter in the lists. She took a firm grasp on the hilt of her sword and pointed the blade at him.

"I don't know that I care for your tone," she said, mustering up all the haughtiness she could.

"We don't have time to argue about it," he said shortly. He thrust out his hand. "Come with me."

"Where?"

He looked at her as if she'd lost all sense. "Well, to the priest, of course."

"Priest?"

"So we can be wed," he said impatiently. "Saints, Gwen, why else would we need one?"

"To bury Alain?"

"He's not going anywhere. My head, however, *will* be if we don't get on with this business before something else disastrous happens—such as the king arriving and finding out what I'm about."

Gwen found her hand in his and her feet trotting to keep

up with him as he strode across the courtyard to the tiny
chapel. He hadn't bothered to sheath his sword, and she
hadn't had the time. She looked at Alain's priest and
watched his eyes roll back in his head at their approach.
Unfortunately they didn't approach quickly enough to
catch him before he slumped to the ground.

"Damnation," Rhys grumbled. "What else can happen
to us this day?"

"A visit from the king?" John asked from behind them.

"A downpour?" Montgomery suggested.

"Ahem," Geoffrey said, trying to insert himself bodily
between Gwen and her love, "I believe now that Alain—
may his dim soul rest in peace—is gone, *I* should be the
one to care for Gwen and what is hers. I am, after all, a
powerful baron in my own right—"

Gwen watched as Rhys elbowed Geoffrey out of the
way and took a firmer grip on her arm.

"Montgomery," Rhys said shortly, "rouse the priest.
And find my grandsire, would you?"

"I am here, Rhys lad," came the crusty response.
"Rude you are, young one, not to take into consideration
an old man's sore knees." He clucked his tongue. "Such
unseemly haste."

Gwen looked to her left to find Rhys's grandfather
standing there. He looked anything but decrepit, and she
could tell by the twinkle in his eye that he mightily enjoyed giving his grandson as much grief as possible. She
found her chin grasped in surprisingly gentle fingers.

"Let me have a look at the girl," he said. He turned
Gwen's face this way and that. "Aye, she'll do."

"Thank you," Gwen said dryly.

"Nicely fashioned ears," Sir Jean added, lifting her hair
to peer at the appendages in question.

"Your grandfather, Rhys," Gwen said, never taking her
gaze from Sir Jean's, "is a man of discriminating taste."

"He's as blind as a bat if you ask me," Geoffrey grumbled from behind her. "Not even a wimple of the stiffest
fabric could pin those enormous flaps to the sides of her
hea—"

Sir Jean threw him a steely look that had no doubt quelled many a braver soul. Geoffrey apparently found other things to do besides speak, for he said no more. Gwen's affection for Sir Jean grew tenfold.

"We need the priest propped up," Rhys interrupted. "John, go over and help Montgomery."

Gwen turned her attention back to the matter at hand and found that though the priest had regained his senses, he didn't seem to have the strength to stand on his own. She took pity on him and resheathed her sword. She thought to suggest the same to Rhys, but she could tell by the way he was clutching the hilt that he had no intentions of releasing the weapon any time soon.

"By the saints," John complained, "is there aught this man does save eat?"

The priest was rotund, and he seemingly had little interest in helping himself stay afoot, as it were.

"Where are those damned Vikings?" Sir Jean muttered. "If I'd known what weak-stomached women they were, Rhys, I never would have left you in their care. 'Tis a wonder you turned out tolerably well at all."

Gwen found, quite suddenly, that the impossibility of the situation in which she found herself was finally beginning to sink in. Rhys planned to wed her. Their priest either was too lazy or too terrified to stiffen his knees and stand on his own. Geoffrey was muttering under his breath behind her, Sir Jean was stalking off to rouse the Fitzgerald brothers, and Montgomery and John were arguing over whom the priest should be foisted upon. Nicholas and Robin were fighting with their wooden swords, and the whole of Ayre's garrison had gathered in a group behind them, all watching with wide, incredulous eyes. Rhys's mercenaries, the ones he had taken with him and the ones who had followed Geoffrey from Fenwyck, had all gathered themselves into a fierce little group of thirty, their hands on their swords as if they intended to seriously injure any soul who sought to thwart the plans of their paymaster. Rhys was fingering his own sword as if he prepared to fling himself into the midst of a battle, not matrimony.

Oh, and then there was Alain, who lay dead not fifty paces from them, victim of his own fury.

"Am I the only one," she asked no one in particular, "who finds this odd?"

"You think this is odd?" Rhys asked grimly. "Just wait, Gwen."

She looked up at him. "What more could happen to improve upon these events?"

He pursed his lips. "The king could arrive and discover what I'm about. You could find yourself widowed twice in one day."

Gwen blinked. "Then he did not give you leave—"

"He gave me many things, but you were not among them."

"Rhys!"

"Do you love me?"

She swallowed, hard. "Desperately."

"Then it is enough."

"Did you give him all your gold?" she demanded. "Did he take it all and merely thank you kindly?"

Rhys shook his head. "I gave him a bit to sweeten his humor and a bit more for his tax coffers. There is still enough yet in France to fund our escape should we need to leave England in a rush. For now, though, let us be about our business. The king's temper will see to itself eventually."

She sighed. "I suppose this means we will be riding very swiftly north."

"We'll have to pause long enough to consummate the marriage, my lady. You can rest then."

"The very romance of the thought leaves me breathless," she said dryly.

He spared her a scowl before he turned back to the priest. "Up on your feet, man! We've a wedding to hasten through."

"Here," Sir Jean said, shepherding the twins in front of him, "be of some use, you great mewling babes."

Rhys waited until the twins had settled themselves on either side of the priest, who suddenly found that his feet were sturdy enough to keep him upright and therefore there was no need to lean on either of the rather crusty and noisome-smelling men flanking him, then cleared his throat.

"Wed us," he commanded.

"But—" the priest spluttered.

"Robin," Rhys called. "Come name your mother's dowry."

Robin sighed as he put up his sword. He came to stand in front of Rhys, who turned him around to face the priest.

"Artane," Rhys supplied, "is hers alone."

Robin looked at the priest. "She has Artane, Father." He looked back up at Rhys. "Is that enough, do you think?"

" 'Tis more than enough for me," Rhys said.

"Perhaps she should have what she had before she married Alain of Ayre," Robin said, as if he talked about someone besides his father. Gwen listened to him discuss the advantages of such a thing with Rhys as if he'd been managing such vast holdings his entire young life. Evidently his journey to France had been instructive.

"All she brought with her before," Robin decided, turning to the priest. "It can go to Lord Rhys. I'll keep Lord Alain's lands. Lord Rhys can see to them for me until I'm of age."

Gwen blinked. She wasn't sure what surprised her more, Robin's tone of authority or his mistake in Rhys's title. She put her hand on his shoulder gently.

"Robin," she said softly, "much as you might like to call Rhys lord, he is but—"

"The newly made earl of Artane," John supplied cheerfully. He smiled at Gwen. "A successful chat with the king and all, you know."

"Do not forget your lands in France," Sir Jean added with a grunt.

Gwen looked at him in surprise. "Land there as well?" She turned to stare at Rhys. "Did you know of it?"

"Not a bloody thing 'til a se'nnight past," he said, sounding none-too-happy about the delay in receiving the tidings.

Sir Jean shrugged. "Could have told him about it sooner, I suppose—"

"Aye, you could have," Rhys agreed with a growl.

"But I wanted to see what he'd make of himself," Sir Jean finished with a wicked smile sent his grandson's way. "Nothing like a little lust for land to make a man into a man."

"Grandpère, had I time, I would take you to the lists and show you what a man I've become."

Sir Jean looked greatly tempted. "Unfortunately you haven't the time, whelp, but don't think I'll forget the offer. In a fortnight or two after we've reached your wasteland in the north and you've recovered from your saddlesores, we'll see who is the man in truth."

"Earl?" Gwen said, looking up at Rhys.

"Gift from the king for valiant service and bravery," John said.

"As well as for a chest of gold," Rhys muttered.

"Earl?" Gwen repeated.

"It was a very large chest."

"Yet still he would not give me to you?" Gwen asked.

"He said he would think on it," Rhys said shortly, "which left me wondering if I would do better to return to France for more funds or merely tempt him with a barrel or two of peaches."

"You could have threatened to make off with his cook," Sir Jean suggested.

"I had considered that, believe me," Rhys said dryly.

"Rhys, what will we do!" Gwen exclaimed. "If he has said you nay—"

"That was before he knew you were a widow," Rhys said, reaching down to take her hand, "and I'm sorry I've left you no time to grieve—"

The one who possibly would need it was Robin, but he seemed more preoccupied with standing as close as possible to Rhys. And it wasn't as if he'd spent more than what amounted to several days with his sire. Perhaps grief would be the last thing on his mind.

"But haste is of the essence," Rhys finished. "I hope the king will be too busy chasing Rollan to pay us much heed until we're safely ensconced at Fenwyck, where I am certain Geoffrey intends to offer us hospitality."

"Hospitality," Geoffrey snorted. "Think again! I *always* have regrets when I indulge in it."

Rhys ignored him and looked down at Gwen. "John reappropriated Artane and gave it to me. I told him not to, but he insisted I should have something for my trouble since I wasn't to have you."

"And now that you'll have me?"

"I'll keep it, if you don't mind, and build you a very fine hall upon it."

It mattered, she found, very little to her whom the land belonged to on the king's rolls. All that mattered was that she and Rhys now seemed destined to live in the same place, hopefully as man and wife. Assuming the king didn't reach them first and deny them what they'd waited so long to have. Gwen turned to the priest.

"Wed us," she commanded. "Now."

"Um," the priest began.

"Scribe!" Rhys bellowed.

A rather thin, sickly-looking soul was thrust into their midst, endeavoring to balance parchment, ink, and quill. The scribe was instructed to record what had transpired, under the watchful eye and drawn sword of the newly made earl of Artane.

The contract was signed by all parties involved, then the priest was sent on his way to see to the less pressing matter of arranging the former baron of Ayre's burial.

Gwen thought Rhys might find it an appropriate time to kiss her to seal their marriage, so she turned toward him, closed her eyes, and lifted her face up accordingly. But instead of kissing her, Rhys took her by the shoulders and set her aside.

Then he hit Geoffrey of Fenwyck full in the face.

"*That,*" he said, "is for slobbering upon *my* wife's

hand.'' He looked down at the baron of Fenwyck, who lay sprawled in the dust. ''Never do it again.''

Geoffrey could only gape at him, speechless.

Rhys looked about him, flexing his fingers. ''Who should be next? I daresay I have many scores to settle this afternoon, especially with those who couldn't seem to follow my simplest command.'' He frowned at the Fitzgeralds. ''Don't know that I'd want to touch them in their current condition.''

''Montgomery?'' John suggested politely.

Rhys shook his head. ''That would leave me having to prop up the twins. He should be repaid as well, though. I left him with instructions to see Gwen remained at Fenwyck.''

Gwen winced at the glare Montgomery threw her way.

''She vowed by the Rood,'' Montgomery said. ''How could I doubt her word?''

Rhys snorted. ''You know her as well as I do.''

''If someone would care to hear my side of the tale,'' Gwen interjected. ''I came to save your gold,'' she said to Rhys before he could open his mouth. ''We received another missive at Fenwyck, you know.''

''I know all about it, as I had the pleasure of intercepting your messenger in Dover,'' Rhys said. ''That changes nothing. Fenwyck could have come in your stead.''

''I am better at disguise.''

''And very vulnerable should Rollan have caught you unawares.''

''I've been working on my swordplay,'' she argued.

''You promised me you would stay behind.''

''My plans changed.''

''You know,'' John put in, ''we should likely gather our gear and be on our way. Should the king decide to come to Ayre in the near future, I daresay we don't want to be here to entertain him.''

Gwen looked at her former brother-in-law. ''There are many who will attest to Rollan's murdering of Alain. You've no need to fear.''

John smiled. ''Oh, I have no fear for myself. 'Tis Lord

Rhys who must worry about his sweet neck."

"There is that," Sir Jean agreed. "Powerfully fickle is that king of yours. Never know what he's intending."

"By the saints, Grandpère," Rhys grumbled, "I wish you had told me of the lands before we left London."

"Wanted to see what—"

"—I'd make of myself, aye, I know," Rhys finished sourly. "Have you any suggestions on what I might do to secure my bride?"

"Well, you've already wed the girl. Best bed her as quick as may be. Johnny Lackland can't argue with that much."

Rhys nodded. "Very well. Won't take but a moment or two."

"It will if you value your ability to sire any children," Gwen warned.

"I'll woo you later—"

"You'll woo me now."

"I've no need to woo you now—I've just wed you!"

"Too long out of polite company," John said, shaking his head sadly.

"I could give you a courting idea or two," Geoffrey offered, leaning up on his elbows in the dirt.

"Let the boy work it out himself," Sir Jean said. "We'll see what sort of imagination he has. 'Tis the last test I have before I tell him the last of the family secrets."

Rhys opened his mouth to say something, then shut it and shook his head. "I don't want to know any more. I've learned too much today as it is."

"I have something that might aid you."

Gwen looked at Montgomery to find him fishing about in the purse attached to his belt. He pulled forth a very faded green ribbon and handed it to Gwen with a smile.

"Oh," Rhys said, his breath catching on the word. "Then you had it?"

"Thought you might want it eventually," Montgomery said with a smile.

Gwen took the ribbon she had once given Rhys and gingerly tied it about his arm again. "I don't suppose," she said softly, "that this counts for you wooing me, but it is a most romantic thing just the same."

He drew her into his arms and smiled down at her. His eyes were very bright and seemingly filled with a stray tear or two.

"If you only knew how long I've waited for this moment," he said softly. "If you only knew what I felt the first time you tied this ribbon about my arm, and how desperately I prayed that some day you would be mine."

"You can tell me of it . . . um . . ."

"During?"

"After."

And with that, he closed his eyes, bent his head, and kissed her softly and sweetly on the lips. Gwen felt the world about her fade until there was only the man with his arms about her. No king, no gold, and no others. He angled his head and kissed her more deeply. His hands began to roam over her back and up into her hair. Her plait was loosened and her hair soon flowed freely over her shoulders.

"Oh, by the saints," a crusty voice said in faint disgust, "find a chamber, won't you?"

Rhys spared his grandfather a glare before he smiled down at Gwen again. "Should we?"

She blinked to clear away the haze and gave the matter serious thought. She suddenly felt the eyes of every man in the company turned upon her. Even Ayre's guardsmen were looking upon the scene with great interest, as if they each were counting on her to make the correct decision.

Gwen looked at Rhys.

"I know just the place."

It was only a short time later that she stopped in front of a vaguely familiar door. She smiled at her newly made husband.

"This might be appropriate."

Rhys pushed it open, then pulled a torch from the passageway and found a place for it inside. "I believe, however," he said as he drew her in behind him, "that you were wearing John's clothes the last time we were here. And you were not so liberally smudged."

Gwen felt her mouth fall open. She had completely forgotten about her condition. She had just been wed in garments covered with horse manure and three weeks' worth of travel.

Rhys laughed, as if he understood what she'd been thinking. "Not even that detracts from your beauty, my love."

"As if flattery comforts me!"

"Flattery?" He shook his head. "A knight never lies, so you must believe I speak the truth. Besides, smudged or not, the very sight of you leaves me weak in the knees." He shifted. "I can scarce believe you are mine."

She sighed and looked down at her filthy clothes. "This isn't exactly how I'd envisioned our nuptials."

"Nor I. I had thought even to attempt a song or two."

"The saints preserve me," she said with a laugh. "Perhaps my ears should be grateful for your haste."

He scowled. " 'Tis hardly my fault that I cannot hear the notes aright. My skills simply lie in a different area."

"Dicing."

He smiled at that. "Perhaps later."

She looked around her. Not even a blanket or two to throw upon the floor. She looked at Rhys.

"Well?" she asked.

He took a pair of steps toward her, reached over her, and shoved the bolt home. "That should assure us privacy."

"For a moment or two," she agreed.

He looked down at her and smiled faintly. "If you had any idea how badly I want you, you'd realize a brief moment or two may be all you'll have from me at present."

She wasn't exactly sure what he meant by that, but she had the feeling she was soon to find out.

"I will woo you properly," he said as he pulled her into his arms. "Soon."

"The very thought is almost enough to induce me to bathe," she said as he kissed her.

And then she found that the condition of her clothing and her person mattered not at all, except as it served for a bed.

The floor was just as uncomfortable as she remembered it being. At least this time she had no fear of being interrupted. There was something to be said for a band of mercenaries to do her husband's bidding.

Her husband. Gwen could hardly believe it. Widowed and wed within moments. And what a ceremony it had been—

"Gwen," Rhys said with a sigh of resignation.

She winced. "Forgive me. No more thoughts."

He took her face in his hands and kissed her thoroughly. And then kissing led to touching and that led to all clothes being used as a bed, which led to Rhys promising between more long, sweet kisses that he would filch Fenwyck's finest goosefeather mattress at his earliest opportunity. Gwen started to say that it mattered not, then she realized she was several years older and the birth of two children more mature than the last time they'd lain upon such scant padding, and a goosefeather mattress was beginning to sound very pleasant.

And then thoughts of goosefeathers and children and uncomfortable floors began to fade and all she was left with was the man in her arms she'd never thought to have there again. And the thing that fair brought tears to her eyes in truth was the realization that his touch was no more practiced, his loving no more skilled than it had been the last time they'd lain together. He was all enthusiasm and unschooled passion—certainly not a lover who had spent countless hours lazing in his mistress's bed.

The saints be praised for that.

And if his hands trembled now and again when he touched her and he seemed not to know what to do with his knees or elbows on occasion, it did nothing but make her smile and clutch him to her the tighter.

He made her his with a positively mercenary-like laugh of triumphant possession.

And when he managed to breathe again, he rolled away with a groan. He sat up and gingerly planted his backside against the cold stone of the floor, rubbed his elbows and knees simultaneously as best he could, and smiled happily at her.

"That was exceedingly uncomfortable," he said cheerfully.

Gwen was quite certain she would never walk quite as easily again, but she had to agree just as merrily. "I don't know that I can manage that again here."

He paused. "We could filch a few more garments and things from about the castle."

"That would necessitate leaving the chamber. Dressing. Combing our hair."

"Enduring a thorough teasing from my grandsire."

She met his gaze and found herself nodding along with him.

"Best to stay here," he stated.

"We might manage with what we have."

And, unsurprisingly to either of them, they did.

39

Rollan of Ayre wished desperately he'd somehow managed to snatch Alain's crop before he fled the keep. Merely kicking his stallion in the sides was not producing the desired speed.

He looked behind him, but saw no riders following. He knew that reprieve wouldn't last long. They would send men after him, and then he would find himself languishing in some hellhole. He doubted that even he, with his superior charm, could talk himself out of such visible familial murder. John had never had much use for Alain, 'twas true, but the king would likely have preferred something a bit more subtle.

Where to go now? What to do? Whom to blame for his current condition?

The last was the easiest. This was de Piaget's fault. Rollan had counted on the gallant Sir Rhys to slay Alain in defense of Gwen's honor. Things would have been so much simpler that way. Rollan would have slain Rhys, then disposed of Robin and Amanda soon enough, and thereafter found himself lord of Ayre with a beautiful aqua-eyed bride at his side. Gwen would have found herself tamed in time. Indeed, he was certain she would have enjoyed the taming.

And now his scheme was completely ruined because of de Piaget's wagging tongue.

He would have to pay for his words, of course.

Rollan found himself heading west. And once he realized where he was heading, he smiled. Perhaps his plans could be salvaged. He hadn't killed Alain outright, had he? If anyone could it would be John who could understand the frustration of having an elder brother possess what should have rightfully come to him. Alain's death was an accident, an accident precipitated by de Piaget's rash goading of the former lord of Ayre.

Perhaps his schemes weren't for naught after all. Rhys could be finished off. Robin could meet with an unfortunate accident. Lads were always dying of one thing or another.

And Gwen could be convinced in time that they had always been destined to be together.

But first the greatest obstacle must be removed. And Rollan knew just who would be most helpful in doing so. Rhys's true parentage wasn't widely known. Indeed, Rollan suspected that there were only two people on the entire island who knew of it—and Bertram of Ayre had carried the secret to his grave.

And Rollan of Ayre had held the knowledge close to his heart since the moment he'd overheard his sire discussing the matter with Rhys's grandfather.

Ah, but eavesdropping was such a useful skill.

He altered his course and set his mind on his goal.

Sedgwick.

40

Rhys pulled the hall door shut behind him and was glad to do it. Though he had fond memories indeed of a certain tower chamber inside the keep, he would not be sorry never to see it again. He knew he would have to come to Ayre with Robin occasionally to assure himself that the lad's holdings weren't being overrun, but he was more than happy to be leaving the place behind him at present. He'd imagined up in his mind scores of times just how it might feel to walk through Ayre's doors with Gwen as his.

The reality of it was almost more than he could bear.

His company was waiting for him in the courtyard. His mercenaries looked appropriately fierce, not hesitating to send Ayre's guardsmen intimidating looks whenever possible. Rhys hadn't yet decided what he would do with the lads. Perhaps he could be forgiven for having had more on his mind than their futures for the past few days. Matters hadn't improved for his poor head—especially after having passed a long night of intimate deliberations with his beloved. Perhaps 'twas for the best that he keep them about for a bit longer until he could again concentrate on something besides thoughts of where and when he might have his lady alone again.

He gestured for the company to mount up. That much he could do with the small portion of his wits left him. He looked at Gwen and found that she was smiling shyly at him. He grinned back, then heard his grandfather begin to chuckle. A blush came from nowhere and applied itself industriously to his cheeks. He turned away before the entire company, and more particularly his grandfather, could see it and humiliate him with their teasing.

He turned to check the straps that held the Fitzgerald brothers to their mounts and gave them both an encouraging smile.

"One last time, my friends. I promise no more traveling."

"The travails we go through for you," Jared groaned. "Tending your hurts and sorrows—"

"Riding from one end of this barren wasteland to the other—" Connor added.

"Puking 'til there's naught left to puke—"

"I ask you, brother," Connor said, turning his head to look at his twin, "is this worth the pain?"

"Nay, it is not."

"I say we let him go north on his own."

"Aye, brother. You have that aright."

"Too late," Rhys said cheerfully, firmly cinching the rope that bound Jared to his horse.

"I'd rather walk," Connor groused.

"I'd rather stay *here*," Jared complained.

"You would miss me overmuch," Rhys assured them. "Courage, friends. The journey will be swift."

He walked away before more Viking curses could be heaped upon his head.

Gwen was mounted already, as was Nicholas. Rhys looked to find Robin holding Rhys's mount's reins. He looked sick with apprehension. Rhys walked over and ruffled his hair.

"Not to worry."

"But what if the king comes after us?"

Rhys squatted down and looked at Robin seriously. "Think you I would let you go?"

"But the king—"

"Will be perfectly happy for me to claim you when the time comes. He values my sword, Robin, just as he will value yours in time—should he manage not to eat himself to death. I daresay he would rather keep us here on the isle then see us all go to France."

"But we've properties there, haven't we?" Robin asked anxiously. "Just in case?"

Rhys threw his grandfather a dark look. "Aye, and they're large enough to keep us traveling over them for quite some time."

"Perhaps we should go to France and look at them," Robin suggested, sounding as if he would have sold his soul to do the like. "Then we won't lose our heads."

Rhys smiled. "We won't lose our heads anyway, Robin. We'll hasten north and begin the building of our keep."

And with luck what you won't see is your soon-to-be adopted father's head on a pike outside those yet-to-be built gates, Rhys thought to himself.

"Besides, your uncle John has been pressed into service as keeper of Ayre until such time as we return to visit your inheritance. He will be the one to face the king's wrath."

Said keeper was none too happy about the duty, but Rhys had promised to return and knight him before the new year. John was nothing if not practical about such things.

Of course, there would be a great amount of groveling on his own part in the future, but hopefully by then the king would see the wisdom of what Rhys had done. He would be there to keep watch over the northern borders. With any luck, John wouldn't become so angry that he reappropriated Gwen's lands for the crown's pleasure. In his wildest dreams Rhys had never dreamed he would be lord over so much. He was loth to give any of it up.

Though if it came to that, he would take Gwen and the children and hasten to France. It wasn't as if they couldn't have lived quite comfortably there as well.

But all that would come later. First would come a swift

journey north, then preparations for building. He could at least start the construction with the gold he had left. He would manage to finish it somehow. All he knew for a certainty was that the fashioning of his home couldn't happen quickly enough.

He could almost see his banner, flying merrily in the breeze.

And what a beautiful sight it was.

The child stood on the side of the road and watched the company pass by her. She would have to go north with them, that much she knew. But her grief was still heavy upon her, and that made it hard to muster up the courage to stop one of the knight's fierce companions and beg for a ride.

Her tears had finally blinded her completely when she felt rather than saw a horse stop. A man dismounted and soon she found herself staring into pale gray eyes.

"*Chérie*," the knight said, "what do you here, dressed for travel? Where is your grandsire?"

"He's gone," she whispered.

Then she wept in earnest.

The knight drew her into his arms and cradled her close. The child then felt the hands of the knight's new lady wife and found herself soon sheltered in soft arms.

"Rhys," the lady said, "we must take her with us if she will come. She cannot remain here."

"*Chérie*," the knight said, laying his hand atop the child's head gently, "will you come?"

The child nodded, unable to speak.

"And your grandfather's things. Surely you should bring them along?"

The child patted the manuscript that she had bound to her small self with strips of cloth. It was the most impor-

tant thing, and her grandfather had labored long over the
scribbling of his potions. But having his pots and pouches
would be a comfort as well.

"I'll see to it," the knight said, and then he walked
away, calling out orders as he went.

The child soon found herself riding in her knight's company behind an old man who reminded her not at all of
her grandsire, but who had a gentle smile just the same. It
was enough to ease her.

She clutched her pieces of glass in her hand and rode
into her future, dry-eyed.

Gwen thought bathing just might be a fatal activity—for
the five girls ignoring their work in the kitchens, that was.
She sat on a stool near the tub and glared at the daughters
of Fenwyck's cook. They took no notice of her. They had
even ceased their chopping, mixing, and stirring to admire
the man who currently tarried in the water, seemingly
oblivious to the commotion he was causing.

Rhys was, unfortunately, too large to fit into the tub, so
his arms were dangling over the sides, and his knees bent
over the sides as well. There was *far* too much of him
exposed for her peace of mind.

She suspected, as she threw the handful of drooling
wenches another warning look they paid no heed to, that
she was even less enthusiastic about this visit to Fenwyck
than she had been about the last one.

Though even she had to admit that loitering in bed with
her love was much more pleasant when they had a goosefeather mattress beneath them. Said goosefeather mattress
of Geoffrey's had been relinquished promptly after Rhys
had invited Fenwyck's lord to decide the matter in the lists.
Geoffrey's attachment to his bed had been clearly shown
by his willingness even to set foot on the dirt. Unfortunately for him, said attachment had been summarily sev-

ered. He'd gulped most audibly when Rhys had drawn two
swords, then snarled out a curse straight from his bruised
pride when Rhys put one of the blades away with mock
dismay over Geoffrey's agitated state.

Matters had not improved much from there for the lord
of Fenwyck.

Gwen had watched Rhys enough in the lists that she
knew when he was toying with an opponent and when he
wasn't. She could hardly believe her eyes when she saw
that Rhys was dragging the entire affair out much longer
than he needed to, but then she supposed that since it was
Geoffrey's finest mattress that she would be sleeping upon
for a pair of fortnights, saving what was left of Geoffrey's
pride was the least Rhys could do.

"By the saints, you are a lazy pup, Grandson."

Gwen shifted on her small stool that she might have a
better look at Rhys's grandsire. Rhys didn't even open his
eyes.

"I've earned the rest, Grandpère," Rhys said, sounding
just as lazy as his grandfather claimed he was. "An exhausting fortnight, to be sure."

Sir Jean looked appraisingly at Gwen, and she found
herself blushing in spite of her best efforts to look indifferent. Then he turned his attentions to the kitchen's maids
and gave them a stern look from beneath his bushy eyebrows.

"Someone stands to lose fingers," he said pointedly, "if
she does not attend better to what she is doing."

Evidently the wenches were better impressed with Sir
Jean's growls than they had been with Gwen's glares, for
they turned back to their work promptly.

Sir Jean pulled up a stool and sat next to Gwen. "Guarding your treasure, lady?"

"I thought it wise."

He laughed at her, and Gwen saw where Rhys had come
by some of his charm. Never mind that the man was old
enough to be—oddly enough—her grandsire, he was exceedingly charming. She found herself returning his smile

and feeling as if she had known him far longer than a month.

"Was he worth the wait?" Jean asked, inclining his head toward Rhys.

Gwen found that even Rhys had opened one eye to see her answer.

"Aye," she said. "Well worth it."

"A good lover then?"

"Grandpère!" That at least seemingly had Rhys fully awake.

Jean only shrugged. "Want to make certain you aren't tainting your name." He looked at Gwen and winked. "Fine lovers, all those de Piaget men are."

"And how would you know?" Rhys asked with a scowl. "It isn't as if you've been with scores of women for them to tell you."

"I had my share before I met your grandmother."

"And after she died?" Rhys prodded.

"I have a very fine memory of former praise," Jean said haughtily. "And who are you, whelp, to question my prowess?"

"You questioned mine," Rhys replied.

Sir Jean began to finger his sword hilt. "I daresay I should plan on seeing you in the lists shortly. You're far too cheeky for my taste."

Gwen suspected, and she had the feeling she had it aright, that Sir Jean would have used any reason to face his grandson over blades. They didn't cross swords a single time that the man wasn't grinning madly, as if he'd been the one to teach Rhys everything he knew about swordplay. Such was a grandfather's pride, she supposed.

"Later," Rhys said, leaning his head back and closing his eyes again. "Perhaps tomorrow."

Jean shook his head. "Lazy," he said, clucking his tongue. "Lazy and soft. Your sire would be appalled were he here to see this."

"I am newly wed but a pair of fortnights," Rhys said, sounding not at all troubled by his idleness.

"You should be wielding your sword daily," Sir Jean

instructed, "and that does *not*—forgive me Gwen for saying so for only a fool would rather be in the lists than with you—that does *not* mean the sword you wield in bed!"

Rhys opened one eye and looked balefully at his grandfather. "When do I appear in the lists?"

"Just after sunrise."

"And leave them when?"

Sir Jean chewed on the inside of his cheek before he pursed his lips and answered. "Late in the day."

"And then spend my time how?"

"Plotting and scheming how to leave the table early," Sir Jean groused.

"Today is the first day of leisure I've taken, and you'll not goad me into being sorry for it. For all you know, I'll crawl from this tub and pass the rest of my day in bed."

Gwen jumped at the frown Sir Jean threw her way. "Disobedient pup. Did you teach him that?"

She held up her hands in surrender. "It wasn't me. He was already grown by the time I had the keeping of him."

"Things are progressing as they should," Rhys assured his grandfather. "I've sent to Mother for the rest of my gold, and you know 'twas one of your own men who is seeing to the message. Montgomery is readying the men for our journey on the morrow to Artane. The children are tearing Fenwyck's hall to bits without my having to encourage them, and Lady Joanna—"

"Ah," Sir Jean said, stroking his chin, "now there is a handsome enough woman." He looked at Gwen. "Would she want me, do you think?"

"Well . . ."

Rhys threw a handful of water at his grandsire. "She has no interest in a lover your age."

"I'll have you know my sword is as mighty as it always was—"

"No doubt—" Rhys interrupted dryly.

"And I've still a pleasing visage—"

"Never said you didn't. . . ."

Sir Jean jumped to his feet and drew his sword with relish, sending most of the kitchen maids and lads scurrying for cover. "Out to the lists with you, insolent whelp!" he bellowed. "I'll not be disparaged thusly!" He took Gwen by the arm and pulled her from the kitchen. "You'll come with me and judge the victor. And bring your mother."

Gwen looked over her shoulder to find Rhys crawling from the tub with a resigned sigh. Half a dozen young women hastened to help him dry himself off, which was almost enough to make Gwen reach for Sir Jean's sword.

He stopped once they reached the great hall, sheathed his sword, and smiled at her. "Got him out of the tub, so now I might enter it. Shall we have a cup of ale first, do you think?"

She could only stare at him, unsure if she should laugh or not.

"You'll come sit on the stool in the kitchen and keep the little wenches at bay for me as well, will you not?" he asked, a twinkle in his eye.

"Well—"

"Better yet, send your mother. A passing handsome woman, that one."

Gwen let him lead her over to the table. She hadn't indulged in but half her cup before her husband arrived, dressed and grumbling. He spared his grandfather an irritated look before he tugged Gwen to her feet.

"Come with me."

"Don't forget your mother," Jean called as Rhys dragged Gwen from the hall. "Send her to the kitchens."

"The saints preserve her," Rhys muttered under his breath.

Gwen laughed as he led her to the bedchamber Rhys had appropriated for them. He pulled her inside, shut the door, and shoved the bolt home.

"You don't think I should call my mother—"

"I do not," Rhys said, backing her up against the door.

"But your grandfather—"

"Can fend for himself. He's been doing it for years. I, however, am perfectly helpless and will need much watching over for the rest of this day."

"You pitiful man," she said, clucking her tongue sadly. "I suppose you'll need my full attention?"

"I fear that is the case."

Gwen wrapped her arms around his neck. "How have you managed all these years without me?"

His mouth came down on hers. She suspected, as he soon lifted her up and carried her to the bed, that such a question was not one he cared to answer. Indeed, he seemed determined to make up for all the years that she hadn't had him to watch over, if the tenacity with which he kept her in his bed was any indication.

Evening fell and Gwen managed to escape long enough to light a candle or two. She returned to her husband's arms and sighed in contentment as she rested her head against his shoulder. He ran callused fingers over her back, and she remembered idly the first time he had touched her hand and how even then such a touch had affected her. Things had not changed.

"Gwen?"

"Aye, love," she said.

"I wish this day would never end."

He sounded so wistful, she lifted her head and looked down at him. "We'll have many more such days, surely."

He smiled, a pensive smile that touched her heart. "I hope so, my love. I do."

"We will," she said. "I am convinced of it."

"Then convince me," he asked. "And take your time at it."

She saw the twinkle in his eye and laughed.

Then she bent her head and kissed him, determined to do just that.

41

"Have patience with an old man," the old man said, "and explain to me once again why it is I shouldn't run you through for interrupting my supper."

Rollan admired Patrick of Sedgwick's callousness. Indeed, he understood it well and had no fears for the continuation of his head resting atop his neck. The old man was naught but bluster. Rollan knew he was intrigued, and he also knew Patrick would have slit his own throat before showing it. This was the kind of man he could reason with.

It had taken him a fortnight to reach Sedgwick after his flight from Ayre, then another fortnight to manage to get himself inside the gates. These were not trusting souls.

"I know where your niece is," Rollan repeated. *Or at least the general vicinity—that vicinity being the whole of France.* There was no need for specifics with this man. "And I know who her son is." There was no one else in the solar, so there was no need for secrecy anymore.

Patrick snorted. "I have no niece. She was stolen by ruffians and murdered."

"She was snatched away by a wandering healer. She bore him a son before he was burned as a heretic in France."

Patrick regarded him narrowly. "Foolishness."

"The healer was Jean de Piaget's son, Etienne," Rollan pressed on. "Etienne met Mary of Sedgwick in this very hall and fled with her in the dead of night."

"She was snatched—"

"She wanted to go," Rollan corrected. "To escape a very violent household, or so I've heard."

He wondered, idly, if that was more truth than Patrick wanted to hear. The man had begun to finger his swordhilt. No matter. Rollan knew Patrick was more than ready to listen now. He would live until the full tale was told, and hopefully by then he would have convinced Patrick of his further usefulness. After all, there were some details even he wasn't prepared to share as of yet.

"Go on," Patrick growled.

Rollan suppressed his smile. "Mary wed with Etienne and they returned to France."

"And then what happened?"

"Etienne was not just a wandering healer and a some-time minstrel. He was a highly skilled knight with a gift for taking on the mores of many vocations. He had, as you might imagine, his share of enemies, and most of them were very powerful. One of them paid clergy to accuse him of heresy. Or perhaps he truly was in league with the devil." Rollan shrugged. "His get certainly has prowess that might be seen as unnatural."

Rollan watched closely for Patrick's reaction. His hand moved from his sword to rub distractedly at his knee. Old battle wound, Rollan surmised. A sure sign of some kind of discomfort.

Interesting.

"Etienne was put to death, or so the story goes."

"And their child? How would I know him?"

Rollan wanted to roll his eyes. By the bloody saints, was he doomed to be surrounded by imbeciles?

"De Piaget?" he prompted. "Rhys de Piaget?"

"Oh." Patrick's mouth shaped the word, but no sound came out. The realization of just who stood to claim Sedg-

wick and all it entailed dawned, and it was followed hard
on the heels by what appeared to be no small measure of
consternation. Patrick only held Sedgwick by virtue of his
brother having died without issue. That his brother's
daughter should have had a son, and such a son indeed . . .
obviously Patrick had just divined who might come knocking at his gates, demanding his inheritance.

"Now you see the necessity of paying him a small
visit."

"Aye."

"He, oddly enough, knows nothing of his parentage, but
who knows how long that might last?"

Patrick didn't seem to have any trouble understanding
precisely what Rollan meant by that.

"There is no sense taking the risk of him finding out,"
Rollan continued.

Patrick nodded.

"His mother, however, is of no consequence."

Patrick nodded again, and Rollan heaved a silent sigh
of relief. In truth there was little Mary de Piaget could do
to wrest control of Sedgwick from her uncle, but it galled
Rollan deeply that he could not discover her whereabouts.
Much as he tried, he'd been unsuccessful in trying to wring
that out of his father on his deathbed. He had no one but
himself to blame for that. He'd been unskilled with poisons
in those days. But how was he to have known too much too
quickly would leave a man in agony, yet unable to
voice it?

"He will be going north," Rollan continued. "Traveling with a woman and a lad. I will see to those two."

"And I will see to him," Patrick said, standing up suddenly. "We'll leave as soon as I can gather enough men
for war."

"Unprovoked?" Rollan mused. "I wonder about the
wisdom of that."

"You said he's responsible for your brother's death.
That's reason enough to see him repaid."

Rollan smiled faintly. He'd only implicated Rhys

slightly in the deed, so he could hardly hold himself responsible for Patrick's incorrect assumption. Besides, someone should pay for Alain's untimely demise.

Why not Rhys?

42

Rhys sat at the base of a partially completed wall and stared out over the sea. The stone was cold against his back, the sun was warm on his face, and the breeze smelled sharply of brine.

He thought he just might die from the pleasure of it.

The keep was progressing slowly, though he suspected that any progress that didn't have his hall up and livable overnight would seem slow to him. They'd been at Artane for almost three months, and what they'd accomplished was truly remarkable.

They had the beginnings of outer walls. The great hall and chapel already had foundation stones laid. The outbuildings and such were to be made of wood and some of them had already been started. Even winter grain had been planted in hopes that they actually might have something more to eat than what they'd brought with them from Fenwyck. Rhys didn't relish having to spend the winter traveling from one of Gwen's keeps to the next to avail themselves of the larders. Even though Gwen's mother had returned to Segrave and offered to see things sent to them, Rhys had little wish to accept of her generosity. If they could finish enough of a temporary hall, they could winter there and keep working.

"We have to train if we want to earn our spurs. And to train together we *both* have to be knights."

"But, Robin—"

"Don't you want to be a knight?"

Rhys heard the voices coming from the other side of the wall and found that he was somewhat grateful that at least this part of the defenses had been built up far enough to hide him. Robin had seemed pleased enough with his new home, but one never truly knew what went on in that young lad's head. No sense in not knowing what was going on. Whatever scheme Robin was about, Nicholas was sure to be dragged into. Nicholas had turned out to be too much the peacemaker to go against Robin's wishes. Poor lad. He would have to find his own footing eventually, or find himself in scrapes he no doubt would have preferred to avoid.

"I would be a better mercenary," Nicholas offered hesitantly. "Much better than a knight."

"You *can't* be a mercenary," Robin insisted. "We both have to be knights, *good* knights. *He* expects it."

Nicholas was quiet for so long, Rhys was tempted to peek over the wall and see what was going on.

"He doesn't expect it of me," Nicholas said finally. "I'm not really—"

"Of course you are," Robin interrupted.

"He's just being kind—"

"A proper knightly virtue," Robin said promptly.

"But he didn't really mean—"

"A knight never lies. He said he wanted you, and he wouldn't lie about it."

"But my blood isn't noble."

Rhys wondered if Robin's ensuing sigh hadn't blown Nicholas over. He found himself smiling in spite of his faint dismay. Hadn't he claimed both boys before the envoy King John had sent north? By the saints, he'd done nothing but congratulate himself for the se'nnight following for the cheek he'd displayed. The envoy had expressed in few, but pointed, words the king's displeasure. Rhys had responded calmly and clearly, stating his position and enlightening the envoy as to why the king should leave him be—with Gwen and her children. He hadn't mentioned Nicholas then, but Gwen had elbowed him firmly later when he'd put his wishes down on paper. Robin, Nicholas, and Amanda. She would accept nothing less.

"Nicholas, he claimed us both before the king," Robin said, seemingly trying to muster up the patience to go through something he obviously had said before. "Maybe we aren't his in truth, but he's acting as if we are. He wouldn't do it if he didn't mean it."

There was another lengthy silence. Then Nicholas spoke.

"If you're sure," he began.

"I'm sure," Robin said firmly. "And we'll prove to him that he didn't choose poorly. Now, are you going to be a knight, or not?"

"All right," came the answer.

"I'll wager I reach the lists first!" was Robin's enthusiastic reply.

Rhys managed to heave himself to his feet and peek over the wall in time to see Robin and Nicholas racing to what would eventually be the lists. 'Twas a good place for them. At least there Robin could work no trouble for Nicholas to follow him into.

That left him with only the three girl children in his care to wonder about. Amanda had acquired a foster sister in the person of Anne of Fenwyck, and the two were forever trying to escape some piece of Robin's mischief. Geoffrey had seemingly sent his daughter to Artane with a sense of relief. Rhys wondered if Geoffrey thought himself unskilled with women unless they were over a score in years. Whatever the case, it had provided Amanda with a companion, and Rhys was pleased about that.

The other little one he seemed to have acquired was Socrates's granddaughter. The child had ridden north with them yet asked nothing in return. Gwen had fussed over the girl and tried to include her in the family, but the girl had accepted only a small tent of her own where she could live amongst her grandfather's pots and pouches. The only other thing she had accepted from Gwen was the promise that Gwen would teach her how to read, that the girl might finish her grandfather's book of potion recipes. Rhys could not deny her skill as a healer, despite her tender years. He was glad to have her about for as long as she contented herself to remain with them.

Rhys saw a movement to his left and realized then that his lady was coming toward him. And, as he usually found himself doing, he sighed in sheer relief that she was his. He leaned his elbows gingerly on the uneven wall and waited for her to arrive. By the saints, he did not deserve this boon, but he wasn't about to refuse it.

"Lazing about again?" she asked when she reached the opposite side of the wall.

"What else?" he asked.

"Your grandfather is searching the lists for you."

"I don't doubt it. You would think I'd never lifted a sword with the way he is ever nagging at me about it."

She smiled and leaned over to kiss him firmly on the mouth. "He's trying to make up for all the years he was unable to watch you work."

Rhys only snorted.

"He is," she insisted. "I pried the truth out of him."

"Did you resort to torture?"

"Nay, I had a go at him myself in the lists," Gwen said.

Rhys felt his mouth fall open. "You did? When?"

"When you were off with Montgomery, scouting out the borders. Your grandfather was endeavoring to induce me to reveal all my secrets, so I thought to distract him with a bit of swordplay."

"Leave any scars?"

She reached out and tugged sharply on his ear. "I did not—and what little faith you have in my skill. Perhaps 'tis just as well I never offered myself to you as a mercenary."

"It would have been the end of me," he said, with fer-

vor, then reached out and managed to snag a bit of her
sleeve before she had, in her irritation, pulled completely
out of his reach. "Not for any lack on your part, of
course."

She paused and waited. "Aye?"

"I would not have managed to concentrate on anything
save you," he said.

"Well," she said, sounding somewhat appeased. "That
sheds a different light upon the matter."

He smiled, then held out his hand. "Care to join me?"

"Are you surveying your domain?"

He shook his head with another smile. "Staring out over
the ocean and dreaming of glorious things in the future."

"Your keep?" she asked.

"You naked for the afternoon?" he suggested.

She laughed and didn't argue when he invited her to
step over the wall and join him. He resumed his perch with
his lady sitting next to him. He put his arm around her and
drew her close to his side.

"Do I dream," he asked, "or are you really mine?"

She nestled more closely to him. "I can scarce believe
it myself."

He closed his eyes and leaned his head back against the
stone. He'd thought, when he made his lady his, that he
could not be more content, nor more satisfied with his life.
He'd imagined, after they'd reached Fenwyck without
having the king come after them, that his life could not be
any better. When the work was begun on his keep and he
saw the walls even outlined in stone, he was certain he
could not be happier.

But as he sat with his lady and enjoyed both the chill
of the breeze and the warmth of the sunshine, he began to
realize that thinking his life had reached its crowning moment was futile. He suspected that things could only improve.

Assuming, of course, that the king did not choose to
travel to Artane, sever Rhys's head from his shoulders, and
carry his head back to London without the rest of his form.

"I am certain, Connor, that I saw her come this way."

"And *I* tell *you*, Jared, that there is nothing save a steep descent to the sea on the other side of this wall. Why would she heave herself over it?"

Rhys sighed. It looked as if his moment of reflection was passed. At least the twins couldn't see him. Perhaps they would tire of speculating about Gwen's whereabouts and be on their way shortly.

"You don't think," Jared began slowly, "that she heaved herself over the wall apurpose. Do you?"

Connor's gasp of horror was clearly audible. "Whyever for?"

"Perhaps young Rhys—"

"Impossible."

"The children then—"

"Fling herself over the wall to escape them?" Connor demanded. "Have you lost your wits, brother?"

There was a long bit of silence during which time Rhys exchanged a look of amusement with Gwen.

"You look," Jared whispered.

"I will not," Connor returned. "*You* look."

"I will *not*. For all I know you'd heave *me* over the side!"

"Me? I wouldn't. But I wouldn't trust you not to do the same."

"I wouldn't," Jared protested. He paused, then cleared his throat. "We could both look at the same time. Then there would be no heaving of either of us."

"Save our stomachs," Connor groused, "and I've no mind for any more of that. For all we know, they've snuck off the other side of the hill where 'tis less steep and gone off for a bit of—" He paused, then coughed. "Well, *you* know."

"Without us?" Jared demanded, outraged.

"I know," Connor agreed darkly. "Difficult to believe, but there you have it."

"Such gratitude."

"You'd think she would think of us—" Connor said.

"Or at least he might give us a bit of consideration—" Jared agreed.

"I say we take them *both* to the lists," Connor said sternly, "and—"

"Oh, not our little Gwen," Jared interrupted. "Never her. 'Tis likely all Rhys's fault anyway. *She* would never think to leave without us. But he—"

"Very well, then, we'll take *him* to the lists. Once we find him, that is—"

As their voices faded, Rhys was spared the knowledge of what the twins intended to do with him for his cheek. He suspected he was far better off not knowing, but there was something to be said for being prepared. He promised to remind himself to continue to carry both swords for the next little while.

Gwen leaned up suddenly and kissed him.

"What?" he whispered with a smile.

"We could sneak off," she suggested, lifting her head from his shoulder. "No sense in disappointing the twins."

"As if you could," Rhys grumbled. "You, my love, are seemingly firmly ensconced in their good graces. Though I cannot blame them, for I am just as enamored."

"Are you?"

"I am."

"Perhaps you could show me," Gwen said, resettling her head against his shoulder, "later. 'Tis too peaceful here right now to move."

Rhys couldn't have agreed more. He gathered his lady more closely and closed his eyes.

Bliss.

It was, however, bliss he never suspected would last overlong. His life had been too easy for the past few months, and he knew something would have to go awry sooner or later.

He rolled over and put his fist repeatedly into a stubborn clump of feathers. He could hardly believe he hadn't bothered to check what sort of mattress Geoffrey had sent along as a wedding present. Obviously it had been his worst one. Rhys put that away in his mind as something he would have to repay Fenwyck for the next time he saw him.

Rhys looked at the woman lying so peacefully next to him. She didn't look uncomfortable. He frowned. Was it possible that the mattress had been constructed so only his side was so lumpy?

Such a thing wouldn't have surprised him in the slightest.

"Rhys?"

Rhys sat up at the sound of Montgomery's voice. Then Montgomery himself put his head inside the tent.

"Did you not think you might be interrupting something?" Rhys asked with a scowl.

Montgomery's teeth were a flash of white in the predawn gloom. "Your children are scattered all over you like puppies. And your lady was snoring."

"I do not snore," Gwen said distinctly as she burrowed deeper into the blankets.

"What is it?" Rhys asked, already rising. "Something I should see?"

"Nothing of import," Montgomery said. "I was actually just looking for a bit of company on my watch."

Liar, Rhys thought to himself as he kissed his lady and then watched Nicholas immediately gravitate into the warm spot he'd just vacated. He left the tent and walked several paces away with Montgomery.

"We have company," Montgomery said bluntly, "and I daresay it isn't company we want."

"Your eyesight is not a blessing at times, is it?" Rhys asked.

"You can decide that," Montgomery said, "once you've seen this for yourself."

Rhys followed him to the outer walls, or what existed of the outer walls. And once he'd seen what was gathering below them on the plain, he wished the walls were finished. The keep sat on the only knoll for miles, true, but what good did it do them to sit perched up on a hill when they couldn't defend the hill?

Especially against the number of men he was seeing camped on the ground below.

"I would guess they want us to know they're there, else they would have just come up and attacked by now," Montgomery mused. "What think you?"

Rhys nodded in agreement. "Any idea who our guests might be?"

Montgomery sniffed. "I smell Rollan. The stench is unmistakable."

Rhys laughed in spite of himself. "Ah, but there is no love between the two of you, is there?"

"He killed my liege-lord, who was also a friend. Nay, there is no love between us."

"Did he in truth?"

Montgomery shrugged, though the movement was far from indifferent. "I have no proof, but my heart tells me 'tis so. There was no need for Bertram to fail as he did. He wasted away as if from some inner poison. If that doesn't describe his second son, I know not what does."

"All the more reason to see him captured. Perhaps we should see him escorted to London, where the king might see to him at his leisure."

Montgomery frowned. "I wonder where it is he acquired so many men." He looked at Rhys. "And why does he need them?"

"To kill me?"

"Surely, but for what reason? He never does anything without a reason, especially a reason that leaves him looking pure and innocent."

Rhys strove to count the number of tents spread out below, but he was the first to admit he had not Montgomery's eyes. Obviously he had no choice but to wait and see what the daylight would show him.

"We should prepare the men just the same," he said finally. "And place them as best we can to make up for our lack of numbers."

"Our position is a boon," Montgomery offered.

"At least this," Rhys said with a wave at what lay before them, "is our only concern."

Montgomery clasped his hands behind his back. "Care for a walk along the seaward wall?"

Rhys felt his heart sink. "You jest."

Montgomery laughed. "I can do nothing but laugh, for our straits are dire indeed."

"By sea as well?" Rhys asked incredulously.

"A single ship only, if that eases your mind any."

Rhys clapped a hand to his forehead. "What else can this day bring?"

"Rhys, my friend," Montgomery said, putting his hand on Rhys's shoulder and smiling, "that is not a question a man in your position asks."

"At least I don't have Fenwyck coming at me as well." He paused and looked at Montgomery. "Do I?"

"It doesn't appear so. You might perhaps wish for aid from him, though."

"Aye, let us see if a message cannot be sent." Rhys left Montgomery to see to the sending for aid and returned to his tent to rouse his lady. Already his mind was far ahead of his feet, wondering just where he might put those that were dearest to him that they might not be overrun. And he began to wonder if his troubles wouldn't include two small boys who seemed to think their wooden swords were quite powerful indeed.

And the saints preserve him if Gwen took up her own blade. Damnation, but he knew he should have forgotten it at Fenwyck. He strode back through the predawn light, cursing under his breath.

Rollan had best pray he wasn't behind this foolishness. The saints alone could help him if he was.

43

Rollan stood in front of his tent and stared up at the half-finished walls silhouetted against the early-morning sky. He cursed heartily. Things were not working out as he had planned. He'd tried to convince Patrick to attack under cover of darkness, but Patrick had refused. Rollan suspected that Patrick was indulging in an old man's curiosity to see his posterity in the flesh, never mind that Rhys was not his direct descendant.

A pity the king hadn't been a likely one to choose for an ally. Rollan had contemplated it seriously, once he'd seen for himself that Patrick of Sedgwick was not the warrior he purported being. Attacking mid-morn. What kind of plan was that? By the saints, not even Alain would have attempted something so stupid.

The sky began to lighten and Rollan scowled. He much preferred the darkness for his deeds, and 'twas obvious his own plans would have to be put off yet another day. It was best that Gwen not know he was nearby. He had told Patrick to keep silent about his whereabouts, though considering Sedgwick's inability to hold a thought past the duration of a meal, Rollan did not hold out much hope that he would remain anonymous.

He put his shoulders back. Let them know he was near. It might make the game even more interesting. Sedgwick had brought many men with him. It was quite possible that de Piaget and his mercenaries would be overcome, but that would surely not be before night fell. If that came to pass, Rollan would snatch Gwen away before Patrick had the chance to lay eyes on her.

Of course, things could happen quite differently. Rollan was well acquainted—from a safe distance, of course—with de Piaget's skill. And he'd had an eyeful of the mercenaries. It wasn't inconceivable that Rhys could come away the victor, though Rollan suspected that, too, would not come before night had fallen. And while Rhys was about the long, unpleasant business of deciding by torchlight just who the dead were, Rollan would snatch Gwen away before Rhys had the chance to lay eyes on her again.

Either way, Rollan knew he would have Gwen before another dawn. He had lost Ayre, true, but he would have the true prize. He could earn bread enough through his wits, if not his sword. She would not starve. He would give her other children. He suspected, and this had troubled him at first, that he might even be happy with her at his side.

Unsettling a thought if ever there were one, but he'd become almost accustomed to the idea.

He saw Patrick sharpening his sword and rolled his eyes in disgust. Imbecile. One old fool leading a camp of younger fools to their deaths, no doubt.

Rollan pulled his cloak more closely about him and turned away, knowing he was doomed to spend another day waiting.

But when night fell . . .

44

He would need her to guard his back. Gwen had decided that the moment Rhys had ducked back into their tent. He hadn't said aught, instead merely beckoned to her. She had known immediately that something was amiss.

She had stood shivering in the faint light of dawn and listened calmly as he'd told her what he'd seen. Men on the plain below them. A ship anchored off their coast. And only unfinished walls to protect them.

She hadn't been surprised.

He'd told her where he intended for her and the children to shelter while he fought the battle. He'd reminded her that the twins would be standing guard. He had absolutely forbidden her to do aught but wait until the battle was won. But she wondered, as she'd heard him sigh as he turned away to plan his strategy, if he could possibly believe she would do as he'd asked.

She had immediately retrieved her blade and donned a concealing cloak. She'd been tempted to relieve Robin and Nicholas of their wooden swords, lest they think them adequate protection, then she'd thought better of it. They had knives to use, should worse come to worst and they stand in need of defending themselves. And the swords would make them feel more confident.

She'd pacified the twins with soothing words about her need to wear hose and a tunic just in case she needed to flee. Indeed, she had made such a long and thorough argument for the scheme that she almost convinced herself 'twas more sensible to wear hose than a gown. The Fitzgeralds had merely blinked at her, either overwhelmed by her logic or the sheer number of words she had spewed at them.

Now 'twas midday and the only thing that had come to pass was the discovery that the ship off their coast contained Rhys's mother and a collection of nuns. There was no movement on the plain. The council of war, however, was proceeding in the center of what would eventually be the inner bailey. She approached confidently. Better that than slinking up and hoping to eavesdrop. Montgomery, Rhys, and Sir Jean were huddled together, obviously plotting their strategy.

"He wants to *what?*" Rhys was asking Montgomery incredulously.

"Who?" Gwen asked.

Montgomery ignored her. "He wants to parley. Says he has aught to discuss with you."

"Such as why the hell he's chosen to encamp his men under my keep?" Rhys asked in exasperation. "What is this old fool about?"

"Who?" Gwen asked again.

"Patrick of Sedgwick," Rhys answered, then realized who had asked the question. Gwen felt the intense heat of his glare, but she ignored it. It was best she know what he was up against so she knew how best to defend him.

She looked at Sir Jean, who had shifted. He didn't look uncomfortable. He didn't even look afraid. He had merely shifted his weight from one foot to another, but she had never seen him do that before. She contemplated his action and wondered if it indicated something she should be aware of.

Rhys shot his grandfather a look of irritation. "Do you

know aught of this you haven't cared to share with me as of yet?''

"What would he know?'' Montgomery asked.

"Aye,'' Gwen put in, "what would your grandfather know?''

Sir Jean looked about him as if he searched for something else to stare at besides his companions. Then he smiled suddenly. "Oh, look, Rhys. There's your mother finally arrived off her little boat. Isn't it a relief to know that 'twas her come to visit and not Johnny?'' He pointed right before Rhys's nose, giving his grandson no alternative than to look where he indicated. "And it would appear she has brought aid with her.''

Gwen looked over her shoulder to see a woman who was obviously a nun of some sort coming their way. She was followed by several more nuns of varying shapes and sizes. There was, however, a sister of such great height that Gwen almost winced. What trouble they must have had fitting her with the proper garments.

"Aid?'' Rhys snorted, looking thoroughly displeased to see his mother. "She brought herself, a herd of helpless women, and no doubt a great amount of my gold. Why should I consider this aid? What I need is aid from Fenwyck, who has not bothered to show his sorry face in my hall yet!''

Sir Jean looked unimpressed by Rhys's outburst. "Your good mother can care for herself.''

"Grandfather, she may spy well enough for Phillip, but she cannot wield a sword, and what I need at the moment is swordsmen, not nuns!''

Gwen looked at Rhys in surprise. "Your mother is a spy?''

"As is my grandfather,'' Rhys said shortly, "which is why I am wondering what he is doing standing here instead of loitering with the lads below, discovering their true intentions.''

"Your grandfather is a spy?'' Gwen looked at Sir Jean, who only smiled uncomfortably and shrugged. Then Gwen looked at Montgomery, who looked as surprised as she did. Then she finally fixed her gaze upon her husband and frowned. "And you could not see fit to trust me with this?"

"Well—" Rhys began.

"For whom does he work?" Gwen demanded.

"Ah," Sir Jean said slowly, "well, love, that would take a great deal of explaining—"

"Phillip," Rhys said briskly. "Phillip of France, to whom I am a great disappointment, for I have no lust for subterfuge. All I want"—and he encompassed them all with his glare—"is to know what in the bloody hell Patrick of Sedgwick wants from me so badly that he's willing to march his men across the whole of England to have it!"

Gwen wished she had something to sit down upon. Jean was a spy for the French king? Rhys's mother was a spy as well? Somehow it made the fact that Rhys's father had been burned as a heretic seem a mild thing indeed. Gwen couldn't decide if she should be horrified by the family she'd married into, or incensed by the fact that Rhys hadn't trusted her with the truth. She decided on the latter, as the former was not something she could change.

"You could have told me," she said to her husband, hoping it had come out as coldly as she'd intended.

"I've been trying to forget it," Rhys said with a sigh. He looked at her and attempted a smile. "It isn't much, truly."

"It isn't much?" she echoed. She found herself with the intense urge to throttle him. "It isn't much?" she said again, much louder this time. "Your family is full of spies!"

"Good ones," Jean offered, "if that matters."

"And you couldn't tell me?" Gwen bellowed. She was tempted to draw her sword and use it not on the men below, but on the man across from her. "Why didn't you tell me?"

"I didn't think—"

"Obviously!"

"Gwen . . ."

She folded her arms over her chest and glared at him.
"What else haven't you told me?"

"Nothing," he began slowly. "You know it all."

"Do I?"

"You do."

"She doesn't," Sir Jean said.

Gwen looked at Sir Jean. So did Rhys, for that matter.
She caught sight of her husband's face and found that his
glare was much more intimidating than hers. She would
have to work to improve her expression, for 'twas a certainty that she would have need of it if the day's events
were any indication of events to come. It would be very
handy to have the skill of causing the kind of trembles in
others that Rhys did.

There was a thunk to Gwen's right. That overly large
sister had set down a chest. Rhys's mother, and Gwen
could only assume that such was she, stepped around the
chest and gave Rhys a kiss.

"Sorry we're a bit behind, love," she said, smiling.
"You likely could have used your gold to aid you in your
little war."

"Mother," Rhys said shortly, "I do not remember asking you to come."

She reached up and patted his cheek. "Once I heard you
had begun work on your keep, I knew you would want the
rest of your funds. I made as much haste as possible."

"Many thanks," Rhys grumbled.

"Now, love"—his mother laughed—"no need to be so
ill-tempered." She patted him again on the cheek, then
turned to Sir Jean and leaned up to kiss his wrinkled cheek
as well. "Father."

"Daughter," Jean said, embracing her heartily. "You
look to have survived the crossing well enough."

"Curiosity over my new daughter," Rhys's mother said.
"Rhys, introduce me to your bride."

"Mother, Gwen. Gwen, my mother, Mary." Rhys
scowled at the both of them. "Why do you not remove
yourselves to a safe place so I might return to the business
of planning my war?"

Gwen found her hands taken by Mary de Piaget. "God's blessings upon you, daughter," Mary said, leaning forward to brush Gwen's cheek with her own. "I can only wish I had arrived at a more auspicious time. It would seem there is a bit of a misunderstanding to clear up on the plain before we can relax and chat in peace."

Gwen couldn't help but smile. Rhys looked very little like his mother, but they shared the same smile.

"Hopefully it won't take long," Gwen said. "And I fear I have little to offer you. We are a bit on the thin side here as far as our larder goes—"

"Oh, by the saints," Rhys exclaimed, "we're at war!"

"I'll sit on the chest," Mary said, promptly doing so, "and bide my time until you finish up with your business. Go ahead, Rhys, love. I'll wait."

Gwen watched her husband gather his patience about him like a cloak. Then he very calmly turned to his grandsire and managed something akin to a smile. It looked more like a great baring of teeth, but Sir Jean seemed disinclined to quibble.

"Grandpère," Rhys began slowly, "you seemed to know what Sedgwick is about."

Mary stiffened. Rhys noted it immediately and turned to her.

"What?" he demanded.

The large nun came up behind Mary and put a hand on her shoulder. Mary looked at Sir Jean.

"You didn't tell me Sedgwick would be here."

Sir Jean shrugged. "Didn't know it."

"What—" She took a deep breath and then spoke again more calmly. "What do they want?"

"That," Rhys said, through gritted teeth, "is what I am trying to ascertain if someone would just go down and find out!"

There was silence. Gwen looked at those gathered in the small circle and wondered why no one seemed inclined to volunteer to go. Montgomery was still too busy gaping at Sir Jean, likely trying to decide if he looked the part of a spy. Sir Jean was shifting again, more uneasily this time,

and looking anywhere but at Rhys. Mary sat on the chest
of gold with her head bowed. And the very tall nun with
the very large feet still rested a hand on Mary's shoulder.

It was, oddly enough, a very hairy hand.

Gwen looked up and met that sister's eyes.

And she saw, to her complete astonishment, a pair of
gray eyes peeping out at her from inside a hood, a pair
of gray eyes that she had definitely seen somewhere before.

Or, rather, a pair like them.

She looked at Rhys. Nay, it couldn't be.

She looked the nun over and saw what could have been
mistaken for the lump of a sword hilt hiding beneath the
woman's habit.

Woman? Gwen shook her head. That was no woman.
She wondered why she was the only one who had seen it.

She looked at her husband. He had turned to look out
toward the plain, his face scrunched up in a formidable
scowl. Then she looked at Sir Jean only to find him staring
at her. He shifted again.

"I haven't enough men," Rhys said with another curse.
"And I *definitely* haven't got one willing to go down and
find out what the bloody hell Sedgwick wants!"

Gwen turned the puzzle over in her mind. Mary seemed
somewhat overcome by the knowledge of who stood to
attack them. She was comforted by one who could only
be Rhys's father—who even Rhys assumed was dead. But
what had that to do with what was happening down upon
the plain? It wasn't as if those below would have known
Mary and her husband were arriving.

Did they?

Nay, not even Rollan could be so clever—assuming
Rollan was behind the mischief.

Gwen looked at Sir Jean. Of any of them, he most likely
knew what was behind the day's events. It was obvious
Rhys was having no answers from him. Gwen suspected
she might be the best one to wring the truth from him,
given that she had already intimidated the old man in the
lists quite thoroughly.

"Sir Jean," she said clearly.

He looked at her, apparently saw her intention in her eyes, and swallowed. Uncomfortably.

"Aye?" he said, looking about him for some avenue of escape.

Gwen put her hand on the hilt of her sword and gave Sir Jean a look of promise. "Where is your son buried?" she asked bluntly.

"Ah . . ."

"The location, good sir," Gwen said. "Where exactly is the location of his grave?"

"Ah . . ."

"And is he in it?"

Rhys turned around at that. He looked first at Gwen, then at his grandfather. Sir Jean looked supremely uncomfortable. Gwen sincerely hoped he was a better spy than that when he was facing those who weren't his family.

The large sister with the hairy hand had even shifted. Gwen decided that before they could plan their war, they needed to know at least who the players were upon the hilltop. She leaned up on her toes and pulled back the hood from, and this came as no surprise to her, Etienne de Piaget's dark head.

He was, she had to admit, a very handsome man still. It was no wonder Rhys was so pleasing to look at. She looked at her husband to find that his jaw had gone slack.

"Father?" he whispered.

Gwen pushed Montgomery out of the way and put her arm around Rhys's waist to hold him up, lest he feel the need to faint.

Etienne was seemingly as affected as his son was, so Gwen turned her attentions to other matters. Why was Mary so overcome by the thought of Patrick of Sedgwick lying in wait below them? Gwen had never cared much for anyone from Sedgwick, and she had suffered through a supper or two with Henry of Sedgwick at her father's supper table. Not a pleasant man. The only thing noteworthy about him had been the rumor that his daughter had disappeared one night and no one had seen her thereafter.

His daughter, Mary.

And Henry had died not a year after that. Some said he had died of his grief. Others said he had died of wounds his brother's knife impaling itself between his ribs had given him. However it had come about, he had left a daughter behind whose whereabouts were a mystery.

Gwen looked at Mary and frowned. It couldn't be. She transferred her gaze to Jean and found that he was, amazingly enough, licking his lips. As if he were nervous. She gave him the sternest look she could muster.

"You know why Sedgwick is here, don't you?" Gwen asked.

"Ah," Jean stalled.

Gwen adjusted her husband's weight. "Well," she said impatiently, "tell Rhys. Tell him why Patrick of Sedgwick has come pounding on his gates."

"We don't have any gates," Rhys whispered, still gaping at his father.

"Well," Jean said, shifting uncomfortably again.

Gwen sighed in exasperation. She opened her mouth to speak only to find Rhys's mother had already begun to do so.

"Henry of Sedgwick was my father," Mary said, looking at Rhys wearily. "And that would make you, love," she continued, "heir to Sedgwick and all that entails. And I suppose Patrick of Sedgwick has come pounding on gates you have yet to build so that you might not come pounding upon his."

Gwen felt Rhys stiffen, then begin to sway. And then she decided that perhaps there was more of him than she could hold up alone, so she didn't protest when Sir Jean offered his aid. 'Twas the least he could do. She had the feeling it was the beginning of the favors he would be doing his grandson to make up for the startling revelations of the day.

45

Rhys found himself sitting upon a portion of his great hall wall with his head between his knees and his grandfather holding it there.

"Breathe, whelp," Jean said gruffly. "And keep your head down. No need to faint in front of your lady."

Rhys didn't want to faint, he wanted to retch. For the first time, he thought he might have sympathy for the Fitzgeralds and what they endured on horseback.

"Father?" Rhys croaked.

"Aye, son."

Rhys managed to lift his head far enough to look at the sister who had always guarded his mother's dining hall.

"You're a nun," he wheezed.

Etienne smiled weakly. "When it suits me."

"I could kill you for this," Rhys managed, "if I could just get to my bloody feet without puking."

"How could I tell you?" his father said softly. "I have too many enemies for that, Rhys. They thought I was dead and you ignorant of my doings. They would have killed you otherwise."

Rhys didn't want to weep, though he was damned close

to it. His father was alive. His mother had known. His grandfather had known.

And they had let him suffer anyway.

"It was better that way," Etienne said firmly. "You were safe, Rhys, and that was worth any price." He smiled. "Besides, I've watched you over the years when I could manage it."

"That eases me greatly," Rhys snapped. "It would have been a comfort to have watched *you!*"

"You did often enough."

"In skirts!"

Etienne shrugged. "One does what one must."

Rhys managed to sit up straight. He realized Gwen was standing nearby, and he jerked her onto his lap and wrapped his arms around her.

"Forgive me, my love," he said, "for not telling you what kind of family you stood to ally yourself with. Allow me to make proper introductions. That is my grandfather, the spy. That is my mother the abbess and sometime spy. And this is my father, the sister of the cloth."

Rhys watched his father take Gwen's hand, bend low over it, and kiss it politely. "How fortunate my son is to have wed a woman who is beautiful and yet deadly. I understand you have a wicked manner with a blade."

Rhys had no idea where his father had heard such drivel, but it certainly served him well, for Gwen immediately seemed to soften toward his father.

And Rhys found he wished he could do the same. But, by the saints, he'd been a lad of seven when he'd last seen his sire! How could he be happy when he was so bloody furious?

Etienne reached out and ruffled Rhys's hair as if he'd been that lad of such tender years. "We'll talk, my son. I will do what I can to make recompense for the years we've lost. But now we must decide what you will do about your uncle."

"I've acquired an entirely new family this day," Rhys said in disgust, "and I've yet to decide if it pleases me or not. I knew I should have stayed abed this morn!"

"At least Patrick wishes to talk," Sir Jean said calmly. "He could merely wish to stick you."

"And you think he does not?" Etienne laughed. "Father, you've obviously led too comfortable a life the past month and it has softened you. Of course he wishes to slay Rhys. Patrick has no desire to lose his keep."

"Why would young Rhys want it?" Jean returned. "Pitiful place."

"Whether or not Rhys wants it matters little," Etienne said firmly.

"I know," Jean grumbled. " 'Tis that Rhys could come take it from him if he chose. I'm not so old as all that, whelp," he said, with a glare thrown his son's way, "that I cannot divine that."

Rhys looked at Gwen. She at least was no longer grumbling at him, or about him. In fact, he thought he just might have detected a bit of softness in her expression.

"How fair you look today, my love," he said, tucking her hair behind her ears. She had ears made for just such a thing, but he chose not to tell her as much. "Shall we go for a walk along the shore later?"

She smiled and put her arms around his neck. "I love you."

"As do I," he returned. He kissed her, then pushed her gently to her feet. "Well, let us be about our business and have an end to it. Then perhaps we can return our lives to something somewhat normal."

Then he looked about him and sighed.

His wife was dressed as a mercenary, his father was in skirts, and his mother sat upon a fat chest of gold as if she were a chicken determined to defend her eggs to the death.

Rhys sighed again and put his arm around his wife. "You stay here."

She agreed far too readily, but he could do nothing about it. He looked at his grandfather.

"You come with me."

He nodded. "Of course."

Rhys looked at his father, opened his mouth to speak,

then shut it again and shook his head. "You do what you like."

"I always do."

"So I see," Rhys said. "Since I cannot seem to find anyone willing to see just what it is Sedgwick wants, I suppose I'll have to go myself."

By the saints, the day could just not worsen from there. He was sure of it.

Gwen pulled the hood of her cloak close around her face, grateful for the darkening sky and arrival of more inclement weather. The hood also kept her from having to smudge soot on her face to complete her disguise, for which she was most thankful. She would have less to explain if Rhys were to catch her. He thought her safely tucked away up on the hill, being protected along with the children, his mother, and his chest of gold.

Evening shadows had fallen and with them had come a face-to-face meeting with Patrick of Sedgwick. Gwen had wondered at the wisdom of it, but Rhys hadn't hesitated. He had taken with him his father, grandfather, Montgomery, and the Fitzgerald brothers. Evidently he considered them protection enough.

She didn't.

Hence her intention to take up her position outside the tent that contained her husband and his uncle.

She swaggered her way toward the appropriate tent, her hand on the hilt of her sword. Obviously she had improved her mercenary mien, for no one stopped her to question her having business in the area. She came to a stop near the tent and sat down casually, as if this had been her goal all the while. With one last look about her to make sure she wasn't being overly observed, she put her ear to the cloth and strained to hear the voices inside.

And she heard nothing. This was not helping her in her cause. With a curse, she rose to her feet and looked about her for a better solution. She walked around the tent, only to find the entrance under heavy guard. The Fitzgerald brothers stood to one side of the flap with Montgomery pacing in front of them, while the other side was guarded by men she did not recognize. She pulled back, but not before Montgomery had caught sight of her.

Obviously her disguise needed more work.

"Well, lad," he said, coming around the tent and looking at her pointedly, "don't you have duties that require you to remain atop the hill?"

She scowled at him and remained silent.

"I'd be about them were I you," he warned.

She shooed him away with her hand, but he only folded his arms over his chest and frowned at her. With a sigh she turned and walked back behind the tent, hoping he would think she had relented and returned to the keep. Obviously, she would have to make do with her current position. She stretched out on the ground and lifted the bottom edge of the tent a fraction. With any luck, in the dark, anyone who passed by would just think she had imbibed too much, and leave her in peace.

"Let me understand this," a deep voice said. "My niece is an abbess?"

"Aye," Rhys answered, "and very happily engaged in her vocation."

With her husband standing guard at her door, Gwen thought to herself. She wondered in the back of her mind if Mary and Etienne still lived as husband and wife.

Patrick grunted.

"No intention of returning to England?" Patrick asked sharply.

"None," Rhys assured him. "And, more particularly, no intention of returning to Sedgwick."

"And what of you?" Patrick demanded.

"Well," Rhys drawled, "I suppose that depends."

"Upon what?"

"Upon whether or not you remove your men from my land before sundown tomorrow."

"And if I do?"

"Then you may remain upon my inheritance," Rhys said pleasantly.

Patrick gasped in outrage. "Why, you insolent pup—"

"Insolent and fully capable of lopping off your head where you sit," Rhys assured him. "And if you think I will not do it, think again."

"And I am to remain there by your good graces?" Patrick was, by the sound of him, not happy at all with the idea.

"You should be grateful that I allow you to remain at all," Rhys retorted. "You and your heirs may have the keeping of Sedgwick, but you will have it as my vassals. If this is not acceptable, you are free to find yourself another keep to inhabit."

Gwen wished desperately that she could have seen Patrick's face. There was a great amount of snorting and swearing, as if Patrick strove to reconcile himself to his fate. Then there was the sound of a final, hearty curse.

"Damn you," Patrick snarled. "I don't want to do this."

"Nor do you wish to move your bed," Rhys finished dryly. "I accept your fealty."

There was the sound of more cursing from Patrick, but no further threats. She could have sworn she heard Patrick grumble something about Rollan and his foolish ideas, but then again she might have been imagining it. She put the tent flap back down and crawled to her feet, feeling somewhat relieved.

She started to walk back toward the path up the hill, then paused. The feeling she'd had of needing to protect her husband had not dissipated. Patrick's words might have been well-spoken, but that didn't guarantee that his men felt the same way. And who knew how many men Rollan had been able to sway to his twisted way of thinking.

She had her sword. There was no reason not to shadow her husband and be prepared to use it.

46

Rollan stood a safe distance away from Patrick's tent and waited for the outcome of the meeting. It had taken all the daylight hours for the negotiations to reach the point where a face-to-face meeting had happened. At least now Rollan had the cover of darkness under which to work.

That a meeting between Rhys and Patrick had actually taken place was a most disastrous turn of events. Patrick should have been planning his assault on the hill, not exchanging pleasantries with his niece's son. It showed a serious lack of commitment on Patrick's part, one Rollan was certain he would have to compensate for.

He fingered the crossbow and handful of quarrels he had brought with him for just such an emergency. If Patrick lacked the ballocks to slay Rhys, Rollan would do it in his stead.

He might even do Patrick in as well. Ayre was out of his grasp, but Sedgwick might be his as a reward for exposing to the king the clandestine activities of the de Piaget men.

He stiffened in anticipation as Rhys and Patrick came from the tent. He searched their bearings, hoping the torchlight would reveal whether anger or friendship was written there.

They weren't laughing. But they weren't snarling, either. And then he watched Rhys extend his hand. It wasn't a friendly gesture, but it was one of agreement. Patrick took it.

And then he knew what he would have to do.

He loaded the crossbow and lifted it. He sighted down the arrow, allowing himself the time to relish the thought of ending the life of the man he had hated from the moment he'd clapped eyes on him and realized Rhys de Piaget was everything he himself would never be.

Rhys and Patrick stepped away from the tent. Rollan allowed it. It would be more of a challenge to put his arrow through Rhys's heart without the light of the torches to aid him.

He watched Montgomery of Wyeth and the Fitzgerald brothers fall into step, saw Rhys's grandfather take up his place on Rhys's side, then saw a nun move to Rhys's other side.

A nun?

The mystery of it was almost enough to make Rollan stop, for he wondered if that could possibly be Rhys's mother. But so tall? Impossible.

It was a mystery he would have to leave unsolved. Rollan watched as another of Rhys's followers stepped directly behind Rhys. Rollan snorted to himself. How had the man acquired such a following? Didn't they realize that Rhys came from a long line of spies? Didn't they realize that Rhys himself hadn't had the courage to follow in his father's spying footsteps? It had to have been a lack of courage—that and that annoying desire for chivalry.

It was best he rid the world of the fool. King John would likely thank him for the service. Rollan found himself smiling. He would gather Gwen up and take her to London. The king would be pleased to see her freed of de Piaget's lecherous hands. Perhaps Rollan would find himself master of all her lands. It would be just recompense for having lost Ayre.

And then he would find himself master of Gwen herself.

The thought was enough to make his hand unsteady on the bow.

He clamped down upon his passions and took aim again. The little mercenary had stepped aside, leaving him a clear view of de Piaget's back. He let out his breath, then held it as he depressed the trigger.

"Damn," he said viciously.

The bloody mercenary had moved again behind Rhys's back and taken the arrow himself. Rollan quickly cranked the bow back again and fitted another arrow to the string. Then he watched Rhys turn and bend, then heard a scream.

"Gwen!"

Rollan shook his head. Surely he was hearing things.

"Merciful saints above, 'tis Gwen!" Rhys cried out.

Rollan found himself moving toward the fallen mercenary. It couldn't be. It was just a fool who had chosen to follow Rhys. It was just a boy, a dispensable soul who would likely have died in battle just the same.

Someone fetched a torch. The circle was parted enough that Rollan could see inside it.

He saw the arrow protruding from the dark cloak.

He saw the face of the mercenary as it lay turned on Rhys's knee.

It was Gwen.

Rollan stumbled back. The quarrels fell from his hand to the ground. The sound seemed to explode in the night.

He looked up and found himself staring into Rhys's tortured face. He met his enemy's eyes and saw the tears there. And, to his great surprise, Rollan found that his own eyes were swimming with tears.

"I never meant—" he began, but he couldn't finish.

He'd never meant to harm Gwen. He would have cared for her. He was certain he was the only one who loved her as she deserved.

And now he'd destroyed the one thing he ever could have loved.

Rhys didn't move, but his men rose and started toward him. They could have been running. Their faces were full of rage and hate. Rollan couldn't blame them.

But they moved slowly.

And he moved more quickly.

He turned the bow on himself.

And with one last look of agony at Rhys, he squeezed the trigger.

47

The child stood at the edge of what would in time be the great hall of Artane and looked on the tragedy.

Artane's lady had been laid softly on a bed of hastily arranged cloaks. Those who loved her were gathered about her, some with tears on their cheeks, some with heads bowed in prayer.

"The arrow must come out, Rhys."

The child looked up to find Lord Rhys's mother standing next to her son with her hand laid lightly upon his arm.

"Shall I do it?" she asked gently.

The child looked to Lord Rhys.

"Nay," he said hoarsely. "I will see to it."

"Rhys, 'tis a less grievous wound than you fear." This came from a nun who knelt at the lady Gwennelyn's side—though the child surmised by the large feet and powerful hands that this was no sister of the cloth. It took no gift of seeing to mark that man as Lord Rhys's father. The resemblance was uncanny.

"You'll need a poultice," Lord Rhys's father said. The way he gently examined the injury convinced the child that he had much experience in the healing arts.

"Yarrow," Lord Rhys said absently, his face full of

grief and disbelief. " 'Tis good for staunching wounds."

"Aye, son," his father said softly, " 'tis good for that indeed."

"Someone add to the fire," the mother instructed. "She needs warmth."

"Someone go see to the children," the grandfather added. "Tell them 'tis but a simple wound that will heal quickly enough."

The child listened to all the voices, caught up in grief and anger that filled them, and wished she had foreseen what had been about to befall her lady. Her gift was a fickle one for now, and again the future was dark to her.

She felt the weight of someone's gaze upon her, and she looked up to find Lord Rhys staring at her. He beckoned and she approached the circle cautiously. She'd thought to have stood fully in the shadows so as not to disturb, but evidently he'd seen her just the same.

"Have y—" He cleared his throat and swallowed with difficulty. "Have you," he said carefully, "any yarrow about you?"

The child nodded. She'd brought what was needful from her tent, that luxurious place where she lived blissfully amongst her grandfather's things.

"And can you . . . can you . . ." He didn't finish.

He didn't need to. She knew what he asked. He wished her to ease his lady's pain. She knelt down next to his lady and bent close so only he could hear. She took a deep breath, hoping that her mother's gift might not fail her.

"Her pain I can ease," she whispered. "But her life is in your hands."

And so it was. There were many things beyond the power of her modest art. But she would do what she could.

The knight, now a lord, nodded with a jerky motion, then prepared to do what he must. The child grieved only for what he suffered, for she had seen the end of the night and knew what would transpire before dawn. But he would think her fanciful, so she kept what she'd seen close to her heart and gave him the aid he asked of her.

The lord put his hand on the arrow and made ready to

pull. The child could feel the weight of the love and concern bear down upon the lady of Artane and ease her, though she knew it not.

The lord pulled and the arrow came free.

The lady breathed out the smallest of sighs, and those about her wept.

But she did not open her eyes and she spoke no word.

The child knelt with her small hand covering her lady's and did what she could with her modest art. But, as she had told her lord, there was only so much she could do.

The lady Gwennelyn's life was in other hands besides hers.

She turned away to gather the things she had brought and be about the work of mixing her poultice.

Rhys sat with his head hanging between his knees, his hands dangling limp beside him. It occurred to him that he'd found himself in that position more than once over the past se'nnight. The first had been after realizing that his father lived still. He had yet to repay his father for the shock of that. He would have to do so eventually. Perhaps he would, when he could move himself from his present position. It had been four days since he'd last stirred himself to leave the tent, so the likelihood of moving in the future was rather slim.

"Rhys?"

That rough, low voice came from the door of the tent. Rhys managed to lift his head to stare at his grandfather. Even that effort was considerable. "Aye?" he croaked.

Jean entered the tent that had been hastily erected to shelter Gwen from the elements. "How fares our lady?"

"She breathes still, though she has not spoken," Rhys whispered.

"Your mother prays for her," Jean said, kneeling down beside Gwen and resting his hand against her cheek. "Her fever has abated at least."

Rhys nodded, but found that a small comfort.

Jean smiled gravely. "Your sire's skill continues in you."

"For all the good that does my lady."

"The little wench's potions have not eased her?"

"Socrates's granddaughter is a fine healer," Rhys said with a sigh, "and I feel certain she has eased Gwen's pain. But she can work no miracles. None of us can."

His grandfather gently smoothed Gwen's hair back from her face with his age-spotted hand. Rhys watched him continue to do so for several moments and knew that his grandfather had no answer for him. What could Jean tell him that he didn't know already?

The arrow had struck bone and remained fixed there until Rhys had removed it. The only stroke of good fortune had been realizing that it hadn't pierced heart or lung. Either Rollan was a poorer shot than they had thought, or he had been aiming for Rhys's heart and the true-flying arrow had found Gwen's shoulder in its way instead. Rhys suspected it was the latter, and he was relieved somewhat by the thought of it. At least Rollan had not been training his sights on Gwen's back. How could he have known? Rhys remembered vividly the horror in Rollan's eyes, horror he could only assume had come by virtue of whom he had struck.

Rhys pushed aside thoughts of that night. The only thing good to have come of the whole encounter was that Rollan had but wounded Gwen and not killed her. But even that bit of good fortune had not caused Gwen to open her eyes any sooner. Rhys could only pray that she would do so in time.

Jean cleared his throat. "The family is settled, if you're curious."

Rhys nodded, mute.

"Borrowed a few tents from Sedgwick," Jean said, sounding as if such a thing would have amused him greatly another time. "Your mother and father are safely tucked away with your gold and your children. The men patrol your walls. Montgomery and your Viking keepers pace about with expressions of great concern upon their faces."

"The children? How do they fare?"

"We've told them that Gwen merely rests. Seeing her sleeping has eased them, though I suspect Robin and Nicholas fear the worst. Amanda only knows she cannot have her mother, and I fear she finds Mary a poor substitute."

"A pity we do not have Joanna with us," Rhys said absently. "Amanda is very fond of her." He looked at his grandfather. "Word should be sent to her, I suppose."

"What word?" Jean asked in a sharp whisper. "That her daughter is recovering nicely?"

Rhys couldn't answer. He didn't dare. He was too afraid that when Gwen did wake in truth, she wouldn't wake to herself. Her fever had been hard upon her, despite their best efforts. If he hadn't known better, he might have suspected the arrow had been poisoned. Knowing Rollan, it likely had been.

"There is no need to tell Joanna that, not that I wouldn't mind looking on her again. Let her come for a visit in a few weeks. Gwen can show her the scar herself then."

Rhys nodded in agreement, simply because he could do nothing else. *Please let her awake whole. We've had such a short time together.*

Jean rose to his feet. "Do you need aught?"

Rhys shook his head. "Nay."

"I could remain—"

"Nay," Rhys interrupted. "I'll stay."

"You do her little good in this state—"

"I'll stay," Rhys repeated. He looked up at his grandfather and attempted a smile. His face was too stiff with worry for any success at it. "My thanks just the same."

Jean nodded and rested his hand briefly on Rhys's head before he ducked out of the tent.

Rhys was once again alone with his lady, with naught but his love and prayers to aid her. He could only hope it would be enough.

He found himself speaking to her before he realized what he was about. He reminded her of all the reasons she had for remaining by his side. He told her of his visions of a magnificent keep to shelter her and her children from

elements and enemies alike. He reminded her of the sounds
of the sea and the sea birds, of the smell of the air and the
chill of the wind. He spoke of his parents and how they
currently both prayed for her recovery. He knew he bab-
bled, but he could do nothing but continue, recalling for
her every scratch and bruise Nicholas had earned while
finding himself caught up in Robin's mischief, every tear
and stomping of feet Amanda had indulged in thanks to
worms and snakes down her dress.

And when he had exhausted that list, and it was a very
long list indeed, he spoke of his love for her, of how he
had spent so many hours over the course of his long life
dreaming of her, longing for her, hoping that one day she
would be his. When that provoked no response, he reminded her that she had said on more than one occasion
that they would have a long and happy life together.

But still she spoke no word, gave no sign that she had
heard any of his heart poured out so fully.

Rhys bent his head again upon his knees and let his
hands rest limply at his sides. Perhaps they had been too
confident that merely removing the arrow and packing the
wound would be enough to cure her.

Perhaps he would spend the rest of his days with only
her children to remind him of her. Much as he loved them,
the very thought of that was almost enough to break his
heart.

So many dreams yet to be grasped and turned into life.
Rhys would have wept, had he the energy for it. They
could not end thusly, those dreams that they had dreamed.
They could not end on a barren rock on the northern coast
with the wind howling and the waves crashing against the
shore. Rhys simply could not bring himself to believe that
their chance was already past and that his life would stretch
out before him with Gwen not in it.

Nay, he would not even allow himself to think it. Gwen
would awaken in time. She had to.

He knew he would not survive if she did not.

He felt something skitter across his foot and he cursed.
That was all he needed, rats now to plague him.

The rat was bold enough to try again, and Rhys seized it by the tail.

Only it was no tail he held. It was a finger.

He whipped his head up. The motion almost sent him toppling forward onto his lady. It might have, had she not tightened her grip upon his hand.

"Rhys," she whispered, stretching, then catching her breath at the pain. "The arrow?"

He almost shuddered with relief. She was speaking. She remembered what had befallen her.

"The arrow is out, my love," he said, feeling the tears stream down his face.

She smiled and the sight of it broke what heart he had left.

"I've been . . . napping?" She yawned, as if she'd been doing nothing more than just that. She looked at him and frowned. "You need . . . one."

"A rest? Aye, my love, I suppose I could."

She shifted, but flinched at the movement of her injured shoulder. "It pains me."

Rhys stretched himself out and carefully placed his arm over his lady. "Rest then, my love," he said. "I'll not leave your side."

"Pleasant dreams," she whispered.

"If you only knew," he said with feeling. That they would have another chance to dream was not a gift he would take lightly.

He waited until his lady had drifted back off to sleep before he allowed himself to relax. She held his hand still and her grip was strong and sure. He knew he would have to rise soon and inform those without that Gwen had awoken, seemingly sound of mind and body, but for the moment he could do nothing but lie beside her and fair drown in the wave of gratitude that washed over him.

Gwen stirred, murmured his name, then slept again.

Rhys closed his own eyes and sighed in relief.

48

Six months later . . .

Gwen worked steadily upon the parchment, copying carefully the ingredients and amounts she had been given. And once she was finished, she sat back and smiled at the child standing next to her chair.

"There," she said, satisfied. "A proper addition to your grandsire's manuscript." She smiled at the girl. "This is a potion of your own making, is it not?"

"Aye, my lady," the child answered.

" 'Tis very palatable," Gwen said with a smile. "And I should know as I have ingested enough of it over the past few fortnights."

The child blushed and Gwen smiled. The girl was never boastful of her skill, but Gwen knew from her own experience that it was great. They were blessed to have such a healer there with them. And, most important, the child could brew a potion that contained no specks of unmentionable substances—or at least none that Gwen could see. That was enough to convince her that this was a healer they would wish to keep about them as long as they could.

"We should sign your name, child," Gwen said. She

realized, with a start, that she had never asked it. She had referred to the child as "Socrates's granddaughter" to those about her, and used the name "wondrous healer" on the girl herself. "How are you called?"

The child bowed her head. "Berengaria," she answered softly.

"Berengaria," Gwen said, laying her hand upon the girl's head. "A beautiful name. Berengaria of Artane. Will that suit you for the moment?"

"Aye, my lady. It will."

Gwen suspected the girl would not remain there always, but perhaps for the foreseeable future it would be enough. Gwen carefully gathered up the manuscript pages she had written out that day and handed them to Berengaria.

"Will you not sup with us tonight?"

Berengaria shook her head. "When your hall is built, perhaps, if it pleases my lady."

"So that then you might be less noticed?" Gwen asked with a dry smile. "Aye, my girl, if that suits you better. I'll see you have something proper in your tent."

"You always do, my lady."

And with that, the girl kissed Gwen's hand as if she'd been the queen and scampered from the small building that served as great hall at present.

Gwen rose and drew on her cloak. Even though it was almost spring, it was still chilly so near the sea. She winced at the ache in her shoulder. It had been six months since Rollan's arrow had felled her, and still she had pain when she put on her clothes. At least she lived. It was something she was grateful for each morn she awoke. Montgomery had told her that Rollan had seemed devastated enough by the thought that he might have killed her, but none of them would know the truth now. She wanted to believe that it had been a mistake, but if that were the case, then it meant that he had been attempting to kill Rhys.

It was a puzzle she didn't dwell on much.

She stepped out into the bailey and shivered. Winter was hard upon them, but still the work went on. Rhys's gold was building an impressive keep. It hadn't hurt that his father and grandfather had done their share of contributing as well. It would likely take a pair of years yet to finish the castle completely, but she felt certain 'twould be worth the wait and the expense. Rhys was determined to build something not even John could take by force.

Messages had flown from Artane to London and back, with the king growing less irritated with each one. Finally John had tersely informed Rhys that he had intended all along that Rhys should take Ayre's widow as his wife. Gwen smiled at the memory of Rhys's reaction to that. He had, however, quickly agreed with the king that his superior wisdom and foresight had indeed provided Rhys with a fine bride in the end.

A bride and children, that was. Robin, Nicholas, and Amanda had been officially claimed and duly recorded to Gwen's satisfaction. Robin was determined to live worthily of his newly made sire's name. Nicholas seemed still to be stunned by the turn of events and spent most of his time trailing after Robin with a dazed look upon his face.

Amanda, however, seemed to think her father had never been other than Rhys, and Gwen understood perfectly. It wasn't as if Alain had done more than hear the babe was a girl and promptly forget about her. Rhys, on the other hand, was lavish with his affections for all three children, though he would be the first to admit that he held a particularly soft spot for his only girl.

Gwen wondered what Rhys would do when she informed him that in a few months he might just have another babe competing for his affections.

She tucked that tidbit away to share later, tucked her hands under her arms, and went in search of her love.

She found him, unsurprisingly, standing atop his walls, staring out over the sea. She made her way to him, then leaned against the wall and slipped her hand into his.

"Staring into the future again?" she teased.

He squeezed her hand. "For all you know, I might be."

"More than likely, you're imagining how it will be to finally have the hall finished where we might retreat to our place before the fire and be warm for a change."

He put his arm around her and snuggled her close. "There is that as well," he said with a smile. Then he shook his head and looked back out over the sea. "I was just standing here, marveling over my life and the gifts I've been given and wondering what I have done to deserve them."

"Well, for a start," she said, "you saved Lord Bertram's life."

"A happy bit of luck," he said modestly.

"Well," she said, "you rescued me from a piggery."

"Now that," he said with a thoughtful nod, "did surely earn me all that I have now."

"I should think it did. It was a horrible stench you endured to save me."

His rich laugh washed over her. "Ah, sweet Gwen, the prize was well worth the effort." He hugged her to him. "It was indeed a most fortuitous bit of chivalry."

Gwen closed her eyes and sighed in contentment. She could indeed do nothing but agree with him and it amazed her that such a simple thing as wading through pig manure to liberate a child from her prison could have led to such happiness. Rhys once again enjoyed the company of his father from time to time when Etienne, Mary, and Jean ventured northward. Her children were blessed with a father who loved and cared for them. Her own mother had full control of Segrave without worrying that she might lose her home at someone's whim.

And there Gwen herself stood with the walls of a magnificent keep beneath her feet, her children safe within those walls, and the love of her heart standing next to her with his strong arms about her. She'd imagined so often how it might be, but the truth of it made her realize just what a poor imagination she had.

"I love you," she whispered, looking up at Rhys.

He smiled down at her. "What brought that on?"

"Just your nearness," she answered with a smile of her own. "I will never forget how fortunate I am."

"You?" he asked with a laugh. "Why, lady, I am the fortunate one. I have obtained the dream of my youth."

As had she, though she didn't say the like. It would have interrupted one of the most overwhelming kisses of her life and she prided herself on knowing when to speak and when to remain silent.

And so she closed her eyes, held her words, and gave herself up to the magic of her husband's mouth upon hers. It was a sweet kiss full of love, passion, and promise. Her life had become the stuff of dreams.

She was content.

MACLEOD

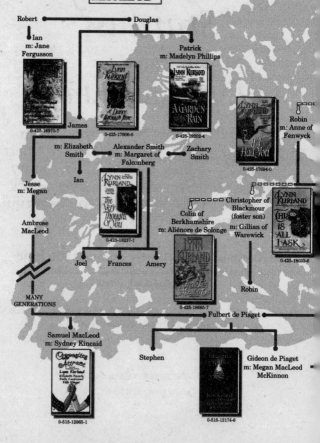

Robert — Douglas

Ian
m: Jane
Fergusson

Patrick
m: Madelyn Phillips

0-425-16970-7

0-425-17906-0

0-425-19202-4

0-425-17694-0

Robin
m: Anne of
Fenwyck

James

m: Elizabeth   Alexander Smith   Zachary
Smith   m: Margaret of   Smith
Falconberg

Ian

Jesse
m: Megan

The Very
Thought
Of You

0-425-18237-1

Christopher of
Blackmour
(foster son)
m: Gillian of
Warewick

Colin of
Berkhamshire
m: Aliénore de Solonge

THIS
IS
ALL
I ASK

0-425-18033-6

Ambrose
MacLeod

Joel   Frances   Amery

0-425-18685-7

Robin

MANY
GENERATIONS

Fulbert de Piaget

Samuel MacLeod
m: Sydney Kincaid

Stephen

Gideon de Piaget
m: Megan MacLeod
McKinnon

0-515-12865-1

0-515-12174-6

family lineage in the books of
LYNN KURLAND

DE PIAGET

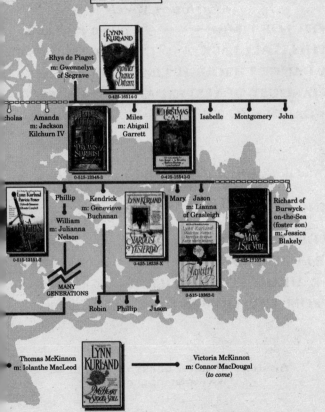

Rhys de Piaget
m: Gwennelyn
of Segrave

Another Chance to Dream — 0-425-16514-0

...cholas | Amanda
m: Jackson
Kilchurn IV | Miles
m: Abigail
Garrett | Isabelle | Montgomery | John

If I Had You / Dreams of Stardust — 0-515-13948-3

Christmas C·A·T — 0-425-15542-0

Phillip

William
m: Julianna
Nelson

A Knight's Vow — 0-515-13151-2

MANY
GENERATIONS

Kendrick
m: Genevieve
Buchanan

Stardust of Yesterday — 0-425-18238-X

Mary

Jason
m: Lianna
of Grasleigh

Tapestry — 0-515-13362-0

Richard of
Burwyck-
on-the-Sea
(foster son)
m: Jessica
Blakely

The More I See You — 0-425-17107-8

Robin   Phillip   Jason

Thomas McKinnon
m: Iolanthe MacLeod

My Heart Stood Still — 0-425-18197-9

Victoria McKinnon
m: Connor MacDougal
(to come)